MYSTERY
OVER THE
MERSEY

A BERNIE FAZAKERLEY MYSTERY

JUDY FORD

MYSTERY OVER THE MERSEY

Published by
Bernie Fazakerley Publications

ISBN-10: 1-911083-29-5

ISBN-13: 978-1-911083-29-0

DEDICATION

To the staff of the Royal Liverpool and Broad Green University Hospitals NHS Trust: "Delivering the highest quality of healthcare driven by world class research for the health and wellbeing of the population."

'To hands that work and eyes that see.
Give wisdom's healing power
That whole and sick and weak and strong
May praise you evermore.'

Edward H. Plumptre (1821-1891)

DISCLAIMER

This book is a work of fiction. Any references to real people, events, establishments, organisations or locales are intended only to provide a sense of authenticity and are used fictitiously. All of the characters and events are entirely invented by the author. Any resemblances to persons living or dead are purely coincidental.

CONTENTS

v

ACKNOWLEDGEMENTS

I would like to thank the authors of a wide range of internet resources, which have been invaluable for researching the background to this book. These include (among others):

- Spinal Injuries Association (http://www.spinal.co.uk)

- Wikipedia (https://en.wikipedia.org)

- Google Maps (https://www.google.co.uk/maps)

- Mersey Ferries (http://www.merseyferries.co.uk)

- Disability and Jesus (http://www.disabilityandjesus.org.uk)

- Singing the Faith Plus http://www.singingthefaithplus.org.uk

The title of this book is inspired by the song "Mist over the Mersey" composed by Jack Owen. His website may be found here:

http://www.jack-owen.co.uk/.

Many of the hymns from which the chapter titles are derived, may be found in *Singing the Faith*, published on behalf of the Trustees for Methodist Church Purposes by Hymns Ancient & Modern Ltd, 2011.

I would like to thank Gillian Gilbert for reading the manuscript, giving helpful comments and pointing out typographical errors; and Helen Ashcroft for her helpful suggestions for Liverpool locations and handy hints on the finer points of Facebook.

Every effort has been made to trace copyright holders. The publishers will be glad to rectify in future editions any errors or omissions brought to their attention.

GLOSSARY OF LIVERPUDLIAN PHRASES

For those unfamiliar with the dialect spoken in Liverpool, some of Bernie's language may be difficult to understand. Here are just a few frequently-used words and phrases.

Ace– Excellent (e.g. 'He's dead ace, he is!') It may also be used to congratulate someone: 'Ace!' means, 'Well done!'

Across the water– On the Wirral side of the Mersey (e.g. in Birkenhead or Wallasey).

Boss!– Good! Marvellous! Wonderful!

Chocka– Full, busy

Cracking the flags– Very hot (literally, hot enough to crack paving stones)

Dead– Very (e.g. 'dead good', 'dead awful', 'dead handy')

Footy– Football (i.e. soccer)

Flags– Flagstones (i.e. paving stones)

Givin' it bifters– Doing your best, making an effort, working enthusiastically.

Gorra– Got a

Gorra cob on– Fed up, in a bad mood.

Lavvy– Toilet

Me 'ead's chocka– Literally, 'my head's full'. This indicates mental overload or disquiet.

Our– Used to indicate that a person is a member of the family or a close friend. E.g. 'Our Bernie', 'Our kid', 'Our Dad'. May be used when speaking of someone or when speaking to them.

Our kid– Brother, often, but not always, the youngest of the family.

Over the water– On the Wirral side of the Mersey (e.g. in Birkenhead or Wallasey).

Ozzy– Hospital

Proddy– Protestant

Scouse– Used as a noun, this means either a type of stew, usually eaten with hunks of bread, or the dialect spoken in Liverpool. Blind Scouse, is scouse without any meat in it. Used as an adjective, it indicates that a person or object comes from Liverpool or is associated with Liverpool.

Scouser– Someone originating from Liverpool – a Liverpudlian.

GLOSSARY OF UK POLICE RANKS

Uniformed police

Chief Constable (CC) – Has overall charge of a regional police force, such as Thames Valley Police, which covers Oxford and a large surrounding area.

Deputy Chief Constable (DCC) – The senior discipline authority for each force. 2nd in command to the CC.

Assistant Chief Constable (ACC) – 4 in the Thames Valley Police Service, each responsible for a policy area.

Chief Superintendent ('Chief Super') – Head of a policing area or department.

Police Superintendent – Responsible for a local area within a police force.

Chief Inspector (CI) – Responsible for

overseeing a team in a local area.

Police Inspector – Senior operational officer overseeing officers on duty 24/7.

Police Sergeant – Supervises a team of officers.

Police Constable (PC) – 'Bobby on the beat'. Likely to be the first to arrive in response to an emergency call.

Crime Investigation Unit (CID) – Plain clothes officers

Detective Superintendent (DS) – Responsible for crime investigation in a local area.

Detective Chief Inspector (DCI) – Responsible for overseeing a crime investigation team in a local area. May be the Senior Investigating Officer heading up a criminal investigation.

Detective Inspector (DI) – Oversees

crime investigation 24/7. May be the Senior Investigating Officer heading up a criminal investigation.

Detective Sergeant (DS) – Supervises a team of CID officers.

Detective Constable (DC) – One of a team of officers investigating crimes.

These descriptions are based on information from the following sources:

[1] Mental Health Cop blog, by Inspector Michael Brown, Mental Health co-ordinator, College of Policing. https://mentalhealthcop.wordpress.com /, accessed 31st March 2017.

[2] Thames Valley Police website, https://www.thamesvalley.police.uk , accessed 31st March 2017.

1 SHALL WE GATHER AT THE RIVER?

'Morning father! What can I do for you?' said the woman in the booking office at the Pier Head ferry terminal cheerily.

'Just a boarding card, please,' the young priest replied, holding up his Trio season ticket, which confirmed that he was entitled to unlimited travel on buses, trains and ferries throughout Merseyside.

'Here you are, love!' She printed the boarding pass and handed it across the counter. 'Don't forget you have to break your journey on the other side.'

The priest nodded rather absently, picked up his ticket and walked away. Behind him in the queue, Bernie Fazakerley moved up to the counter to claim boarding cards for herself, her husband, Peter, and her daughter, Lucy. Then she led the way out of the booking hall to where passengers awaiting the next crossing were standing by the gates to the landing stage, watching for the ferry to arrive.

It was more than three decades since Bernie had visited her home town. That had been to attend her father's funeral, after which there had seemed to be nothing there to make it worth her while going back. And she had not wanted to remind herself of the happy times of her childhood or give her numerous uncles, aunts and cousins an opportunity to commiserate with her over the death of her fiancé and her subsequent failure to find a replacement for him. They had all busily played happy families, sending her cards to announce births, marriages and, increasingly in recent years, deaths, while Bernie had lived alone for the best part of twenty years, devoting herself to her role of Tutorial Fellow at one of the lesser-known Oxford Colleges.

Marriage, when it did eventually come, had been to a police superintendent nearly nineteen years her senior, and Bernie had not felt it necessary or desirable to introduce him to the few remaining relatives with whom she still maintained sparse correspondence. She was beyond the age when she might have liked to show off her conquest and she was well aware that few would consider Richard Paige to be much of a catch. When he died a mere two years later, none of Bernie's Liverpool family attended the funeral, and only a few sent cards of condolence. Although she remained fiercely loyal to her native city, Bernie's life and friends were in Oxford – something that became increasingly clear after she gave birth to Richard's posthumous daughter, Lucy, and, at the age of forty-two, finally joined in the game of motherhood, which her Scouse cousins had been playing for so long without her.

Now Lucy was sixteen and was

demanding to see the city that her mother always declared to be 'the best in the world'. Bernie, already feeling guilty at having neglected her family for so long, agreed to take her for a visit to see the sights and to meet her few remaining relatives. As always, her second husband, Peter, had come along for the ride – or more accurately, had come out of a mixture of affection for his stepdaughter, of whom he was extremely fond, and a sense of obligation to meet his in-laws, albeit rather distant ones.

The young priest looked rather out of place in his clerical collar and dark suit among the tourists in summer holiday garb eagerly anticipating their *River Explorer Cruise*. This was the rather grandiose description in the ferry company brochures of the round trip from Liverpool to two destinations on the Wirral side of the Mersey and back to the Pier Head. Bernie had shaken her head as she read the information and declared scornfully that this was not what it had been like in her day, when the ferries had been packed with workers travelling from homes on the Wirral to Liverpool, or conversely, travelling from Liverpool to the shipyards of Birkenhead. Then she had seen the price and had felt a mixture of pride in the ability of her fellow-Scousers to rip off the visitors and annoyance that she had become one of the victims of the racket. Finally, she had discovered that, for less than the cost of the so-called cruise, a *Saveaway* ticket could be purchased that allowed unlimited travel on rail, bus and ferry services for a day. That was more like it! And they could take the train to West Kirby or Port Sunlight – two fondly-remembered day-trip destinations from her childhood – for nothing.

The gate opened and they streamed down the slope towards the floating landing stage. The priest stumbled over the metal plate that covered the join between the ramp and the shore, allowing the landing stage to rise and fall with the tide. He seemed to be preoccupied and not watching his feet. He righted himself and walked briskly down to join the passengers queuing below. Bernie thought that he looked very young – quite unlike the ageing priests that she remembered from her childhood, with lined faces and grizzled grey hair; but perhaps that was just a sign of her own age, she mused, like what they said about how you knew you were getting old when the policemen started looking young. Lucy also watched the incident, noting subconsciously that, although the ferry brochure had boasted full accessibility, wheelchair users would need to take care during the process of boarding.

MV Snowdrop approached the landing stage and Bernie was afforded yet another opportunity to declare *it wasn't like this in my young day*! Not only had the ferry been re-named, but it had also been re-painted in a garish colour scheme as a *Dazzle Ship* – part of the World War I commemorations.

'It says here,' Lucy said, reading

from her smartphone, 'that ships were painted like this in the war to make it more difficult for them to be targeted by German aeroplanes and U-boats.'

'Hmm!' her stepfather murmured, staring at the brightly patterned hull with a sceptical expression on his face. 'I understand the theory. It's like zebras having stripes to confuse the lions by breaking up their outlines; but I can't help feeling that if I was manning the periscope on a U-boat I'd have no difficulty spotting all that red and yellow.'

'My gran used to tell us about the Mersey ferries going off to fight in the First World War,' Bernie told them. 'Not this one – they were steam ships in those days. And a couple of Dad's brothers went down in ships that were torpedoed in the Second World War. They were in the merchant navy bringing supplies from across the Atlantic.'

The ferry docked and passengers started to disembark. Then, shortly afterwards, the queue began to move and soon Bernie, Lucy and Peter were walking up the ramp on to the lower deck.

'Where shall we go?' Lucy asked

'There'll be a better view from upstairs,' Bernie told her, 'and I think you'll see more of the shore from the starboard side'.

So they climbed up to the stern deck and looked around for somewhere to sit. It was crowded and they could not see three seats together.

'Let's try the bow end,' Bernie suggested, leading the way forward, past the covered seating to what Peter, who was rather ostentatiously demonstrating that he had no pretentions to nautical knowledge, would insist on calling *the pointy end* of the boat. As they passed the door from the forward stairs Bernie collided with the priest from the booking hall who was stepping out on to the deck, his head bowed.

'Sorry father,' Bernie apologised.

'No, no,' he murmured absently. 'My fault. I wasn't looking where I was going.'

Bernie stepped back and allowed him to go ahead of them. He took up a standing position at the front of the boat, leaning against the rail. Bernie watched as he reached into his pocket and took out a string of beads, which he raised to his mouth and kissed. He must be planning to spend the crossing praying the rosary. Bernie wondered briefly whether this was a regular discipline – a way of making use of time that would otherwise be wasted during a routine journey that he made, perhaps every week – or if it symbolised a particular need for prayer at this time. The young man had seemed distracted right from when she had first stood behind him in the queue at the booking office. Bernie strongly suspected that there was something very particular on his mind and she felt curious to know with what intention he was offering his prayers.

They sat down on a bench seat facing the rail on the starboard (or as Peter put it, the right-hand) side of the vessel. An automated voice welcomed them aboard and went through a list of safety instructions. The sound of the diesel engines increased and they were off.

As they travelled downstream past the famous Liverpool waterfront, Bernie had to compete with the public address system in pointing out landmarks to Lucy and Peter. She also pointed out the folly of the ferry company in choosing a voice that could have come from anywhere to provide their commentary. 'If they're trying to give tourists a flavour of Liverpool, they could at least have got a Scouser to record it!'

'Maybe they thought it was more important to make it intelligible to everyone,' Peter suggested. 'Like the way they provided English commentaries at tourist attractions when we were in Portugal. It's all very well for us, because we've brought along our own interpreter, but your average Japanese tourist wouldn't have a clue what they were saying if it was in the local dialect.'

The boat turned, giving them a view of the estuary, and the disembodied voice invited them to look to see New Brighton and the lighthouse beyond. It went on to promote the Floral Pavilion theatre, which it claimed had recently enjoyed a revival of its fortunes.

MYSTERY OVER THE MERSEY

'We used to go for days out in New Brighton,' Bernie told Lucy. 'There used to be a ferry from the Pier Head that went there, but they stopped them when I was about twelve. I think they finally realised that New Brighton was not destined to become a major seaside resort!'

It was not long before they were drawing up alongside the landing stage at the Seacombe ferry terminal. Passengers walked past them on their way to disembark.

'Do we get off here?' Lucy asked.

'No. We'll stay on to Woodside,' her mother told her. 'I want to show you the street where my posh Aunty Margaret lived. She thought she was a cut above the rest of the family because she married an insurance broker and went to live across the water. They had a house near Birkenhead Park. It may even still be there.'

Lucy disappeared round to the other side of the boat and leaned on the rail, looking down at the landing stage, as passengers disembarked and a new group came aboard. Most of them headed for the larger stern deck, leaving only a handful of passengers in the bow area. Bernie glanced forward to see if Lucy was coming back, and noticed that the priest was still there, leaning against the rail, apparently engrossed in his prayers.

The ferry moved off again, turning round so that it was travelling upstream with the Wirral shore to their right. Bernie went to join Lucy on the port side of the boat, in order to show her the view of Liverpool from this side of the river. The Priest did not look up as she passed him.

After only a few minutes, it was time to make their way down to the lower deck ready to disembark. Lucy and Bernie walked back again to join Peter, who had remained in his seat overlooking the starboard side of the boat.

'I'm sorry to disturb you, father,' Bernie said to the priest as they passed, 'But we're nearly at Woodside. You have to get off here.'

He did not reply. Bernie touched him gently on the shoulder to attract his attention. Immediately, she knew that there was something wrong. He remained completely unmoving – unnaturally so. She shook his shoulder, gently at first and then more strongly. He twisted round and slipped to the floor. For a moment, Bernie and Lucy stood there staring down at him. He lay on his back staring up with lifeless eyes, his right hand still clutching the rosary of brown wooden beads.

They knelt down to examine him. Bernie undid the buttons of his jacket with the idea of helping him to breathe. As she did so, she felt a stickiness on the black shirt beneath. She looked at her fingers and saw that they were smeared with blood. There was a small hole in the shirt, which Bernie tore wider, trying to find the wound. Lucy, realising what she was doing, reached over to help. They both looked at the pale flesh beneath the clerical shirt and then looked at each other in stunned disbelief.

'Peter!' Bernie called out sharply. 'He's been stabbed – in the chest.'

Peter ran over, looked down briefly and then turned to go.

'Stay here,' he ordered. 'See nobody moves anything. I've got to make sure no-one gets off the boat.'

2 YE WHO HAVE WAITED LONG

'Please return to your seats,' came the announcement over the public address system. 'There has been a serious incident on board and we are awaiting the arrival of the police. Until then, no one is permitted to disembark. Mersey Ferries apologises for the inconvenience that this may cause.'

Bernie relinquished the body to two members of the crew, who stood guard over it, fending off passengers who crowded round wanting to know what was going on. After a few minutes of jostling, one of them tied ropes across the deck to keep everyone except Lucy, Bernie and the two guards away from the bow area.

Meanwhile, on the lower deck, Peter watched as the gangway was secured again in an upright position to prevent anyone leaving the vessel. He was glad that he had been able to intervene in time and that the deck hands in charge of docking the ship and supervising the disembarkation had accepted his authority as an ex-policeman and immediately suspended their operation. They summoned the first officer, who hurried upstairs to see the casualty for himself. Having confirmed that the young man was dead, he relayed the news to the captain, who summoned the police and ordered everyone to stay on board until they came. Now the first officer and one of the deck hands were standing awkwardly by the body, to which their eyes kept being drawn involuntarily, and giving non-committal answers to questions from passengers who wanted to know when they would be allowed to leave the boat.

Bernie and Lucy sat down on one of the wooden seats on the bow deck, trying to keep out of the way and look inconspicuous.

'Are you alright?' asked the first officer, looking anxiously towards Bernie.

She followed his eyes downwards and saw for the first time that her own shirt was stained with blood. It must have been transferred as the body slid down past her when she disturbed it.

'Yes,' she assured him. 'This isn't my blood – it must have come off him when I tried to attract his attention. I didn't realise he was dead,' she went on, trying to explain what she had been doing. 'I thought he just hadn't noticed we'd got to Woodside, and I was afraid he was going to forget to get off. So I put my hand on his shoulder and then he fell over.'

'It must have been a bit of a shock for you,' the first officer observed. 'Would you like me to get you a drink to steady your nerves?'

'No thanks. I'm fine.'

'This isn't the first time we've seen

a dead body,' Lucy informed him. She had been disappointed at not being allowed to examine the wound more closely and wanted to make it clear that there was no need to shield her or her mother from the grim reality of violent death. 'Mam is personal assistant to a DCI and she sees murder victims all the time. And I'm going to be a forensic pathologist,' she added, 'so this is really good experience for me.'

'Are you now?' the first officer said, smiling indulgently.

'You'd better believe her,' Bernie said firmly. 'She's got it all planned out. And she's deadly serious when she talks about getting experience. She's already managed to persuade a friend of ours to let her sit in on a post mortem. So my advice is – don't mess with our Lucy, if you know what's good for you!'

'I'd better check if the police are on their way.' The first officer excused himself and left them.

They sat for a few minutes in silence. Then Lucy turned to her mother with a puzzled frown on her face.

'How come nobody noticed him being killed?' she wondered. 'I mean, there were people about – us for a start – and yet we didn't see or hear anything.'

'I suppose we weren't watching,' Bernie answered. 'And there weren't that many other people out here after we left Seacombe.'

'But you'd have thought he'd have

shouted out,' Lucy persisted. 'I mean, it must have hurt, mustn't it? But I don't remember hearing a thing.'

'I don't know. Maybe you don't feel much if the knife goes straight into your heart. Or maybe it killed him so quickly he didn't have time to call out.'

'Could he have done it himself do you think?'

'I'd be surprised,' Bernie shook her head. 'For starters, he's a Roman Catholic priest. He must have had it drummed into him that suicide is a mortal sin. And I doubt if it's possible to kill yourself by stabbing yourself through the heart. It must take some force to do it. I don't know, but I think your reflexes would probably stop you. And whoever did it pulled the knife out again afterwards. Why would you bother if you were killing yourself? But if you're a murderer, you want to get rid of the murder weapon. And,' she continued, pointing towards the priest's right hand, which still clutched the rosary, 'he couldn't have held a knife in his right hand because it was already full.'

'What will the police do next?' Lucy wanted to know. 'I suppose they'll want to interview us?'

'They're bound to,' her mother agreed. 'But the first thing they'll want to do is to secure the crime scene, to make sure that no evidence is lost. Those ropes are a start, but the whole ship will have to be checked over by a forensics team. Whoever did it is likely to have blood on them somewhere, so they may want to check everyone's clothing. It's all going to take a long time, I'm afraid. Somehow I fancy we may not be going to get to see Aunty Margaret's house today, after all.'

'Never mind. This is much more exciting,' Lucy said, getting up and going over to look at the body more closely. She stood over it, staring down. 'I think you're right about it not being possible for him to have stabbed himself. If he had done, the hand that he'd held the knife in – which would have had to be his left hand – would be covered with blood. I mean – look at how much you've got on you, just touching him. His clothes are soaking in it.'

'Mmm. That's what makes me think the knife must have gone straight into his heart – or at least a major artery. Either the killer was dead lucky or he knew exactly what he was doing.'

'I don't suppose they'd let me sit in on the PM?' Lucy suggested, knowing already that the answer would be negative but determined not to allow the opportunity to pass without any attempt at taking advantage of it.

'No. I'm sure they wouldn't. And it's no good asking me or Peter to lobby on your behalf. It was all very well with Mike Carson, who knows us, but here we're just a couple of civilians who have no business getting involved. Besides, we are both witnesses, which means that it would be improper to allow you access to any additional evidence in case it biased your own testimony. In fact,' Bernie added, remembering an aspect of police procedure that she had forgotten in the excitement, 'we shouldn't really be discussing what we saw in case we influence each other's memories.'

Bernie's long association with the police, first through marriage and, during the two years since her retirement from academia, as the personal assistant to DCI Jonah Porter, meant that she had accumulated a large amount of knowledge about good practice in criminal investigation. She ran through in her mind the steps that the team from Thames Valley Police would have taken in these circumstances.

'I bet all the other passengers are discussing what they saw,' Lucy said combatively. 'So I don't see why we shouldn't.'

'It's all a matter of making sure that our evidence is independent,' Bernie explained. 'According to the psychologists, witnesses naturally like to agree with one another, so what you say you saw might influence what I remember seeing. We don't like to feel that what we are saying is inconsistent with what other people tell us they saw. And then, precisely because our evidence is consistent, juries tend to believe that what we think we saw was what actually happened. Ideally, witnesses would all be kept in complete isolation until after they've given their statements to the police.'

'That must make everything take an awfully long time,' Lucy observed. 'I thought they'd interview the three of us all together.'

'They shouldn't,' Bernie said firmly. 'However, in your case they're in a bit of a bind, because there's also a rule that says that you can't interview minors without an appropriate adult present – which would normally mean me or Peter. You have to have someone there to look after your interests and see that they don't bully you.'

'Anyway, we'll have plenty to talk about with Cousin Joey and the rest of them tomorrow,' Lucy said, obediently seeking a topic of conversation that could not be construed as prejudicial to the enquiry. 'I bet they've never been witnesses to a murder.'

'No, I don't suppose they have –

although the way some people talk, you'd think it was the sort of thing that happened every day in their part of Liverpool – and I'm not that overjoyed that we are, either,' Bernie said sharply. 'Before you get too excited about the whole business, please try to remember that somebody has actually died here.'

'Sorry, Mam,' Lucy tried to feel remorse. 'But we didn't know him and you have to admit it's interesting to try to think how someone managed to do it under our noses like that – and why they'd want to, as well. What harm could a priest have done to anyone?'

'And that's another thing,' her mother answered, refusing to be drawn into speculation. 'Two of Joey's uncles and one of his brothers are priests, so it's entirely possible that they could have known this one. So be very careful what you say to the family tomorrow.'

'Who exactly is it we're meeting?' Lucy forced herself to move the conversation on to safer ground. 'I get so confused trying to work out who everyone is.'

'Joey is my cousin. His dad was my dad's brother, so he's another Fazakerley. He and his wife, Ruth, have invited us over. Joey's mum is a widow and getting on a bit, so she lives with them and I expect we'll see her too. Her name is Rose. Then Joey and Ruth have three kids: James, Chloë and Dominic. They're all still living at home as well.'

'How old are they?'

'I can't remember exactly. Dominic was just a baby when I married your dad. I remember because that was Joey's excuse for not coming to the wedding. So I suppose he must have been born in ninety-six or maybe early in ninety-seven. He's the youngest, by quite a few years.'

'So they're all a lot older than me.'

'It depends what you mean by *a lot*, but yes, they're all in their twenties. You have to remember that my dad was the youngest in his family and then I left it rather late to have you, so the surprising thing really is that there isn't a bigger age gap.'

'So aren't there any *young* relations for me to meet?'

'Not that I know of. At least … there must be lots, but they've probably moved away. The only people I've kept up with are Joey and Aunty Dot. She's one of my dad's sisters. She never married, so she helped us out when my mam was diagnosed with motor neurone disease. She was a bit like a second mother to me. We're going to see her tomorrow as well. She's in a care home in Wavertree. Joey's going to take us over there tomorrow afternoon.'

'Your attention please,' the captain's voice sounded over the public address system again. 'The police have now arrived and arrangements are being made for you to disembark. Please remain in your seats for further announcements. Once more, I would like to apologise for the delay to your journey and the inconvenience that it will cause.'

'I bet he's glad it will be the police's job to break it to them all that getting off the ship is only the start of things,' Bernie muttered. 'I imagine there's a lot going on clearing the ferry terminal and finding somewhere to accommodate us all while we wait to be interviewed and fingerprinted and stuff.'

'Jonah will be green with envy when he hears that we've got involved in a murder without him,' Lucy said, smiling at the thought of their friend from Thames Valley CID, whom they had left behind in Oxford. 'This is just the sort of thing he'd enjoy investigating.'

'Too right, he would,' her mother

agreed, smiling at the mention of DCI Jonah Porter, who played a big part in both of their lives. 'Which means it's a good thing he stayed at home this time. If he was here, I'd have my work cut out preventing him from trying to take over – which would *not* be likely to endear us to the local CID.'

'I wonder how he's getting on at home with Nathan looking after him,' Lucy mused. 'He said he was going to give Nathan lots of jobs to do in the garden to keep him out of his hair, but I think Nathan was expecting to be fully occupied seeing to his personal care.'

'I expect they'll rub along OK. Nathan's a good lad. He's just never managed to stop being over-protective, that's all.'

MYSTERY OVER THE MERSEY

A bullet in the neck, more than seven years previously, had left Jonah severely disabled. He had fought back and had demanded to be allowed to continue his police work. This was made possible by dint of an array of technological devices and by having Bernie as his constant companion during working hours. After his wife's death, Bernie and her family had played an increasing role in his care, culminating in his moving in with them on a full-time basis. Nathan, his younger son, was very willing, but found it hard to allow his father the same freedom to take risks as he enjoyed when Bernie was in charge. Lucy was quite correct in thinking that a week's annual leave in the care of his son, without the stimulation of his police work, would be a trying ordeal for him.

'I'll send him an email,' Lucy said, reaching in her pocket for her smartphone. 'It'll cheer him up to have a nice juicy murder to think about.'

'You'll do nothing of the sort,' Bernie retorted firmly. 'First off: you've no business telling anyone about this until the police say you can. And second, what business do you have suggesting that Jonah needs cheering up, just because he doesn't have you there to keep him amused? For all you know, he and Nathan are having a whale of a time!'

Lucy looked sceptical, but replaced her phone in her pocket.

'I bet none of the other passengers

are maintaining radio silence,' she muttered. 'They'll all be on to their friends and relations saying,' – and here she switched to an exaggerated version of her mother's Liverpool accent –, 'Get this, Our Kid. I've got a right cob on with this malarkey. It's cracking the flags down here and we've got to stay on this ferry boat while the filth faff about asking questions.'

'Not so much of the cheek, our Lucy!' Bernie pretended to be offended. 'Never mock a Scouser – we have long memories. Seriously, though, I'm glad that we're the only people who actually saw anything. It'd be awful if his,' – here she looked down at the dead priest lying at their feet –, 'family got to hear rumours before he's been officially identified.'

3 AN EVER PRESENT HELP AND STAY

Back in their house in Headington, on the outskirts of Oxford, Jonah was contemplating an escape plan.

The previous evening had been fine, he admitted to himself. Nathan and his fiancée, Georgia, had arrived in plenty of time to enable his friends to set off for Liverpool at the scheduled time. Then they had spent a pleasant time chatting about the arrangements for their forthcoming wedding, which was now only two weeks away. Georgia had tactfully left when it was time for Nathan to start the process of washing Jonah and preparing him for bed. And Nathan had carried out his caring duties in a business-like manner.

The night had passed uneventfully, although Jonah had been conscious of Nathan's presence looking down on him on several unnecessary occasions – presumably checking in case he was being smothered by the bedclothes or had unaccountably stopped breathing. They had got through his morning ablutions and breakfast with only minor irritation on Jonah's part when Nathan had insisted on waiting for his tea to cool down to a safe temperature before putting it within his reach. Jonah had been about to remonstrate with him about treating him as if he could not be trusted to judge such things for himself, but managed to restrain himself, knowing that his son was only acting for the best – and probably following guidelines provided to him by professional carers.

Now they were out in the garden, taking advantage of the good weather to enjoy some fresh air and sunshine. Jonah, who had been a keen gardener before his injury, set Nathan to work on a list of jobs, while he sat in the shade of a large oak tree – one of the trees that been growing here before Richard's grandfather had built this house for his family in the early years of the twentieth century – following an online forensic science course on the computer screen attached to his electric wheelchair. He was studying a photograph of fingermarks collected from a crime scene and trying to decide whether or not they matched any of the sets of prints from three suspects in an imaginary robbery, when Nathan came over to check that he did not need anything. Jonah did his best to sound grateful for the attention, but assured his son that there was nothing that he could do for him.

Nathan returned to tying up the wisteria that covered half of the back wall of the house, winding round the kitchen window and dangling across the window on the half landing at the head of the stairs. For about ten minutes, Jonah was able to concentrate on new techniques for showing up fingermarks on porous surfaces. Then Nathan stepped down off the stepladder and came over to him again.

'Everything OK?' he asked cheerily. 'Are you sure there's nothing I can get you?'

'What I'd really like is for you to mow the lawn for me.'

And so it had gone on. It seemed to Jonah that, no sooner had he got fully engaged in the next part of his course, but Nathan would come over and interrupt his thoughts to check that all was well with him. In the end, he decided to make a getaway. He waited until Nathan was engrossed in his latest gardening task and then exited from the online course and started the chair gliding silently across the patio.

'I'm just going to pop out to the shops on London Road,' he called out to Nathan, as he headed off towards the gate at the side of the house. 'The bird feeder is out of peanuts.'

'Don't worry about that,' Nathan responded, dropping the shears with which he had been trimming the grass round the edge of one of the wide flower borders and walking quickly across the lawn to intercept his father. 'I'll go later and get them for you.'

'I'd rather go myself,' Jonah argued patiently. 'You've got plenty to keep you busy here and it'll do me good to get out of the house.'

'You *are* out of the house,' Nathan pointed out.

'You know what I mean.'

'No, I don't really. It's a beautiful day. Why don't you just sit back and relax and enjoy the sunshine?'

'Because I'd rather keep active. I don't want to stagnate.'

'I thought you were working on your computer?'

'I was.' Jonah forced himself not to add, *but I keep getting interrupted*, and instead went on, 'but it's time for a break.'

'That's a good idea,' Nathan agreed, brightening up. 'I could do with one too. I'll put the kettle on.'

'I didn't mean a tea break,' Jonah said, keeping his temper with some difficulty. 'I just meant a change. A walk over to the shops will give me a chance to mull over what I've been learning about before going on to the next module.'

'But it won't be a walk for you, will it?' Nathan argued, taken aback by his father's use of the word to describe an expedition in his electric wheelchair. 'You're talking about a mile or more and how do you propose getting across the by-pass?'

'There's a pedestrian crossing.'

'How will you press the button?'

'I can reach with my nose if necessary, but there are usually people about who do it for me.'

'What if the battery gives out before you get back?'

'It won't. You put it on to charge overnight, remember?'

'I still think it would be easier for me to go, but if you really want to get out for a while, that's fine by me. I'll just go and wash my hands before we set out.'

'No.' Jonah's patience was stretched to the limit, but he was determined not to allow it to show. 'I'd rather go on my own and let you finish the grass. I want the garden to be looking its best when the others get back.'

Nathan hesitated. He knew that his father valued his independence and he recognised that he was probably being excessively cautious in not wanting to let him out of his sight, but he still found it difficult to allow him the freedom that he demanded. In Nathan's mind, the trip to the shops was full of dangers for Jonah. What if a car failed to stop at the lights? Or if his chair broke down while he was crossing the road? Suppose someone were to decide to rob him? All they needed to do was to move his left hand off the controls of the wheelchair and he would be completely at their mercy. What about uneven pavements and tree roots that might upset the chair? He forced himself to ignore all these concerns and to reply calmly.

'OK Dad. Have it your own way. I'll keep my mobile in my pocket, so if you do need anything just give me a bell.'

'Thanks.'

Nathan watched as Jonah expertly steered the chair down the side of the house, pausing for the automatic gate to open to allow him through and then continuing out into the front garden. He was hidden from view as the gate closed behind him. Nathan stood for a few moments gazing at the back of the gate, undecided what to do. Then he made up his mind. He put the long-handled shears away in the shed. Then he went inside and locked the patio doors and the kitchen door before going out through the front door. He looked down the long drive, checking that his father was out of sight before pulling the door closed behind him.

Then he ran down the drive and peered out round the tall copper beech hedge. Jonah was moving away from him along the pavement, driving his chair at a brisk walking pace. Nathan waited until he turned the corner into the next road before coming out from behind the hedge and hurrying to follow.

The garden at the end of the road was bounded by a low wall. Nathan crouched down so that it shielded him as he peered round the corner. He saw his father some distance away, crossing the road, taking advantage of the lowered kerb at the edge of a driveway. He remained crouching until Jonah had reached the pavement on the other side and set off again, heading towards a path past a wide grassy area, which Nathan knew separated the residential area from the Eastern By-pass. This fast-moving dual carriageway, part of the ring road that encircles Oxford in an attempt to keep through traffic out of the city centre, separated the part of Headington where Jonah and his friends lived from the small shopping centre to which he was bound.

Jonah passed out of sight once more, beyond a high hedge and metal railings, which marked the boundary of the grounds of a small engineering firm. Nathan stood up and followed, keeping close to the hedge to avoid being seen. When he was far enough round the curve of the hedge to see Jonah once more, he stopped, pressing himself against the railings so as to watch without being observed.

There was no-one else around. Jonah manoeuvred his chair expertly to stand close by the control panel that allowed pedestrians to signal their desire to cross the busy road. He was unable to move his hands or arms to press the button. However, the three working fingers of his left hand, with which he controlled his wheelchair, enabled him to adjust the height to bring his face level with the panel. He leaned forward and pressed his nose against it. The display lit up: *WAIT*.

'Mummy! Can I press the button?'

Nathan turned at the sound of a child's voice behind him. He saw a young woman with a baby in a buggy and a small boy walking beside her.

'OK.'

The boy ran on ahead, reaching the crossing just as the *WAIT* sign went off and the green man lit up to indicate that it was safe to cross the first half of the dual carriageway.

'Stop there, Noah! Wait for me!' his

mother called anxiously, hurrying to catch up with him.

Jonah hesitated, wondering whether to cross. He looked at the boy, who was pressing the button vigorously, wondering why it did not make the sign light up as it usually did.

'The cars have already stopped for us,' Jonah pointed out to him. 'But we'd better wait for your mum to join us before we go across.'

'It's OK. I'm here now,' the boy's mother arrived in time for them all to cross safely to the central reservation together.

'Do you think you could press the button for me this time?' Jonah asked Noah seriously. 'It would be a big help if you could.'

Noah nodded and reached up eagerly, smiling with delight as the light came on instructing them to *WAIT*. Soon they were all stepping on to the pavement on the other side. Seeing that Jonah was engaged in conversation with his new acquaintances, Nathan risked stepping up to the crossing and making his own request for the traffic to be stopped. It seemed like a long time before he had negotiated both carriageways and Jonah had already disappeared from view by the time he was able to follow him into a road lined with a mixture of genuinely old buildings and modern houses built from imitation Cotswold stone, designed to blend in with their surroundings. Nathan hurried along, keeping close to the tall, moss-encrusted stone wall on his left, trying to be as inconspicuous as possible.

He stopped as he saw Jonah and his friends waiting at a junction. They crossed the road and then their ways parted. The children were bound for the small play area at the corner of the recreation ground. As soon as his mother released her hold of his hand, Noah raced ahead, eager for his turn on the slides and swings. Jonah turned to the right to reach a narrow passageway between houses, which opened out to become a path along the side of the recreation ground. It was a shortcut, but tricky for Jonah in his wheelchair because of the slalom at the entrance, which had been installed to deter cyclists.

Nathan waited at the entrance to

the path, peering gingerly round the wall, watching as his father progressed down the long, straight strip of tarmac. Eventually he turned a corner and disappeared again down a short passage between two houses. Nathan ran to catch up. He was not sure which way Jonah would go when he came out to the road. Either direction would take him to the shops – eventually. Nathan felt that he had already come quite far enough in the heat of a sunny August day and wondered why his father had been so keen to make this unnecessary journey.

By the time Nathan reached the corner, Jonah had already disappeared, so he ran on to reach the end of the path. Looking to left and right, there was still no sign of his quarry. To the right, the road was straight for some distance, whereas to the left it curved round almost immediately. Nathan deduced that this was, therefore, the more likely direction; so he turned that way and hurried along, watching out all the time for any sign of Jonah and his wheelchair ahead. He came to a T-junction and looked hopefully to the right, which was the direction that Jonah would have to go, assuming that he had chosen this route.

There he was! Not far off now, but heading away at a faster rate than Nathan's accustomed walking pace. London Road, where Jonah was bound, was only a few hundred yards ahead now. Nathan could see the cars and buses passing across at the junction. First however, there was a smaller cross-roads to negotiate. Jonah glided down the wheelchair-friendly section of pavement where the kerb had been lowered and continued across the road and up the other side.

Then he turned to the left and started across the road along which he had been travelling. *Why did he do that?* Nathan wondered as he watched Jonah heading away again, this time on the left-hand pavement. He followed suit and soon realised the purpose of his father's apparently unnecessary manoeuvre. A little further on, a side road emerged on the right. Its kerb had not been lowered and might have been problematical for Jonah's wheelchair.

Jonah had reached the main road now. Nathan ran to catch up and then stood at the corner, grateful for the rather overgrown hedge surrounding the end house, which concealed him from view as he watched his father heading off towards the row of shops. There were more people about now, so Nathan risked following, assuming that Jonah would be unlikely to notice him among the other pedestrians if he were to look round. Seeing him disappear into a shop on the left, he looked around for somewhere to wait. There was a bus shelter almost directly opposite the shop. He could sit down there, inconspicuous among the cluster of people waiting for the bus, and keep an eye on the shop entrance. He crossed the road and settled down on one of the benches in front of the stone wall that surrounded a small park.

The woman in the pet shop knew Jonah and greeted him warmly.

'What can we do for you on this lovely summer day?'

'Just a bag of peanuts for the birds. Or ... perhaps I might as well have some more sunflower seeds too, while I'm here.'

She selected the items and went round to the back of Jonah's chair to put them in the storage bag that was built in behind the backrest.

'Is your credit card in the usual place?'

'That's right. It's a new contactless one, so you won't even need to get me to type in the PIN.'

She reached into the bag, located a small zip-up compartment inside, and extracted the card. The sale completed, she returned it to its place and fastened the bag closed.

'There you are. All done! Have you got anything exciting planned for the weekend?'

'I've got my younger son staying for a week, while the rest of the family go off to Liverpool for a break,' Jonah told her, trying to sound as if this were a treat for him. 'He's getting married in two weeks, so we'll have a lot to talk about.'

'How exciting! Give him my congratulations.'

Nathan watched impatiently from

across the street. The purchase of a few nuts for the birds seemed to be taking a surprisingly long time. Could he have missed seeing his father emerge? Could Jonah have come out while that bus was stopped, blocking his view, a few moments before? He stood up and started along the road towards the shop. Then he froze and stepped back behind two elderly women with shopping bags, who were standing in the middle of the pavement chatting. To Nathan's surprise instead of turning to set off for home, Jonah crossed the wide pavement outside the pet shop and approached the zebra crossing, which linked the row of shops to the park entrance. Almost immediately, the traffic gave way and he set off across the road and in at the park gate. *What was he up to now? Why couldn't he go home, where he would be safe from all the unpredictability of the streets?*

Nathan peered cautiously round the wall to see Jonah heading off along the path that stretched out diagonally towards the right. Nathan stepped through the gates and concealed himself behind a tree. A golden retriever ran across the grass, alerting Nathan to yet another potential threat to his father's safety. Nathan knew to his cost that dogs often attacked cyclists, and he imagined that the canine reaction to a wheelchair might well be similar. However, the dog was intent on retrieving a ball thrown by its owner and raced past Jonah without even turning its head.

Jonah continued for a hundred yards or so and then moved off the path to take up a position in the shade of one of the large trees that were dotted about the grassy parkland. Nathan watched for a while. Then, seeing that he appeared to be engrossed in something on his computer screen, he started to work his way closer, taking cover behind trees and shrubs to avoid being seen. Eventually he found a bench that afforded a clear view of Jonah's position, while being screened by a small clump of bushes. He sat down and prepared to wait until his father decided to set off again.

His mobile phone buzzed in his pocket. He fumbled to extract it and looked down at the display. It was

Jonah. What could he want? Nathan could see from here that there was nothing obviously wrong. He answered the call.

'It's alright Nathan,' came his father's cheery voice. 'You can come out now.'

He looked up and saw that Jonah had turned his chair to face the bench where he was sitting and was looking straight towards him. Nathan got up and started to walk over to him.

'You may be an excellent barrister,' Jonah greeted him, 'but you are hopeless at covert surveillance.'

'How long have you known I was following you?' his son asked with a rueful grin. 'I thought I'd been so careful not to let you see me.'

MYSTERY OVER THE MERSEY

'I had my suspicions from when the traffic on the ring road stopped again so soon after we'd crossed. After that, I was on the lookout and I spotted you before we'd got to the end of Beaumont Road.'

'But how? You never turned round.'

'I didn't need to. There are all sorts of surfaces around that act as mirrors – especially on a sunny day like this. I caught sight of you first reflected in the rear window of one of the parked cars. Then I double-checked in the wing mirror of another and after that, I knew I could rely on you following along like a good little puppy dog until we got to the shops. It wasn't a bad idea to join the bus queue, but then you really blew it coming right out into the open just as I was making my getaway. You need to cultivate more patience if you're ever going to be any good at shadowing people.'

'I thought I must have missed you. A bus came past while you were in the shop and I thought maybe you'd come out while it was blocking my view.'

'It was very amusing watching you trying to cross the park,' Jonah went on, smiling. 'It reminded me of the cartoons I used to watch when I was about six. There you were waiting your moment to dash from one piece of cover to the next and then standing rigid behind each tree, hoping I couldn't see you.'

'But you were reading the computer screen,' Nathan protested. 'I made sure you were looking down each time before I made a move.'

'Aha! But you were forgetting the camera facility. The lens is in the back of the screen. When you thought I was busy doing my forensic science course, I was actually watching your antics.'

'I suppose you think I ought to have stayed at home and let you go on your own,' Nathan said in a resigned tone.

'Absolutely, you should! I've done it dozens of times before.'

'I know. I'm sorry. The thing is, I can't help thinking about all the things that could go wrong.'

'If anything did go wrong, I've got a tongue in my head – I could always ask someone to help. And, so long as the mobile phone app was still working, I could have rung you to come and sort me out.'

'Not much good if you're crushed under a lorry on the by-pass or pinned to the ground by a pit bull.'

'Both of which could perfectly easily happen to you as much as to me.'

'Not *as* easily,' Nathan argued, unwilling to give way completely. 'Look, I know you want to be independent, and I can respect that, but I do think you ought to be more willing to recognise the risks and to accept that people worry about you.'

'Might you not try to accept that it's up to me to decide what risks I want to take?' Jonah asked mildly. He had rather enjoyed leading Nathan on a wild goose chase and was consequently feeling less irritated by the argument than he would normally have done.

'But it's not, though,' Nathan persisted. 'Why don't you try looking at it from my point of view for once? If anything did happen to you, what am I supposed to say to Gran or Reuben? – or to Bernie and Peter and Lucy, for that matter? They handed you over to me in good faith and they'll be expecting to get you back in good condition.'

'They wouldn't blame you, if anything *did* happen. They know how stubborn I am.'

'Maybe not, but I'd blame myself. And we'd all be upset if you got hurt. Why can't you see that?'

Jonah sighed.

'I'm sorry, Nathan. I know what you mean, and I *don't* take silly risks – but you must let me do ordinary things that everyone else does. Things like walking to the shops on my own. And before you start,' he went on, seeing that Nathan appeared to be about to protest, 'remember that there's no such thing as a risk-free existence. A vehicle is just as likely to jump the lights on the ring road when *you're* crossing as when *I* am. And you won't come off any better from an argument with a ten ton truck than I would. In fact, I might even do better than you, because the chair would probably absorb some of the impact.'

'You're still more vulnerable in lots of ways,' Nathan continued to argue. 'And I don't think it's fair of you not to take into account other people's feelings about you. Lucy, for example,' he said, with a flash of inspiration, knowing how fond Jonah was of the girl who had played such a large part in his life since his disabling injury shortly after her ninth birthday. 'She'd be devastated if anything happened to you.'

This hit home. For a few moments, Jonah did not know how to respond.

'They don't try to stop me going out on my own,' he said at last.

'Only because they know you wouldn't listen to reason and they've got to live with you afterwards.'

'And *I'd* be devastated if anything happened to Lucy,' his father went on, trying to think of a better argument to justify his stance, 'but I don't tell her not to do risky things like riding her bike or punting or swimming or climbing trees or …'

'OK. OK. I can see I'm wasting my breath,' Nathan sighed. 'Let's call it quits and go home now, shall we?'

4 THY WOUNDS THEY ARE DEEP

After what felt like hours, but which was only in fact a matter of minutes, a further announcement told passengers aboard MV Snowdrop that the police had arrived and that the gangway was being lowered to allow officers on board. The disembodied voice reminded them that this did not mean that they were free to go and asked them to stay seated and not attempt to disembark.

Peter positioned himself near the

exit and watched as the barrier was removed and the gangway lowered. A man in a navy blue business suit came up behind him and tried to pass. Peter put out his hand to restrain him.

'Stand back please, sir,' he said, falling back into the tone of polite authority that he had gained through forty years in the police force.

'I've got to get off,' the man said forcefully, pushing past and striding towards the gangway.

The deck hand operating the barrier stepped forward and stood in his way.

'I'm sorry,' he said firmly 'We have orders from the police not to allow anyone off.'

'But I have an important meeting,' the man insisted. 'There could be thousands hanging on this. It could mean people's jobs at stake.'

'I'm sorry, sir–,' Peter began again, but he was interrupted by the arrival up the gangway of two uniformed officers. The businessman turned to appeal to them, but one of them spoke first.

'If you would just return to your seat please sir: we need to have a look around and then we'll tell you what is going to happen next.'

'But you don't understand. I'm already late for a very important meeting.'

'I'm very sorry sir, but we've received a report that a man has been killed and we have to investigate before anyone can be allowed off the boat. Please bear with us and go and sit down.'

The man appeared to hesitate as if considering another attempt at getting past the barrier. Then he changed his mind and went back into the covered seating area. The sergeant turned his attention to Peter.

'And perhaps you could also return to your seat please, sir?'

'Detective Inspector Peter Johns,' Peter introduced himself by way of explanation. 'At least, I'm retired now, but I might be able to help. I was one of the people who found the body. Would you like me to show you?'

'Sergeant Tom Pullinger – and my colleague, PC Janet Morecambe. You must be the guy who raised the alarm. Yes please – you lead the way.'

Peter took them up the stairs to the stern deck and held the rope up for them to pass under. The deck hand who had been left guarding the body looked towards them with an expression of relief on his face. Pullinger and Morecambe strode across and stood looking down at the corpse. Peter followed them, but his attention was on Lucy and Bernie who were still sitting on the seat close by.

'You alright?' he asked.

'You betcha!' Bernie grinned up at him. 'I've been explaining to our Lucy all the reasons why she can't be allowed to sit in on the PM.'

Sergeant Pullinger straightened up from where he had been crouching down to examine the body.

'It definitely looks like foul play,' he murmured. Then louder, 'we'd better get CID and a team of SOCOs over here. Jan – you stay here and make sure nobody tampers with the crime scene. I'm going to see about clearing the booking hall and finding somewhere to keep everyone while we get statements from them.'

He turned to Peter, 'It's a good thing you were there to step in and stop people leaving. Now if you could come with me ...'

His voice trailed off as he noticed Bernie and Lucy for the first time. He looked them up and down, taking in the smears of blood on Bernie's pale blue polo shirt and the red stains on the palms of her hands.

'May I introduce my wife, Bernadette Fazakerley – Bernie – and her daughter, Lucy? Bernie was the one who actually discovered that he was dead.'

'Hence the bloody appearance,' Bernie added. 'He sort of rolled against me as he fell over. He was propped up against the railings, you see.'

'Ah!' Pullinger nodded. 'I think you three had better all come with me.'

Leaving his colleague to guard the body, he led the way back down the stairs. There was a cluster of people at the bottom, arguing with the first officer, who had joined the deck hand at the exit to help prevent any of the increasingly disgruntled passengers from forcing their way past. It appeared that the smartly-dressed executive was not the only person who thought that they had special circumstances that warranted their being allowed off. They stared at Bernie's blood-stained shirt, hands and face, as she followed the uniformed police officer off the ferry and down to the landing stage. Lucy giggled when she heard them whispering together that it looked as if the police had already made an arrest.

The inside of the terminal building was buzzing with activity. The public had been cleared from the booking hall and police officers in uniform were helping staff from the café to set out piles of stacking chairs to provide seating for the ferry passengers when they disembarked. One of them came up to Pullinger.

'DI Latham is on her way,' he reported. 'She said to get the passengers off the ferry and make them comfortable here until we can process them.'

Pullinger ushered them into the café and indicated to them to sit down at a table in the corner.

'I'm afraid there may be a bit of a wait,' he apologised, 'but I expect you'll be some of the first that the inspector wants to speak to when she gets here. I'd get yourself a coffee if I were you. I should think you could do with something to drink.'

'What I could do with more,' Bernie replied, 'is a clean shirt and to wash my hands. Is that allowed?'

'I've got blood on my hands too,'

Lucy added. 'From where I helped to rip his shirt open.'

Pullinger hesitated then nodded. 'You can both go and get washed in the Ladies. Come back here when you're done. I'll see what I can do about another shirt.'

Peter ordered a pot of tea for three and waited. He heard vehicles outside and saw a group of about a dozen police officers coming into the booking hall. Then the automatic doors opened again and a tall woman in plain clothes entered. The sea of blue uniforms parted to allow her to walk briskly through, followed by a shorter, less authoritative figure in a grey trouser suit and pink blouse. Peter watched as one of the police officers, who had been arranging chairs when they arrived, stepped forward and greeted the two women. This must be DI Latham and her assistant, Peter deduced.

Just then Bernie and Lucy returned, looking a little less like violent criminals now that their hands were clean and the smears of blood, which Bernie had managed to transfer on to her face, were gone. They sat down and Peter poured tea for all of them.

'It looks as if the DI's here,' Peter observed, nodding towards the door of the café.

They followed his gaze and saw the familiar figure of Sergeant Pullinger speaking with the two women whom Peter had seen arriving. They saw him gesticulating in their direction.

'He's telling her about these suspicious characters who claimed to have found the body but who are probably really the perpetrators of the crime,' Bernie said with a grin.

'Don't joke about it,' Peter warned. 'It may come to that if they can't find anyone else to pin it on.'

'That is an extraordinarily cynical attitude for an ex-policeman.'

Pullinger came over and made the introductions.

'This is DI Sandra Latham,' he said, looking towards the tall woman, whom Peter could now see had short brown hair and pale brown eyes of an almost identical shade. He judged that she was in her mid-forties and, by her confident air, that she was an experienced investigating officer. 'And this is DS Charlotte Simpson,' Pullinger continued, turning towards the younger woman, whom Peter categorised in his mind as a bit of a greenhorn, probably a graduate on a fast-track scheme who had been promoted ahead of getting much hands-on experience.

They all shook hands. Then the two plain-clothes officers pulled up chairs and sat down at the table with them. Pullinger remained standing, looking a little uncomfortable. Then a female constable in uniform approached and held out a plastic carrier bag towards him.

'This is the best I could do,' she said. 'It's a size twelve. I hope that's OK.'

Pullinger took the bag and held it towards Bernie.

'Constable Evans has been out to get a new shirt for you. I hope this fits.'

'Thanks.' Bernie took the bag and peered into it. Then she pulled out a blue and green floral-patterned blouse with short sleeves and, to her mind, a rather low neckline. 'That will do fine,' she assured them. 'Can I go and change into it now?'

'How much do we owe you? Peter asked, as Bernie disappeared in the direction of the toilets once again. He got out his wallet and there followed a brief argument over who should pay for the garment or whether it could be legitimately charged to police expenses. Peter won in the end and handed over to PC Evans the price of the blouse, generously rounded up.

By the time Bernie returned, wearing her new blouse and carrying the soiled polo shirt in the carrier bag, the other passengers were being escorted off the ferry and directed to find seats in the booking hall and café. There was a buzz of conversation as everyone found places to sit and chattered about what was going on and how it would affect their schedule for the day.

'Mrs Fazakerley?' DI Latham said to Bernie. 'Sergeant Pullinger tells me that you found the body. I'm afraid that means that we are going to have to ask you a lot of questions and it may take some time. And we'll need to interview you each separately – you, your husband and your daughter.'

'It may make things easier for everyone,' Bernie answered, 'if I tell you that Peter, here is an ex-DI and I work for Thames Valley Police in a support role for a DCI. So we know the drill. The other thing to get straight is our names. I'm Dr Bernie Fazakerley – if I'm Mrs anything I suppose it would be Mrs Johns. That's Peter's name. And Lucy's surname is Paige, which is her father's name. Sorry that everything's so complicated.'

'I see. So, just to be sure I've got this right: you are Dr Bernadette Fazakerley, DI Peter Johns –'

'You can forget the DI,' Peter interjected, 'I'm retired now.'

'– and Lucy Paige. And Lucy, you are how old?'

'Sixteen,' Lucy answered.

'In that case, one of you had better be present when we interview your daughter,' Latham said, turning to look at Bernie. 'Will she be alright with one of our female PCs while we interview you and your husband? Then we'll be able to save time by interviewing you both at the same time, and then afterwards you can be there when we interview your daughter.'

'I don't need a minder,' Lucy objected. 'I'll be fine here on my own while you interview Mam and Peter. There's Wi-Fi in the café here, so I won't be bored.'

'I was thinking more that you might

be more comfortable having someone around, after what you saw on the boat,' Latham began, but, seeing Lucy's scornful expression, she went on, 'but, if you're sure? You wait here and your mum and dad will be back shortly.'

'But remember,' Bernie warned, 'all this is still confidential. So no pasting pictures of the crime scene on Facebook or messaging all your friends.'

'I wasn't going to,' Lucy protested, 'but can't I just tell Jonah? He won't spread it around.'

'I'm sure you're right,' Peter agreed, 'but better stick to the rules. That's the way rumours get started – at each stage someone tells someone in strictest confidence and soon the whole world knows.'

'Oh, alright,' Lucy mumbled, looking disgruntled but accepting the argument. Latham looked round at each of them in turn and then addressed Peter and Bernie.

'Good. Now, I'd like you both to come with me. We have a couple of offices that the ferry company is allowing us to use for interviews. I'd like to speak with you, Dr Fazakerley, and Sergeant Simpson will take a statement from Mr Johns.'

'Now, Dr Fazakerley,' Latham began a few minutes later, leaning back in her chair and putting her notebook down on the desk in front of her. 'If you don't mind, I'd like you to describe, in your own words, exactly what happened on the ferry this morning.'

'Of course. But before we go on, can we make it *Bernie*?'

'If you prefer. Now, please start from the moment you boarded the ferry and include anything you remember, however trivial it may seem. Close your eyes, if you think it might help, and picture the scene.'

'It's OK,' Bernie said with a grin. '*I've* done the *Cognitive Interviewing* course too. Actually, my evidence starts before that – in the booking hall at the Pier Head. I was behind the priest – does he have a name yet, by the way? – in the queue for boarding passes.'

'According to his driving licence, his name is Father Nicholas Allerton of St Wilfrid's Presbytery, Dingle. Does that name mean anything to you?'

'No. I remember St Wilfrid's. Some of my family used to live in Dingle. But that was all years ago. I haven't been back since eighty-two.'

'Never mind. Carry on with your story.'

'I noticed that he was getting a free boarding card with a *Trio* pass. That's how I knew he must be intending to get off on the Wirral side and not going on the round trip. I got our boarding passes and we went to wait for the gate to open to let us down on to the landing stage. He was waiting there with everyone else. I remember thinking how young he looked. He seemed a bit distracted, as if he had something on his mind. He tripped up on the way down, as if he wasn't watching where he was going. And, later on, we bumped into one another – literally – after we'd gone on board. I noticed then that he was carrying a rosary – or, no, maybe he got it out later. Yes, I think that was it. He went over to the side of the boat – well, the front, right up by the flag on the bows – and stood there, leaning on the rail, gazing out across the water, and he took out a rosary and started praying.'

'Out loud?'

'No. But I could see him moving the beads in his hand as he went through the prayers in his head.'

'Are you a catholic?' Latham asked unexpectedly. Bernie looked at her, wondering what reason she might have for the question.

'That rather depends on how you define it,' she answered after a short pause. 'My dad was a catholic and he brought me up to it, but my mum was in the Salvation Army and thought it was all a bit too close to idolatry for her liking. I haven't renounced anything, but I'm a member of the Methodist Church now, which in some people's eyes ought to bar me from the mass – not that I let that bother me. I don't have anything against catholic priests, if that's what you're getting at.'

'No – not at all. You seemed to know a bit about the ritual, that's all. I wondered how you knew what he was doing with the beads. Now, go on – what happened next?'

'Nothing much. He stayed there, leaning against the rails, and we sat down as per the safety instructions, until the ferry moved off. Then we were busy looking out at the sights until we got to Seacombe. The bow deck more or less emptied then – apart from us and the priest, everyone seemed to be getting off there. We watched the new people getting on, but none of them came up to where we were, and then the boat moved off again.'

'Go on.'

'When they announced that we were getting to Woodside, we got up to go down. Hang on! No. Before that, Lucy went round to the other side, and then I went as well, to show her the view of Liverpool. Then, when the announcement came over the Tannoy, we went back past the priest – Father Nicholas, was it you said? – and it occurred to me that it was strange that he wasn't getting ready to go too. That's why I said it was important you knew about me overhearing him getting his boarding card. I thought maybe he was so absorbed in his prayers that he hadn't noticed that we'd arrived, so I tapped him on the shoulder and told him it was time to go.' Bernie paused as she recollected the surreal scene that had unfolded after this.

'Go on,' Latham repeated. 'What happened then?'

'He didn't react. Looking back, I think I sort of instinctively knew there was something wrong. But I didn't think of it like that at the time. I shook him by the shoulder, thinking he must be so deep in thought that he hadn't noticed me, and then … well … he sort of toppled over and rolled on to the deck.'

There was a knock at the door and DS Simpson entered.

'I've taken Inspector Johns' statement,' she told Latham. 'Would you like me to talk to his daughter now?'

'Is that alright with you?' Latham asked Bernie. 'Or would you prefer to wait until we've finished and you can be the one to sit in on the interview? It would help us if we didn't have to wait, but you know best what would be better for your daughter.'

'I'm quite certain that Lucy will be delighted to have Peter as her chaperone,' Bernie assured her, 'and she won't want to be kept hanging about. I'm sure she's just itching to tell you what she saw.'

'Good. Sergeant Simpson: take Mr Johns to collect Dr Fazakerley's daughter and, so long as they're both happy with it, take her statement. I'll join you as soon as I can.'

Simpson nodded and withdrew. Latham turned back to address Bernie.

'Going back in time a bit – to while the priest was still alive – did you see anyone with him? Did anyone go up and speak to him at all? Or stand alongside him?'

'Not that I remember,' Bernie

frowned in concentration. 'As I said before, there was nobody else at that end of the deck after we left Seacombe. I don't think. Or ... I don't know,' she went on slowly. 'There was a young couple. I thought they got off at Seacombe, but maybe I'm misremembering. He was a Scouser and she was a southerner by her accent. I guessed that this was her first visit to Merseyside and he was showing her the sights. I remember them leaning on the rail and him pointing across and saying something about Bootle. And then, after we'd turned to face the Wirral, they went up to the front and he stood right next to Father Nicholas to point out something over there. I didn't catch what they were saying then.'

'Would you be able to describe them to me?'

'Young – student age. I thought maybe they'd met up at university. He was wearing an Everton jersey. I can't remember what she had on. He was taller than the priest, but not by a lot. He probably thinks he's got a beard, but to me he just looked as if he hadn't got round to shaving for a week or so. It was a sort of pale brown, so I suppose his hair probably was too. That's about all I remember.'

'Don't worry. Do you think you'd recognise them if you saw them again?'

'I don't know. I wasn't exactly studying them. Probably if I saw them together, but one at a time? – probably not.'

'And was there anyone else at all who came near to Father Nicholas during the journey?'

'I don't think so,' Bernie shook her head. 'Certainly not after we left Seacombe. Before that it was quite busy around where he was standing.'

'Did they speak to Father Nicholas?'

'I don't think so, but they may have done.'

'I see. OK. Go on – what happened after you touched Father Nicholas and he fell to the floor. Presumably you realised then that something was wrong?'

'Yes. I thought maybe he'd fainted or was having some sort of epileptic fit.

I knelt down and tried to loosen his clothing and I saw a hole in his shirt. And the material was sort of wet and sticky. And then I saw that there was blood on my hands. So I tore the hole bigger to see what was underneath. Lucy got down and helped me. When we saw the wound in his chest I looked at his face and I was pretty sure he was dead, but I checked by feeling for a pulse in his carotid artery. If you find blood on his neck, that will be where it came from.'

'And you raised the alarm? Is that right?'

'Yes. I called Peter over as soon as I saw the blood – it didn't show up on his black shirt, so I didn't see it at first – and Peter went down to stop the crew letting anyone off the ferry.'

'And while he was gone, what did you and your daughter do?'

'Once we were sure there was nothing we could do for him, we sat down on one of the seats and waited. We knew we shouldn't do anything to disturb the crime scene.'

'It must have been very traumatic for you both.'

'Well yes and no. As I said, I've seen murder victims quite a few times now.'

5 AS WE QUESTION

DS Simpson showed Peter and Lucy into another room behind the booking office. She moved a second chair from against the wall and placed it in front of the small desk that stood in the centre of the room.

'Sit down, please.'

They sat. DS Simpson walked round the desk and sat down opposite them. She reached into a bag that she was carrying and took out an A4 pad and two ballpoint pens. Then she looked across and smiled at them.

'Now Lucy,' she began, in what she evidently intended to be a kindly manner, but which Lucy considered to be patronising. 'I know you've had a big shock, but we need you to think hard and tell me everything that you can remember about what happened. Your Dad will be here all the time, but I want you to tell me what *you* saw without asking him about it. Do you understand?'

'You mean you don't want my evidence to be contaminated by the co-witnessing effect,' Lucy said, unable to resist the temptation to show off her knowledge. Bernie's words concerning the proper conduct of interviews with eye-witnesses had prompted her to look into the matter. While she was waiting for it to be her turn, she had been doing some research into forensic psychology on the internet.

'Yes. That's right,' Simpson agreed, taken aback but trying to remain calm. 'So, now Lucy, can you tell me what happened, starting from when you got on the ferry?'

'We went in and turned left to go upstairs to the stern deck. It was full there; so then we went back along the upper deck to get to the bow. We went back inside the covered area and past the top of the stairs that come up the other way – towards the bow – the ones we would have got to if we'd turned right instead of left when we got on. The priest came up the stairs and bumped into Mam as she went past. She was in front, and then me, and

Peter was bringing up the rear.'

'I know my place,' Peter muttered to no-one in particular.

'They both apologised and then he went out of the door into the open, and we all followed. There's like a passageway there with a bench running along the side of the cabin, facing outwards, and room to walk between that and the side rail.'

DS Simpson turned to a clean page of her pad and pushed it across the desk.

'Do you think you could draw me a plan of the boat, to show me?'

Lucy took the pen that DS Simpson was holding out to her and started drawing the outline of the ferry.

'The covered area comes out right

to the sides in the middle of the boat,' she explained, drawing it in. 'So you can only get from the outside at the back to the outside at the front by going inside. I can't quite remember how the stairs go, but there was one staircase that went to the back – the one we came up – and another that came out into the covered area at the front. Then there was a door in the side to get out on to the deck at the bow.'

She drew it in.

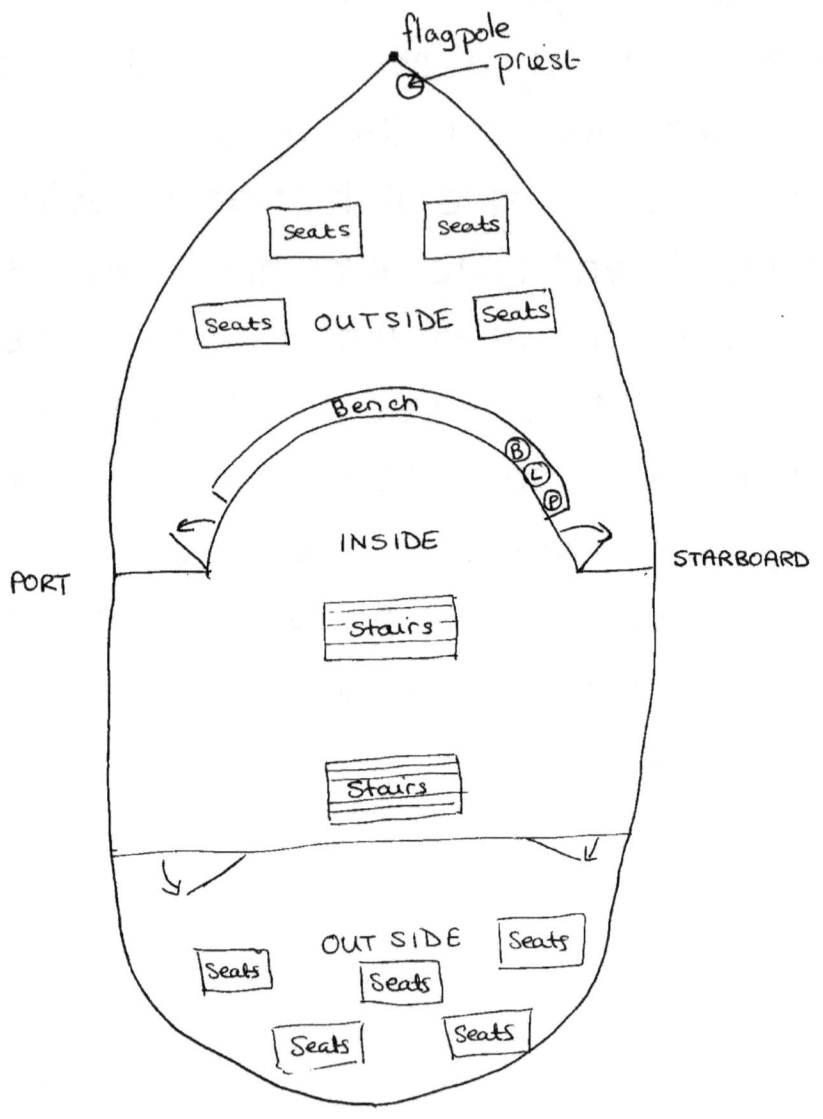

'And that gets you out into a sort of
passage round to the open seating

area at the front. We bumped into the priest between the stairs and the door on the starboard side.'

'And by *starboard* you mean, which side? DS Simpson interrupted.

'The right-hand side, looking forwards,' Lucy explained, wondering how anyone could have risen to the rank of sergeant without such basic knowledge. Admittedly, Peter was making a show of ignorance of nautical terminology, but he was perfectly aware of the meanings even if he chose to pretend otherwise.

'Right,' Simpson nodded. 'I just wanted to be sure we both knew what you meant. Carry on.'

'The side of the indoors part of the boat curves round like this, and so does the bench. So when we sat down we were facing the starboard rail, but Mam, who was furthest towards the bow, was partly facing forwards. Peter was nearest to the door, so he was facing straight out over the side rail.'

Lucy added circles to indicate where each person was sitting. Simpson looked down at the drawing with interest.

'Sitting there, you must have seen everyone who came out on to that part of the deck,' she said thoughtfully. 'They would have had to walk past you.'

'Well, there's presumably another door on the other side to match,' Lucy pointed out. 'So, on average, only half of the people would have come past us. And we didn't stay sitting down all the way. Quite a lot of the time, we were standing up looking over the rail, so anyone who walked past would have been behind us.'

'Yes. I see. Sorry – I interrupted you. Go on: you were just saying that you followed the priest out to the open area at the front of the boat.'

'He didn't sit down with us; he carried on and went and stood by the rail at the very front of the boat. There was a flagpole sticking up at the front, with a union jack on it. The red ensign was flying at the back,' Lucy added, to make it clear that she understood the difference between the two flags. 'He was standing right by the pole, leaning on the rail and looking out over the water.'

'Did you see anyone come up to him at all while he was there?'

'No.' Lucy shook her head. 'But there were lots of people milling around on that part of the deck, so I probably wouldn't have noticed – not until they got off.'

'OK. You all settled down on the bench and the ferry went off. What happened after that?'

'Nothing much. We went off down the river and Mam talked a lot about the things we could see on the bank. Then they announced that we were soon going to be docking, and people started getting up and heading off downstairs, ready to get off. I asked Mam if we were getting off too, because the announcement said it was *the gateway to New Brighton* and she'd said something earlier about how we might go to New Brighton later. But she said we were going to stay on to the next stop. So I went round to look out over the port rail, where I could see the men tying up the boat and letting down the gangplank. Lots of people got off and not so many got on. Then they cast off again and the ferry moved off. Then Mam came round to that side to point out the *iconic Liverpool waterfront*, and we stayed there until the boat turned round again to dock at Woodside.'

'All three of you?'

'No. We left Peter on the bench, with the bag.'

'The story of my life,' Peter

muttered under his breath.

'Nobody must have come up to the bow end when they got on at Seacombe. At least, when I looked round, it was deserted except for the priest. He was still standing, leaning against the rail and the flagpole. We looked across the river and Mam pointed out the Royal Liver Building – again – and the two cathedrals. Then they announced that we were approaching Woodside, so we started back to pick up Peter and go down. As we passed the priest, Mam said something to him. I think it was *you've got to get off here* or something like that. I wasn't taking much notice. Then the next thing I knew, he was lying on the ground. He looked like he was staring up at us – except that there wasn't any expression on his face, if you know what I mean. And it was very white. Mam got down to see if she could help him and I did too. There was a rip in his shirt – on the front, about here.'

Lucy put her finger on Peter's chest to indicate the position.

'Mam tried to tear the shirt to see what was underneath, but it wouldn't. So I pulled at it too and it ripped open and we saw that he'd been stabbed. At least,' she corrected herself, remembering how cautious their family friend, forensic pathologist Mike Carson always was about making definite statements concerning bodies that he was examining, 'there was a wound in his chest that looked to me as if it was consistent with stabbing. It was about this long,' she held her thumb and forefinger about two centimetres apart. I took a picture on my phone. Would you like to see?'

'Er, yes.' Simpson hardly knew what to say. This interview was not turning out at all as she had envisaged it would.

Lucy got out her smartphone and found the photograph. She laid it down on the desk so that Peter and the police officer could both see the close-up of a slit wound in pale flesh liberally smeared with blood.

'Thank you, Lucy. Now you won't go sharing that picture with anyone, will you?'

'Of course not! At least,' Lucy hesitated. 'I would like to show it to DCI

Jonah Porter – he's a friend of ours – and to Dr Mike Carson, who's a forensic pathologist we know. I'm sure they'd be interested; and I'd like to know what they think about it. I'm hoping to become a pathologist myself so this would be a good opportunity for me to get some experience.'

'But this isn't their case,' Peter objected gently. 'We ought to leave it to the Merseyside Police to investigate.'

'OK,' Lucy agreed reluctantly. 'But I bet everyone else has already been sharing their photos all over the internet.'

'But only you and your mam had the opportunity to take pictures of the victim,' Peter pointed out. 'That's the difference.'

'We'll be asking everyone to give us any photographs they've taken while they were on the ferry this morning,' Simpson told her. 'After this interview is over, I'll take you back to where we've got a team of people processing all the passengers. We're asking everyone to allow us to take pictures off their phones and cameras, just in case there's anything in them that might help with the enquiry. Now, I want you to think back again to while you were on the deck of the ferry. Did you see anyone speaking to the priest or coming up alongside him?'

'No.' Lucy shook her head. 'I wasn't looking. And, until they all got off at Seacombe, there were lots of people between him and us.'

'Not to worry. And, after you left

Seacombe, you say the front deck was empty, apart from the priest?'

'Well, it was as far as we could see. Of course, there could have been someone sitting on the bench round the other side. We wouldn't have been able to see them.'

'Yes,' Simpson said thoughtfully. 'You couldn't see them and they couldn't see you.'

'You mean the killer could have been waiting there and could have come out and stabbed the priest and gone back that way without knowing that there was anyone else on the deck?' Lucy asked eagerly.

'Yes, well, it's too early to say,' Simpson said hurriedly.

'Don't worry,' Lucy grinned at her. 'I

won't go shooting my mouth off to the press!'

'Now,' Simpson resumed, trying not to be put off her stride by this disconcerting witness, 'before we finish, is there anything else – anything at all – that you want to tell me?'

'No. I think that's it.'

'Or any questions you want to ask me?'

'Lots!' Lucy grinned. 'But I'm sure you wouldn't be allowed to answer any of them.'

'Well, if you think of anything else we ought to know about, your dad has my number so just ask him or your mum to give us a ring.'

DS Simpson got to her feet, glad that this interview was over.

'Now, I expect DI Latham will have finished with your mum, so I'll take you back to her and then it won't be long before you can go home.'

6 THE STRIFE OF TRUTH WITH FALSEHOOD

Bernie was waiting for them in the café, which was doing a brisk trade in coffee, cakes and sandwiches for the passengers waiting to be interviewed by the dozen or so police officers who had been assigned to the task

'Now you've both made your statements,' she greeted them, 'our instructions are to join the queue to be photographed and fingerprinted – assuming that we aren't planning to insist on our right not to co-operate! Oh – and we're to have our phones and your camera ready for them to copy across any pictures we took while we were on board.'

She led the way back out into the booking hall, where they attached themselves to the end of a line of people, who were all talking excitedly about what had happened.

'Someone told me they'd already made an arrest,' a middle-aged woman was telling her neighbour. 'So I don't know why they need to keep us all hanging about here.'

'I heard they thought it was a terrorist gang,' a man cut in, eager to have his say. 'They want to be sure that they don't let the accomplices get away.'

'Who was it who was killed?' another man wanted to know. 'I saw them carrying the body away, but it was all covered up.'

'Mr Johns! Dr Fazakerley!' DI Latham noticed Peter and Bernie and hurried over to speak to them, conscious that it was only a matter of time before someone recognised them as the couple who had been escorted from the ferry ahead of everyone else. She did not want them to be interrogated by curious by-standers. 'Come with me. You don't need to wait your turn. I'll get someone to see to you right away.'

She led them to the head of the queue and stood with them, waiting for the photographer to be ready for his next client.

'I've brought in as many officers as we can spare,' she explained to Peter, 'but it's still going to take a long time to get through everyone. I'm only glad it was the first round trip of the day and the ferry wasn't full.'

It was not long before Bernie, Peter and Lucy had all been photographed. Then they went into the next room to have their fingerprints taken. Finally a young man, sitting at a desk strewn with cables and other bits of kit associated with computers and electronic devices, asked for "any cameras, phones, iPads etc." to be handed over. Lucy waited impatiently as he downloaded all the photographs that she had taken that morning on to a laptop computer before disconnecting her phone and giving it back. Then DI Latham told them they were free to go and offered to arrange for a car to take them back to their hotel.

'Don't be daft!' was Bernie's reaction to this suggestion. 'We don't want to waste our Saveaway tickets. We'll grab some lunch in Birkenhead and then decide what to do with the rest of the day. We can get the train back to Lime Street when we want to go home.'

DI Latham hesitated, wondering whether to insist on a police escort away from the ferry terminal. She decided against it. Not only might it antagonise the only real witnesses that they had, but the cluster of journalists waiting outside for news might be more likely to follow a police car transporting members of the public away from the crime scene than an innocent-looking family leaving on foot.

'Very well. Just don't hang around outside giving interviews to the press.'

As they emerged into the bright sunshine, they saw that the police had erected barriers to hold back the crowd that had gathered in the small car park outside. They walked in single file down the path between them, self-consciously looking straight ahead to avoid the eager demands for information. Bernie led the way, walking briskly out to where the road swept in a loop around a line of bus stops. A young man holding a microphone stepped in front of them and tried to accost them, but a police officer held him back. Two more gentlemen of the press detached themselves from the crowd and followed them across the road.

'Change of plan!' Bernie called over her shoulder. 'Follow me.'

She ran towards a bus, which was waiting at the second stop in the row, and climbed aboard. Peter and Lucy followed. Bernie showed their passes to the driver.

'Can you close the doors now?' she said urgently. 'We're rather keen not to have any more company.'

He hesitated just long enough for a young woman in jeans and a tee-shirt to get on. She rummaged in a brightly-coloured patchwork shoulder bag and extracted a *Trio* monthly pass, which she showed to the driver before walking past them to sit down near the back of the lower deck. Then, seeing a group of four or five young men breaking away from the crowd and heading across the road in pursuit, the driver did as Bernie had asked.

"Bout time we were off anyway,' he said, releasing the hand brake and moving out from the bus stop.

'Where are we going, Mam?' Lucy asked.

'By the look of it, Birkenhead bus station in the first instance,' her mother replied, watching out of the window, trying to spot familiar landmarks amongst the new buildings that had sprung up since she had last been here. 'Did anyone happen to notice where this bus is going?'

'New Brighton, love!' the driver called out, 'stopping at Birkenhead Park and Seacombe ferry terminal.'

'It looks as if we're going to New Brighton, then. At least we should be able to get fish and chips there for lunch.'

'What's going on at Woodside, then?' asked the driver. 'I heard they've cancelled all the ferries.'

'Someone's been killed on the ferry,' Peter told him, thinking that he had to give some sort of explanation for the large police presence. 'The police are investigating. We've been told not to talk about it to anyone.'

At Birkenhead, the bus filled up with morning shoppers on their way home for lunch. These gradually thinned out again as it headed through Wallasey and on towards New Brighton. Progress was slow, with passengers boarding or alighting at practically every stop. After a little over half an hour, Bernie announced that they were there and they stepped down on to a wide pavement opposite a supermarket, which Bernie declared had not been there in her day.

It took longer to find a fish and chip shop than Bernie had anticipated. The roads and shops had all changed from what she remembered and the tastes of the residents seemed to have shifted towards kebabs and pizzas. However, by two-thirty they were sitting down on a bench overlooking the marine lake with their delayed lunch on their laps.

The warm sun had brought people out on to the promenade and the line of benches was well-populated. A woman in jeans and a purple tee-shirt came up to them, a can of coke in one hand and a large bread roll – or, as Bernie would have described it, a *barm cake* – in the other.

'Do you mind if I join you?' she asked.

They shook their heads, murmured inconsequential words of acquiescence and moved a little closer together on the bench. The woman sat down, putting the barm cake on her lap while she used both hands to open the can.

'I'm Lauren,' she told them, looking

at each of them in turn, clearly expecting to be introduced.

'Bernie,' Bernie said, to break the awkward silence. 'And this is my husband, Peter, and my daughter, Lucy.'

Lauren nodded and smiled towards each of them.

'It's a lovely day,' she said conversationally.

They agreed that the sunshine was very pleasant.

'I came over from Liverpool on the bus,' the woman continued. 'I was intending to go back on the ferry, but it says they've been cancelled until further notice. Do you have any idea what's up?'

'There's been an incident on one of

the boats,' Peter told her. 'The police are investigating.'

'That sounds interesting. It must be serious to stop the ferries. Do you know what happened exactly?'

'The police will make a statement in due course.'

'Oh! I see! They've told you not to speak about it to anyone. You were there, weren't you?'

'We were, but, as you correctly say, we are not at liberty to talk about it.'

'I'm afraid it's a bit late for that,' Lauren said, taking out her smartphone and holding it out so that Peter and Bernie could both see the screen.

They looked down and, to their concern and annoyance, saw a photograph of Bernie being escorted off the ferry by Sergeant Pullinger. The bloodstains on her polo shirt were clearly visible.

'One of your fellow passengers took it and put it on their Facebook page,' Lauren told them. 'And then he sent a link to the Echo. According to him, you are the perpetrator of a vicious and fatal stabbing. However, I rather fancy the police would have kept you in custody if that had been the case, so my guess is that you found the body. Am I right?'

Bernie nodded miserably.

'Would you like to help me put the record straight?' Lauren asked, reaching in her pocket and holding out a plastic identity card for them to read. 'I'm with the Echo and we want to tell our readers what really happened.'

'You followed us on to the bus,' Lucy said indignantly. 'I remember you now. You sneaked on and went and sat at the back.'

'That's right,' Lauren admitted, smiling graciously at Lucy. 'I thought you'd prefer me to wait for a more opportune moment to start asking questions.'

'I really think you ought to stick to the official police statements,' Bernie said, determined not to co-operate with what she saw as press intrusion.

'Even if we do, that won't stop the picture going viral on social media,' Lauren pointed out. 'Surely it's better to tell me the truth than to have everyone believing you're a killer?'

'OK,' Peter intervened. 'I can see we'll have to give you a story, but you *must* get it cleared with the police before you run it. The person to contact is DI Latham. Here's her card. You can keep it – we've each got one.'

He handed over the card that DS Simpson had given him. Lauren pocketed it and then turned back to speak to Bernie.

'Tell me what happened,' she urged, getting out a tablet computer from her shoulder bag.

"There's not much to tell,' Bernie said, determined to give away as little as possible. 'He was leaning on the rail as if he was looking down at the water. When we got to Woodside, I tapped him on the shoulder, because I thought he'd forgotten to get off, and he fell over. That's when the blood got on my shirt. Peter raised the alarm, and then we just waited for the police to come. That's about it, really.'

'You say *he*?' Lauren said eagerly, tapping away on her tablet as she spoke. 'Do you mean that the victim was a man?'

'Yes,' Bernie said shortly.

'What did he look like? Do you know his name?'

'I can't say.'

'Do you mean you recognised him? Was he someone famous?' Lauren asked, reading into Bernie's evasive answer the possibility that she was hiding something sensational.

'We can't possibly answer that sort

of question until after the police have informed his relatives,' Peter told her, speaking in the authoritative tone of an ex-police officer. 'Look – I know you people always want some human interest, so how about this.' He paused to marshal his thoughts and remember the type of phraseology used by the press when reporting anything from a lost bus-pass to multiple rape and murder. 'A nostalgic trip home to her native Merseyside took a dramatic turn for Dr Bernadette Fazakerley, originally from the Toxteth district of Liverpool, when she took her daughter on the famous *ferry 'cross the Mersey*. Shortly before they were due to disembark at Woodside, she made the grisly discovery that one of her fellow-passengers had been stabbed to death by an unknown assailant. Her husband, ex-copper Peter Johns, raised the alarm and the police were soon at the scene. Our Bernie, as she is affectionately known, has been exiled in Oxford for more than thirty years and this is the first time that she has returned to the city of her birth since …'

'Nineteen eighty-two,' Bernie filled in the gap as Peter paused to think. 'And I suppose you'd better include a soundbite purporting to be my own words, to give it a feeling of authenticity. How about: *It wasn't the homecoming I was expecting, but the police have been very supportive and I'm sure it won't be long before they find out who did it.* And you'd better finish with *thoughts and prayers* from everyone for the victim's family.'

'Of course, this isn't the first time Our Bernie's been in the Liverpool Echo,' Peter went on, still trying to divert Lauren's attention from her quest for more details of the priest's death and suddenly remembering some press cuttings that he had seen in a drawer where Bernie kept her father's last remaining personal effects. 'She got an honourable mention back in seventy-six when she won an open scholarship to Oxford.'

'Really?' Lauren wrote this down.

'That was sister Dorothea's doing,' Bernie said. 'She was mortified when the photographer came round to my house instead of going to the school and I insisted on dressing up in my Salvation Army uniform!'

Lauren made a mental note to look for the picture in the newspaper's archives.

'And then,' Peter continued, beginning to enjoy leading Lauren up the garden path, 'there's a rather sweet picture a few years earlier of Bernie on a picket line with her dad.'

'He was a docker,' Bernie explained. 'You're too young to remember what it was like in the seventies, with twenty percent unemployment in some places and the threat of casual labour undermining what jobs there were. And the Port of Liverpool was in decline, with trade switching from the Commonwealth towards Europe. Things had to change, but there must have been better ways for the employers and government to go about it.'

'That's great,' Lauren said, getting it all down. She held out the tablet to Peter and allowed him to check what she had written. He nodded and passed it back.

'Thank you very much. And now, Lucy,' Lauren said, addressing her for the first time, 'do you have anything you'd like to say? It must have been quite an experience for you.'

'My mam always told me not to speak to strangers,' Lucy said primly, grinning across at Peter, who had opened his mouth to protest at this attempt to interview a minor without prior permission from her parents.

'Quite right too,' Lauren agreed, recognising that she was not going to get anything further from the family. Never mind. She had still managed to steal a march on her press colleagues, including some from prestigious national papers and one particularly irritating co-worker at the Liverpool Echo, who would be livid when he discovered her scoop. 'Thank you all for your time.'

They watched as she walked away, already speaking excitedly on her phone. She was presumably reporting to her boss at the local daily newspaper that she had an exclusive.

'I hope we've done the right thing,' Bernie murmured.

'I don't see we had any choice,' Peter assured her. 'But, I'll just give DI Latham a ring to warn her what's coming. It's about time they had a proper press conference – before the speculation really starts getting out of hand.'

'And I'd better get on to my cousin Joey and get him to warn the family about what's likely to be on the front page of their papers when they open them at their breakfast tables tomorrow morning,' Bernie nodded in agreement. 'Did you have to go quite so much to town on the *local working class kid, made good* angle?'

'And *now* can I tell Jonah?' Lucy pleaded. 'Before he sees Mam on the news and starts wondering what's going on?'

7 WHAT'S THE NEWS?

A box appeared at the foot of the screen, interrupting Jonah's perusal of the next module of his course. It announced that an email had arrived from Lucy. Delighted to have an excuse to set aside for a while the comparison of tread marks from different makes of tyres on a variety of surfaces, he opened his email client and clicked on the new message.

MYSTERY OVER THE MERSEY

Hi Jonah!

You'll never guess what we've been doing today! And when you find out you'll wish you'd come with us after all. We're the key witnesses in a suspicious death! You can read all about it in the Liverpool Echo, which, according to Mam, is the newspaper that EVERYONE in Liverpool reads. There's a picture of us on their website. Some idiot decided that Mam must be the murderer because she got blood all over her when she found the body, so he took a picture of us being taken off the ferry by the police and posted it all over the internet. But this girl, Lauren, from the Echo followed us and got us to give her the real story. Peter insisted on telling her a load of stuff about when

Mam was a kid in Liverpool. He says it's because he doesn't want her messing up the police investigation by revealing things that the public aren't supposed to know about. I'd better go now. Mam wants us to look and see if there's still a funfair at New Brighton.

Love,

Lucy

Jonah read the words rapidly. Then he re-read them to make sure that there could be no misinterpretation of their meaning. Finally, he opened a browser and selected the BBC news site from his list of bookmarks. *Mersey ferry stabbing victim named* was the headline over a photograph of MV

Snowdrop. Beneath the picture there was a paragraph identifying *Father Nicholas Allerton of St Wilfrid's RC Church* as the body that, as had been reported earlier, had been found on the ferry shortly before it docked in Birkenhead. Jonah clicked on the headline to read the whole story.

Merseyside Police have declared the entire vessel to be a crime scene and it has been taken out of service while forensics officers are carrying out a minute examination of every part. DI Sandra Latham, the officer in charge of the investigation, gave a statement confirming that they believe that Father Allerton was the victim of a deliberate attack and that they are currently interviewing the more than two hundred passengers who were on the ferry at the time of the murder. Members of the church where he had been working since June are devastated by the news. They told journalists that Father Allerton, who was ordained priest only three months ago, was sympathetic and hardworking, and well-liked by all his flock. The Parish Priest at St Wilfrid's, Father Liam Cosgrave, has been summoned back from retreat to provide pastoral support. In his absence, the Archdiocese of Liverpool issued a statement expressing sympathy for Father Allerton's family and the people of St Wilfrid's.

There was not much here to tell Jonah what had happened or who might be responsible. He entered *Mersey ferry stabbing* into the search box and selected a page from the Liverpool

Echo website. Again, the bright colours and striking patterns on the hull of the dazzle ferry took centre stage, below a headline claiming an exclusive interview with the *Liverpool mother who found the body*. He scrolled down, and was treated to the sight of the photograph that Lauren had shown to Bernie. Beneath it was the caption, *Mother of one, Bernadette Fazakerley (58) leaves the ferry with the police after discovering the death of Father Nicholas.*

Subconsciously noting that Bernie's fifty-eighth birthday was not for another three weeks, Jonah read on. He learned several facts about Bernie's past life that were new to him, but finished the article knowing very little more about the young priest's death.

Of course, that was precisely what Peter had intended when he fed the journalist all those snippets of information that would titillate the readers' interest without revealing anything about the police investigation. He re-read Lucy's email. What exactly did 'all over the internet' mean? Social media, presumably. He turned to Twitter. It did not take long for his search to produce another copy of the photograph of Bernie in her blood-stained polo shirt. The author had not needed his full quota of 140 characters to convey his belief that he had snapped the perpetrator of a bloody crime being taken into custody.

The post contained a link to a Facebook page, where Malcolm Blackler (Ground Lighting Technician at

MYSTERY OVER THE MERSEY

Liverpool John Lennon Airport; studied at Liverpool John Moores University; went to Roby Comprehensive; from Liverpool; married to Ellie Blackler) had posted a sequence of updates, chronicling his day. Jonah read the caption that accompanied the snap of Bernie. Amidst a plethora of typographical errors and a liberal sprinkling of exclamation marks, was a clear message: *this woman is a murderer*. Scrolling upwards, Jonah was treated to detailed descriptions of Malcolm being photographed and fingerprinted and finally – after what Malcolm considered to be an inordinately long time – interviewed by 'a woman PC who looked like she was only just out of high school'. He was evidently very proud of having got his photograph into the Echo and mentioned this achievement several times. Jonah clicked on one of the links and discovered that the news page had been updated.

Someone had evidently been busy trawling the newspaper's archives. Two more photographs had appeared. One showed a girl of about ten with long, fair plaits and a determined expression on her face, adding wood to a brazier, surrounded by men holding placards. The other was a press cutting with the headline, 'Oxford scholarship success' and a photograph of the same girl, older now but still with the same plaits and look of determination. He smiled. Old Peter's diversionary tactics appeared to be working. He wondered what the staff of the convent grammar school named in the clipping had thought of seeing their star pupil gazing out from under an old-fashioned Salvation Army bonnet. Trust Our Bernie to turn even her academic success into an act of defiance! He was about to return to his Google search when he noticed, in the *breaking news* column on the right of the page, a new headline: *Apology from man who wrongly accused woman of ferry murder.*

He clicked on the headline and the article opened. There was the picture of Bernie being led away by Sergeant Pullinger and, below it, he recognised the Facebook profile picture of Malcolm Blackler. Reading on, he saw that most of the article was a reproduction of a new post from Blackler's Facebook page, in which he apologised for having jumped to conclusions and expressed a hope that Bernie – described by the paper as *retired Oxford don, Dr Bernadette Fazakerley MA DPhil* – would accept that he had not intended to cause upset or embarrassment to an innocent person.

'How're you doing, young Jonah!'

The greeting interrupted Jonah's thoughts and made him look up. Bernie's old friend, Stan Corbridge, had arrived, letting himself in through the side gate. He was a keen pigeon racer, but the yard at the back of the house in Cowley where he lived with his wife, Sylvia, was too small to accommodate his flock of birds, so Bernie had invited him to erect a loft at the bottom of her large garden. He had come to attend to them, as he did every day. Sylvia appeared round the corner of the house, carrying a square cake tin.

'Not so bad,' Jonah responded cheerfully. 'Come over here and have a look at this.'

Stan and Sylvia crowded round Jonah's chair and peered over his shoulder at the screen. He took them through the pages that he had been looking at.

'I remember Bernie in that uniform,' Stan said, pointing at the scholarship photograph. 'That's what she was wearing the first time we met her. I remember saying to Sylvia afterwards that our Stephen could do a lot worse than marrying a Sally Army girl.'

'You weren't so chuffed, as I recall,

a couple of days later when she invited us back to her room and you saw that crucifix she had up over her bed,' Sylvia reminded him with a smile.

'You're right enough there,' Stan agreed, giving a laugh. 'And she saw my face and went right off and got out her rosary beads and started going on about Hail Marys and the five joyful mysteries and all that. I began to think Stephen had found himself an apprentice nun for a girlfriend!'

'She was only testing us,' Sylvia laughed. 'And making sure we wouldn't go putting our foot in it with her Dad when we met him.'

'Does she still sleep with a crucifix over the bed?' Jonah asked, momentarily diverted from his quest to find out more about the *Mersey Ferry Mystery,* as the case was already being dubbed in the media. 'I can't see Old Peter being comfortable with having the *Lamb of God who takest away the sins of the world* looking down on him all night.'

'It's on the wall above the desk in her study,' Stan told him, 'together with a collection of icons and a holy water thingy.'

Jonah raised his eyebrows in interrogatory fashion.

'I suppose it's probably got a proper name,' Stan explained, 'but I don't know about such things. It's got like a cross, hung up on the wall, with a container at the bottom in the shape of a scallop shell. Bernie told us it was for keeping holy water in.'

'A holy water stoup,' Sylvia said. 'And it was a present from one of her aunties. She doesn't actually put holy water in it.'

'My dad thought I was halfway to Rome when we had the boys baptised as babies,' Jonah observed, smiling. His father had been a Baptist pastor. 'Goodness knows what he would have thought if I'd hitched up with a girl who believed in rosaries and holy water!'

'Hi there!' Nathan called out, pulling off his gardening gloves as he came over to greet Sylvia and Stan. 'Sit down and I'll get us all a drink. I could do with one after weeding that border. It's a lot bigger than it looks.'

'You sit down and have a breather,'

Sylvia insisted, putting down her cake tin on the large wooden table in the centre of the patio. 'I'll make us all a pot of tea. I baked a cake,' she added, looking towards the tin. 'I thought you might enjoy it, Jonah. Might as well make the most of it, while the diet police are away!'

It was a standing joke among Jonah's close friends that Bernie and Lucy, mindful of the increased risks of cardiovascular disease associated with spinal cord injury, were uncompromising in the way that they controlled his eating habits. Sylvia, who was of the *a little of what you fancy does you good'* school, delighted in sneaking treats to him behind their backs.

'Here Nathan,' Jonah said, turning

back to his computer screen and scrolling to the top of the news report. 'Have a look at this.'

Nathan stood behind his father and looked over his shoulder, reading the words silently to himself.

'Trust Bernie to be the one to make the discovery,' he said, when he got to the part where Bernie approached the priest to tell him it was time to go. 'Why couldn't she just leave the guy to make up his own mind when he wanted to get off?'

'It's a good thing she didn't,' Jonah observed. 'If they'd let everyone go before they found the body there'd be no chance of catching whoever did it. As it is, it must be only a matter of time before they turn up evidence to link one of the passengers with the killing. You can't knife someone like that without getting some trace of blood on you.'

'Hmm.' Nathan wondered whether to voice the thought that immediately sprung into his mind, namely that there was certainly one passenger with plenty of blood on her hands – and on several other places about her person by the looks of things. While it looked as if the police were accepting her account at present, how long would it be – if no other suspect were found – before they started to wonder if she had reported the incident in order to cover up her own involvement in it? He went and sat down at the table, opened the cake tin and looked inside. 'This looks good!' he exclaimed, hoping to distract his father from thinking about the goings-on in Liverpool. 'I wish someone made this sort of thing for me.'

'It's quite surprising really that nobody seems to have been taken in for questioning,' Jonah murmured, refusing to be deflected. 'It says here that the body was discovered at 10.30 this morning. It's nearly four now. They must surely have finished checking all the passengers by now. Something like this would warrant getting a big team of officers out there to get things done quickly.'

'Not everyone has your *get everything done by yesterday* attitude, Dad.'

'Hmmph!'

'Yes, I know you think you'd have

got it all wrapped up by now if you were in charge,' Nathan sighed. 'But this isn't your case. You'll just have to trust that Merseyside Police know what they're doing – which I'm sure they do. Now, how much of this cake do you think I ought to allow you to have?'

He picked up the knife, which Sylvia had brought from the kitchen, together with a pot of tea and four cups, saucers and plates. Soon they were all sitting round the table enjoying the snack. Nathan cut Jonah's slice into small pieces and fed them to him, taking bites out of his own slice in between. Jonah switched to the BBC News channel so that they could all hear the headlines as the hourly news summary began. They listened impatiently to the top stories – which might have seemed important had they not been waiting for the one item that interested them – and then the background changed to show library pictures of a ferry leaving the Pier Head and setting off across the river. The newsreader's voice summarised the facts: Father Nicholas Allerton had boarded the ferry at Liverpool and had been found dead shortly before it docked at Birkenhead.

Then the scene changed to live coverage from outside the ferry terminal at Woodside. DI Latham emerged and gave a short statement to the waiting press: investigations are ongoing … we are ruling nothing out … the ferry has been taken away for a detailed forensic examination … we would like to thank the public for their help. Questions centred on possible motives for the attack – the police had not identified any yet – and the posting of Malcom Blackler's photograph and accusation on social media.

'Why did you allow passengers to take photographs and post them on Facebook?' demanded an earnest young journalist in black spectacles, representing the Guardian.

'There were nearly three hundred people on board the ferry,' Sandra Latham explained. 'Most of them will have had phones. Many of them, quite understandably, were sending texts and emails to people to explain why they were delayed on the ferry. Our priority was securing the crime scene and caring for the family who found the body.'

'Huh!' Sylvia snorted derisorily. 'She obviously doesn't know them if she thinks they needed caring for. I'll bet Lucy will have been demanding to attend the post mortem and Peter will have been making sure nobody messes things up for the police and our Bernie will have been wanting to be the one who breaks the news to the lad's mother.'

'No, but that was a clever answer,' Jonah said thoughtfully. 'In a single sentence she's made it clear that she believes Bernie's story that she found the priest already dead and that Bernie wasn't alone when she found him – making it more likely that she's telling the truth – and that she's a mother, which always makes people more sympathetic and less likely to believe the worst. I'm beginning to think that this DI Latham knows what she's doing.'

'Well thank God for that!' Nathan said with feeling. 'Now perhaps you can relax and leave it to her to solve the mystery and stop hankering after going up there to take charge yourself!'

'I wonder what could have made someone want to kill the lad,' Stan mused. 'It said he was only twenty-five and presumably for the last half dozen or so of those years he's been shut up in some seminary somewhere. I can't see how he'd have had the opportunity to upset anyone.'

'Could it have been sectarian?' Nathan asked, reluctantly accepting that the subject was not going to go away and thinking that at least this speculation was keeping his father from dwelling on any possible repercussions for his friends.

'I shouldn't think so,' Sylvia said. 'My impression is that in Liverpool they mostly see themselves as with their backs against the wall united against an unfair world that doesn't understand them.'

'I agree,' Stan backed her. 'You only have to look at pictures of the Hillsborough memorial and count the Everton scarves to see that. People who can set aside their football loyalties like that aren't about to start killing one another over a little thing like religion!'

'How about Islamic State?' Nathan

suggested. 'Like that French priest the other day[1].'

'It doesn't sound like a terrorist attack,' Jonah said. 'They're usually more dramatic. A quiet stabbing and then slipping away into the crowd isn't really their style. The whole purpose is publicity.'

'Why then?' Nathan asked. 'I suppose you have your own theory.'

'As the great Sherlock Holmes used to say,' his father replied, knowing full

---

[1] On 26 July 2016, two Islamist terrorists attacked the congregation attending mass at a Catholic church in Saint-Étienne-du-Rouvray, Normandy. They took hostages and later killed 85-year-old priest Jacques Hamel, by cutting his throat.

well that this response would irritate his son, but unable to resist the temptation to tease him, 'it is a capital mistake to theorise before you have all the evidence.'

8 O HAPPY HOME

Cousin Joey's home was a three bedroomed semi-detached, with small gardens front and rear. Bernie reflected that, while it was a step up from the two-up two-down terraced house opening directly on to the street, which she remembered his family living in when they were children, it must be very cramped for a family with three grown-up children and an aged mother. Joey welcomed them into the front room, which doubled as lounge and dining room, so that the back room could be used as a bedroom for Mrs Fazakerley senior, whom Bernie remembered as *Aunty Rose*.

She was sitting opposite the door, in a high-backed chair with a walking frame positioned in front of her. She looked much smaller than Bernie remembered. At the age of eighty-six, she was very frail and unsteady on her feet. She had come to live with Joey, who was her youngest child and the only one still living in the UK, after a series of falls made it clear that she was unsafe living on her own in the small terraced house in which she had brought up her three sons.

Joey's wife, Ruth, introduced their three children, none of whom had met their cousin Bernie before. James and Chloe were both established in their careers and hopeful of soon being able to afford their own homes. Dominic, who had been something of an afterthought, arriving some five years after his sister, was studying at Lancaster University. He looked Lucy up and down, unsure what to make of this self-assured girl who somehow appeared older than her sixteen years. They all sat down. The three Fazakerley youngsters squashed together on a small settee while Ruth insisted that Bernie and Peter should take the two easy chairs. She and Joey declared themselves very comfortable on two of the dining chairs, while Lucy reclined on a large beanbag.

'I'm very pleased to meet you at

last,' Joey greeted Peter. 'I'm sorry we didn't make it to the wedding, but it seemed like just one thing after another that year and we just couldn't make the time.'

'People think,' Ruth explained, 'that when you're self-employed you can take time off just whenever you like. What they forget is that when you're not working, you're not earning. And if you get a reputation for letting people down or for turning work down that's offered to you, you soon don't have any business left.'

'How *is* the business?' Bernie asked, grateful for the prompt. It was difficult to think of things to talk about with people whom she had not met for more than thirty years.

'Not so bad. The recession hit us pretty badly as far as new installations are concerned, but when you get a leak or your boiler breaks down, you still need a plumber to fix it. And we're getting a bit more contract work with local builders now that our Jamie's qualified so we can offer plumbing and electrics together.'

Everyone nodded and murmured agreement. Then there was silence. Nobody could think how to continue the conversation.

'Mass is at eleven fifteen,' Ruth said at last. 'We wondered if you'd like to come with us. We usually try to get along. At least,' she continued rather hesitantly, 'we do our best, but someone always needs to stop behind with Mum. So we sort of take it in turns.'

'Lucy was hoping I'd show her the church I used to go to,' Bernie answered, 'so we'd both like to go. But I think Peter would probably rather not. He's not used to it.'

'I'd be very happy to stay with your mother-in-law,' Peter suggested. 'If that's alright with you,' he added turning to speak to Rose. 'Then you could all go together, if you'd like to.'

Ruth was clearly delighted at this suggestion. Bernie fancied that James and Chloe might have preferred to have been given the option of volunteering to stay with their grandmother, but they politely avoided saying so outright. The situation reminded Bernie very much of how it had been for Joey and his brothers when they were growing up. Rose had set great store by the whole family attending church regularly and Joey had often complained about his lack of freedom. It seemed, however, that he had chosen a wife from the same mould and was content to bring up his own children in the same tradition.

'It's another mixed marriage, I gather,' Rose observed, looking at Bernie. Clearly, her physical frailty had not affected her strength of mind. 'Your mother was a good woman, I won't deny it, but I always wished she'd given up that Salvation Army stuff and become a catholic. I don't hold with husband and wife having different religions. How are the children supposed to know what to think?'

Bernie laughed. 'We just have to think things through and make up own minds. You should just be glad Mam didn't persuade my Dad to leave the church and join the Army. But I won't argue with you, Aunty Rose. If you were going to come round to my way of thinking, you'd have done so by now. Don't worry, I'll be a good girl and I won't corrupt your grandchildren with any nasty proddy ideas!'

As they walked through the once-familiar streets, Bernie gazed around trying to get her bearings. Everything seemed to have changed. Rows of Victorian terraces had been pulled down and modern buildings erected in their place. Many of the roads seemed wider, and there were open spaces that she did not remember. Landmarks that she recognised appeared surprisingly amidst unexpected surroundings. It was all very confusing.

The redbrick exterior of the Catholic Church, where she and Joey, and numerous other cousins, had been taught their catechism and taken their first communion, was one thing that did not seem to have changed at all. As they fell silent and walked solemnly in, blinking as their eyes adjusted to the gloom after the bright sunshine, Bernie felt that she would not have been surprised to feel her father grasping her by the hand as he always used to do.

Ruth led the way, pausing by the holy water font to dip her fingers and sign herself with the cross. Joey and their three children did the same. Bernie hesitated and then followed suit. This was one of the rituals that her mother used to dismiss as *Roman Exhibitionism*, but which her father had embraced with a simple trust that Bernie could not help but admire, even though she could not truly understand. She looked at Lucy, who was at her side and whispered in her ear, 'When in Rome ...'

Lucy giggled at the appositeness of the quotation and reached out her hand to administer the blessing. Although they were members of a Methodist church in Oxford, Bernie had made a point of taking Lucy to Catholic services regularly during her childhood so that she would *understand her heritage*, as she put it. However, they had always adopted a minimalist approach to ritual and Bernie had been very clear that water was just water, wherever it might come from or whatever words might have been recited over it. So this was the first time that Lucy had performed this particular ritual since the occasion of her first communion when she had entered the church in the company of half a dozen of her contemporaries under the watchful eye of her catechist.

They were too many to sit together in one pew, so Bernie, Lucy and Dominic found themselves seated behind the others. When the priest prayed for the soul of Father Nicholas and for repentance from his killer, Dominic looked sideways along the row to see what reaction this might provoke from his cousins. Both Lucy and Bernie kept their heads resolutely bowed and their eyes closed. They had no intention of drawing attention to themselves or to their involvement in the tragedy.

After the mass was over and they were leaving the church, it was another matter, however. Joey introduced them to their parish priest, Father Nathaniel, as his cousins, Bernadette and Lucy. Father Nathaniel shook hands warmly and said some words of welcome. Then he broke off and looked at Bernie more closely.

'Bernadette Fazakerley?' he asked. Bernie admitted that this was correct. 'Would that be the Bernadette Fazakerley who found poor Father Nicholas on the ferry yesterday?'

'Yes. Did you know him, then?'

'Certainly I did. St Wilfrid's is the next parish. When he went on retreat, Father Liam asked me to keep an eye on the young fellow. He's only been in the priesthood a matter of months and this was the first time he'd been left in charge.'

'Can you think who might have wanted to kill him?' Dominic asked eagerly. He had been wanting to broach the subject of the killing ever since Bernie had arrived at their house that morning. Now he did not intend to miss this opportunity to find out more.

'Certainly not,' Father Nathaniel said firmly, giving Dominic a disapproving frown. 'I've had nothing but good reports of him from St

Wilfrid's and he came with quite excellent recommendations from his seminary. Are you quite sure it could not have been some sort of accident?' he asked hopefully, turning back to Bernie.

'I'm afraid not,' Bernie shook her head.

'He had a deep wound to his chest,' Lucy put in eagerly. 'It looked to me as if a knife had passed up under his rib cage and probably reached his heart. The blood was very red, so it may have punctured the left ventricle or the aorta – or I suppose it could have been oxygenated blood from the lungs.'

'Lucy is hoping to do a medical degree,' Bernie cut in hastily, digging her daughter in the ribs to indicate that she had said enough. 'So she's studied this sort of thing. Of course, we shouldn't really talk about it. The police will give a statement when there's something definite to report.'

'It must have been quite a long knife,' Dominic said, ignoring Bernie's efforts to close down the subject. 'So it would be quite hard to conceal it.'

'*Afterwards-*,' Lucy began, but Ruth interrupted.

'That's enough, Dom,' she said sharply. 'You've been told not to talk about it. Think of poor Father Nicholas's mother. She doesn't want every Tom, Dick and Harry going on about how her son died.'

'Sorry, Mum,' Dominic mumbled, making a mental note to try to get Lucy on her own later to find out how much else she could tell him about this exciting event. Fancy her knowing all that about knife wounds and stuff!

'Will we be seeing you at the youth group this evening?' Father Nathaniel asked, changing the subject.

'I'm not sure,' Dominic answered slowly. 'We've got visitors …'

'Why don't you bring the young lady along with you?' the priest turned to address Lucy. 'It's just a social thing, really, for young people. They play table tennis and computer games and I come along in the middle and lead a bit of discussion over coffee.'

'Like a Bible study?' Lucy nodded. 'OK – unless we're doing something else?' She looked towards her mother who nodded and smiled.

'You go along, love. It'll be less boring for you than sitting around hearing me and Joey reminiscing about how things ain't what they used to be.'

Over lunch, crowded round the small table in the front room, Dominic did his best to steer the conversation round to the *body on the boat*, as he privately described it to himself. His parents, however, were determined to keep away from the subject for fear of upsetting Rose, while Peter and Bernie were steadfastly sticking to their rule of not discussing ongoing police investigations in public. Dominic caught Lucy's eye across the table and smiled at her. He would bide his time and see what he could get out of her when they were alone together on the way to the youth group.

As his wife cleared away the dishes, Joey looked at his watch.

'I told Aunty Dot we'd be there about two,' he said to Bernie. 'So we'd better be going. The home doesn't like too many visitors all at once, so I'll just take you two and Lucy. You kids,' he added looking round at Chloe, James and Dominic, 'can do the washing up while we're gone.'

'Tell me again who Aunty Dot is,' Lucy entreated her mother, as they climbed into Joey's van, arranging themselves around the boxes of tools and lengths of copper pipe that lay strewn around the interior.

'She's my Aunt,' Bernie explained. 'As I've told you before, my dad was the youngest of thirteen. Joey's dad was three or four years older. There was a girl in between; I don't remember her name. She married an Irishman and went to live in … Donegal, I think it was?'

'That's right,' Joey agreed. 'Aunty Lizzie. She died a couple of years back.'

'Aunty Dot was the only one of Dad's sisters who never married,' Bernie resumed. 'When my Mam was diagnosed with MND she stepped in and helped Dad with looking after me. So she was like a sort of second mother, if you like – which is why I feel so guilty about having neglected her all these years.'

'So she's my great aunt?' Lucy queried.

Bernie nodded. 'That's right.'

'And so is Aunty Rose?'

'Yes.'

'OK. Now – what relation are Dominic and Chloe and Jamie to me?'

'Well …,' Bernie thought for a moment. 'Joey and I are first cousins. So I *think* that makes them my first cousins once removed and your second cousins.'

'I see …,' Lucy said slowly. 'And that's because …?'

'Joey and I share a pair of grandparents,' Bernie explained. 'You have to go up two generations to get to the common ancestor. The rule is that you subtract one and that makes us first cousins. Whereas–'

'Dominic and I have to go up *three* generations to get to the common ancestor,' Lucy broke in. 'So, when you subtract one that makes us second cousins. Now, what about *removals*?'

'That's when cousins aren't from the same generation. The degrees of removal give the difference in generation between the two. So you're one generation down from me, which means that you and Joey are first cousins – because that's what Joey and I are – once removed, because you're a generation further down the family tree.'

'I see,' said Lucy, starting to become excited at this new knowledge.

'So, if I had children, they'd be Joey's first cousins twice removed and Dominic's second cousins once removed?'

'That's right. And Aunty Dot would be their great, great aunt.'

'And you would be their grandmother,' Peter added. 'Don't forget that!'

'Thanks for that – granddad!' Bernie retorted. 'I've got a good few years to go before I'll be old enough to become a granny, thank you very much.'

'What I don't get,' Lucy said, coming back to the subject of her Liverpool relations, 'is: if your dad had twelve brothers and sisters, where are all my other uncles and aunts and cousins?'

'Well, you have to remember that he was the youngest,' Bernie pointed out. 'So most of the uncles and aunts are dead by now.'

'Three of them were killed in the war,' Joey added. 'They were all in the merchant navy serving on the same vessel in the Atlantic convoys when it was torpedoed by a U-boat.'

'Your *Dad*'s uncles were all killed in the war too,' Bernie continued. 'His father was the only one, out of a family of five children, who survived long enough to marry and have kids.'

'Then there were two brothers who both entered the priesthood,' Joey said, thinking back. 'Reggie and Albert, I think they were called.'

'And we certainly hope *they* weren't

responsible for any cousins,' Bernie grinned.

'And then the others all emigrated,' Joey concluded, 'which just left my dad and Bernie's dad and Aunty Dot.'

'There wasn't much work in Liverpool in the sixties and seventies,' Bernie explained. 'We'd lost the empire and trade was moving away from America and the colonies towards Europe. The port of Liverpool was in decline. All the jobs were down south.'

'But, as far as our family was concerned, that wasn't what started it,' Joey argued. 'What about Uncle Frank? He served in Italy during the war, married an Italian girl and settled there with her family.'

'So I've got relations all over the

world?' Lucy asked with interest.

'Yes,' Bernie agreed. 'You must have – but I've lost touch with them all over the years. You've got to remember that most of them went away before I was old enough to take much interest.'

Miss Dorothy Fazakerley looked very small, sitting in the large, high-backed chair in the lounge of the Care Home. The thin, almost skeletal hand, which she held out to each of them, had gnarled knuckles and prominent veins and trembled uncontrollably. Her voice was thin and high-pitched and her fluffy white hair was thinning. Her blue eyes, however, were bright and piercing and her smile infectious.

'So you've deigned to come to see us all at last!' she greeted Bernie, in a voice that made it clear that she bore no malice for her niece's long period of neglect. 'And this is young Gerard's granddaughter, I assume,' she added looking Lucy up and down critically and then appearing to like what she saw. 'It would be too much to expect, I suppose, that you've brought her up as a good Catholic?'

'We all went to mass this morning,' Joey assured her, but his aunt looked to Bernie for an answer.

'You wouldn't expect me to abandon my ecumenical principles would you, aunty? We're both pretty bad Catholics and equally bad Methodists and other things besides. But the pope seems rather keen on building bridges too, so I hope we're not quite beyond the pale.'

'And you, young man,' Dot said, turning to Peter, 'must be husband number two, I assume? A police officer, I believe? Probably as well – our Bernie needs someone to keep her in line.'

'I'm retired now, but, yes – I was a detective inspector.'

'I hope she's looking after you a bit better than the other two,' Dot observed with a twinkle in her eye. 'You really have been remarkably careless with husbands over the years, haven't you Bernadette?'

'I'm doing my best to keep this one in good condition,' Bernie assured her. 'I've handed over all the cooking to him for a start!'

Lucy, who had been expecting a woman of ninety-seven to be out of touch and quite possibly gaga, was surprised to be drawn into a lively conversation covering a range of topics including: her anticipated GCSE results, their recent holiday on the Algarve, her ambitions to become a forensic pathologist, her mother's work with Jonah in Thames Valley Police and, finally, the death on the ferry and their involvement in the discovery of the body. To Lucy's utter amazement, at that point, her great aunt reached across to a drawer in her bedside cabinet and took out an iPad.

'I saw all the fuss on Twitter,' she told them, 'opening a browser and immediately reaching the Liverpool

Echo's news page. 'And the apology from that silly man who accused you. Of course, if you will go round disturbing corpses, left right and centre, what can you expect!'

'I was only trying to be helpful,' Bernie defended herself, but grinning at her aunt at the same time. 'How was I to know he was dead?'

'And do you have any theories about who killed him?' Dot wanted to know.

'None at all,' Bernie shook her head. 'It doesn't make any sense to me.'

'You didn't see any likely suspects hanging around near him?' Dot pressed her. 'Come on, girl! This is the first chance I've had of first-hand involvement in a real murder and you tell me you saw nothing! You do realise that my street cred with the old dears in the Bingo club will be rock bottom if I have to admit that you didn't tell me *anything*.'

Bernie reflected that the *old dears* were probably mostly younger than her aunt and that it was unlikely that most of them had any idea what *street cred* meant. What a pity that she had left it so long to renew her acquaintance with the relative whom, as she now realised, had been an important factor in shaping her own personality and outlook on life.

'That's pretty much what the DI who's in charge of the investigation said too,' she said. 'I could see she was hoping I'd be able to pinpoint some suspicious-looking character lurking around, but really … first there were too many people to spot one particular one, and then everyone got off at Seacombe and he was all on his own as far as I could see.'

'I've got some pictures,' Lucy said suddenly. 'Would you like to see them? I've got them on my phone.'

'Yes please!' Dot sounded eager. 'Could you post them on my Facebook page?'

'Yes, well … I'm not sure.' Lucy, taken aback by the suggestion, looked up at her stepfather for advice.

'Better not,' he said. 'The police may still want to keep the details away from the public. Better just show them on your phone.'

Dot looked down with interest at the photographs of the dead priest, turning the phone round in her hands to view the wound from different angles and zooming in to look in greater detail.

'It looks like a single stab and then the wound was enlarged as he pulled the knife back out,' she said at last. 'See there – at that end of the slit? The way the skin is torn?'

Lucy inspected the picture closely. Yes, the two ends of the wound did look a little different from one another.

'I'd forgotten you used to work in A&E,' Bernie said, remembering that her aunt had been a nurse at the Royal Liverpool Hospital. 'I suppose you must have seen a few of these in your time.'

'Don't forget I was a nurse all

through the war,' her aunt replied. 'There's not a lot I haven't seen as far as traumatic injuries is concerned.'

Time passed quickly and soon Joey was looking at his watch and reminding them that they must get back in time for the meal that Ruth would have ready for them. Bernie and Lucy kissed Dot goodbye and promised to pay her another visit before they returned to Oxford.

Peter gave a low whistle as they walked across the small car park at the front of the care home.

'Now I see where you get it from,' he said to Bernie. 'I always imagined it was your mother who was the role model for your unconventional behaviour. Now I see it came from the other side of the family!'

'No,' Bernie laughed. 'You were right first time. Aunty Dot was quite straight-laced compared with Mam!'

'I think she's awesome,' Lucy declared. 'How old did you say she was?'

'Ninety-seven, going on twenty-one,' Bernie answered, highly delighted that her daughter and aunt had got on so well. 'She always was interested in new things. She was the first in the family to get a television set – and then the first to switch to colour when it came out. I'm glad the old girl hasn't lost her marbles. It always seems so awful when someone's mind deteriorates faster than their body.'

MYSTERY OVER THE MERSEY

It was a somewhat smaller party that sat down to enjoy the magnificent high tea that Ruth had prepared for them. Chloe and Jamie considered that they had done their bit as far as entertaining the long-lost relatives was concerned, and had excused themselves, choosing to spend time with friends of their own age. Dominic, still hoping to get an opportunity to discuss the murder with one of the eye-witnesses, played the part of the dutiful son, laying the table and helping his grandmother into her seat. Then he sat down next to Lucy and started making conversation about the youth group, in the hope of breaking down her reserve and making her receptive to more direct questioning, once they were alone.

They were still eating when the telephone rang. Joey got up and went out to the hall to answer it. A minute or so later, he came back in.

'It's Father Nathaniel,' he announced, catching Bernie's eye as they all looked towards him. 'He'd like to speak to you, Bernie – something about Father Nicholas.'

Bernie got to her feet and followed Joey out to the hall.

'Hello?' she said, putting the receiver to her ear. 'Bernie Fazakerley here. You wanted to speak to me?'

'Yes. This is Father Nathaniel – we met at mass this morning.'

'Yes.'

'I've got Father Liam here with me. He's been talking with Father

Nicholas's mother. She's very upset, as you can imagine. He was wondering … That is to say, I told him that you'd been at the mass this morning and he thinks … Well, Mrs Allerton – Father Nicholas's mother – would very much like to meet you – with you being there during his last moments, if you understand me.'

'I'd be happy to meet her,' Bernie said dubiously, 'But I don't know that there's much I can tell her. I mean, apart from colliding with him as he came up the stairs, I didn't really have any dealings with him until he was dead.'

'I know. I know. It's just that – when Father Liam heard that you were a Catholic he thought you might be able to give her some words of comfort –

perhaps reassure her that his body was treated with respect – that sort of thing.'

'Well, as I said, I'll be happy to meet her – just so long as she isn't expecting me to be able to give her his dying words or anything like that. Where would I need to go?'

'She's stopping overnight at the presbytery – at St Wilfrid's, I mean – so I'll hand you over to Father Liam now and he can make the arrangements with you.'

Bernie agreed to meet the grieving mother the following morning at 9.30. When she reported this to the others, Dominic immediately volunteered to act as guide to Peter and Lucy in her absence.

'I'll come to your hotel,' he said

eagerly, 'and take you off round the sights. We can all meet up later when Bernie's finished her mercy mission.'

'Thank you,' Peter said, smiling at the young man's enthusiasm and glancing towards his stepdaughter, who was eating a slice of Ruth's Victoria sponge apparently oblivious of Dominic's efforts at ingratiation. 'We'll look forward to it.'

9 FAITH OF OUR MOTHERS

Dominic arrived promptly at nine the following morning and found his cousins waiting for him in the hotel lobby. After a brief discussion of their itinerary, they agreed that he would take Peter and Lucy to see the cathedrals and the university, while Bernie went on her errand to St Wilfrid's presbytery. They would take the bus, while Bernie set off on foot. The Anglican Cathedral was within walking distance of Dingle, and Bernie would meet them there when she had finished talking with the dead priest's mother.

As she made her way across Princes Park, looking around at the dewy grass sparkling in the morning sunshine, Bernie wondered what she was going to say to Mrs Allerton when they met. What was the young priest's mother hoping that she would be able to tell her? What possible comfort could she give to a mother who had just lost her son?

Small groups of trees stood tall and stately, spaced out across the rolling parkland. Bernie recognised oak, ash and beech. There used to be elms, she recalled, but they had presumably been killed by Dutch Elm disease years ago and all trace removed. That copper beech, near the path – could it be the one where Joey's brother, George, had carved his initials on his twelfth birthday? He had been given a Boy Scout penknife and was looking for something to try it out on. You would never think of giving a knife to a twelve-year-old these days. She stepped off the path and walked round the tree, inspecting its trunk. No, there was no sign of the wobbly *G.F.* that she had seen gouged out of the bark all those years ago.

Time to get on. She had said *nine-thirty* and it must still be fifteen minutes' walk to St Wilfrid's. She returned to the path and set off at a brisk pace. She came out of the park and saw the row of imposing houses opposite. They looked cleaner than she remembered. Perhaps they had recently been painted. There was a church on the left, which she vaguely remembered. There were builders' boards around it now, hiding the frontage, but you could still see the impressive arched windows and carved stonework. Was this another church that was being converted to new use, or just some renovation work?

She hurried on, through Toxteth and across the main road, which, in her own mind at least, marked the boundary with the adjacent district of Dingle. She turned into a side road and was presented with a view downhill to the river and the Wirral peninsula beyond. In the distance, she could make out the Welsh mountains. She was nearly there now.

As Bernie pressed the bell on the wall beside the front door of St Wilfrid's presbytery, her apprehension over what she was going to say to the bereaved mother returned. She waited anxiously on the doorstep, going over in her mind alternative opening phrases and rejecting them all.

The door was opened by a woman in her fifties, who introduced herself as Maureen Henderson, housekeeper to Father Liam and Father Nicholas. She listened intently as Bernie explained who she was and why she had come. Then she invited her in and showed her to a long wooden bench, which extended along the wall of the left-hand side of the hall.

'If you don't mind waiting here,' she said, 'I'll tell Father Liam you're here.'

Bernie sat down and waited. Mrs Henderson disappeared into a room opposite and closed the door behind her. After a short while, the door opened again and she reappeared, followed by a small man in clerical costume. Bernie noted his grey beard and reflected that it was odd that it had become unusual these days to see a clean-shaven clergyman. In this respect, Father Nicholas had been an exception – a throwback to an earlier age. At that moment, the doorbell rang again and the housekeeper hastened to answer it. She stepped back to allow the entry of a small group of people.

Father Liam spoke briefly to Bernie before hurrying to greet the newcomers.

'I'm so sorry, Dr Fazakerley. I'll be with you presently. I must just have a word with Mrs Solari and her boys. Her youngest died on Friday and they are here to discuss the funeral arrangements.'

Bernie nodded understandingly and murmured something suitable. Then she watched the priest speaking to the family, taking them each by the hand in turn. There was a woman of about the same age as Bernie, who was presumably Mrs Solari, the mother of the two young men who accompanied her. She was about middle height with grey hair and high cheekbones. Her dark eyes looked out from beneath black eyebrows. Her two sons both had dark curly hair, deep brown eyes and rather swarthy complexions. That, together with the surname, made Bernie suspect that they had Italian ancestry. The fourth member of the party was a complete contrast. She was a blonde goddess, as tall as the young men and considerably taller than their mother. Her face was heavily made up with a pale foundation and bright red lips. Her slim figure and unexpectedly large bust were accentuated by her close-fitting blue and gold dress, which was very different from the long, full skirt worn by Mrs Solari, and contrasted starkly with the sombre colours in which both mother and sons were attired. Her footsteps sounded loud on the tiled floor and Bernie looked down to see that she was wearing high-heeled sandals with wooden soles. The toenails that protruded from the open toes were painted red to match her lips.

For a few moments the hall felt very crowded and Bernie drew back to make room for them to stand in front of the bench where she was sitting. The young woman stumbled as her foot made contact with Bernie's walking boots, which she had donned that morning in anticipation of a long day of pedestrian sight-seeing. She steadied herself by grasping the bench, and their eyes met as they muttered apologies.

'If you could all make yourself comfortable in my study,' Father Liam was saying, opening the door through which he had emerged a few minutes previously. 'I'll be with you shortly. Mrs Henderson will bring you some tea and biscuits.'

They all filed through the door and Father Liam closed it behind them. As the door closed, Bernie became aware of one of the young men looking back through it. He seemed to be staring directly at her. For a moment, she wondered why, and then she realised that he must have recognised her from the pictures on the internet and in the press. She hoped fervently that this was not a sign of things to come. What a nuisance that man was, posting his stupid photograph for all to see!

'Dr Fazakerley!' Father Liam said, coming over and stretching out his hand towards Bernie. 'I'm sorry to keep you waiting. Father Nick's mother is in his study. I'll take you and introduce you. I'm so glad you agreed to come. I blame myself,' he added. 'I should never have left Father Nick on his own so soon after he started his ministry. He was very earnest and conscientious; I feel sure he must have somehow put himself in danger through his zeal and inexperience. His mother is a widow, so naturally she feels the loss enormously.'

'I'll do my best,' Bernie assured him, 'although I'm not sure what I can say that will help.'

'Just knowing that there was someone with him who understands will help, I'm sure. When she heard that you were a Catholic, it made a big difference.'

Bernie wondered whether she ought to come clean and explain her ambivalence on that score, but decided against it. If it helped the young priest's mother to think that he died in the presence of a co-religionist, what could be gained by disillusioning her?

Father Nicholas' study was a large airy room at the back of the house. The sunlight was streaming in through the window, which looked out over a large garden comprising a lawn surrounded by shrubs. As they entered, a tall thin woman got up from one of the easy chairs that were grouped around a small table near the centre of the room, and came forward to greet Bernie.

'Thank you for agreeing to come,' she said gratefully, taking Bernie's hand in hers.

Bernie held the proffered hand between her own two in a gesture that she hoped was sympathetic.

'Don't mention it,' she said awkwardly. 'I just hope you aren't expecting too much. I mean, I really didn't … I mean, I only said a couple of words to your son before …'

They sat down and looked at each other in silence across the table.

'Well, I'll leave you two to it,' Father Liam said, backing towards the door.

'I'll send Mrs Henderson in with some tea for you both.'

For a minute or two, they continued to sit in silence, looking at one another. Mrs Allerton looked anxious. She appeared about to speak and then seemed to change her mind. Her expression reminded Bernie of how her son had looked in the minutes before his death. She was more and more convinced that he had been mulling over something in his mind, unable to decide on the best course of action.

'I'm not sure what you wanted from me,' she said at last, feeling obliged to break the silence and somehow get a conversation started. 'Would you like me to just tell you what happened? I warn you – it isn't much.'

'Yes – yes, please. Or, well, no. What I really want is to know … I'd like to feel sure that he was in a state of grace when he died.'

'Aaah!' Bernie took a long, slow intake of breath and thought hard how to answer this. 'Well, of course nobody can ever know about that sort of thing for sure, can they?' she said hesitantly, playing for time. Then she remembered something and went on more confidently. 'But I can tell you one thing that might help. I'm sure he was praying when he died. He was holding a rosary in his hand. I think he was praying all the time he was on the ferry and that's why he didn't notice whoever it was coming up and attacking him.'

'Really?' Mrs Allerton's expression

changed from anxiety and uncertainty to what Bernie could only describe as sorrow mixed with cheerfulness – or perhaps *joy* would be a better word. Trying to make sense of it, Bernie thought back to her childhood and remembered how important it had seemed to her grandmother that a priest had visited her grandfather to anoint him before he died. Her mother had dismissed it as *superstitious nonsense* but her father had gone out in the rain (it was before they had a telephone at the house) to summon Father O'Leary to come out. Like Mrs Allerton, he had believed that death was not something to be fearful of – only of dying without the assurance of being at one with God.

They were silent again for several minutes, but this time the silence was peaceful rather than awkward.

'Was Nicholas your only son?' Bernie asked at last, becoming curious to know more about the young man and his mother. Surely if she had other children they would be with her now.

'Yes. His father died you see, when he was only a few months old.'

'I'm sorry.'

There was another long silence. Bernie tried to think of something else to say. She was grateful for the interruption when Mrs Henderson entered with a pot of tea, a milk jug, two cups and a plate of biscuits.

'Shall I be mother?' Bernie asked,

as the housekeeper left, closing the door behind her.

Mrs Allerton nodded and Bernie poured tea for them both.

'My first husband died six months before our daughter was born,' Bernie ventured, desperately trying to think of something more to say.

'So you understand!' Mrs Allerton sounded so grateful that Bernie began to feel guilty at having mentioned her own past bereavement.

'But I was lucky,' she went on hastily. 'I had some wonderful friends to help me and eventually her godfather became my second husband. It must have been much harder for you, if you were left to bring your son up alone.'

'I don't know. It didn't seem hard. He was such a joy to have around the house. And, like you, I had so many friends who all wanted to help. And the church was a great comfort to me. Didn't you find that, yourself?'

'I – I – certainly my faith made a big difference,' Bernie struggled to give an honest answer without embarking on elaborate explanations of her own complex religious journey.

'I was so proud when Nicky told me he was going to be a priest – although, at the same time, I would have liked to have grandchildren.' A brief look of regret passed over her face and then her features crumpled. 'And now …,' her voice tailed off into tears.

Bernie leant forward and took both

of Mrs Allerton's hands between hers. She could not think of anything to say. They stayed like that for perhaps a minute before Mrs Allerton pulled her hands away and, reaching inside her sleeve, drew out a paper handkerchief and started dabbing her eyes. Looking round the room, Bernie saw a box of tissues and brought them over to her. She looked up and smiled her thanks.

'I'm sorry,' Mrs Allerton apologised when she had composed herself a few moments later. 'I didn't mean to give way like that.'

'Don't be daft!' Bernie shrugged and shook her head. 'I can't imagine what I'd be like if anything happened to our Lucy.'

'That's your daughter? Tell me

about her. Is she married? Do you have any grandchildren?'

Bernie was taken aback by the other woman's eagerness, but she decided that this was at least a safe topic.

'Well, she's only sixteen and has just taken her GCSEs,' she began. Then, seeing the surprise on Mrs Allerton's face, she paused before continuing. 'I was a bit slow off the starting blocks in the marriage stakes,' she explained. 'I didn't meet Lucy's father until I was thirty-eight and I was nearly forty when we got married, so Lucy was an unexpected bonus.'

'So sad that her father didn't live to see her.'

'Yes.'

'Nicky's father had cancer. Typical man – he didn't go to the doctor until it was far too late to do anything. At one stage, *we* weren't sure he was going to make it to see Nicky born, but he did. All those stages you go through when you've got a baby – first smile, first tooth, first words – were extra precious for us because it seemed like an achievement for Mike to have lived to see them.'

'It must have felt very strange,' Bernie suggested, tentatively, 'watching your son developing and at the same time seeing your husband deteriorating. I had a friend who died of cancer and it was heart-breaking to see her.'

'What about your husband? How

did he …?'

'He fell off a roof. He was a police officer. He was chasing a suspect who tried to escape by getting out on to the roof of one of the Oxford colleges. Richard went after him and …'

'It must have been a terrible shock.'

Bernie nodded. Silence descended on them again.

'Dr Fazakerley?' Mrs Allerton said, at last.

'Bernie. Everyone calls me Bernie.'

'Really? I'm Bernadette too. At least – it's Mary Bernadette, but there are always so many Marys, so people call me Bernadette. But what I was going to say, Bernie, was, if your husband was in the police, do you know anything about police procedure? I mean, what happens now, do you think? They took me to identify Nicky's body, but they said I couldn't take him away until after they'd done a post mortem. What exactly does that mean? I don't like the idea of him being kept there in the mortuary like that. It's so … cold … and … impersonal. And when can I start planning the funeral? And they've been through all his things in here and in his bedroom. What do you think they were looking for? It feels like they're treating him like a criminal!'

'No,' Bernie tried to be reassuring. 'It isn't like that at all. They're trying to work out why anyone would want to kill him. They were probably hoping that there might be something here to suggest a motive. If he'd received threatening letters, for example – or – or – if he was planning to do something that someone wanted to stop – or …,' she tailed off, unable to think of any plausible reason for wanting to kill such an apparently inoffensive young man.

'I see.'

'Can *you* think of any reason why someone would want to hurt him?' Bernie asked tentatively.

'No.' Mary Bernadette shook her head, a look of puzzlement on her face. 'I don't understand it at all. Everyone liked him. He never did anyone any harm.'

'He looked to me as if he had something on his mind when he was on the ferry the other day. Do you have any idea what that might be? Had he talked to you about any big decisions he needed to make?'

'No. We'd spoken on the phone only a couple of days before – Thursday evening it was – and he seemed fine. He was a bit nervous of being left in charge over the weekend, but I think he was looking forward to it in a way too. He was proud that Father Liam trusted him. He told me he wouldn't be able to get over to see me this week because he couldn't leave the parish. That's what was so strange.'

She broke off, apparently deep in thought. Bernie waited in silence for her to go on.

'I don't understand why he was on

the ferry at all. He said he had to stay in the parish in case anyone needed him while Father Liam was away. He had an evening mass on Saturday and he had to hear confessions in the afternoon.'

'So he wasn't on his way to see you, then?'

'No. He specifically said he wouldn't be coming. He often does pop across for a visit, but not usually at the weekend, and definitely not *this* weekend.'

'Is there anyone else he might have been coming to see? If he lived across the water with you before he was ordained, maybe he has friends there. Is there anyone he might have gone to for advice – if he had a problem?'

'I suppose he might have wanted to talk to Father Aidan. He's the parish priest at our church in New Brighton. He's been there since before Nicky was born and Nicky has always seen him as something of a role model. I think perhaps if he was worried about something to do with his work as a priest, Father Aidan might be the person he'd turn to – especially with Father Liam being away.'

'Have you told the police about that?'

'No. I've only just thought of it now – when you asked me.'

'I think maybe you ought to mention it to them. If your Nicky was on his way to see Father Aidan, then he might be able to tell them what it was about, and

245

that might help them find out who killed him.'

'I don't know,' Mary Bernadette sounded unsure. 'Father Aidan came to see me as soon as he heard, and he didn't say anything about it. Don't you think he would have said if Nicky had arranged to meet him?'

'Maybe, but you never know.'

10 I COME TO THE GARDEN ALONE

Bernie looked at her watch as she set off up the road from St Wilfrid's presbytery – nearly ten minutes past ten. They would have time to look round the cathedral before lunch. The meeting with Mrs Allerton had not taken as long as she had thought. Turning a corner, she was presented with a view of the magnificent Anglican mother church rising up behind the houses, shops and trees. It looked as if it could have been there for centuries, but Bernie could remember it being completed in 1978. Her catholic friends, she remembered, had expressed a certain amount of superiority over the fact that it had taken the Church of England more than half a century to complete the building, while the Roman Catholic Cathedral had been constructed in a mere five years.

She quickened her pace as she strode up the long straight road that led uphill towards St James Mount, where the cathedral was situated. Not far now. Should she ring Peter again and let him know where she was? No. He already knew that she had set out from the presbytery; it would make more sense to wait until she was nearly there.

Bernie came out on to Upper Parliament Street and crossed at the pedestrian crossing outside Toxteth library. The railings that surrounded St James' Gardens were ahead of her. She turned to the left to find the entrance. As a child, she had often climbed over the railings and then scrambled down the steep bank to reach the path, or else skirted round through the undergrowth, following the boundary to where the trees gave way to a grassy path high up above the gardens, from which there was a magnificent view of the cathedral towering above. Now, however, she had become more observant of the rules that dictated that the railings were there for a purpose and entry should be by the approved route.

The gate was not far away – certainly not far enough to justify the effort of scaling the fence; but then, saving time or effort had never been part of the equation when she and her childhood friends had chosen the less orthodox entry method. She turned in under the stone arch and entered a tunnel of shade created by the trees growing on either side of the path. Walking briskly on, she soon came out into the sunshine again. She passed a domed memorial, which seemed familiar but she could not remember what or whom it was commemorating. The left-hand side of the path was now lined with gravestones, standing upright, hard against the sheer rock face, which reared up above the path. They must have been moved and put there at some time, she thought. This can't be where the graves are – all crowded together in a line.

A grassy area opened before her and she saw more gravestones and some more elaborate memorials in the shape of obelisks, pillars and pyramids. She would bring Lucy down here later, she decided, and they would have a look around and see if they recognised any of the names. The thought of Lucy made her remember that she had intended to ring Peter to let them know she was approaching the place where they planned to meet up. She took out her phone and made a brief call.

'Shouldn't we be going to meet Mam now?' Lucy asked as they walked round the inside of the unusual circular building that was the Metropolitan Cathedral of Christ the King. 'She said she was on her way.'

'Not yet. It must be a good twenty or twenty-five minutes' walk from St Wilfrid's to the cathedral,' Dominic told her. 'And it's less than half that for us. You saw how close it was when we were outside, looking along Hope Street. 'Now, see the way the light shines in through the coloured glass? As the sun moves round, the colours change. We ought to come back after lunch and you can see what I mean.'

Peter's mobile phone rang and he fumbled in his pocket to silence it. It was Bernie.

'I'm just coming through to the cathedral from St James' Gardens,' she reported.

'OK. Hang on.'

Peter relayed this information to Dominic.

'Tell her to wait at the main entrance and we'll be there in ten minutes,' he said. 'She must walk quicker than I thought.'

Peter passed on the message and put his phone back in his pocket. Then they made their way outside, blinking in the bright sunlight as they emerged on to the long flight of steps that led down to the street.

'You're right,' Lucy observed, looking across at the Anglican cathedral, which appeared to be only a few hundred yards away behind a row or two of buildings. 'It doesn't look far.

Will it really take us ten minutes to get there?'

Bernie followed the path round to the left, skirting the bottom of the cliff upon which the cathedral was built, and came to a short tunnel through the rock, which she knew would bring her out near to the main entrance, where she had agreed to meet Peter and the others. She stepped into the darkness and could at once see the light at the other end, above her and slightly to the right.

Without any warning, someone grabbed her from behind. A hand covered her mouth, jerking her head backwards. It felt as if a plastic bag was covering her mouth and nostrils, preventing her from drawing breath. She could not cry out. She tried to struggle, but whoever was holding her was strong and managed to keep hold of her head, suffocating her with the pressure on her mouth and nose. Bernie felt a hard impact against her chest and then suddenly there was a terrible pain in her left side. She slithered to the ground clasping her right hand over the place where it hurt, panting and trying to call for help, but no sound came and everything seemed misty and faraway.

11 QUESTIONS WITHOUT ANSWERS

As Peter and Lucy walked along Hope Street, pausing for Dominic to point out the Philharmonic Hall before hurrying on so as not to keep Bernie waiting, an ambulance passed with its siren wailing and lights flashing. They saw it turning right at the end of the road. The siren became fainter and then stopped suddenly. As they approached the junction, a police car flashed past from left to right. It looked as if it must be heading for the same incident as the ambulance – a traffic accident, perhaps.

They turned right along Upper Duke Street and crossed over to reach the cathedral entrance. They could see blue flashing lights through the railings that surrounded the cathedral grounds. Then, as they came to the open area in front of the main entrance, they saw two police cars and an ambulance parked close to the building. Had someone been taken ill while visiting? A heart attack following the exertion of climbing the tower, perhaps? But, if so, why the need for a police presence?

They hurried across the paved area and joined a small group of onlookers, who were watching as two figures in the green uniforms of the North West

Ambulance Service headed off down a path to the side of the cathedral. They stepped over the blue-and-white police tape, which indicated that this was a crime scene, and disappeared.

'What's going on?' Dominic asked.

'Someone's been stabbed in the tunnel,' a woman in her fifties told him. She was wearing a badge that indicated that she was employed in the cathedral bookshop. 'A woman. A couple found her lying there about ten minutes ago. There they are – over there, with the police.'

Peter turned to look where she was pointing. He saw a man and a woman sitting together on a low wall. A policewoman was sitting next to them, and another officer was standing nearby holding a notebook. They looked to be in their fifties, Peter judged, Bernie's age or a bit younger. Sightseers, he supposed, who had got a bit more excitement than they had been bargaining for. Another stabbing! Was this par for the course? Or could it be in any way related to the murder of the young priest? He had better not let Bernie catch him speculating on the possibility that violent crime might be commonplace in her native city! Which reminded him – where *was* Bernie? According to Dominic, she should have arrived here before them.

The same thought seemed to have occurred to Lucy. Peter looked across at her and saw that she had her phone to her ear, evidently waiting for a call to be answered.

'Where is this *St James' Gardens*,' he asked Dominic. 'Is it through there?'

'Yes. That's right. There's a sort of tunnel – you can just see it from here.' Dominic pointed over the police tape to where the path disappeared downwards into darkness.

'Constable!' Peter addressed the police officer who was standing in the centre of the path just beyond the tape. 'How long have you been here?'

'Not long, sir. Why?'

'My wife rang about ten minutes ago to say she was just the other side of your crime scene. I was wondering if she's stuck there.'

'I don't know about that, sir. That must have been about the time we got the call to attend the scene. I shouldn't worry, sir. Sergeant Farrow is at the other end, directing people to come round by the road.'

'I see,' Peter said slowly. Somehow, this reassurance did not reassure him. Why hadn't Bernie rung them to say that she was delayed? The woman with the cathedral badge had said that a woman had been stabbed. And now Bernie was not answering her phone. 'Now, can you tell me, constable …?' he left the sentence hanging, waiting for the officer to fill in the gap.

'O'Connor, sir,' he replied obligingly. 'PC John O'Connor.'

'Constable O'Connor,' Peter resumed, 'can you tell me–'

He was interrupted by the return of the paramedics, wheeling a trolley between them. A young-looking police constable walked alongside holding up a drip. At least it was a stretcher and not a body bag, and the face was uncovered.

As the trolley passed the little crowd of onlookers, everyone's eyes fell on the victim, curious to see what sort of person it was who had been assaulted in broad daylight in the grounds of the cathedral. Peter and Lucy gasped as they recognised the unconscious face.

'Bernie!'

'Mam!'

For a moment they stood there, staring in disbelief as the scenario that had been playing in Peter's head for the last few minutes turned into grim reality. Then Lucy ran after the ambulance crew, shouting to attract their attention. They ignored her and continued with the task of loading their patient into the back of the ambulance. Peter hurried in pursuit, calling out as he went.

'Hey! Wait! We need to come with you!'

The police constable handed over the drip to one of the paramedics and turned to face Peter.

'Stand back, please, sir,' he instructed.

'But that's my wife you've got there,' Peter argued, taking hold of the door and making to climb in.

'I'm sorry, sir,' the constable was firm. 'We have to get her to A and E right away. Stand back now.'

He spread his arms wide and stepped forward, shooing Peter, Lucy and Dominic back on to the pavement. The ambulance siren started up again and the vehicle moved off. The constable watched it out of sight before turning to speak to Peter again. Peter, however, was not there. He had gone over to tackle the police officer guarding the taped-off area at the side of the cathedral.

'Who's in charge here?' Peter demanded, his heart racing as he tried to make sense of what he had seen.

'DI Lucas is on his way. Until then, it's Sergeant Farrow. If you're still worried about your wife–'

'I am *not* worried about my wife,' Peter said, keeping his temper with some difficulty and speaking with the exaggerated calm and clarity of someone struggling not to give way to emotion. 'I am *distraught* about my wife. I have just witnessed my wife being taken away unconscious in an ambulance. I have been told that she has been stabbed. I do not know where she has been taken and I was not permitted to accompany her. And you ask me if I am worried about her?'

'I'm sorry, sir,' Constable O'Connor stammered. This was a new situation for him and he was not sure how to handle it. 'I had no idea, Are you sure it was her?'

'Of *course* I'm–,' Peter began, but Dominic interrupted.

'They'll have taken her to the

Royal,' he told Peter, pulling at his arm. 'It's not all that far. 'Don't you remember? I pointed out where all the cranes are – you know – building the new hospital. Why don't we just go over there and find her?'

'Because I want to know–,' Peter answered, pulling away from Dominic's grasp and facing Constable O'Connor. He got no further, however, because he was interrupted again, this time by a tall woman in police uniform who introduced herself as Sergeant Sarah Farrow. She sent O'Connor back through the tunnel to guard the other end of the crime scene and turned to speak to Peter.

'Can you tell me your wife's name, please?'

MYSTERY OVER THE MERSEY

'Dr Bernadette Fazakerley.'

'Yes,' Sergeant Farrow looked at Peter and then at Lucy and Dominic. 'That agrees with the credit cards that we found in her pocket. 'I'm very sorry, but it looks as if your wife was the victim of a knife attack. Fortunately, we don't think she was lying there long before she was found, and the ambulance got here within a few minutes, so there's a very good chance—'

'Never mind all that,' Peter broke in. 'Just take us to her, can't you?'

'Yes. Of course.' The sergeant turned and waved at the police officer who had been helping the paramedics. 'Constable Jones!'

The young man hurried over.

'This is the victim's husband and …?'

'Daughter,' Lucy chipped in.

'And cousin,' Dominic added.

'I want you to drive them to the Royal. Thomas is already there. I'll let him know to expect you.'

It might not be far to the hospital, but to Peter it seemed to take forever. The traffic lights all seemed to be against them and the roads appeared to be packed with slow-moving vehicles and drivers who did not know where they were going. Why didn't Constable Jones use the siren and lights to clear a path for them? However, even Peter had to admit that this was not such an emergency as would justify this action.

Bernie's fate was in the hands of the staff at the hospital and it would make no difference how long it took him and Lucy to join her there. The chances were it would be some time before the doctors would allow them to see her anyway. But what if there were nothing they could do for her? It might make the difference between arriving just in time or just too late to say goodbye – something that had been denied him when his first wife was killed in an eerily similar unprovoked and pointless attack. Oh, put your foot down, can't you, Constable Jones!

At last, the police car pulled up outside the emergency entrance of the Royal Liverpool Hospital. They all tumbled out and headed towards the door. Constable Jones hurried after them, calling out to his colleague, who stepped forward from under the canopy.

'I'm PC Robert Thomas,' he introduced himself. 'Sergeant Farrow asked me to look after you. I'll take you through to the waiting area.'

'How is she?' Peter demanded, striding ahead through the automatic doors and staring round. It seemed very dark after the bright sunshine outside.

'She's with the doctor now,' PC Thomas told him. 'They said that they're stabilising her and then she'll probably go to theatre. The best thing is for you to take a seat and I'll let them know you're here.'

Peter looked round. The room was

crowded and it was difficult to find space for them all. Eventually he spotted three seats together. He walked across the room with Lucy and Dominic following. They passed a woman with short brown hair, sitting with her head bowed, apparently deeply engrossed in a book of Sudoku puzzles. She looked vaguely familiar, but Peter could not place her.

They sat down, but Peter was unable to settle. After a few seconds, he got up again and started pacing around the room. Then he seemed to recollect himself and he sat down again, twisting his hands together in his lap and fidgeting with his wedding ring. Lucy watched him anxiously. She had never seen her stepfather like this before. Usually he was the epitome of composure, coping with the most difficult situations with a quiet confidence that radiated calm and inspired peace of mind in all around him. He saw her watching him and forced a brief smile.

'Don't worry,' he said, without conviction. 'She's in good hands.'

'That's right,' Dominic put in. 'The Royal is one of the best hospitals in the country. You don't need to worry about your mum now she's here.'

Lucy nodded and sniffed. She put out her hand and felt for Peter's, whether for comfort for herself or to offer comfort to him, she was not sure. He took hold of her left hand in his right one and gave a gentle squeeze. Dominic felt the movement and looked down. Then he stretched out and took hold of Lucy's other hand.

'Don't you worry,' he repeated. 'We Fazakerleys are tough. I bet Our Bernie'll be fit as a flea in no time.'

'Father Nicholas wasn't,' Lucy pointed out. She was becoming a little annoyed with her cousin's reassurances. She was used to her mother's *tell it as it is* bluntness and did not find Dominic's groundless optimism comforting.

Peter put his arm round Lucy's shoulders and drew her closer to him. He felt angry with himself for being so taken up in his own shock and worry that he had not paid sufficient attention to his stepdaughter, whose trauma must be so much greater than his own.

He was also resentful of her cousin's attempts to offer her the solace that he saw as his own personal prerogative. He rested his chin gently on her head and murmured softly.

'But he was already dead when your Mam found him. There's every possibility that they'll be able to patch her up.'

'Yes. I know, but ...'

'There's no point thinking about that,' Dominic said, putting his other hand on Lucy's so that he was holding it between his two.

At that moment, PC Thomas returned.

'Your wife has regained consciousness,' he reported, 'but they've sedated her again so that they can investigate the injuries. It'll probably be another half hour or so before you can see her. Would you like me to get you some coffee or something while you're waiting?'

'No thank you,' Peter began, but Lucy cut across him.

'I think Mam would say we need a brew,' she said, trying to put on a brave face. 'Can we have three teas, please? Nice and strong.'

12 OUT OF THE DEPTHS

Bernie struggled to open her eyes. The lids felt heavy and, when she did persuade them to open, the bright light hurt. She screwed up her eyes, peering out from half-closed lids, trying to make sense of her surroundings. She was lying on her back. There was a white ceiling above her, so she must have been taken indoors. Yes! She remembered now. This was a second awakening. There had been a doctor – a middle-aged woman with black curly hair, turning grey at the edges – who had said something kind and then told her that they needed her to go to sleep again. Bernie had tried to argue, but no-one had listened. She must try to get them to take notice now.

She twisted her head round, trying to see more. A blue shape to her left came slowly into focus and became a nurse's uniform. Its wearer looked down at Bernie and smiled.

'Dr Fazakerley?' she enquired.

'Yes,' Bernie nodded weakly and then lay back on the pillow. She could not believe that such a small movement could leave her feeling so exhausted. She braced herself to speak again, but someone else got in first. It was the curly-haired doctor again, speaking from the other side of the trolley on which Bernie was lying. At the sound of her voice, Bernie made an effort and turned her head to meet her eyes.

'Don't worry if you feel light-headed,' she said. 'You've lost a lot of blood, but we've got that under control now. I'm Elvira Yorke. I'm the surgeon who is going to get you sorted out.'

'Peter!' Bernie said urgently, angry with herself at the weakness that made even speaking a struggle. 'Where's Peter?'

'Peter?' the nurse asked, sounding puzzled.

With a great effort, Bernie turned her head the other way again to answer her.

'My husband,' she explained laboriously. Every word felt like climbing a mountain. 'I was supposed to be meeting him. He'll be wondering where I am.'

'Don't you worry,' the nurse assured her brightly. 'He's here – waiting outside. You can see him when the doctor's finished with you and we've got you up to the ward.'

'No!' Bernie gathered all her strength and managed to raise herself to a half-sitting position. A searing pain started up in her side and she flopped back. She gathered her strength for another try. 'Get him in here now!'

'That really isn't a good idea,' the doctor said, with the firm kindness that doctors reserve for dealing with awkward patients, while the nurse tidied the sheet, which Bernie had disarranged in her agitation. 'Much better to wait until you look a little less like death warmed up. No point frightening the poor man. The police have already told him you're safe.'

Bernie closed her eyes and concentrated on breathing. She must stop the pounding in her head that made it so difficult to think. And she must ignore the pain in her side, which was thankfully receding again, now that she was lying flat once more. How was she going to convince them that they were wrong?

She opened her eyes slowly and looked towards the doctor, who was busy studying papers on a clipboard.

'Listen to me, please!' she begged, speaking as loudly as she could manage, determined to get someone's attention. 'You don't understand.' She paused to get her breath back before continuing, speaking faster now that she had decided what to say. The words came tumbling over themselves in her anxiety to get her message across. 'Peter's first wife was killed in a knife attack. He saw her – lying there on her kitchen floor. He had to identify her body. Can you imagine what he's thinking now? Do you really think he's going to believe everything's OK? You've got to get him in here right away.'

The doctor's face changed. The benevolent smile was replaced with a look of anxiety. She was no longer humouring a patient who did not understand what was good for her.

'I see,' she said after a moment's thought. 'I think you're right.' She turned to address another nurse, whom Bernie had not noticed before. He was on the other side of the room, apparently checking the contents of a trolley loaded with surgical instruments. 'Glenn, go out to the waiting room and see if you can find Dr Fazakerley's husband and bring him in here,' she said briskly.

The young man nodded, left what he was doing, and crossed the room, heading for the door, which was in the wall behind Bernie's head. As he passed, he gave her a grin. 'Don't you worry: I'll have your old man in here in two ticks.'

Bernie forced a smile and tried to relax. She heard the door close and thought she could hear footsteps receding down the corridor outside. She closed her eyes and waited.

'Is there a Mr Peter Fazakerley here?'

At the sound of his surname, Dominic looked up. Then he looked round in surprise, wondering if the nurse who had appeared at the door of the waiting area was calling for some distant relative of his whom he did not know.

'Peter Fazakerley?' the young man repeated, looking round the room expectantly. 'Your wife is asking for you.'

'Peter!' Lucy said, digging her

stepfather in the ribs. 'He means you. Mam mustn't have told him Fazakerley isn't her married name.'

Peter stood up, feeling rather foolish and hoping that Lucy was right in her diagnosis of the problem.

'I think you mean me,' he said.

'Is your wife Dr Bernadette Fazakerley?'

'That's right. Is she OK? Did you say I could see her?' Peter started out across the room, stumbling over Dominic's outstretched feet in his eagerness.

'She's going to be absolutely fine,' Glenn assured him. 'She's a feisty lady – and determined that you should be there to see the worst. Just come through here and I'll take you to her.'

As Peter followed the nurse down the corridor, a pang of guilt suddenly struck him. What was he thinking of, leaving Lucy behind like this? He ought to have asked for her to be allowed to come too. It was too late to say anything now; Glenn had opened a door on the left and was ushering Peter into a small treatment room. He looked round, taking in an empty couch against the wall, with a trolley of medical stuff in front of it. Where was Bernie?

Then he looked to his right and saw a nurse standing over a patient trolley. She seemed to be adjusting the flow from a bag of blood hanging from a drip stand. Then he looked down and saw Bernie's face, so white as to be almost unrecognisable. She smiled up at him.

'So they let you in at last.'

Peter stepped forward, pushing the nurse out of the way in his eagerness. He stood looking down at Bernie's face, trying to think of something to say and wondering what to do with his hands. Her left arm lay outstretched, with a cannula in one of the veins and a tube snaking across to the drip stand. Her other hand was hidden beneath the sheet. He wanted to hold her, but did not dare touch; she looked so small and vulnerable – quite unlike the usual irrepressible, and apparently indestructible, Bernie.

'Bernie!' he said at last. 'Thank God you're OK.'

'Here,' a voice spoke behind him and Peter half turned to see a woman in a doctor's white coat holding a plastic chair. 'Sit down,' the surgeon instructed. 'You can have five minutes and then I want to take your wife into theatre to finish repairing the damage. You're lucky,' she added, looking at Bernie and smiling. 'That is, if you take it as read that you've been knifed in the chest. There's no damage to anything vital. We should be able to stitch you up and you'll be good as new in a few weeks.'

'You're sure of that?' Peter asked anxiously.

'As sure as I can be – and I've seen a good many knife injuries in my day.'

Peter subsided into the chair and leaned forward to kiss Bernie gently on the cheek. She waited for a few moments to give him time to get used to the good news. Then, mindful of the short window of time before he would be ushered out again, she spoke urgently.

'How's Lucy?'

Lucy! Another wave of guilt washed over Peter. In his delight at finding his fears unfounded, he had forgotten her again.

'She's fine – upset, of course, but fine. She's outside in the waiting room – with Dominic. I think he's rather enjoying looking after her.'

'Yes,' Bernie smiled again. 'I rather got the impression that he's somewhat taken with her. I can't decide whether I approve or not.'

Lucy fidgeted in her seat. It seemed like a long time since Peter had left them. Was that good news? If her mother needed urgent treatment, they would have sent him away, wouldn't they? But, if she had taken a turn for the worse, if they had decided there was nothing they could do for her, might they have allowed him to stay, to be there with her so that she would not die alone? Then again, he wouldn't have forgotten her, would he? He would have insisted that she be called. Or would everyone have thought she was too young?

'Don't worry,' Dominic said, tentatively venturing to put his arm around her as he had seen Peter do. 'They said she'd been asking to see your dad, so she must be OK.'

Lucy pulled away and stood up. She liked her cousin well enough but she was not ready to allow him to take such liberties. She stood, watching the double doors through which Peter had departed a few minutes earlier. They opened, and his familiar figure stepped through. He immediately saw her and hurried over. He took her in his arms and swept her off her feet, hugging her fiercely before setting her back down.

'The doctor says it's not serious,' he told her. 'They just need to do a bit of needlework to make sure it all heals up right. She's gone to the operating theatre now, but she'll be out and on one of the wards very soon. They said we ought to get some lunch and by the time we've finished we'll probably all be able to go and see her.'

'And you've seen her?' Lucy pressed him. 'It's not just what the doctor's say?'

'Yes. She's not exactly sitting up in bed and taking nourishment yet, but she was awake and asking after you.'

Lucy's face lit up as she dared to believe that everything was going to be all right. She hugged Peter round the waist, holding her face against his chest.

'I told you she'd be OK,' Dominic could not resist saying. 'It takes more than a mad knifeman to kill us Fazakerleys! Now, let's get something to eat, like the man said. I'll show you where the restaurant is – or there's a place over the road that specialises in real scouse. How about that?'

'Sounds good to me,' Peter said. Now that the crisis was over, he felt a little sorry for Dominic who had been doing his best to help and not getting much encouragement.

They trooped out of the waiting room. As they passed the woman with the Sudoku puzzles, she glanced up at them and followed them with her eyes until they disappeared through the door. Then she got up, pushed her book into her shoulder bag and went out after them.

'This isn't the same as the scouse that Mam makes,' Lucy said, after the first few mouthfuls.

'There are lots of different recipes,' Dominic told her. 'It's really just any sort of stew.'

'I looked it up in a dictionary,' Peter added. 'Like a lot of traditional recipes it was originally designed as a way of using up leftovers.'

Lucy ate rapidly. After all the excitement, she suddenly discovered that she was hungry. Dominic looked on, surprised at the speed with which Lucy's food was disappearing. Peter noticed and smiled.

'At home, it's usually Lucy's job to help our friend, Jonah, with his food; so she tends to be in a bit of a rush to eat her own,' he explained.

'Jonah? Is that the–'

Dominic broke off as a woman approached their table carrying a tray of food.

'We meet again!' she greeted them. 'Do you mind if I join you?'

Peter looked up and recognised Lauren Schofield, the journalist who had interviewed them in New Brighton. His immediate instinct was to tell her that he *did* mind and he would thank her to go away and leave them in peace. However, on reflection, he realised that if he did this she would simply sit down somewhere close enough to eavesdrop on their conversation and they would have no control over what she put in the report that she was, no doubt, already preparing in her mind for the next edition of the Echo.

'Be my guest,' he said in the pleasantest voice he could manage.

Lauren unloaded her tray on to the table and put it down on a shelf that ran along the side of the room. Then she pulled out a chair and sat down. She smiled round at them. Lucy glared back, wondering why Peter had not told the journalist to go away and leave them alone.

'Won't you introduce me?' Lauren said brightly, looking towards Dominic.

'This is my wife's first cousin once removed,' Peter explained. 'He is one of the relatives that we came here to see. He's been showing us round.'

'My name's Dominic,' Dominic added. 'Dom Fazakerley.'

'Pleased to meet you, Dom. I'm Lauren Schofield. I work for the Echo. You probably saw the bit I wrote about your cousin.'

'Yes,' Dominic agreed eagerly. He had never met a journalist before and was excited at the prospect that he might feature in the newspaper that his family would be reading over their breakfast toast the following morning.

'Thank you for giving me all that background info the other day,' Lauren went on, addressing Peter, with a friendly smile. 'It made all the difference to my report of the stabbing on the ferry. I'm sorry to hear that your wife seems to have been the killer's next victim.'

'No you're not,' Lucy said rudely, putting down her knife and fork and pushing her empty plate away. 'You're just pleased to have another story to write about. That's what you're here for, isn't it? You were there, weren't you, in the waiting room, watching us? And now, my mam's in the operating theatre and you've followed us over here to get us to talk to you.'

'Well, that *is* what newspapers are all about.' Lauren spoke in a mild, reasonable voice, conscious of the need not to antagonise her potential interviewees. 'Reporting the news, I mean. And, give me my due; I did get that awful man to retract his accusations that your mum had stabbed the priest.'

Lucy did not answer. She sat, staring down silently at the table. Lauren turned to Peter again.

'Do you have any idea *why* your

wife should have been targeted?' she asked.

'It's far too early to speculate,' Peter answered shortly. He was on familiar territory here, having honed his skills in parrying journalistic attempts at extracting information while he was a serving police officer.

'But you must have an opinion?' Lauren suggested, smiling sweetly, first at Peter and then at Dominic. 'Do you think this could be someone who saw those dreadful Facebook posts and is attempting to avenge the death of the priest by killing your wife?'

'As you said,' Peter replied shortly, 'you scotched those stories.'

Dominic opened his mouth as if to add something, but then changed his mind. He would have liked to have been quoted in the Echo giving his opinion on the motives for the attack on his cousin, but he realised that Lucy would probably never forgive him for such *fraternising with the enemy*, as she seemed to view it.

'In that case, do you think whoever killed the priest attempted to silence your wife too? Could it be because of something she saw?'

'I told you,' Peter got up and walked towards the door, motioning to the others to follow him, 'it's far too early in the case for any such speculation. The two attacks may not even be linked.'

'Surely that would be too much of a coincidence–,' Lauren began.

'The reason we have a word for it,

is because they do happen,' Lucy said, striding out into the open air with her head held high, delighted to have thought of a put-down for the annoying journalist.

Peter's mobile phone rang and he took it out of his pocket and looked at the screen. Then he tapped it to answer the call.

'Jonah! How are you doing?' he said, trying to sound upbeat and natural.

'What's all this about Our Bernie being knifed?' Jonah demanded, ignoring Peter's greeting. His voice sounded anxious and a little annoyed.

'Where did you hear that?' Peter gasped, trying rapidly to assemble his thoughts.

MYSTERY OVER THE MERSEY

'The Liverpool Echo Twitter feed. I've been following it since your murder case kicked off. *Witness to fatal ferry stabbing fighting for her life after second knife attack* is what it says, and there's a picture of Bernie being carried out of an ambulance on a stretcher. What's going on up there?' Jonah tried to keep the rising panic out of his voice, but Peter could tell that he was seriously worried. He tried to work out the best way of breaking the news.

'The first thing to tell you is that Bernie's going to be alright,' he said, trying to speak calmly and fighting back growing anger at the newspaper for having broadcast the news so soon, and at himself for not having anticipated it and taken steps to inform Jonah himself. 'I've seen her and she's not seriously hurt. They're patching her up and we're on the way back to the hospital now to see her again.'

'Are you sure? It said–'

'Yes. I told you; I've seen her and spoken to her,' Peter said firmly. 'Look I can't talk now, but as soon as there's more news, I'll–'

'But I need to know–'

'I'm sorry. I've just got to get rid of a journalist and then I expect Bernie will be ready to see us. I'll ring you right away after that.'

Peter ended the call and put his phone away. Then he turned to face Lauren.

'How dare you write that stuff about my wife, without checking that all her friends and family knew about it first?'

he exploded. 'Don't you journalists have some sort of code of conduct about that sort of thing?'

'I'm sorry,' Lauren apologised, 'but, you and your daughter knew what had happened. I assumed that if there was anyone else, you would have told them yourself.'

'Next time, wait until the police give you an official statement,' Peter growled. 'Now if you'll excuse us, we have to get back to the hospital.'

'DI Lucas would like a word,' PC Thomas greeted them as they walked under the canopy at the entrance to the hospital. 'If you would just step this way?'

He led them through the large

revolving doors into the main foyer of the hospital, where a tall man in a dark suit stepped forward with his hand outstretched. Peter had the unusual experience of looking upwards in order to see a clean-shaven face with brown eyes and a rather pointy nose, topped off with reddish brown hair. It somehow put Peter in mind of a fox.

'Mr Fazakerley?' he greeted Peter, shaking his hand in a rather stiff, formal manner. 'My name is Detective Inspector Chris Lucas. I'm in charge of investigating the attack on your wife.'

'Fazakerley is my wife's name,' Peter explained, fighting back his impatience. Was this officer going to insist on questioning him now, instead of allowing them to visit Bernie on the ward as the doctor had promised? 'I'm

Peter Johns.'

'*DI* Peter Johns,' Lucy added forcefully. She was keen that the inspector should realise that her stepfather was his equal and should be treated with respect.

'Retired from Thames Valley Police,' Peter told Lucas, in response to an enquiring look from the tall police officer. 'What can I do for you? We were just on our way to find out how my wife's doing,' he added, hoping to put off any police interrogation until after they had seen Bernie and satisfied themselves that she was safe after whatever procedures the surgeon was performing in the operating theatre.

'I can give you an update on that,'

Lucas replied. 'She's in a side room on Ward 4A. The surgeon said to tell you that everything went fine and she'll be good as new in a matter of weeks.'

'Can we see her now?' Lucy asked eagerly. 'Where's ward 4A?'

'Just a minute,' Peter interrupted, becoming aware of a presence behind his left shoulder, which turned out to be Lauren Schofield, clearly listening in on their conversation. He turned to face her.

'Constable Thomas!' he said sharply to the uniformed officer, who had followed them into the foyer and now stood waiting for orders from his superior. 'I wonder if you could escort Ms Schofield off the premises. And perhaps you could explain to her that the press will be given a statement at the appropriate juncture.'

Rob Thomas smiled and nodded, but before he could say anything, Lauren held up her hands and backed away towards the door.

'OK. OK,' she said. 'I get it. I can see you need some space. I'll back off.'

Then she seemed to remember something and she felt in her pocket for a business card, which she held out towards Dominic, who was closest to her.

'If there's anything the Echo can do for you, there's a phone number and an email address where you can get hold of me, on this.'

'Thank you,' Peter said coldly, taking the card from Dominic's hand

and pocketing it. Then he turned back to DI Lucas. 'I know you need to talk to us, but can you just give us a few minutes to go to the ward first? Lucy hasn't had a chance to see her mum yet.'

'The ward sister asked for us not to come up until after lunch has finished,' Lucas answered. They have very strict rules about protected mealtimes for patients. So, if you would just come with me, I've been given the use of an office on the fourth floor link corridor, which is right by Ward 4A. So, please, come with me and let me take down some basic facts and then, after that, we can see your wife.'

13 HASTE THE DAY WHEN MY FAITH SHALL BE SIGHT

Jonah sat staring at the blank screen in front of him. What did Peter mean by '*going to be* alright' and 'not *seriously* hurt' and 'patching her up'? He flicked back to the Liverpool Echo news page to see if anything had been added since he last checked it. No. It still simply reported that Bernie had been attacked by an unknown assailant in St James' Gardens and taken to the Royal Liverpool Hospital.

He searched for the hospital's website and found a list of consultants in the Trauma and Orthopaedics department. His late wife had been a trauma surgeon and it was always possible that one of her friends might now be working there. He looked at the list of names. No, none of them was familiar – or, yes! Perhaps this one was. Elvira Yorke? Elvira was an unusual name; he was sure he had come across it somewhere before. Elvira Yorke, Elvira Yorke – no! Not Elvira Yorke, Elvira Baker. It was coming back to him now. Elvira Baker had been his wife's registrar. This must be the same person. It was far too great a coincidence for there to be two Elviras both training as trauma surgeons. Yorke must be her married name. He looked back at the list – yes, it said clearly *Mrs Elvira Yorke*. And there was a telephone number for her secretary.

Jonah started keying in the number, intending to telephone and ask to speak to the surgeon, but then he hesitated. He could not remember whether he had ever actually met her all those years ago when she was training under his wife. Even if she did remember him, she would not be able to reveal any information about a patient. Moreover, in all probability Bernie was being treated by a different consultant altogether.

Nathan came into the living room, asking solicitously if there was anything he needed. Jonah flicked back to the Echo report of the assault on Bernie and turned the screen round so that Nathan could see it.

'Look at this,' he said. 'I've been on to Old Peter, but he's being cagey because there's a journalist hanging around. He *says* she's going to be OK, but I don't know if he's just not wanting to worry me.'

'If Peter says it's OK then I expect it is,' Nathan said, bending over to read the screen. 'The newspaper has to make it all sound more dramatic than it really is to make people want to read it.'

'But is says *fighting for her life*,' Jonah objected. 'What if they're not exaggerating?'

'I'm sure Peter would have told you if it was that serious.' Nathan sat down on one of the easy chairs so that he was on a level with his father. He looked him in the face, adopting an expression intended to convey understanding for Jonah's anxiety while suggesting that it was unfounded. 'What did he say was happening now? Is he with Bernie?'

'He said he'd seen her and he was going back to see her again now.'

'There you are then! I bet he'll be on the blower again any minute to tell you everything's fine.'

For a few moments, neither spoke, then, seeing that his father was still not satisfied, Nathan continued.

'Look: there's absolutely nothing *we* can do to help; so there's no point in getting het up about it, is there?'

He was doing his best to be reassuring, but to Jonah he sounded like a nursery school teacher reasoning with a wayward toddler. It was always the same when he was left in the care of his son; sooner or later Nathan would say or do something that just slipped over the border from *caring* to *paternalistic*.

'I want to go up there,' Jonah said suddenly. 'I want to see for myself.'

Nathan was so taken aback that, for a moment or two, he could not think of a reply. Surely, his father could not be serious? It must be nearly two hundred miles – more than a hundred and fifty, anyway. He remembered Bernie saying that it would have taken three hours or more to drive. He shuddered at the thought of the alternative, which would be a long train journey, probably with changes to be made. And that would only be the start of it. They would need somewhere to stay – with disabled facilities.

'Oh Dad! Don't you think they've got enough on their plate without you to worry about?' he chuckled at last, deciding to make light of the proposition in the hope that Jonah would abandon it when he saw that his son was not taking it seriously.

'I'm serious,' Jonah retorted, trying to keep the annoyance that he felt out of his voice. 'You can come too. You said you were entirely at my disposal this week. I want you to dispose yourself to driving me up to Liverpool. You do the packing and I'll sort out where we're going to stay.'

'Don't you think you're getting a bit ahead of yourself, Dad? At least wait until Peter rings again. For all you know, they may decide to come home as soon as Bernie's discharged from hospital.'

'I suppose so,' Jonah agreed reluctantly. 'Still, there's no harm in making plans. I'll check out hotels and you can start packing the car. We can always unpack later if we change our minds. There's a list of everything we need on the noticeboard by my desk.'

'Hang about! What's all this *we* business? Things *we* need – if *we* change our minds. As far as I'm concerned, my mind is completely clear that traipsing all that way up there is total madness.'

'Well, if that's your attitude, you'd better get out of my hair and go and do something useful,' Jonah said petulantly, turning his chair so that Nathan could no longer see his face. He could see the force of Nathan's argument but he was loath to abandon his plan. Not only was he very fond indeed of Bernie, but he also depended on her to provide the support that he needed in order to continue working in the job that he loved and which gave him a sense of worth. While he knew that he ought to trust Peter to keep him informed, nothing could replace seeing with his own eyes that Bernie was safe and on the road to recovery. And, in the final analysis, if things were more serious than he had been led to believe – doctors were sometimes overoptimistic in their prognoses – he wanted to be there to say goodbye and to console Lucy. 'The front hedge needs trimming. Go and get on with that and leave me in peace.'

Recognising that there was no point in prolonging the argument while his father was in this mood, Nathan silently went out and fetched the electric hedge clippers from the garden shed. The boundary between the front garden and the road was marked by a thick copper beech hedge about four feet tall. It would take a couple of hours at least to cut it and dispose of the clippings. Maybe by that time Dad would have come to his senses – or Peter would have rung with definitive news that would convince him that all was well.

Jonah stared morosely at his

computer screen, wondering what to do next. It was intensely frustrating to watch a disaster unfolding in front of him and to be unable to do anything to help. He was accustomed to taking charge of emergency situations, and inaction was anathema to him. He checked his email, in case Peter or Lucy might have sent him a message with news on Bernie's condition. Nothing. What about Lucy's Facebook page? Only a status update saying that she was at the Royal Liverpool Hospital with Peter Johns (fancy Peter having a Facebook account!) and Dominic Fazakerley.

Dominic Fazakerley? That was a new name – presumably some relative of Bernie and Lucy. Jonah clicked on the link and a new page opened in his screen. Dominic Fazakerley, it appeared, was quite liberal with the information that he shared with the public about himself. Jonah was able to discover that he was twenty years old, studying English Literature and Religious Studies at Lancaster University and lived in Liverpool. He too was currently at the Royal Liverpool Hospital and was in the company of Lucy Paige. Jonah studied the profile picture critically. It showed a young man in an Everton shirt standing in front of a modern-looking building, which might be a university hall of residence. Jonah zoomed in to see the face more clearly, but the definition was poor and he could only be sure that the young man in the picture had rather unkempt mousey brown hair and eyes that might be either green or pale brown. He could not detect any family likeness to either Bernie or Lucy, but then this must be some quite distant cousin, so no surprise there.

He felt an irrational pang of jealousy at the realisation that this nondescript young man was currently in the thick of it and, moreover, in the company of Lucy – for whom he had a deep fatherly affection – while he was stuck at home hundreds of miles away from the action. He looked at the time displayed at the bottom of the screen. Why hadn't Peter rung yet? Surely he must have some more news by now? What if the news was bad and Peter was unsure about breaking it to him? On the other hand, perhaps it was a simple delay. Hospitals often seemed to underestimate the time that procedures would take. Maybe he should ring Peter to find out? But then again, hospitals often had blind spots where there was no mobile phone signal – which could, of course, be another reason why Peter had not yet called.

He was interrupted in his deliberations by the sound of the front door opening, followed by voices in the hall.

'Come in!' he heard Nathan calling. 'I'm really glad you've come. Perhaps you can knock a bit of sense into Dad for me. He's got it into his head that he wants to go up there himself. As if that wouldn't make things ten times worse for Bernie and Peter.'

The door opened and Stan and Sylvia entered the room. Jonah turned his chair to face them, forcing a smile and hoping that they would not fall in with Nathan's request.

'Peter rang us,' Sylvia told him, walking over and sitting down in the easy chair next to Jonah. She looked into his eyes with an expression of compassion mingled with anxiety. 'He was about to be interviewed by the police, so he could only give us the bare bones, but he seemed sure that Bernie was going to be alright.'

'I know,' Jonah said, as calmly as he could. 'He said the same to me, but I'd rather see for myself.'

'I'm sure you will,' Nathan said, also keeping his annoyance in check with some difficulty, 'but that doesn't mean you need to go running off up to Liverpool. They've got Wi-Fi in the hotel. As soon as Bernie's discharged, you can have a chat with her on Skype.'

Jonah said nothing, but looked dissatisfied. Nathan turned to Stan for support.

'Go on Stan,' he urged. 'Tell him what a big mistake it would be imposing himself on them when they've got enough to handle already.'

Stan looked round at each of them in turn, taking in Nathan's anxiety tinged with irritation, Sylvia's compassion, and Jonah's defiance, which he suspected was a cover for genuine distress.

'Have you asked Peter what *he* thinks?' he asked at last.

'No,' Jonah answered, before Nathan could speak. 'We haven't had the chance yet.'

'But he'd be bound to say they didn't mind,' Nathan cut in quickly. 'Even though it's obvious that it would only make things more difficult for them.'

'Why?' asked Stan with characteristic directness.

'Well, isn't it obvious? I mean they'd feel responsible for him – and Bernie would probably insist on doing things for him – and, well …'

'One of us could come with you, if you don't think you'd be able to cope,' Sylvia suggested quietly.

'That's ridiculous! There's no need for you two to get involved. I just think–'

'Well, I'm going to ring Peter and find out what's going on,' Jonah declared, sensing that what Nathan was about to say would exasperate him all the more, and seeking to close down the conversation before he lost his temper. 'Then we can decide what to do, with all the facts in front of us.'

14 I CANNOT TELL

'I'll try not to keep you long,' DI Lucas said, motioning them all to sit down in the cluttered office. 'I just need some basic facts from you. First: can I just have your full names and addresses, and your relationships to Dr Fazakerley?'

It took a few minutes to get this information straight. Lucas found it hard to comprehend how Lucy could have a surname that was different from those of both her mother and the man whom he had assumed to be her father. Then, when it came to Dominic, Lucy launched into a lengthy explanation of the correct method for calculating the degree of kinship for cousins, which left him feeling considerably confused.

'I'll just put down *cousin*,' he said in the end. 'I don't think we need to bother about removals and all that. Now,' he said turning to Peter, 'I understand you spoke with your wife by phone shortly before she was assaulted ...'

'Yes,' Peter affirmed. He took out his phone and found the call history screen. 'Here you are. It's this incoming call here – at ten twenty-nine.' He held out the phone so that Lucas could see the entries. 'She said she was in St Johns' Gardens. We were at the other cathedral and we'd agreed to meet her at the main entrance, so we set off right away.'

'We expected her to be there first,' Dominic added. 'She only had to walk through the tunnel from the gardens. We'd thought it would take her longer to get there from Dingle, or we would have started off sooner.'

'And what was your wife doing in Dingle?' Lucas asked Peter.

'That's something I wanted to tell you about,' Peter answered. 'And I think you really ought to bring in DI Latham. Presumably you are aware that my wife is the key witness in the case of the stabbing of the priest on the ferry two days ago?'

Lucas did not answer Peter's

question, but something about his face and the tone in which he spoke next, suggested to Peter that this was news to him.

'Are you suggesting that the two cases are connected?'

'Not necessarily, but it has to be a possibility – and I think you ought to be aware that the press are already making the connection.'

'Is that what that journalist was sniffing around about?'

'Yes. That's one reason why it's so important to bring in DI Latham and show the public that the police are properly joined up.'

'Thank you for your advice, Mr Johns. However, as you have pointed out, you are now retired, so if you could allow us to do our jobs in our own way and confine yourself to answering my questions, I'd be grateful. You haven't told me why your wife was in Dingle, while the rest of you were sightseeing.'

'She was talking to the mother of the young priest who was killed. She – the mother – asked to speak to the person who was the last to see him alive. The other priest – the more senior one, who worked with him – asked Bernie to come to the church to see her; so she did.'

Lucas noted this down. Then he looked round at all three of them again, studying their faces as if he expected to deduce something from their expressions.

'Now,' he said at last, 'apart from

the theory that there might be some connection with the ferry stabbing, do any of you know of anyone who might have wanted to hurt Dr Fazakerley?'

They all shook their heads.

'Bernie hadn't been back to Liverpool for years,' Dominic pointed out. 'If she had any enemies they'd be down in Oxford, not here.'

There was a uniformed officer standing outside the door when Lucas led them through the ward to the single room that had been assigned to Bernie. He looked rather bored, but snapped to attention as he saw DI Lucas approaching, followed by Peter, Lucy and Dominic. Peter recognised him as the constable who had driven them to the hospital earlier.

'I've put PC Jones here as a precaution,' Lucas explained. 'This was probably just a random attempted robbery, but just in case it was a personal attack on your wife, this is protection to make sure they can't have another go.'

Lucy's heart started beating faster as the realisation dawned on her that this incident might not yet be over. The very solid and real presence of PC Jones suddenly made the gravity of the situation horribly real. What if there was someone out there intent on killing her mother? They couldn't have police protection forever. She slipped her hand into Peter's and he squeezed it gently.

'If it *is* someone trying to prevent her talking about something she saw on the boat,' he said, forcing himself to speak more calmly and optimistically than he felt, 'then surely they'll give up now. Once you and Latham have interviewed her again, they can't possibly think she's still holding anything back, can they? But thanks all the same,' he added hastily, anxious lest Lucas mistake his attempts at reassuring Lucy for a request to have the protection removed.

Bernie turned her head and smiled at them when they entered. She was propped up in bed with both hands lying in front of her on the blue hospital blanket. Peter thought that she looked considerably better than when he had last seen her. A little colour had returned to her cheeks and her face looked less haggard. The drip, which was still attached to her left arm, now contained a colourless liquid. For Lucy, however, her mother's appearance was a shock. She looked from the pallor of Bernie's face to the bag hanging on the drip stand and her eyes opened wide. She forced herself to smile back, but Bernie had seen her consternation and hurried to allay her fears.

'That's only plain saline,' she told her, looking up at the drip bag. 'It's only to keep the vein open, just in case they need to give me anything intravenously, but the plan is to take it out later this afternoon. They reckon my blood count and hydration are OK now.'

Lucy nodded and forced another

smile. She still did not trust herself to speak.

'Take a pew,' Bernie invited. 'I told the nurses we'd need at least three chairs, so they brought in a couple of extra ones.

Lucy and Peter took seats of either side of the bed. Dominic picked up a plastic chair from a pile of two that stood under the window, moved it next to Lucy and sat down on it. DI Lucas remained standing. Peter ventured to take Bernie's right hand in his, squeezing it gently. For a few moments nobody spoke. Then DI Lucas cleared his throat.

'Dr Fazakerley,' he said apologetically, 'I am Inspector Chris Lucas. I'm in charge of investigating your assault. I'd like to start by saying how sorry I am that you have been hurt. I realise that this is a difficult time for you–'

'I don't know about that,' Bernie interrupted, unable to resist the temptation to wrong-foot the big police officer, whose attempts at a sympathetic approach merely irritated her, and hoping by this facetious approach to dispel Lucy's evident anxiety. 'It's all been rather interesting. Presumably you'll have been comparing notes with DI Latham in case the two incidents are related?'

'– however I do need to ask you some questions to enable us to track down the person who did it,' Lucas continued, apparently oblivious of Bernie's interjection into the preamble which he always used when interviewing crime victims. 'I'll be as brief as I can and then I'll leave you to talk to your family.'

'Right you are then – crack on!' Bernie answered cheerfully, determined to appear as normal as possible in front of Lucy, and also taking secret delight in trying to surprise Lucas by refusing to accept a victim role. 'Where would you like me to start?'

'Let's begin by checking a few facts.' Lucas opened his notebook and flicked through the pages. 'Your phone showed that you made two calls to your husband this morning.'

'That's right. I had an appointment at St Wilfrid's Presbytery – you know, the RC church in Dingle – so Dom was taking them round a few of the sights, and then we were going to meet up for lunch. I was finished by ten-ish, so I rang Peter to let them know. We agreed to meet at the front entrance to the Anglican Cathedral. I reckoned it would take twenty or twenty-five minutes to walk, so I suppose it would have been – what? – ten twenty-five or thereabouts when I rang to tell him I was nearly there.'

'You walked from St Wilfrid's to St James' Gardens?'

'Yes. Do you have a problem with that?' Bernie detected a touch of incredulity – or was it disapproval? – in Lucas' voice. She wished that he would sit down, instead of towering over her like that. Didn't he realise how intimidating it was to see his piercing brown eyes staring down on her from above?

'Well, I certainly wouldn't allow *my* wife or daughter to walk alone through Liverpool 8.'

Bernie treated Lucas to a hard stare. She was proud of her native city and did not take kindly to anyone who subscribed to the popular view that its inhabitants were all either thieves, con men, scroungers or thugs.

'You're not from Merseyside, are you?' she said sharply.

'I've been here more than ten years,' Lucas protested mildly, keeping his voice calm despite the dawning realisation that he had blundered. He was afraid that he was losing the goodwill of this crucial witness.

'Where *are* you from?' Bernie persisted. She had been trying to place his accent, but had only got as far as *northern, but not Scouse or Geordie.*

'Rotherham.'

'Rotherham? That's in *South* Yorkshire, isn't it?' Bernie's tone was becoming positively hostile. 'I hope you didn't bring any South Yorkshire Police attitudes with you when you crossed the Pennines.'

'I was never with the South Yorkshire force,' Lucas assured her, rushing to distance himself from the damning findings of the Hillsborough inquests. More than three months on, and twenty-seven years since the incident in Sheffield when 96 Liverpool

Football supporters lost their lives, there was still a deep-rooted feeling of anger and resentment against the police, who had firstly presided over the episode and then tried to shift the blame on to the fans themselves. 'I trained with Greater Manchester before coming here.'

'Did you see anyone following you?' Peter prompted,' trying to get the interview back on track.'

'No.' Bernie shook her head, 'but then I wasn't looking out for anyone.'

'OK,' Lucas took over again. 'Now, I realise this will be painful for you,' he continued, back in *empathetic-handling-of-a-victim-of-violent-crime* mode, 'but I need you to try to picture in your mind exactly what happened in the moments leading up to when you were attacked. Close your eyes, if it helps. Take yourself back to when you entered St James' Gardens. What can you remember?'

Once again, Bernie recognised the Cognitive Interview technique, which she had observed on numerous occasions when acting as Jonah's personal assistant. She grinned and obediently closed her eyes.

'It was sunny,' she said, deliberately trying to think of some irrelevant details to satisfy the inspector that she was entering into the spirit of the exercise, 'but it was shady under the trees. There were conkers coming on the horse chestnuts. I rang Peter when I got in sight of the tunnel. There was a bed of flowers on the left as I went into it. I'd just got inside, out of the sun when someone grabbed me from behind. They put their hand over my mouth and then, I suppose they must have brought their other hand round my waist to stab me in my left side. Then they threw me to the floor – or maybe I just dropped down – and the next thing I remember was someone bending over me and saying something, and then I think I woke up in the ambulance, but I may have been imagining that.'

Bernie opened her eyes and smiled sweetly at Lucas, as if to say, *how was that?*

'Going back to when you were attacked,' he said gently, relieved that his witness appeared to have abandoned her animosity. 'Did you get any feeling for what they might have been like? A man or a woman? Tall or short, for example?'

'Well, they didn't have any difficulty grabbing me around the head, so that might suggest they were taller than me – not that that's saying much. And they managed to cover my mouth and nose with one hand, so maybe they had biggish hands.'

Peter experimented with his own hand, placing it over Bernie's face. He had no difficulty obstructing nose and mouth simultaneously. Then Lucy had a go with her smaller hand, holding her mother's nose between thumb and forefinger while covering her mouth with her palm.

'Hmm!' Bernie murmured, when she

was released. 'Another theory bites the dust! I don't think we can deduce anything about hand-size after all. But I'm sure they were holding my head back against their chest, so they must have been on the tall side – compared with me, anyway.'

'That's good,' Lucas said encouragingly (receiving a withering look from Bernie for his pains). 'Now is there anything else – anything at all – that you can remember about him?'

Bernie shook her head. Then suddenly she remembered something.

'There *was* something,' she said slowly. 'A funny smell. Oh! And the hand that was over my face – I think maybe it had gloves on.'

'What sort of gloves?' Lucas asked

eagerly.

'Smooth – like latex gloves, the sort they use in hospitals.'

'That's very interesting. It suggests an element of planning. Now, can you tell me any more about the smell that you mentioned? Can you describe it to me?'

'It's difficult to describe a smell,' Bernie said, wrinkling her nose in concentration.

'Well, was it an unpleasant smell?'

'Not exactly. No, I don't think so. It was … sort of floral – like you get in air fresheners. A sort of artificial flower smell. And a bit sweet and sickly. It reminded me a bit of Parma violets – or pear drops, maybe. Yes – there was a definite whiff of O' level organic chemistry lessons. I think it must have contained an ester of some sort.'

Lucas jotted all this down, considered whether to press Bernie for any more information and then decided to call it a day.

'Thank you Dr Fazakerley,' he said politely. 'I'll probably need to talk to you again at a later date, but for the time being I'll leave you to recuperate. Your husband has my card, if you think of anything else that might be of help to us.'

He opened the door to leave the room, and then he remembered something and turned back.

'Just one last thing. I've arranged with the hospital to take away your clothes for forensic examination. It may be a few days before we can return them, to you – and if we find anything on them that might give us the identity of the attacker, it's possible that they'll have to be kept as evidence.'

Bernie nodded acquiescence and Peter promised to bring in some clean clothes as soon as they had definite news on when she would be discharged.

15 THE GIFT WHICH HE ON ONE BESTOWS

They sat in silence for a few moments, relief at the departure of DI Lucas being succeeded by awkwardness in knowing what to say now. Lucy was the first to speak.

'Are you really OK, Mam?' she asked.

'That's certainly what everyone keeps telling me,' Bernie asserted boldly. 'Now that they've stitched me together again and topped me up with a couple of pints of blood, it's just a matter of time before I'll be good as new.'

'Well, just make sure you follow doctor's orders and don't think you can behave as if nothing has happened,' Peter cautioned. 'I know you – you simply won't be told sometimes!'

'Do you think it was the same person who killed the priest?' Lucy asked. Now that she was convinced that her mother really was not seriously hurt, her thoughts turned to solving the crime.

'If it's the same person who killed Father Nicholas, you're very lucky to have got away with minor injuries,' Peter observed. 'That seemed to be a very efficient murder – almost instantaneous, no sound, no mess. It was as if they knew exactly where they needed to aim to inflict a fatal blow.'

'Actually,' Bernie said hesitantly. 'They seem to think that Richard may have saved my life.'

'What an Earth do you mean by that?' Peter said in tones of utter amazement, while Lucy's eyes grew wide and Dominic looked round with blank incomprehension.

For answer, Bernie withdrew her hand from Peter's grasp, leaned over and reached out to open the drawer in the bedside locker. She winced as the movement caused a jarring pain in her side. Peter intervened, pulling open the drawer and looking inside. He saw an object that had become very familiar to him since his marriage to Bernie ten years previously. Putting his hand into the drawer, he took it out and held it up.

Lucy and Dominic stared in puzzlement. Hanging over Peter's hand was a loop of ordinary household string. Strung on the loop, there was a gold locket, about an inch across. On either side of the locket were two rings. One was a simple gold band set with a small diamond flanked by two even smaller red stones. The other was made up of an intricate pattern of interwoven strands of gold.

Bernie took hold of the locket and pointed to a deep scratch on the surface, which cut across the engraved pattern of two interlocking hearts that adorned it. Peter bent closer and looked at it carefully. The front of the locket had been bent out of shape by the impact of whatever instrument had made the scratch.

'They reckon the knife hit this and glanced off, so that it just grazed my ribs instead of going through into my chest, Bernie explained.

'But what is it?' Lucy asked, still puzzled.

'I think it must have belonged to your great grandmother,' Bernie told her. 'I found it when I cleared out the room she used to have.'

'You mean Richard's grandmother?' Peter asked.

'That's right. She seems to have had quite a lot of jewellery. I sold most of it, but this didn't look valuable so I kept it.'

Lucy reached out her hand and took the locket from her mother. She studied the outside for a few moments and then opened it and looked inside to see a colour photograph of a man in his late fifties with white wavy hair and pale blue eyes.

'This is my dad, isn't it?' she said. 'It's the same as the one in your bedroom.'

Bernie nodded.

'So *you* put it in there!' Lucy said accusingly. 'That can't have been his grandmother's.'

'No. It was empty when I found it, so I scanned the photo and printed out a smaller version.'

'And you've been wearing this next

to your heart ever since?' Lucy sounded incredulous. Her mother had always appeared to her to be one of the least sentimental people imaginable and the thought that she had been secretly carrying around with her a picture of her late husband came as something of a shock.

'I think that's dead sweet,' Dominic said warmly, putting his arm around Lucy's shoulder to have a closer look at the photograph. 'So that's where you get your lovely curls from, Lucy. All the Fazakerleys have straight hair.'

'And what are these rings?' Lucy asked, ignoring this remark.

'That's my engagement ring,' Bernie answered, pointing. 'The one that Stephen gave me. And the other one is my wedding ring.'

'Which one?' Lucy looked from the intricate gold ring to her mother's empty ring finger and back again.

'I've only got the one. When we got married, Peter and I recycled the ones we'd already got.'

Dominic looked at her in amazement. Then he looked at Peter, who was sitting back with an expression of mild amusement on his face.

'You stood up in church and put another man's wedding ring on your wife's finger?'

'What's wrong with that?' Bernie asked sharply. 'There was no way Peter was going to stop wearing Angie's ring and I can't be trusted to wear one at all, so there wasn't much point going to the expense of buying new ones.'

Her cousin still looked dissatisfied, so she continued.

'I started wearing Stephen's ring round my neck when I discovered that, when you're twenty-something and sporting an engagement ring, people are constantly asking who the lucky man is and then getting embarrassed when you tell them he's dead. Then, after I married Richard, I did try wearing his ring, but I never remembered to take it off when I was doing messy jobs and it ended up permanently filthy; and if I did take it off I'd forget where I'd put it or it'd get knocked into the waste bin by mistake. So I decided it was safer round my neck.'

'It's an unusual design,' Dominic observed, taking the ring from Lucy and turning it round in his fingers.

'It's called a Celtic knot,' Bernie told him. 'Richard's grandmother was Welsh – and so was one of mine, come to that – so it seemed appropriate.'

Lucy leaned across the bed and took hold of Peter's left hand, which was lying on top of the blanket. She gently eased the ring off his finger and studied it. It was plain on the outside, but inside there was an inscription: *Peter & Angela 10/06/78*. Without speaking, she replaced it on her stepfather's finger and sat back in her chair again.

'You might at least have got

yourself a proper gold chain,' she said, handing the locket and rings back to her mother, 'instead of this piece of string.'

'What for? The whole point is that nobody else can see it.' Bernie gave the jewellery to Peter. 'You'd better look after this until I get out of here.'

Peter studied the scratch on the outside of the locket again. 'The police ought to see this. Forensics might be able to work out something about the knife from looking at the marks it's made.'

'OK,' Bernie agreed. She was starting to feel very tired and to hope that her guests might leave soon. 'You do that, will you? I've had enough of DI Lucas for one day.'

Peter nodded and put the locket and rings in his pocket. 'I may wait a bit and give it to DI Latham – assuming that Lucas does have the sense to bring her in on this. He seemed amazingly reluctant to accept that the two cases are most likely related.'

'He seemed remarkably–,' Bernie began, but she was interrupted by Peter's phone. She broke off and waited as he took the call.

'Jonah! I was going to call you in a few minutes. We're with Bernie now. Would you like to speak to her?' Peter handed the phone over to his wife, who took it eagerly.

'Hi Jonah! How're you doing?'

'On tenterhooks waiting for news about you. How are you?'

'I'm f–,' Bernie stopped herself, realising that her knee-jerk response simply would not do. It was patently obvious to everyone that *fine* was not an appropriate description of her current condition and would only convince Jonah that she was hiding something from him. 'I'm feeling a lot better now,' she amended. 'I've been assured that nothing important has been damaged and it's only a matter of time before it all heals up. I've been sewn up by one of the consultant surgeons and she says there's absolutely nothing to worry about.'

'*She*?' Jonah queried. Surgery – especially trauma and orthopaedics – was still a very male-dominated profession. 'It wasn't Elvira Yorke, by any chance?'

'Yes. Do you know her?'

'Not personally, but I recognised the name. She was one of the first registrars that Margaret trained.'

'It's a small world, as they say.'

'Are you *sure* you're OK?'

'Absolutely. Just a bit tired, after losing some blood. Don't you worry – I'll be right as rain by next Monday and champing at the bit to go back to work with you.'

'Rubbish!' Peter intervened. 'You'll wait until the doctors say you're ready.'

'Don't worry!' a younger voice sounded on the phone. Evidently Nathan had been listening in and had heard Peter's exclamation. 'I've already been on to the agency and they say there'll be no difficulty at all about providing carers to accompany Dad when he goes back to work next week. Bernie – you *must* take as long as you need. It won't help Dad if you do yourself permanent injury by going back too soon.'

'Nathan's right,' Jonah agreed, in a tone that Nathan felt was suggestive of surprise at his having come out with something sensible at last. 'And I resent the implication that my only concern is to get my Personal Assistant back to work as soon as possible! My enquiries after your health are entirely motivated by the deep regard in which I hold you.'

'Tell that to the marines!' Bernie teased. She knew perfectly well how genuinely fond Jonah was of her and what agonies he must have been enduring while he waited to hear that she was safe, and she wanted to avoid a display of emotion in front of the younger generation. The incident with the locket and rings had already shown off too much of her softer side and she certainly did not wish to allow Dominic to realise how much affection she had for this other man in her life.

'I suppose it was too much to hope that this near-death experience would have improved your disposition,' Jonah pretended to grumble. 'But I suppose I must assume that your continued failure to listen to reason is a sign that there isn't a lot wrong with you. OK. I'll get off the line and let you get some rest. I know I'll be in trouble with Old Peter for over-exciting you if I'm not careful.'

He ended the call and Bernie handed the phone back to Peter.

'Jonah's right,' he said, slipping it into his pocket. 'We ought to get off and leave you in peace.' He bent forward and kissed his wife, feeling very self-conscious under the watching eyes of Lucy and Dominic. He was not naturally demonstrative and he knew that Lucy would recognise this behaviour as a departure from the norm.

Lucy hugged her mother affectionately round the shoulders.

'Take care,' she whispered, 'and don't overdo it.'

Not to be outdone, Dominic waited until Lucy had got up out of her chair and then leaned over the bed to give

Bernie a peck on the cheek.

'See you later.'

'Try to get some sleep,' Peter advised, turning back at the door. 'We'll come again at evening visiting time.'

16 COMPANIONS ON THE ROAD

No visiting was allowed at the hospital during the morning; so the following day Peter was pleased that Dominic offered to take Lucy to see the redevelopment work on the Anfield stadium. She could do with something to take her mind off recent events. He arrived soon after breakfast, eager to set off. Peter noted with satisfaction that he was no longer wearing the Everton jersey that he had sported the previous day. Although Bernie always insisted that the rivalry between the two clubs was friendly, he assumed that there were limits to their tolerance and suspected that flaunting support for the opposition while actually at the Liverpool ground might fall outside of them.

After the youngsters had left, Peter looked around the room, wondering how to fill in the time. His eyes lit on Bernie's laptop and he remembered his promise to keep Jonah up to date on developments.

'Peter! How's things?' Jonah's face appeared on the screen a few minutes later, somewhat unclear and with imperfect synchronisation between voice and mouth.

'We're expecting Bernie to be

discharged this morning. She's just got to wait for the all-clear from the doctor, but she rang earlier and seemed pretty confident. The drip's out and she's been making a nuisance of herself trying to give Constable Jones the slip so she can wander off round the hospital.'

'Sounds like Our Bernie. And what about you?'

'Oh I'm OK,' Peter assured him, taken aback by the question. 'Just at a bit of a loose end waiting to hear when she's coming out. I sent Lucy out with her cousin, Dominic. I thought it was better for her than hanging around the hotel.'

'How *is* Lucy?' Jonah had been wanting to ask but had been reluctant to do so in case Lucy was listening in on the conversation. 'It must have been a shock for her.'

'She seems to be taking it in her stride. I think she had a bit of a wobble yesterday, while we were waiting to find out how bad things were – we all did – but Bernie was so much better yesterday evening that I think she's ... well, like I said, taking it in her stride.'

'Good.' Jonah paused, trying to think of the best way to approach what he wanted to say next. 'I'm glad she's gone out. I wanted to sound you out about something and it's better that she's not here.'

He paused again. Peter waited patiently.

'I'd like to come up to join you,'

Jonah said at last. 'Nathan thinks it's a mad idea, but …'

Thoughts flashed rapidly through Peter's mind as he tried to process this proposal. There was no denying that it had been pleasant – give or take the discovery of a mysterious corpse and an unprovoked attempt on his wife's life – to be free of the constraints that Jonah's presence usually put on their activities. Since leaving Oxford the previous Friday, they had not had to be constantly thinking about disabled access to venues, or organising their meals to fit in with the rather rigid dietary regime that helped to keep Jonah's digestion functioning well, or turning down invitations to late evening events knowing that Jonah needed an early night. He had to admit that he had also enjoyed having his wife and stepdaughter to himself, instead of sharing their attention with a man whom he knew to be (despite his disability) more charismatic than himself. For a moment, he was tempted to concur with Nathan and to brush aside Jonah's request by telling him that there was nothing to worry about and nothing he could do to help.

Then he remembered how he had felt when he saw Bernie being loaded into the back of the ambulance, and on the journey to the hospital, and during the long, long wait to hear that she was alive and expected to make a full recovery. And he remembered how useless it had been to be told that all was well. He had needed to see for himself.

'I can't see that being a problem,' he forced himself to say, as brightly as he could. 'Will Nathan drive you? If not, we could meet you from the train. We're in a different hotel now. It's hardly any distance from Lime Street.'

'That's great!' Jonah said enthusiastically. Then he added apologetically, 'if you're sure you don't mind. This was supposed to be a respite break for you all, as well as taking Bernie back to her roots.'

'Don't you worry about that! I know that Lucy would never forgive me if she found out you'd asked and I'd put you off.'

'That's why I wanted to talk to you when she wasn't there. Please Peter, be honest. If you'd rather I didn't, just tell me.'

'I *have* told you. We'll be delighted to see you.'

'We?'

'Alright. *I* will be delighted to see you. Are you satisfied now?'

'Yes. Thanks. Sorry. Now, what was that about a new hotel?''

'The police have insisted on moving us into one of the big ones in the centre of the city. It's in case whoever attacked Bernie was deliberately targeting her – perhaps because she's a witness to the killing of the priest – and may try again. They want us where they'll be able to keep an eye on us without it being too obvious. The good thing from your point of view is that it boasts about having accessible rooms and disabled facilities and, as I said, it's easy walking distance from the station.'

'Why not just come home – if they seriously think Bernie may still be in danger? And what about you and Lucy? You were witnesses too.' Jonah refused to be deflected by Peter's attempt to play down the danger and divert attention to the advantages of their new location.

'Do you seriously think Bernie would stand for us running away?' Peter laughed, more cheerfully than he felt. 'Besides, she's still going to be needed to help with the police enquiries. Don't worry. Like I said, it's just a precaution. Nobody really thinks they'll try again. It would be far too risky.'

'Well, I hope you're right.'

For a moment, the two men eyed each other across the ether, both trying to look and sound more confident than they felt.

'When shall we expect you?' Peter said at last.

'That's just it,' Jonah sighed. 'Nathan's still being obstinate. That's why I wanted to sound you out, his main argument being that you'd all be better off without me. Stan and Sylvia have offered to come with me, but it's not fair to ask them if I can't persuade Nathan to help. They're pushing eighty after all.'

'Well, let me know when you've got a plan.'

Jonah logged off and Peter was

again at a loss to know what to do. He switched on the television and flicked through to find the news channel. He was relieved to see that there was plenty of national and international news to fill the bulletins, squeezing out any mention of the *Mersey Ferry Murder* or its aftermath. He switched off again and turned back to the computer. Perhaps he ought to check the Echo website to see what the interfering Lauren had seen fit to write about the attack on Bernie. He had just found the page when his phone rang. It was Bernie herself, sounding very bright and cheerful.

'I've been given the all-clear,' she reported, 'but there's some paperwork to do apparently before I can go. They said to ask you to pick me up from the discharge lounge at eleven. Will that be OK?'

'Of course! I'll organise a taxi.'

'No. Better to ring for one after you get here. You know what hospitals are like. Eleven could easily turn into half past or quarter to twelve.'

'OK. See you later then.'

Peter stood in the middle of the room looking round indecisively. Now he knew for certain that he had an hour or so to kill. He would go out and buy something nice for Bernie to celebrate her return – but what should he get? She disliked cut flowers and disapproved of extravagant gestures of any kind. In Bernie's book, clothes were just something to keep you warm and decent, and she never wore jewellery. It was not easy to find a present for her that she would not consider a pointless extravagance. He sighed. His first wife had not been anywhere near as difficult to give little treats. However, there was no harm in trying. He would go to the market. Perhaps he might find a souvenir of Liverpool or some local speciality in the way of confectionary that she would enjoy.

Jonah meanwhile was having a very unsatisfactory time, trying to convince Nathan that making the journey to Liverpool to see Bernie and the others was both possible and desirable.

'Oh Dad! I thought you'd got over that idea,' Nathan groaned, when he broached the subject. 'Bernie told you herself there's nothing to worry about. And they'll be back in a few days. What on earth would be the point of you going all that way?'

'I just want to be there with them.' Jonah knew that logic was against him, but was determined to argue his case. 'Try imagining it was Georgia instead of Bernie. You'd want to be there, wouldn't you?'

'That's completely different. Georgia is my fiancée. Bernie is married to someone else – and that someone else is there with her. She doesn't need you. And that's even without taking into account the extra work that having you around would make for them.'

'There won't be any extra work if you come with me. And Peter said they'd be pleased to see me.'

'Of course he did! He's far too polite to say anything else. Oh come on Dad! Try to be reasonable.'

'Peter and I go back a long way,' Jonah argued. 'He doesn't have to be polite to me. He was a detective sergeant when I was a mere PC. He'd soon tell me to get lost, if that was what he thought.'

'I don't believe you were ever a *mere* anything,' Nathan retorted. 'Not in your own estimation anyway! If you don't like *polite* then try *kind*. Peter is far too considerate of your feelings to tell you where to get off, the way I'll bet he would have liked to. I'm sorry Dad, but I'm just not prepared to take you off on this ridiculous wild goose chase. It would only make things a whole lot worse for Bernie and Peter, and the chances are it wouldn't do your own health any good either.'

They sat together in silence for several minutes.

Jonah realised the force of his son's arguments but he was still reluctant to give up on the idea – especially after Peter had sounded so welcoming. It crossed his mind – briefly – that he could run away by himself. He could order a taxi – there were firms that specialised in vehicles large enough to accommodate his electric wheelchair – to the station. He could arrange with the rail company to see him on and off the train. And Peter had offered to meet him at the station in Liverpool. He sighed. No. That would be irresponsible and unfair. If he could not bring Nathan round to his way of thinking, he would not be able to go. Besides, he now remembered that there was engineering work going on between Oxford and Banbury, with rail replacement buses. The chances were that they would not be able to accommodate his wheelchair. It was not often that Jonah allowed his disability to get him down, but now he raged silently against the paralysis that prevented him from making the journey as easily as Bernie and the others had done a few days earlier.

Nathan waited, expecting his father to come up with some new counter-argument. He had nothing further to say, but was reluctant to leave the room to get on with the chores without being assured that Jonah had abandoned his travel plans. God only knew what mad new scheme he might come up with left to his own devices.

There was a ring at the doorbell and they looked at one another in surprise. They were not expecting visitors; the postman had already been; and it was still early for casual callers. Jonah manipulated controls in the panel on the arm of his wheelchair to open up communication with the loudspeaker outside the front door.

'Jonah Porter here,' he said. 'How can I help you?'

'Hi Jonah,' replied a voice over the intercom. The speaker sounded young and rather uncertain of himself. 'It's Cameron Price. Remember me? From the Algarve?'

'Yes, of course. I've unlocked the door. Just give it a push and come in.'

'It's the boy whose uncle died falling off a balcony[2] when we were in Portugal,' Jonah explained to Nathan. 'He took a bit of a shine to Our Lucy. I bet he's come hoping to see her.'

'I'll show them in here,' Nathan offered, hurrying out into the hall. A moment later, he was ushering into the room a young man in his teens, wearing jeans and a tee-shirt and with canvas training shoes on his feet. He

---

[2] See DEATH ON THE ALGARVE, © 2016 Judy Ford, ISBN 978-1-911083-16-0.

was accompanied by a smartly-dressed woman of around forty.

'Cameron!' Jonah greeted them. 'And this must be …?'

'Julie Price.' The woman stepped forward and extended her arm to shake hands. Cameron grabbed it and pulled it back down to her side, reddening with embarrassment at his mother's faux pas. Jonah pretended not to have noticed. He was used to people failing to realise – or failing to remember – that he could not move his arms to participate in the traditional greeting. 'I'm Cameron's mother,' she continued. 'I'm taking him on the rounds of universities so he can make his mind up where to apply next year, and he said we couldn't go to Oxford without looking you up. I gather you were all very supportive when my brother-in-law had his accident.'

Jonah took in Mrs Price's immaculately styled hair and well-tailored powder blue suit – its skirt just short enough to show off her shapely legs – with some surprise. This was not at all how he had imagined Cameron's mother to be, based on what he had heard about her from her estranged husband and her sister-in-law. He had pictured her as timid and easily cowed, dominated by her domineering husband – until the moment when the worm had turned and she had left him, taking their son with her.

'Is Lucy around?' Cameron asked, trying, and failing, to sound indifferent.

'I'm afraid not,' Jonah told him

hiding a smile. 'She's gone off to Liverpool for a week with Our Bernie, to look up some distant relatives and find their roots. It's just me here, I'm afraid – and my son Nathan's staying to look after me.'

'But she never said!' Cameron burst out indignantly. 'I mean, she hasn't put anything about it on Facebook.'

'What about–?' began Jonah. Then he stopped abruptly, realising that Lucy's Facebook privacy settings must have allowed him to see the post announcing her presence at the Royal Liverpool Hospital, while blocking it from Cameron. Now was probably not the time to reveal to the boy that Lucy considered him to be a mere *acquaintance*, while affording Jonah all the privileges of a *friend*. 'I daresay she's been too busy with other things to bother with that,' he amended, trying to soften the blow of Cameron's realisation that Lucy almost certainly had considerably less interest in him than he did in her. 'Did you see the news reports about a priest being killed on the Mersey ferry?

'Yes,' Julie Price confirmed, but Cameron looked blank.

'Bernie found the body. She and Lucy have been busy giving statements to the police and things, so it's not surprising she didn't have time for maintaining her social media presence.'

'You're kidding!' Cameron gasped, looking at Jonah, wide-eyed. Then he remembered Lucy's reaction to his uncle's sudden death a few months earlier. 'I suppose Lucy will have been wanting to watch the post-mortem,' he said regretfully. 'I told you she wants to be a pathologist, didn't I?' he added to his mother.

'So, is your friend, Bernie, the *Bernadette Fazakerley* who's being reported in the papers as the attacker's second victim?' Julie asked with interest, ignoring her son's remark. 'Have you heard from her recently? How is she?'

'The latest is that she's being discharged from hospital this morning and she's going to be absolutely fine,' Nathan intervened, before Jonah could answer. He was keen to play down Bernie's injuries to deter his father from re-visiting his plan to travel up to see her.

'What about Lucy?' Cameron asked eagerly, seeing an opportunity for offering comfort to the girl whom he was hoping might become a little more than merely a Facebook friend. Surely even hard-nosed Lucy must be upset and in need of support when faced with a murderous attack on her own mother? 'Was she there when it happened? Is she OK?'

'*Taking it in her stride* was how old Peter put it,' Jonah told him. 'But I'm sure that underneath she'll have been pretty upset about the business.'

'We could go up and see them, couldn't we, Mum?' Cameron turned to his mother, his eyes shining. 'I wanted to check out the Institute for Performing

Arts. Why don't we go there now and leave Oxford Brookes and Reading for another time?'

To Jonah's surprise, and Nathan's annoyance, Julie Price seemed enthusiastic about this idea.

'Why not?' she said at once. Then she turned to Jonah. 'Why don't I drive us all up there? I'm sure you'd like to see for yourself that your friends are OK.'

'That's very kind of you,' Jonah began.

'But it really isn't feasible,' Nathan cut in quickly. 'My father's wheelchair wouldn't fit in your car and we'd need to think about where he could stay when he got there. Not all hotels are disabled-friendly.'

'Peter says the one they're staying in is,' Jonah pointed out. 'He'll organise a room if we let him know we're coming. But you're right, Nathan, we'd need to go in our car. It's specially adapted,' he explained to Julie, 'with space for my chair to be strapped in so I can travel in it.'

'What are we waiting for then?' Julie asked. She looked at her watch. 'It must be – what? – about four hours, do you think? Not much more than that. With a break for lunch, we could be in Liverpool by–'

'Hold on a minute!' Nathan interrupted. 'It's not as simple as that. You're forgetting, my dad can't just drop everything and leap in the car and go off the way you can. There's a load of things we'll need to pack, and we *must* check with Peter that the hotel really does have an accessible room free, and the route needs planning to make sure there are enough stops to give him a rest from being strapped in one position in the chair, and–'

'What my son is trying to explain,' Jonah put in, 'is that we won't be ready to set off until after lunch.' He was highly delighted that Nathan had allowed himself to be carried by the flow into accepting that they were, after all, going to make the trip up to Liverpool to join Bernie and the others. He now wanted to make things as easy for him as possible, without giving way on the main point. 'I suggest that you stay to lunch – unless you need to do some packing on your own account – and we aim to get off early in the afternoon, with a view to arriving round about tea time.'

'OK.' Nathan sighed, accepting the inevitable. 'I'll sort out the packing. Why don't you work out our itinerary?' Then he turned to Julie, 'can I get you something to drink, while you're waiting?'

'That's quite OK. I'm sure you've got plenty to do. Would you like me to fix the lunch for you? We don't need to pack – we've already got overnight bags in the car.'

'That's an excellent idea,' Jonah agreed, before Nathan could turn down the offer. 'Let's all go in the kitchen and I can show you where everything is. Then you can do that while I have a look on Google maps and find the best route. And I'll ask old Peter to book rooms for us.'

'Do you have any theories about who the killer might have been?' Julie asked Jonah a few minutes later, as she washed a lettuce in the sink.

'It's difficult to say from this distance,' Jonah answered. 'I don't have all the facts.'

'Your friends then? What do they think?' Julie persisted. 'Did they get a look at the person who attacked her? And do they agree that it's likely to have been the same person as killed the priest?'

'Stop it, Mum!' Cameron pleaded, feeling embarrassed at his mother's questioning. 'You might at least warn him that you're after a scoop to get you in the nationals.'

'I'm sorry,' Julie apologised. She dried her hands and then took out a business card from her jacket pocket and placed it in front of Jonah. 'Cameron's right. I'd better come clean. I'm a journalist. That's why I knew all about your friend's involvement in the stabbings. I have to keep up with all the news to spot anything that I might be able to make into a story. It would be great to have your point of view. It's a whole new angle. To think that the key witness to a murder, and the victim of a possibly related attack, is also the personal assistant to a famous detective! I'm a freelance,' she went on, 'and this could be the story that gives me the break I need.'

She broke off and looked at Jonah apologetically.

'Sorry. Shall I go home now?' she asked, half seriously. 'I'm really not wanting to take advantage of you. It's just …'

Jonah studied the card; then he looked up at Julie's expectant face. Again, Jonah found himself having to re-calibrate his opinion of Mrs Price. This was definitely not the passive army wife, with no interests beyond her home and family, which he had been expecting. Here was an intelligent and ambitious woman, who knew what she wanted and was prepared to do what it took to get it. No wonder she had found life with her macho and controlling husband intolerable. After a short pause, he laughed.

'Well, I can't say I'm overjoyed at the idea of entertaining a journalist on a four hour drive,' he admitted, 'but I can't very well complain. I've been using you just as much as you've been using me. Until you came along, I was making no headway at all in persuading Nathan to take me up there. So I reckon we're quits.'

'Thanks.'

'However, we do need to agree some ground rules,' Jonah went on. 'And number one is that you won't send anything off to any paper without showing it to us first and giving us a chance to censor it.'

'OK,' Julie agreed with a smile. 'After all, I'm supposed to be taking a few days off to help Cameron choose his options for uni. *Any* story I write will be a bonus. And if you're worried about me applying the third degree during the journey, why don't we take both cars? Then we can be more independent and you can bring your friends back in yours to save them having to come on the train.'

'Good. I'm glad we understand one another. Now, carry on with what you're doing while I ring Old Peter and ask him to organise accommodation for us all.'

17 FACE TO FACE

At Peter's insistence, once he had brought her back to the hotel, Bernie remained in their room for the remainder of the day, ostensibly resting. With some difficulty, he persuaded Lucy that her mother would recover better if she had as few people around her as possible, and she agreed to allow Dominic to take her off on a further round of sight-seeing. By mid-afternoon, Bernie was feeling very bored and was looking forward to

Jonah's arrival.

'I wonder what Dom will make of Cameron,' she mused to Peter, as he fussed around, adjusting cushions to make her more comfortable in the basket-weave chair provided by the hotel. He had tried to induce her to go to bed, but she was having none of it, declaring that she was not going to be treated like an invalid.

'Or how Cameron will react when he sees Dom and Lucy together,' Peter agreed with a grin. 'Perhaps we ought to insist on her wearing a hijab,' he joked. 'I'm sure it's that mass of yellow curls that drives all the boys wild!'

There was a knock at the door and Peter opened it to reveal PC Jones with DIs Lucas and Latham. Seeing them there standing in a line together, Peter was reminded of the old comedy sketch about class divisions and imagined the towering Lucas looking at his colleagues and saying 'I look down on him ...'

'I'm afraid I need to speak to your wife again,' Lucas said. 'Can we come in?'

Peter noted the inspector's use of the singular pronoun and took it to be a deliberate tactic to emphasise that he was still in charge of the investigation. He nodded and opened the door wider to allow them to enter.

'I think you have already met my colleague, DI Latham?' Lucas went on, still pressing home the point. 'She's here in case it turns out that there's a link between the attack on your wife and the ferry incident.'

Peter arranged chairs for the two police officers and then sat down on the end of the bed.

'I'm sorry to intrude on you like this,' Lucas said to Bernie, falling back into his sensitive-treatment-of-the-victims-of-crime routine, 'but I'm afraid with criminal investigation, it's important to act quickly. I'll try to make sure this doesn't take too long. I know you must be tired after your ordeal.'

'Not a bit of it!' Bernie declared cheerfully, determined not to give him the satisfaction of believing that she was grateful for his concern. 'Always happy to help the boys and girls in blue. And we'll be glad of something to liven up our day. What can we do for you?'

'DI Latham would like to show you some photographs,' Lucas told her.

'It's the pictures we took of all the passengers on the ferry,' Sandra Latham explained. 'We'd like you to have a look and see if you recognise any of them – either on the ferry or, more significantly, if you've seen any of them since. Assuming that the two attacks are connected, there's a good chance that whoever knifed you was on the ferry with you on Saturday.'

She picked up a briefcase, which she had put down on the floor next to her chair, and took out a thick file.

'There are rather a lot of pictures to get through,' she said apologetically.

'But please, take your time and we'll take a couple of breaks so you don't get too tired.'

Bernie opened her mouth to protest that there was no need, but Sandra continued.

'It's been proved that a person's attention is significantly reduced after an hour or so of concentrated mental activity; so we always work on the basis of five minute rests every hour.'

Peter grinned to himself as he compared the different approaches of the two officers. He could see that Lucas had irritated Bernie by his overt solicitude, while Latham had skilfully avoided suggesting that she was being treated differently from any other witness. She had thus gained her trust and her full attention. It was going to be interesting to see how this all panned out. His money was definitely on Latham being the more likely to obtain a positive outcome to the enquiry.

Bernie and Peter both studied each picture in turn. Peter identified the businessman who had tried to force his way off the ferry at Woodside. Bernie recognised two of the passengers who had been with them in the queue to have their fingerprints taken. However, most of the pictures rang no bells in either of their minds. Then, after two rest breaks and as Sandra turned to the final page of pictures, Bernie pointed at one of them.

'That's the lad in the Everton shirt that I told you about,' she said to Sandra. 'The one who went and stood next to Father Nick for a while. There was a girl with him … yes! That's her, there.'

She pointed at another photograph. This one showed a young woman – teens or early twenties – with long, black hair drooping over her face.

'I'm glad you recognised them,' Sandra said. 'I rather fancied they might be the ones. They were together and, as you surmised, he lives locally – in Bootle – and she was visiting and being shown the sights. They're both at Bristol University, studying Sociology.'

'Did they remember seeing the priest?' Peter asked, forgetting for a moment that he was not the investigating officer on this case.

'They remembered that there was

someone leaning on the rail at the front of the boat, and one of them remembered him being dressed in black; but they hadn't noticed that he was a priest and they didn't remember seeing anyone approaching him or talking to him.'

'And presumably there was nothing to indicate that they killed Father Nick?' Bernie suggested, certain that if there had been, the two would have been arrested by now.

'No. Their fingermarks were on the rail by where he was standing, but it would be more suspicious if they weren't, given that they admitted having been there. They handed over their tee shirts for testing by forensics and we swabbed them for traces of blood, but nothing came up. As far as we can tell they did nothing more than stand next to him for a few minutes and then move on.'

'Where did they go?' Bernie asked suddenly. 'I mean, they didn't stay on the bow deck, but they obviously didn't get off at Seacombe; so where were they between Seacombe and Woodside?'

'They said that they carried on past where Father Allerton was standing and then back down the opposite side of the boat from where you were sitting and then went downstairs, ready to get off at Woodside.'

'So, I was right that they'd left the stern deck *before* we left Seacombe,' Bernie said triumphantly. Then she pouted her lips as she thought through the implications of this statement. 'Which suggests that my impression that Father Nick was alone on the deck between Seacombe and Woodside, is probably also correct,' she said slowly. 'You know, I think we may be barking up the wrong tree with these photos. What if the killer struck *before* ever the ferry got to Seacombe, and then disembarked. Do you have records of the passengers who got off at Seacombe?'

'We have the CC-TV footage of the passengers disembarking,' Sandra told her, 'but, to be honest, we haven't paid them that much attention. We were assuming that he must have been killed between Seacombe and Woodside. It didn't seem very likely that he could have been dead for upwards of ten minutes and stayed standing there like that.'

'But, he was propped up, with his left arm round the flagpole,' Bernie argued excitedly. 'He only fell down when I disturbed the body by taking hold of his shoulder. If he could stay like that for long enough for the killer to get away out of sight, why couldn't he have been there for several minutes – or even more? He could have been already dead when those two students approached him. You say they didn't take much notice of him.'

'What do the medics say about time of death?' Peter asked.

'The usual,' Sandra said with a wry smile. 'In other words, hedging their bets. We certainly couldn't rule out the possibility that he died any time from when he got on the ferry to when you found him.'

'There you are then!' Bernie said jubilantly. 'The more I think about it, the more convinced I become that we'd have noticed someone coming up to him after we left Seacombe, because there was nobody around at that end of the boat by then. And Lucy and I walked past him – twice – so surely we would have seen if anyone else was there.'

'You may be right,' Sandra agreed. She sighed. 'I'd better get hold of that CC-TV recording and let you have a look at it. I'm afraid the quality isn't great, but you never know …'

'You could try appealing for people

who got off at Seacombe to come forward as witnesses,' Peter suggested. 'The chances are, the killer won't respond, but you never know – they might be afraid that *not* doing so would be construed as suspicious, or sometimes they actually crave publicity.'

'Yes. I'll do that,' Sandra agreed. 'I'll get it out on local radio and in the Echo – that may help to get them off my back,' she added, with another wry smile. 'You never know – someone may have seen one of the other passengers behaving suspiciously, but not done anything about telling us because they assumed that only people who stayed on to Woodside were relevant. The other thing I'll do now, is to go and have another chat with those students and see if they can tell us whether or not Father Allerton could have been already dead when they saw him.'

She put the folder and her notebook back into the briefcase and closed it up.

'I think that's all from me at the moment,' she said, getting up. 'So, unless DI Lucas has anything further to ask ...?' she added, turning to her colleague.

'No – nothing at present,' he replied. 'Thank you both for your time. I'll be in touch if there's any news, or if I need to speak to you again.'

Peter held the door for the two police officers to leave and then closed it firmly behind them.

'Well!' he said. 'You've certainly opened up a nice little can of worms there. 'DI Latham must be delighted to have you telling her that her nice closed group of suspects is wide open after all!'

'Hardly my fault,' Bernie grinned back. 'It'll be interesting to see what Jonah makes of it all when he gets here. I bet he'd have been rounding up everyone who got off at Seacombe as soon as he heard that nobody could confirm that Father Nick *wasn't* dead by then.'

'Or at least, he'll *think* that he would have done,' Peter agreed, with a chuckle. 'And he'll be absolutely certain that in Lucas's place, he'd have called in Sandra Latham the moment we mentioned that you were involved in her case. I certainly don't envy DI Lucas when Jonah starts giving him the third degree over dragging his feet like that. I wonder who decided that they had to work together – not Lucas, I'll be bound!'

18 WE ARE HERE TO HELP EACH OTHER

The telephone in the hotel room rang. It was Reception. They had a Father Liam Cosgrave there, hoping to see them. Was it alright to send him up? Peter's immediate reaction was an urge to send the priest away. He had been hoping to persuade Bernie to have a rest after the session with the police, in anticipation of the excitement of Jonah's arrival, which could not be long off now. However, he caught

Bernie's eye and realised that she had heard the request. He recognised the strong-willed look on her face and concluded that if he did not invite Father Liam up to their room, she was likely to insist on going down to meet him at Reception.

'By all means,' he replied at last. 'We'll be expecting him.'

A few minutes later, there was a tentative knock on the door and Father Liam entered. Bernie recognised him at once and introduced him to Peter. They all sat down and Father Liam looked round, taking in Bernie's still pale face and tired but determined expression, and Peter's anxious look.

'I won't stay long,' he assured them. 'I just felt obliged to call to see how you are – and to thank you again for meeting Mrs Allerton. She told me that it helped her a lot speaking to you.'

Bernie nodded and smiled, embarrassed at the praise and unsure what to say.

'I don't think I said much,' she mumbled, feeling that some sort of reply was expected. 'But she seemed pleased to know that he was saying the rosary when he died.'

'Yes,' Father Liam agreed. 'It seems to be something that she felt deeply about. I always wondered why Father Nick ... I suppose I thought it was odd in this day and age that a young man should use that as his main spiritual discipline. I see now that it was probably that his mother brought him up to it.'

'So, would you say that it was the thing he would resort to if he was seeking guidance from God?' Bernie asked.

'Very probably. Why?'

'Well. I may be making far too much of this ...,' Bernie hesitated before going on, 'but I got the distinct impression that he was worried about something. I'm not sure why, but it looked to me as if he had a decision to make and he was trying to think through what he ought to do. Did he have any big choices coming up?'

'Not that I'm aware of,' Father Liam shook his head and frowned. 'Of course, he was probably upset about the Solari boy's death. It pulls you up short the first time you see someone younger than yourself die – or anyone, come to that – but Ben was only twenty-two; it must have been quite traumatic for Father Nick administering the sacraments for the first time and comforting the family. I wish I'd realised how ill Ben was. I'd never have gone off and left Father Nick on his own, if I'd known.'

'I don't know,' Bernie said slowly. 'I'm probably reading too much into what I saw of him, but I would definitely say it didn't so much look as if he was upset about something as if he was trying to make up his mind about something. An ethical dilemma, maybe?'

'I don't know what it could have been,' Father Liam said, shaking his head. 'He seemed quite settled in that respect when I left. So if he was in doubt about anything, it must be something that cropped up while I was away.'

'His mother thought that, if he had become worried about something while you were away, he might have gone to their own Parish priest for advice,' Bernie suggested. 'We wondered if that could have been where he was going when he was killed.'

'Technically, it might have been more appropriate for him to consult one of the senior clergy at the cathedral, but I can see that speaking to a priest that he knew well and who had known him for many years might be more attractive. And he might feel more comfortable about confiding in such a person if he was worried about whether he had done everything correctly regarding the Solari family – which I do think is the most likely cause of the anxiety that you are describing. Father Nick was very conscientious and he may well have realised afterwards that he had omitted some small element of the sacraments. As I said, he had never administered extreme unction before.'

'Mmm,' Bernie sounded sceptical. Then a thought occurred to her. 'I suppose, if he did think he'd missed out something important, and the family hadn't noticed …'

'Mrs Solari told me that he acquitted himself very well,' Father Liam interjected. 'She had nothing but praise for him.'

'Then he might have been wondering whether or not he ought to do anything to put it right,' Bernie continued. 'Would it be better to leave things as they were – with whatever it was still wrong – or to tell the family that he'd cocked up and offer to do whatever it was again?'

'I don't know,' Father Liam sounded dubious. 'It all seems a bit tenuous to me. But you could be right. Poor Father Nick did have a tendency to worry about things, and to assume that, as a priest, he ought never to make mistakes. I was forever telling him that we are all human and God will judge us by our intentions.'

The door burst open and Lucy walked in, followed closely by Dominic. She stopped short when she saw

Father Liam.

'I'm sorry,' she apologised. 'They said at Reception that you had visitors, so I assumed that Jonah must have arrived already. I didn't realise …'

Bernie introduced them to Father Liam, who greeted Lucy with some kindly remarks to the effect that she must have found the last few days very traumatic, what with finding Father Nick's corpse and then seeing her mother taken off to hospital. Lucy replied politely, but treated him to a look of scorn that made it abundantly clear that she considered herself quite capable of dealing with such incidents and not at all in need of his solicitude.

Lucy sat down next to Peter on the end of the bed and Dominic sat down beside her. Father Liam got up to go, but before he could make his farewells, there was a knock at the door. Peter opened it to let in Joey and Ruth.

'Did you know there's a policeman watching your room?' Ruth asked, somewhat breathlessly.

'We had to show him our ID before he would let us through to you,' Joey added, with a grin that showed that he was amused, rather than worried, by the phenomenon. 'What have you been up to, Cousin Bernadette?'

'Oh, just being the principal witness to a murder and then getting myself knifed in the ribs,' Bernie said airily, returning his grin. 'Nothing to get excited about.'

'It's just a precaution,' Peter

assured Ruth, who was looking rather scared. 'Until they know what the motive was for attacking Bernie, they have to work on the assumption that she could have been specially targeted and that the attacker might try again. Regrettably, it's not that rare for witnesses of crime to be intimidated.'

'Don't worry, 'Bernie added. 'Remember I've got my own personal police protector, as well as having Constable Jones lurking in the corridor.'

'Well, I'll be–,' began Father Liam, making a step towards the door.

'Oh! I'm sorry,' Bernie exclaimed, realising that she had not introduced him to her cousins. 'Joey, this is Father Liam. He's the Parish Priest at St

Wilfrid's. Father Liam – my cousin Joey and his wife Ruth.'

'Pleased to meet you,' Father Liam said, shaking hands with each of them. 'You'll be the Fazakerley family. Father Nat mentioned that you were regular attenders at mass.'

'We do our best,' Ruth nodded.

'Well, I'll be getting on,' Father Liam said, holding his two hands together in front of him and backing away towards the door. 'I hope you are soon fully recovered,' he added to Bernie, 'and that there's no repeat of this dreadful incident. If there's anything I can do, you know my number and there's always a welcome for visitors at the presbytery.'

'We won't stop,' Joey said, as soon

as the priest had closed the door behind him. 'I'm sure you're tired and don't want to be entertaining visitors, but we just had to see that you were alright.'

'And check if there's anything we can do,' added Ruth.

'So we'll just collect Dom and go,' Joey went on. 'I promised Aunty Dot that we'd call in and see her after we'd seen you, to let her know the latest.'

'I'd completely forgotten about Aunty Dot!' Bernie exclaimed. 'How did she find out? Did anyone think to tell her?'

'She read the reports on the internet,' Joey answered, grinning again as he remembered his aunt's telephone call, which she had made to him when she saw the initial doom-laden report on the Echo's website. 'Then she got on to me, wanting to know what *Our Bernie has been up to now*! By then I'd already had Peter's call, telling me that reports of your death had been greatly exaggerated, so I told her not to believe everything you read in the papers.'

'I'm glad she wasn't left in suspense for too long,' Bernie said with a sigh of relief. 'We ought to have realised that she'd have been following things on that iPad of hers, and rung her to let her know things weren't as bad as they were being reported.'

'You mean, *I* should have done,' Joey replied. 'You and Peter had enough on your plates without worrying about ageing aunts.'

Peter smiled with amusement at Joey's pronunciation of the word *aunt*. Catching Bernie's eye, he felt obliged to explain.

'I'm sorry,' he said to Joey, 'I just can't get over the way you northerners say that word. It makes me imagine your father's sister with six legs and a pair of antennae, running around the forest floor picking up bits of leaf litter!'

'Oh Peter!' Lucy squealed, cuffing him playfully around the head. 'You're making that up! Just because they say it differently from us.'

'You mean, just because he never learnt to speak proper,' Bernie joined in.

'It's you who don't speak properly,' Peter objected, waving Lucy away with his hand as if she were an annoying fly. 'It's two words with different spellings, so I can't see the logic in you pronouncing them the same. And that means if you say *ant* I am entitled to think you mean the insect and not a female relative.'

'I'll start saying *aant* when you can explain to me why you say *paaths* and *baaths*, but not *maaths*,' Bernie retorted.

Before they could go any further into the well-worn argument about which regional accents were the most absurd and illogical, Peter's phone rang and Jonah announced the he and Nathan were downstairs at Reception and eager to come up to check on the health of the invalid.

'The room I've booked for you is just across the way from ours,' Peter told him. 'I'll come down now and show you up.'

'I'll do it,' Lucy said quickly, her face lighting up with pleasure at the anticipation of being reunited with their friend. 'Please!'

'We must be going,' Ruth announced. 'Like Joey said, we only came to see you were OK and to collect Dom. I hope he hasn't been any trouble.'

'He's been a great help,' Peter assured her. Then he turned to Lucy. OK. You can go and meet Jonah. Why don't you all go together? Then you can introduce him to your cousins before they leave. I'm sure he'll be interested to see some more Fazakerleys – if only to prove to himself that Our Bernie isn't completely unique.'

Lucy leapt up, smiling broadly, and headed for the door. Ruth, Joey and Dominic bade hasty goodbyes to Bernie and hurried after her. When the door had closed behind them, Bernie looked at Peter.

'Poor Dom!' she said, smiling. 'I think he may suddenly discover that he's been side-lined by a man in a wheelchair!'

19 AND WHY TOGETHER BROUGHT?

'Jonah!' Lucy ran over, put her arms round his shoulders and gave him a hug. 'We've missed you. You should have come with us.'

'Indeed I ought to have,' Jonah agreed, smiling up at her. 'Look at the trouble you get yourselves into as soon as I let you out of my sight!'

'We've booked you a room just opposite mine,' Lucy told him. 'Peter and I checked it out. There are twin beds with plenty of room to get your chair round them. It's got an ensuite shower room and we've organised a chair for the shower, but there's no hoist, so Peter or I will have to help Nathan with lifting you, but that's OK.' She paused to think whether there was anything else of significance that she had forgotten regarding the hotel facilities.

'Thanks,' Jonah said, smiling at Lucy's enthusiastic concern for his welfare. 'It sounds as if you have everything under control.'

'Hi, Lucy!'

Lucy looked up, noticing Cameron for the first time. She had forgotten that Jonah and Nathan had not been travelling alone.

'Hello, Cameron,' she replied blandly without meeting his gaze. She looked round at the assembled company. 'I'm sorry. I was supposed to be introducing everyone.'

She turned to address the waiting Fazakerleys. 'This is DCI Jonah Porter, who lives with us in Oxford; and his son, Nathan, who's staying with him while we're away. He's a barrister. He's usually very busy in his practice in London.'

Joey, Ruth and Dominic nodded and smiled towards Jonah and Nathan.

'And this is my second cousin, Dominic Fazakerley,' Lucy continued, waving an arm in his direction. 'And this is Joey, who is Dom's father and my mam's first cousin, which makes him my first-cousin-once-removed. And Ruth, who is Dom's mother and Joey's wife and my first-cousin-once-removed-in-law.'

'I don't think you bother with in-laws when it comes to cousins,' Nathan said, smiling at Lucy's long-winded explanation of her relationship to the Fazakerley family. 'Like the way you just say *aunt* when you mean someone married to your uncle.'

'That's right,' Joey agreed. 'Or *ant*,' he added, giving Lucy a wink.

'And this is Cameron Price,' Lucy continued, a little reluctantly but determined to complete the task that she had been set. 'We met him when we were in Portugal a few weeks ago. And ...,' she looked towards Mrs Price, not sure how to describe her.'

'I'm Julie Price,' she finished for her. 'I'm Cameron's mother. He's told me a lot about you, Lucy. And he's been itching to catch up with you again ever since he got home.'

Lucy flushed red and tried to hide her embarrassment by giving Jonah another hug. Dominic looked Cameron up and down, wondering exactly what his relationship with Lucy might be. Cameron returned his stare, pondering in his turn upon how things might stand between Lucy and Dom. Her cousin must be a few years older than Lucy, he thought, but then Lucy was unusually mature for her age and had fitted in very well with a group of students that they had met on holiday.

'We're very pleased to meet you both,' Ruth said to Nathan. 'Of course, we admire your dad tremendously for the way he's overcome his disabilities. I mean – most people would just have allowed themselves to be pensioned off, wouldn't they?'

Nathan hesitated. He did not want to appear rude, but he felt he could not completely ignore the fact that, in a couple of sentences, Ruth had become guilty of two of the most common – and most annoying – offences that are committed by able-bodied people when encountering someone in a wheelchair: she had addressed his carer instead of speaking to him direct; and she had suggested that there was something remarkable and heroic about his doing ordinary things that 'normal' people took for granted.

'Stop talking about Jonah as if he isn't here!' Lucy said indignantly, releasing Nathan from the obligation to think of a suitable response. 'If you've got something to say, say it to his face.'

'I'm sorry,' Ruth said, blushing scarlet. She stepped forward and crouched down in front of Jonah's chair so that she could look him in the eye. 'I never thought. I hope you didn't think …'

'Forget it,' Jonah said dismissively. 'Everyone does it sometimes. But take my advice and watch your step when Our Bernie or Our Lucy are around! And speaking of Our Bernie, it's about time we made tracks to find her, before she gets fed up with waiting and insists on coming down to meet us.'

'Peter said to tell you that your room is on a different floor,' Lucy said to Julie and Cameron. 'We booked a twin – like you said.'

'Thank you, Lucy,' Julie answered, while Cameron looked disappointed at the news that there would be little opportunity of just happening to bump into Lucy in the corridor during their stay. 'Now, I suggest that we all go to our rooms and settle in and then, shall we meet up for dinner?'

'We'll let you all get on,' Joey said, leading the way to the exit. 'You must all be tired after your journey. Let us know if there's anything we can do for you.'

The Fazakerley family left. Dominic,

who was bringing up the rear, turned to look back briefly through the glass doors and saw Lucy leading the way to the lift, chattering all the time to Jonah. He could not make out the dynamics here. If some sort of holiday romance had gone on between Lucy and Cameron, why was she almost ignoring him now? And why was she lavishing so much attention on a middle-aged man in a wheelchair? Why did Jonah live with Peter and Bernie instead of with his own son, who seemed perfectly happy to look after him? The whole business did not make sense.

Forty minutes later, they reconvened for dinner in the hotel restaurant. Peter removed a chair from round their table to make space for Jonah's wheelchair. Nathan sat down next to his father and Lucy hurried to appropriate the chair on his other side. Peter annoyed Bernie by pulling out a chair opposite Jonah and motioning her to sit down in it. However, she curbed her instinct to insist on her right to move furniture on her own behalf and sat down without comment. After all, she had at least won the battle to be permitted to eat with them, instead of having something sent up to her room.

Cameron stepped forward to take the seat next to Lucy, but he was thwarted by Peter, who sat there himself. There were now three places vacant around the square table. Cameron chose the seat next to Nathan, which meant that he was directly opposite Lucy. Julie hesitated between sitting next to her son (which might appear the natural thing to do) and taking the other remaining seat, which was next to Bernie (her prime witness) and opposite Nathan (whom she hoped might be persuaded to reveal some interesting snippets of information about the family life of the well-known Disabled Detective). In the end, she decided that Cameron would probably prefer not to have his mother any closer than necessary, and thus she was fully justified in choosing the position most likely to further her career by providing tempting copy for the national newspapers.

'You've certainly been having an exciting time,' she said to Bernie, as she sat down next to her.'

'I told Our Lucy that there's never a dull moment in Liverpool,' Bernie replied with a grin. 'I didn't quite have all this in mind though.'

Hearing this exchange, Peter looked at Julie with renewed interest. Like Jonah, he had been taken aback when he was introduced to Julie, who was so different from the person about whom her ex-husband had complained publicly while on holiday with Cameron. Her appearance was of a businesswoman, not averse to using her good looks and shapely figure to her advantage. Now he saw that she was also a shrewd observer of people, who had correctly judged that Bernie would respond better to this matter-of-fact approach than to sympathy for her injuries or a suggestion that she should be in a state of distress. That was quick work, considering that they had only just met – but perhaps Cameron had briefed her, or else conversation with Jonah might have given her some clues.

The food arrived, and Nathan took his father's plate and started cutting up the meat and vegetables into bite-sized pieces. Lucy gave him a hard look, but a few words in her ear from Peter persuaded her to remain silent and concentrate on her own meal. Julie pretended not to watch as Nathan fed Jonah while, at the same time, trying to eat his own food. Nevertheless, she was making mental notes all the time. She was learning some wonderful background details that would give human interest to her writing. Still keeping an eye on events on the other side of the table, she spoke to her neighbour.

'I suppose they've told you that I'm a journalist,' she said in an apologetic voice. She had sized Bernie up and had decided that a direct approach was the one least likely to antagonise her.

'Jonah did mention it, yes,' Bernie replied.

'This is going to sound as if I'm just trying to exploit your daughter's friendship with Cameron,' Julie went on, 'but I'll come clean and admit that I'm hoping to get a story out of this.'

'I can't give you details of the incidents,' Bernie said quickly. 'The police press-releases contain all the information that they want the public to know.'

'Yes, I realise that, but surely there must be some interesting background that you could tell me? People are always interested in hearing about the people behind the news – often more than the news itself.'

'Yes, I know. It's called *press intrusion.*'

'Don't be like that. I've already promised not to publish anything without getting your permission first. Now, if you won't talk about the stabbings, tell me more about your relationship with DCI Porter. What made you decide to take him into your home?'

'You're not planning another of those *police hero battles against the odds* stories, are you?' Bernie asked suspiciously. 'Jonah had quite enough of those at the time. I thought we'd got past that stage.'

'I was thinking more of looking at things from the point of view of the people around him – a heart-warming story about–'

'If you think I'm going to fall for your flattery, you've got another think coming,' Bernie cut in. '*We* don't want to be set up as heroes any more than Jonah does.'

'Cameron told me about you all,' Julie went on, ignoring the interruption, 'and I'm fascinated to know why you decided to dedicate your life to looking after a ...,' she paused, searching for an acceptable way to describe Jonah.

She had been about to say *cripple*, but remembered in time that this word was considered offensive. '... severely disabled man,' she concluded. 'It must have made big changes to your family life. I'm sure people would be interested to know what motivated you.'

'It's all perfectly simple. Jonah is our friend. Don't you believe in helping your friends?'

'Of course, but this goes a bit beyond ordinary friendship.'

'Does it?'

'Way beyond! It must have changed your whole life. What about your daughter? Weren't you worried about the impact on her?'

'No.' Bernie laughed. 'Lucy was the driving force behind the whole scheme

– but you're not to bring her into anything you write,' she added hastily. Then, seeing Julie's dissatisfied expression she decided that the best solution might be to feed her with something that she could write without doing any significant damage. Inspired by Peter's tactics in dealing with the Echo reporter, she decided to look to the past for a story that could safely be published.

'Look,' she said grudgingly, 'if you *must* write about us how about this? My mam had motor neurone disease and, when I was a kid, I helped my dad to look after her. And I was pleased to be allowed to do it. It made me feel grown up and important. In those days, having a disability was much more restrictive than it is today, so people would probably say that I missed out on a lot of things because of my mam's condition, but I think I got a lot from it as well. So naturally, I didn't have any worries about Lucy when it came to inviting Jonah to live with us. Now, is that enough *human interest* for you?'

While this conversation was going on, Lucy had been eating rapidly, partly out of habit and partly in order to keep her head down and avoid making eye-contact with Cameron, who was sitting opposite her. She finished the main course ahead of everyone else, put her knife and fork neatly together on the plate, and turned to speak to Nathan, whose meal still lay largely untouched.

'Let me take over,' she begged. 'I've finished. Your steak must be getting cold.'

Nathan's first instinct was to decline the offer, but then he reflected that: (a) everyone would be obliged to wait for him to finish before they could move on to the dessert; (b) the sooner they finished their meal, the sooner they could remove themselves from the company of the Prices and relax in the knowledge that whatever they said was not being mentally taken down with a view to publication; (c) Jonah would probably prefer being fed by Lucy, who was more experienced and could give the task her full attention now that she had finished her own food; and (d) both Jonah and Bernie would benefit from an early night.

'OK,' he said, handing over Jonah's fork to Lucy. Then, 'thanks,' as an afterthought.

'Inspector Johns,' Julie called across to Peter, having decided that she was in danger of losing Bernie's goodwill by continuing too long with her questioning. 'What do you think of the way the police are handling this? With all your experience, you must have an opinion.'

'It's not for me to say,' Peter replied curtly.

'But?' Julie prompted. Then when Peter did not reply, 'I feel sure that you must have some misgivings about the way in which a killer was allowed to get away and attack your wife.'

'And what makes you say that?' Jonah intervened. 'What are you suggesting the police could have done?'

'Well, I would have thought that it was obvious that whoever killed the priest must have been one of the ferry passengers. So surely they could have kept an eye on them and prevented them from attacking again.'

'That's ludicrous!' Peter exclaimed. 'There were upwards of a couple of hundred people on board. No police force has the resources to keep them all under 24-hour surveillance.'

'And that's without considering the human rights issues raised by police monitoring of hundreds of innocent citizens,' Jonah added.

'And what about the ones that got off at–,' Lucy began, but she was interrupted by Peter, Jonah and Bernie all speaking at once. They did not want

Julie Price to know that there was a possibility that the murderer was among the passengers who had disembarked at Seacombe.

'If they'd offered us police protection, I'd have turned it down,' Bernie said decisively.

'Nobody could have predicted that the killer would strike again,' Peter declared. 'And we've got good protection now. Don't try calling at our rooms during the night – you'll probably get arrested!'

'What you're suggesting would be turning the country into a police state,' Jonah continued with his argument. 'It's impossible for everyone to be both perfectly safe and completely free.'

Poor Lucy blushed red as she

realised her mistake. She looked down at Jonah's plate and pretended to be very busy loading his fork with a mixture of different vegetables. For a few minutes, nobody spoke as Nathan and Jonah finished their main course and a waiter came round behind them all, collecting the plates and handing out menus for the sweet course.

'I don't think I'm going to bother with a pudding,' Bernie said, setting the menu aside. 'I think I'd rather just go back up to our room.'

She got up and extended her hand rather formally towards Julie.

'It's been nice meeting you. I expect we'll see you again at breakfast. Goodnight, Cameron,' she added glancing across in his direction.

MYSTERY OVER THE MERSEY

Peter got up and followed his wife out of the room. He was surprised at her coming so close to admitting to being tired. Usually she refused to show any sign of weakness. Then it crossed his mind that she was probably thinking about Jonah's need to recuperate after his journey and was intending to provide him with an easy way of getting some rest himself.

Lucy looked towards Jonah, who smiled back at her, understanding that she was waiting for him also to make a move. Then he looked towards Nathan, who also bore a hopeful and enquiring expression. He sighed and decided to forgo the delights of the sticky toffee pudding in the interests of keeping his minders happy. It would also, he reflected, be good to get away from

Julie Price and the need to watch every word that was spoken.

'Yes,' he said at last. 'I think it's time I went up too.'

20 PETER, DO YOU LOVE ME?

'Bernie?' Peter said tentatively, as they lay in bed that night. He had insisted that they splash out on a separate single room for Lucy, in place of the family room that they had occupied in the previous hotel. He thought that this would make it easier for Bernie to sleep peacefully, and so speed up the recovery process. He had something important to say, but he was nervous of disturbing her rest.

'Mmm?' she responded encouragingly.

'Bernie,' he repeated a little more confidently. 'I love you.'

Bernie hesitated before replying. Peter did not often say this sort of thing.

'Yes,' she said at last. 'I know. I love you too.'

'No – I mean I *really* love you.'

'Yes. That's what *I* meant too.' Bernie wondered what this was all about.

'I'm sorry. I'm not explaining properly.' Like his namesake[3], Peter

---

[3] See St John's Gospel, chapter 21, verses 15-19, where Jesus asks St Peter three times 'do you love me?' mirroring Peter's three denials of Jesus, recounted in chapter 18.

felt compelled to repeat the declaration a third time. 'When Angie died, I was sure I could never love anyone else as much as her.'

'I thought we agreed *no comparisons*,' Bernie objected gently.

'But when I saw them putting you in that ambulance, and someone said it was a knife attack ...,' for a moment Peter found himself unable to continue, as the memories came flooding back. He could see in his mind's eye not just the events of the day before, but also the scene, all those years earlier, when he had been called to view his first wife's body after she had been set upon by youths wielding a knife.

'I know. It seems so unfair for it to happen to you twice.'

'No. That's not what I mean.' Peter struggled to put his feelings into words. 'What I'm getting at is … that's when I *knew* how much you mean to me.'

'Oh Peter!' Bernie attempted to roll over and put her arm round him, but the agonising stabbing feeling that this movement produced in her side defeated her and she flopped back with an only partially-supressed gasp of pain. She reached out and took hold of Peter's hand in hers instead. They lay together without speaking for perhaps three minutes.

'There's something I want to show you,' Peter said, breaking the silence and drawing his hand out of Bernie's.

He slipped his wedding ring off his finger and held it out to her. Bernie took it, puzzled.

'Have a look at the inside,' Peter urged her.

She held it close to her face and peered at the inscription. She saw that more words had been added, almost filling the interior surface. It now read: *25/03/06 Bernie & Peter & Angela 10/06/78.*

'Oh Peter! You shouldn't have! I mean – you didn't need to.'

'I went out for a walk while I was waiting for you to be discharged,' Peter explained, 'and I saw this place that said it did engraving while-you-wait; so I got them to do it. I wanted to do something to show that I … well …'

Bernie lay back, turning the ring round and round in her fingers. Then she took Peter's hand in hers and replaced the ring on his finger.

'Thank you, Peter. When we get home, I'm going to print out a photo of you to go in the other side of that locket of mine,' she promised. 'Then we'll be quits.'

'I thought you said it wasn't a competition,' Peter objected.

'No. I know, but oh Peter! I can't go on carrying around mementoes of Stephen, whom I knew for less than three years, and Richard whom I only knew for just over four years, when I've been married to you for nine and we've been friends for twenty-seven. I can't *not* have something of yours as well. And you must have seen Dom's face when I said I didn't even have a ring to signify our wedding.'

'You don't have to make out that I'm as important to you as Richard,' Peter insisted. 'After all, he's Lucy's father. 'You're bound to–'

'I can't even picture Richard's face properly in my mind now,' Bernie interrupted sadly. 'You probably know him a whole lot better than I do. After all, you worked with him for twenty-six years. And if you're going to bring Lucy into it, you've been like a father to her all along, even before Angie died.'

'Well, I had to do something to pay back all that free childcare you gave to us when Hannah and Eddie were young!' Peter said jokingly. 'But seriously, having Lucy has just been a bonus for me. It's just such a pity that Richard never got the chance to see her for himself.'

'Yes. Poor Richard! He got a very raw deal, didn't he? He left me Lucy, and that big house in Headington, *and* his life's savings, *and* a pension – and what did he get out of our marriage? Two years of my company, which must be at best a rather dubious benefit.'

'Well, as you just pointed out, I've survived for nine,' Peter joked, 'and I'm not asking to get out yet!'

They relapsed back into silence. Peter rested his head against Bernie's shoulder – very carefully to avoid hurting her.

'At least now I don't feel quite such a fraud as I did,' Peter murmured a few minutes later, 'I always felt guilty marrying you when I was still in love with Angie.'

'Oh Peter!' Bernie sighed. 'You spend altogether far too much of your time feeling guilty for things that don't matter at all! I always knew that Angie was the only one for you, and we agreed that it wasn't a problem.'

'Yes, I know, but it still didn't seem fair, somehow.'

'Peter! This is ridiculous. You have far more reason to feel that you're being pushed into second place than I do.'

'You just said that you could hardly remember Richard any more.'

'I wasn't talking about Richard. I meant Jonah.'

'Jonah? You're not suggesting that I might feel jealous of him? The guy's in a wheelchair, for goodness sake.'

'Well, he does take up an awful lot of my time – and Lucy's – and yours, for that matter. Not to mention the fact that he's living in our home. A lot of husbands would resent the lack of privacy.'

'And may I remind you that *I* was the one who suggested that he should come to live with us?' Peter pointed out mildly.

'I know, but I've always thought that you were just bowing to the inevitable. I never even got the impression that you even liked him that much.'

'Well, it was a bit different back in the days when we were both sergeants under Richard's command. He always seemed too full of himself, and in too much of a hurry with everything. He never looked before he leapt. And every time he took a leap in the dark, he seemed to fall on his feet instead of getting the comeuppance he deserved.'

Bernie giggled. 'Sounds like Our Jonah!'

'But either he's mellowed,' Peter went on, 'or I've become more tolerant in my old age. He doesn't seem nearly so irritating these days.'

'I'm glad you don't mind having him around. Lucy and I would hate to have to choose between you.'

'Just so long as you don't mind having *me* around,' Peter murmured in Bernie's ear, before kissing her lightly and settling himself down beside her. 'Now, I'm going to assert my husbandly authority and order you to get a good night's sleep. Now that Jonah's arrived, tomorrow is bound to be busy, busy, busy!'

21 MORNING HAS BROKEN

Bernie woke the following morning and sat up, preparatory to getting out of bed. Her incautious movement set off a throbbing pain in her side, forcing her to sit for a few moments with her legs hanging over the side of the bed, breathing deeply. She felt Peter turn over behind her.

'What time is it?' he asked.

'Half past six. Sorry. I didn't mean to wake you.'

'How're you feeling?'

'A bit stiff. That's all. I'll be better when I'm up and about.'

'Well, don't be too proud to take the painkillers they gave you at the hospital. Remember what the doctor said: it's better to take them *before* the pain becomes unbearable.'

'OK. OK,' Bernie grumbled. She hated having to admit to weakness of any kind.

She got to her feet, steadying herself by holding on to the headboard, as another wave of pain passed through her side. Then she strode off to the bathroom, making an effort to walk normally and hold herself upright.

Peter lay back, contemplating the day ahead. DI Latham would, no doubt, be in touch to ask Bernie to watch the CC-TV footage of passengers departing the ferry at Seacombe. Jonah would presumably expect to be in on that. DI Lucas might also be back, hoping to question them all further about the attack on Bernie. Cameron Price was obviously hoping to get some time with Lucy alone – something which both Lucy and Dominic were probably hoping to avoid. And then there was Julie Price, on the lookout for a story. What had induced Jonah to bring those two with him? A journalist and a love-sick teenager were the last things they needed to add to their problems.

Once washed and dressed, and having taken a dose of the prescribed painkillers, Bernie felt considerably better. She no longer felt that the stitches in her side were pulling her down into a stooping posture.

'I'm going over to see how Jonah's getting on,' she told Peter.

'OK.' Peter watched his wife leaving the room and wondered if he dared indulge in the luxury of a few more minutes in bed. Anxiety, coupled with a reluctance to change his sleeping position for fear of disturbing Bernie, had prevented him from sleeping well. He now felt poorly-prepared for the rigors of a day in the company of the irrepressible Jonah – not to mention the need to fend off Julie Price's questions and see that neither Cameron nor Dominic took advantage of his beloved step-daughter.

Sighing to himself, Peter threw off the duvet and swung his legs over the side of the bed. It was no good. If he did not get up and go to join them, goodness only knew what mad schemes Bernie and Jonah might be cooking up together in a misguided attempt to track down the killer.

'Hello Jonah! How's things?' Bernie called cheerfully as she entered the room.

'Not so bad,' Jonah responded. 'How about you?'

He was propped up in bed, drinking his early morning tea from his plastic cup, which Nathan had ingeniously managed to secure within his reach. The cup was balanced on the end of a large book (provided by the hotel for the entertainment of its guests) entitled *Merseyside in pictures*. Nathan had moved a small table so that it stood alongside Jonah's bed, and had balanced the book so that it overhung sufficiently for him to reach the long straw, which protruded from the lidded top. Lucy, fully dressed and eyes sparkling in anticipation of an action-packed day, was sitting on the other side of the bed.

'A bit stiff, that's all. Definitely on the mend.'

Jonah looked sceptical, but decided not to pass any comment on this assertion.

'Lucy's been bringing me up to date on the investigation so far.'

'Ah well! She doesn't know the latest,' Bernie said, smiling mysteriously. 'What with all the visitors we've been having, I didn't get the chance to tell her about DI Latham bringing photos of all the ferry passengers and asking me if I recognised any of them.'

'And did you?' Jonah and Lucy chorused in unison.

'Nope. At least, only the two students who were on deck with Father Nick for a few minutes. Sandra Latham was planning to interview them again, now she knows for certain that they are the ones I told her about. I'm sure they're not our killers, though. What possible motive could they have?'

'On the other hand, what possible

motive could *anyone* have?' Jonah asked. 'Did this Latham woman tell you any more about them?'

'They're both studying at Bristol. He lives in Bootle and she's from Surrey. They were just out for the day, seeing the sights.'

'Hi Bernie!' Nathan emerged from the bathroom. 'Could you ask Peter to come and give me a hand in a few minutes? I'll need help getting Dad on to the toilet.'

'Don't bother; I can do it,' Lucy put in eagerly, before her mother could reply.

'No, Lucy love. Not without a hoist,' Bernie said quickly. 'Peter's a better match for Nathan's height,' she added, to make it clear that this was not a reflection on her daughter's competence.

Lucy sat back in her chair with a look of resignation on her face. She was now taller than her mother, and football training had made her stronger than most girls of her age. She secretly believed that she was at least as capable of heavy lifting as her stepfather, who was in his sixties by now and a pensioner. Moreover, Jonah was lightly-built and Lucy was experienced in caring for him. She had no doubt in her own mind that she could have assisted Nathan without difficulty.

'Peter was still in bed a minute ago,' Bernie said. 'I'll go and see if he's getting up yet.'

She turned to go, but the door opened and Peter came in. He had anticipated that Nathan might need help and had hurried to get ready, it having occurred to him that Bernie might have insisted on doing it herself.

While Peter and Nathan, in the bathroom, took Jonah through the tedious, but necessary, preliminaries to his day, Bernie spoke through the open door, telling him about the discussion with DI Latham the previous day.

'I expect she'll have the tape of the passengers getting off at Seacombe ready for me to look at today,' she concluded. 'Maybe that'll have something on it that jogs my memory. She reckons I must have seen *something* that the killer is afraid will give him away.'

'If that tape's so important, what's taking her so long?' Jonah wanted to know.

'We'd all assumed the killer must have still been on the boat when we got to Woodside,' Bernie explained. 'It was only after I'd been through all of them that it occurred to us that Father Nick could have been dead since before we stopped at Seacombe.'

'It's the investigating officer's job to think about all possibilities,' Jonah replied, still dissatisfied.

'Oh Jonah! You're not to give her a hard time, just because she hasn't done things the way you would have done them – or the way you *think* you would have done them,' Bernie protested. 'Sandra Latham seems pretty good at her job, to me. If you want to have a go at anyone, pick on DI Lucas. *He* thinks the attack on me was just a random mugging, and he made it abundantly clear that he resents having another officer muscling in on his case. If he got his way, I'd never even have been shown the photographs, never mind the CC-TV footage.'

'I suspect someone higher up has told him he's got to work with her,' Peter added. 'And it wouldn't surprise me if they've put her in charge. After all, this murder has got a lot of publicity and – well, at the end of the day, murder is murder. I'd say he's insecure and doesn't like a woman – and a younger woman at that – taking over.'

They went down to breakfast in the hotel restaurant. Nathan, who knew that his father disliked eating in public, suggested having food sent up to their room, but Jonah demurred.

'We agreed with the Prices that we'd all meet up at breakfast,' he pointed out. 'After bringing them all the way up here, we can't just abandon them.'

'What got into you to do that?' Peter asked, voicing the question that had been in his mind since the previous afternoon.

'For one thing, if we hadn't brought them, they'd have come on their own,' Jonah told him. 'Cameron was desperate to see Lucy–'

'Thanks a bundle!' Lucy muttered

under her breath. She had struck up a friendship of sorts with Cameron during their holiday a few weeks earlier, but had no wish for it to turn into a longer-term relationship.

'– and Julie was desperate for her story. At least this way we've got a bit more control over what they get up to. And secondly,' here Jonah looked across at his son, 'certain people weren't being very co-operative about bringing me on my own.'

'I still don't know how I let myself get bounced into this,' Nathan sighed, looking upwards as if seeking divine guidance.

When they reached the restaurant, they found Julie and Cameron waiting for them at the entrance. Julie stepped forward and greeted them, asking after Bernie's health and telling them that she had found a table that would accommodate them all for breakfast. They went in, giving their room numbers to the member of hotel staff on the door, and Julie led the way to a large table near to the window. Nathan removed one of the chairs and stood it against the wall to make room for Jonah.

For a few minutes, they were all busy choosing their preferred breakfast options from the help-yourself buffet.

'It's very bad for me staying in hotels,' Bernie murmured to Peter. 'I always feel I ought to eat as much breakfast as I can to get my money's worth. I probably should skip lunch after this little lot!'

Lucy and Nathan were vying for the right to select Jonah's food, while Jonah was trying to decide whether he would later regret eating the bacon and eggs that he fancied, but which were not part of his normal diet and might upset his bowel-management regime. In the end, he decided to take the risk. He asked Lucy to bring a bowl of cereal and milk, then turned to Nathan and instructed him to select a few rashers, a sausage and a fried egg, to go with the toast that he already had in front of him, and to put tea in his lidded cup.

Once they were all seated around the table, Julie looked round at them all.

'Do we have any plans for today?'

she asked brightly.

'I'm expecting a call from DI Latham,' Bernie told her. 'She said she'd like to interview me again today,' she added, carefully avoiding giving away any details of the purpose of the interview. 'So I'd better stay around here, I suppose.'

'I thought I might go and see the Institute of Performing Arts and see if I can find out about where I'd be living if I came here,' Cameron said. 'Lucy – would you show me round?'

'I think that's a great idea,' Julie said approvingly, before Lucy could think of a suitable answer. 'I'm sure you two would get on better without us oldies.'

'OK,' Lucy agreed, without

enthusiasm, bowing to the inevitable. 'I wouldn't mind checking out the student accommodation, in case I don't get into Oxford and end up coming here instead. I don't know how I'll get on with showing you around, though. I've only been here a couple of days.'

'Dom could help,' Bernie suggested, sensing Lucy's reluctance to be left alone with Cameron. 'He doesn't seem to have anything better to do at the moment.'

Peter's phone rang. It was Sandra Latham. Bernie, sitting next to Peter, leaned closer so that she could hear both ends of the conversation.

'We've got the video of the passengers getting off at Seacombe,' she heard her say. 'I was wondering if your wife could manage to come down to the station to view it? We'll send a car – if you think she's up to it?'

Bernie grabbed the phone from Peter's hand before he could answer.

'Hi there!' she greeted her, cheerfully. 'I can come down, no problem – and you don't need to send a car; we've got our own transport now. Just tell me where to come.'

The police officer explained which police station she needed Bernie to attend, the best route to get there and where they would be able to park. Bernie jotted it all down on a paper napkin.

'Right you are,' she said at the end. 'We'll be over as soon as we've finished breakfast. Just give us half an hour.'

She handed the phone back to Peter and smiled round.

'That's my morning sorted,' she observed.

'Mine too,' Jonah added. 'I want to meet this DI Latham.'

'Da-ad! Nathan protested. 'It's none of your business.'

'If people are going round making murderous attacks on my personal assistant, that's very much my business. Not to mention the fact that Bernie here has just volunteered my transport to take her there.'

'Let him go,' Peter urged in a tone of mock resignation. 'It's only fair to let DI Latham know that her every move is being scrutinised and criticised by Mr *if-*

I'd-been-in-charge-this-case-would-have-been-closed-by-now.'

'OK,' Nathan agreed, realising that Peter was correct in thinking that, if they were to prevent Jonah from attending the police station with Bernie, he would remain determined to find other ways of getting involved in the investigation. 'But that means that I'm going too. This is supposed to be a holiday for you and Bernie. I can't have you taking over looking after Dad, just because he's being pig-headed about interfering in a murder case that doesn't concern him.'

Peter thought for a moment. While he was reluctant to let Bernie out of his sight, he felt that it was hardly appropriate for all four of them to descend on DI Latham. He decided that his wife was unlikely to come to harm in the company of Nathan (who was quite capable of doing the worrying for both of them) and Jonah (whose advice to Bernie on taking it easy and not over-stretching herself was probably more likely to be received favourably than Peter's own suggestions on that subject, which she would probably dismiss as "fussing"). Moreover, he reflected, someone ought to keep an eye on Julie Price and make sure she did not jeopardise the investigation with any thoughtless disclosures.

'Right you are then,' he said at last. 'Nathan – you drive. Since I'm not needed, I'll find something else to keep me occupied this morning, and we'll all meet up again for lunch.'

MYSTERY OVER THE MERSEY

They hurried to finish their breakfast – or, to be more correct, Bernie and Cameron hurried and Jonah instructed Nathan to hurry up with feeding him, while Lucy ate uncharacteristically slowly and unexpectedly embarked on a third round of toast. Peter smiled, as he deduced that she was trying to put off the moment when she would be forced to set off alone with Cameron. Should he offer to go with them? No – that would only delay the time when Cameron realised that he was on a hiding to nothing. In any case, you never knew – perhaps Lucy would warm to him in this new environment, well away from his overbearing father, who had been so intrusive during their holiday.

22 SEEK AND YE SHALL FIND

Bernie pressed the pad to open the door and admit Jonah to the police station. She and Nathan stood back as he manoeuvred his chair inside, and then followed him in. The desk sergeant looked up enquiringly.

'Can I help you?' she asked, carefully directing her question at Jonah, as she had been trained to do when encountering members of the public in wheelchairs.

'We're here to see DI Latham,' Jonah answered. 'She's expecting us.

At least, she's expecting Bernie here.' He nodded in Bernie's direction.

'Bernie Fazakerley,' Bernie added. 'It's about the death of the priest on the ferry.'

'Of course. Take a seat.' Sergeant Mel Wharton indicated a row of plastic seats attached to the wall. 'I'll let her know you're here.'

Bernie and Nathan sat down as instructed. Bernie looked around. The walls were painted in institutional blue emulsion, a little lighter in colour than the functional blue vinyl tiles that covered the floor. There was a slight smell of disinfectant.

'Dr Fazakerley! Thank you for coming in.' Sandra Latham entered from a door to the left of the reception desk and strode over to greet Bernie.

Bernie stood up and shook her hand. Then she turned to introduce the others.

'This is my friend, Nathan. He's acting as our chauffeur. And his father-'

'DCI Porter!' Sandra exclaimed in a voice filled with awe and delight. 'Dr Fazakerley's daughter told us that she worked for you, but I wasn't expecting you to do us the honour …'

'Wait till you've got to know me better before saying it's an honour!' Jonah answered, favouring her with a lopsided grin. 'And call me Jonah. I'm not on duty now.'

'I do admire your courage,' Sandra continued. 'It's an inspiration to us all, the way you-'

'Let me stop you there,' Jonah interrupted politely but firmly. 'The word is *obstinacy* not *courage*, as Nathan, here, will testify. And, if you find me an inspiration, I hope it's for my record in solving crimes, not because I manage to get up and out to work every morning – just like everyone else.'

'Sorry.' Sandra looked rather shamefaced. 'You must get very bored with people going on about it; but I still think it's remarkable what you've done.' She turned back to Bernie. 'Dr Fazakerley–'

'Bernie.'

'Bernie. I'd like you to have a look at the CC-TV footage that I told you about; but first I'll bring you up to date on some developments. If you would like to come with me ...'

She turned to go. Bernie and Jonah followed her. Nathan got up to come too, but his father told him to wait for them there.

'DI Latham won't want us all cluttering up her interview room,' he said. 'I'll give you a bell if I need anything.'

Nathan sat back down, reflecting on his father's presumption that his own presence in the interview room would be welcomed. You would have thought that he would at least have asked her permission before barging in and taking over! Of course, she probably didn't realise yet that he would be taking over – not officially, but, nevertheless, running the show as a persistent backseat driver.

Sandra led them to a room at the back of the building. Bernie saw a large television screen with a video recorder on a shelf beneath it. There were four chairs arranged around three sides of a table, so that they all had a view of the screen. A young woman was sitting in one of them, apparently engrossed in a pile of papers lying on the table in front of her. She looked up as they entered, and Bernie recognised Sergeant Charlotte Simpson.

Sandra introduced Charlotte to Jonah and then moved one of the chairs back against the wall, to make room for his wheelchair. Bernie sat down at his left.

'First up, I've got something to show you,' Sandra said briskly. 'Wait here a minute and I'll get it.'

She left the room, returning after a minute or two with a plastic evidence bag, which she deposited on the table in front of them. Bernie leaned forward to get a closer look. It was a knife. She picked it up by the top of the bag, taking care not to hold the knife itself for fear of damaging any fingermarks that there might be on its surface, and held it up in front of Jonah's face. At a slight movement of his head, she rotated it slowly to give him an all-round view. He nodded to indicate that he had finished his examination, and she placed it back down on the table.

'We found it in St James' Gardens,' Sandra told them. 'It had been pushed down into the soil in the flower bed by the entrance to the tunnel where you were attacked.'

'Fingermarks?' Jonah enquired.

'No,' Sandra shook her head. 'There were smudges of blood that looked like marks from gloved fingers, but nothing that could be used to identify the attacker.'

'I told DI Lucas that I thought they were wearing latex gloves,' Bernie said excitedly. 'Would that fit with what you found?'

'Very likely. We're getting the blood DNA-tested. Assuming that it's yours, it looks as if we've found the weapon.'

'It's a shorter blade than I was expecting,' Jonah observed thoughtfully. 'I can't see this one penetrating the ribcage and fatally piercing the heart, can you? Not reliably, anyway.'

'No,' Sandra agreed. 'The knife that killed the priest must have been longer – and probably wider – than this. But that one is presumably at the bottom of the Mersey by now, so that doesn't mean that it wasn't the same person responsible.'

'It's a flick knife, isn't it?' Bernie said, noticing the button on the handle, which could bring the blade springing out of concealment in an instant. 'I wonder how they got it.'

'Not legally,' Sandra agreed. 'But I'd say it wasn't that hard, if you know the right people.'

'I'd say this suggests this attack

wasn't as pre-meditated as the one on the priest,' Jonah observed. 'This is the sort of knife that could be carried around in someone's pocket all the time; whereas the longer one that killed Father Nick must have been taken along for that specific purpose.'

'Do you think it *was* just random mugging then?' Bernie asked. 'Just a bit of opportunism?'

'No. If they were lying in wait for a victim, and you just happened to come along, then they'd be more likely to have a *really* lethal weapon. I think whoever it was had you in their sights in a general sort of way, but then they spotted you unexpectedly and used the weapon they happened to have about their person – or maybe they just didn't have time to get hold of another long knife, like the one they used on Father Nick.'

'That reminds me,' Bernie said, reaching inside the collar of her shirt and pulling up the string that once more hung round her neck. 'I should have given this to DI Lucas, but I didn't think at the time, and then I forgot. I *had* thought it might help you to identify what sort of knife had been used, but now you've found it, I don't suppose it's much use to you.'

She undid the knot, slipped the locket off the string and handed it to Sandra.

Jonah watched with interest. This was the first that he had known about the knife-marks on the locket – or indeed about the string of trinkets that his friend wore beneath her clothes.

'That indentation on the front was made by the knife. The medics reckon that was what stopped it getting through into my chest cavity. It looks as if it deflected the blade so that the damage was all superficial.'

Bernie re-tied the knot in the string to secure the two rings, and put it back round her neck. Sandra studied the locket closely before handing it to Charlotte.

'Bag this up and give Dr Fazakerley a receipt,' she instructed. 'I'm afraid we'll need to keep this for a while,' she told Bernie apologetically. 'I'd like forensics to have a look at it.'

'Is it really necessary?' Bernie asked. To her own surprise, she realised that she was reluctant to part with the locket. 'I mean – you've got the knife. If that's my blood on it, surely that must be conclusive?'

'You'd think so,' Sandra agreed, 'but we don't know yet whether we've got a definite blood match. In any case, you never know what story the defence counsel might come up with to explain it away. I'd like to check that the marks match and see if there are any traces of gold from the locket on the knife. The more evidence we can find, the more likely we are to get a conviction – if we can once find the owner of this knife.'

Bernie nodded her understanding and accepted the receipt, which Charlotte held out to her.

'When will I be able to have it back?' she asked, feeling at the same time anxious to know the answer and angry with herself for caring about it. It was only a piece of old jewellery, after all. Moreover, up until the day before yesterday, nobody but she – and Peter, of course – was even aware that she had it. 'I mean – will you have to keep it until after the trial? What if it never comes to trial?'

'I'm not sure. We'll take some photographs and that may be enough; but I think the prosecuting counsel may want to be able to show the actual item to the jury. The depth of the mark gives an indication of the force of the blow, which is evidence that the intention was to kill.'

'Yes,' agreed Jonah. 'It's the sort of

thing that barristers like. I can imagine them making a nice bit of theatre out of it. *Do not listen to the suggestion that the defendant merely wished to frighten the victim into giving up her purse!*' he went on, adopting the vocal delivery-style of *Rumpole of the Bailey*[4]. 'See *how the knife has cut deep into the metal of this locket, showing the force with which it was thrust into her defenceless body. Imagine how things might have been had she not–*'

---

[4] *Rumpole of the Bailey* is a television series created by John Mortimer and produced by Thames Television. It features Leo McKern as barrister Horace Rumpole, who is adept at defending hopeless cases, often using dramatic methods to influence the jury.

'OK. OK. I get the picture,' Bernie grumbled. 'You can stop the amateur dramatics.'

'We'll take good care of it,' Sandra assured her. 'I gather it has sentimental value?'

'Yes. I suppose so,' Bernie admitted reluctantly. She did not believe in allowing sentiment to override rationality. She abruptly changed the subject. 'Now, tell me how you're getting on? Did you talk to those two students that I saw?'

'Yes. They didn't have much to add to their previous statements. Nothing that they could tell me about Father Nicholas proved whether he was alive or dead when they came alongside him.'

'You didn't tell them that there's a possibility that he died *before* the boat left Seacombe, did you?' Jonah asked sharply, momentarily forgetting that he was not in charge of this investigation. 'If they go shooting their mouths off about that, it could let the killer know we're looking at passengers who disembarked there.'

'Don't worry,' Sandra smiled, not at all offended at having her methods questioned. After all, this was DCI Jonah Porter, who was famous for solving cases where other officers had failed. It was a privilege to have him working with her. 'I was very careful not to suggest that there was any possibility that he might have already been dead. I just asked them about what he was doing and whether they noticed him saying anything or moving his beads through his fingers. They didn't notice anything – but then, they were probably too taken up with each other to notice much.'

'Good. Well done.' Jonah thought for a moment. 'So, how about seeing that CC-TV footage?'

'We'll come on to that in a minute. First, I wanted to ask about the meeting you had with Father Allerton's mother.' Sandra turned back to Bernie. 'I gather from DI Lucas's notes–'

'Talking of DI Lucas,' Jonah interrupted. 'What exactly is his role in this now? Have the two cases been officially merged, or is he still in charge of the assault, while you're dealing with the murder?'

'The two cases are being treated as separate but potentially linked,' Sandra told him. 'I'm the officer leading the murder enquiry and I also have a remit to explore links with the assault on Dr Fazakerley. DI Lucas is currently looking into possible alternative motives and known criminals who may have been in the vicinity of the incident at the time it took place.'

'I see.' Jonah wondered whether Lucas had chosen to follow this line of enquiry or if he had been instructed to do so by someone more senior. He might be keen to prove right his theory that the assault on Bernie was a straightforward mugging. On the other hand, this could be a clever ploy to give Sandra Latham a free hand in her investigation without officially putting her in charge of both cases.

'We have to keep an open mind,' Sandra went on. 'It's always possible that the two incidents *are* unrelated. As you may have heard in the press, there have been a number of violent attacks in Merseyside recently, including a stabbing in Bootle only last Thursday. However, as I was saying,' she turned to address Bernie again, 'DI Lucas says in his notes that you visited St Wilfrid's presbytery on the morning that you were attacked. Can you tell me why that was?'

'Father Nick's mother asked to see me,' Bernie answered. 'She was hoping I might be able to tell her something about her son's last minutes of life.'

'That's what your husband told DI Lucas,' Sandra confirmed. 'Now, could you tell me a bit more about that meeting? What did you talk about?'

'About what it's like trying to bring up a baby whose father is dead,' Bernie said, struggling to recall the conversation, which now seemed a very distant memory. 'And she seemed very pleased when I told her he was praying the rosary when he died,' she added, at last.

'Anything else?' Sandra encouraged.

'We discovered that our names were the same. ... And ... oh yes! I asked her if she knew why Father Nick was on the ferry and she said that he'd told her specifically that he had to stay in the parish all weekend.'

'Yes. She told us that too.'

'And I told her that I thought he looked as if he was trying to make his mind up about some big decision,' Bernie went on, the memories coming back to her now. 'And she said that he could have been planning to go to see their own parish priest in New Brighton.'

'Really?' Sandra sounded excited at this suggestion. 'She didn't tell us about that.' She turned to DS Simpson. 'Charlie. Find out the name of this parish priest, and then go over and interview him. Find out whether he'd had any communication with the victim in the days before he was killed or if he has any idea what might have been on his mind.'

'I think Mrs Allerton said his name was Father Aidan,' Bernie told them. 'She didn't give a surname, but it'll be easy enough to find out. The archdiocese website has a list of all the clergy.'

'Thank you. That's very helpful. OK, Charlie, off you go. We can manage without you now.' Sandra dismissed the sergeant with a wave of her hand before turning back to Bernie and Jonah. 'Now, is it OK with you to have a look at those CC-TV pictures?'

23 OUR RESEARCHES LEAD US

Bernie watched the screen intently. As usual with recordings from CC-TV, the images were somewhat fuzzy and indistinct. However, some pre-processing had enhanced the clarity and she was reasonably confident that the faces would have been recognisable – if only she had seen any of them before. But they all seemed completely unfamiliar – until ….

'Hang on a minute! Can we go back a bit?' she called out excitedly. 'I think I saw something.'

Sandra stopped the tape and wound it back a little way. Then she pressed *play* again. They all leant forward and watched closely.

'Stop the tape!' Bernie cried. 'Stop it right there!'

Sandra did as she asked and they all sat looking at a still of two young men, wearing black short-sleeved tee-shirts and jeans, striding up the slope that led from the floating landing stage to the shore. They had tanned faces and dark, curly hair. They looked to be in a hurry and one of them was in the act of pushing aside a middle-aged woman in a green dress who was, presumably, walking more slowly than they desired.

'That's the two Solari boys,' Bernie told the others. 'Did I tell you about them being at the presbytery when I was there?'

'No,' Sandra shook her head. 'Who are they? How do you know them?'

'I don't really. I think probably Father Liam may have introduced us, but we'd never met before. They were there with their mother to discuss funeral arrangements for their brother. He died last Friday. Father Nick gave him the last rites. I did wonder whether it could have been something to do with that that was bothering him when he was on the ferry; but Father Liam says that the family were very happy with the way he dealt with it.'

'Even so – this is the first real

connection we've found between you and any of the ferry passengers,' Jonah said excitedly. 'And it opens up all sorts of possibilities. He could have arranged to meet the brothers on the ferry; or they could have followed him there, wanting to talk to him – out of hearing of their mother, maybe?'

'But, I don't think they *can* have spoken to him,' Bernie objected. 'Or not more than a word or two. I'm sure I would have noticed if he'd had a long conversation with anyone – especially a couple of lads as striking as these two. I remember thinking when I saw them in the hall at St Wilfrid's that they looked like a couple of Mafiosi.'

'You said the deck was crowded, up until everyone got off at Seacombe,' Sandra reminded her. 'Don't you think you could have missed them in amongst everyone else?'

'I'm not saying they couldn't have come up to Father Nick. I just don't think they could have held him in conversation, that's all. And if they did, then surely, even if I was looking the other way at the time, someone else would have noticed and told you about it.'

'Not if they also got off at Seacombe,' Jonah pointed out. 'Have you had many people coming forward in response to the appeal?'

'Quite a few, but it's early days yet. We've got a team working on interviewing any that ring in. I'll brief them to look out particularly for these Solari boys – or for anyone who mentions having seen them. And I'll go through all the statements that we've got so far, in case they've already been spotted. Do you know anything else about them? Their first names, for example? Or where they live?'

Bernie shook her head. 'I don't think Father Liam told me their names. I suppose they probably live somewhere in Dingle – or they could have moved away but still see St Wilfrid's as their church. Father Liam would be able to tell you.'

'He might also be able to tell you what time they left the presbytery,' Jonah added. 'If they were responsible for killing Father Nick, and if they thought that Bernie had recognised them from the ferry and would be likely to tell the police, then they could have followed her and tried to silence her.'

For a moment, none of them spoke. Jonah had voiced the thought that they all shared. Here, at last, were two people who could have murdered the priest and then gone on to attack Bernie.

'I've got his phone number here somewhere,' Bernie volunteered, taking her mobile phone out of her pocket and scrolling through her contacts list. 'Yes! Here you are.'

Sandra jotted the number down in her notebook and then got up to reach for a telephone, which stood on a desk at the side of the room. However, before she got there, she was interrupted by a knock at the door. A police officer in uniform entered.

'Excuse me,' she said apologetically. 'I thought you ought to see this.'

She held out an evidence bag, which Sandra took and held up in front of her.

'It was picked up on the shore at Egremont,' she explained. 'It's a pair of latex gloves. It looks like they were pulled off inside-out with one wrapped up in the other, so they stayed together.'

'Is that reddish staining what I think it is?' Sandra asked, studying the contents of the bag carefully.

'We don't know yet. We were going to send it to the lab for analysis, but we thought you'd better see it first.'

'Thank you, Mel. Yes – get it off

right away. If it *is* blood, there's a very good chance these are what the killer used to keep his hands clean.'

Constable Melanie Wharton left the room and Sandra turned back to speak to Jonah.

'Which reminds me,' she said. 'We have some other evidence that you might be interested in.'

'Really?' Jonah asked, raising his eyebrows interrogatively. 'You interest me strangely. Tell me more.'

'We've been going over the ferry with a fine tooth comb,' Sandra told him. 'And we picked up something interesting in the toilet. There were some faint traces of diluted blood in the washbasin – not enough to give us a match with Father Allerton's DNA, or at least not yet. We've called in some experts from another lab who think they may be able to do something with it. Anyway, it looks a bit like the killer may have washed his hands there – or maybe even tried to get blood off his clothes.'

'That would fit,' Jonah agreed. 'There would be a lot of blood from a wound like that. The gloves may not have been enough to keep it off the killer's arms.'

'The rest of his body would be protected by the priest's own body,' Bernie pointed out. 'Father Nick was standing, leaning over the rail, all the time. The killer must have reached round from behind – like he did with me,' she added, suddenly recognising the parallels between the two attacks,

'– and then stabbed with the knife coming towards him like this.'

She got up and demonstrated on Sandra, who was still on her feet, standing by the telephone, ready to ring Father Liam.

'Yes,' agreed Jonah. 'The only part of his clothes that might get blood on them is his sleeve.'

'If it was one of the Solari brothers,' Bernie said, pointing to the screen, which still displayed the image of the two young men alighting from the ferry, 'not even that. They both have short sleeves.'

'OK. So let's assume they got some blood on their arms, up above where the gloves came to. They peel off the gloves and drop them into the river, together with the knife. They can do all that behind the priest's body so that no-one will notice. It'll just look as if they're giving him a friendly embrace.'

'And, if it *was* the Solari brothers,' Bernie added excitedly, 'the other one could stand there blocking people's view.'

'But then he notices that there's some blood on his arm,' Jonah continued. 'So he hurries off to the toilet – whereabouts is it on the boat, by the way?'

'On the lower deck,' Sandra told him. Close by where the gangway connects when it berths.'

'Very convenient,' Jonah commented. 'As I was saying, he hurries down to the toilet. It's not time yet to get off at Seacombe, so there's nobody else going down that way. He washes the blood off his arm and comes out, just in time to disembark, leaving his victim still leaning on the rail and apparently still alive.'

'Yes,' Sandra agreed. 'That's about how we pictured it. But I think he did one other thing before leaving the toilet. There were practically no fingermarks in there – not on the door handle or on the washbasin: just one partial print on the tap. So we think he tried to wipe all the surfaces clean before he left.'

'And the partial print on the tap?' Jonah asked.

'Doesn't match any of the ferry crew or any of the passengers who got off at

Woodside. Nothing so far on the database either, but we're still searching.'

'Good. So that still all fits in with our hypothesis that the killer might be one of the Solari boys,' Jonah said with satisfaction. 'We definitely seem to be getting somewhere now. Let's just check out with Father Liam, what time they left on Monday, and we could have the case closed by the end of the day.'

Smiling at his enthusiasm, Sandra picked up the phone and dialled the number of the presbytery. She spent a few minutes speaking with Father Liam, making notes all the while in her notebook. Then she put the receiver back and turned to face Jonah and Bernie.

'Well?' Jonah asked, trying to keep the impatience out of his voice.

'He confirmed that the Solaris were there on Monday morning. He says they arrived at about half-past nine. Does that fit in with what you remember?'

'Yes,' Bernie confirmed. I got there at half-past and they rang the bell while I was still in the hall waiting for Father Liam. He came out of his study and the housekeeper let the family in. That's when I saw them all. Then Father Liam took them into his study. I remember now! One of the boys was staring at me through the door, before Father Liam closed it. I thought at the time that he must have recognised me from the photos on the web.'

'Whereas, in fact, he probably recognised you from the ferry,' Jonah put in.

'Yes,' Bernie agreed. 'I suppose he must have done. Anyway, Father Liam left them all there while he introduced me to Father Nick's mother. She was waiting in Father Nick's study.'

'And then, when you left, one or both of them followed you until they found a nice quiet place,' Jonah concluded.

'I'm afraid not,' Sandra said regretfully. 'The bad news is that Father Liam was very definite that the Solaris didn't leave until eleven, by which time Dr Fa- Bernie was already in the ambulance and on the way to the Royal.'

24 LOVE THAT WILT NOT LET ME GO

Dominic was waiting for them outside the restaurant. He was gratified when Lucy immediately went over to greet him – and less pleased when he discovered that the plan was for him to act as guide to both Lucy and Cameron on an expedition to explore facilities for students in the city. He accepted the role with good grace, however, and they set off at once, walking three-abreast, the two young men each determined to remain at Lucy's side.

Lucy tried to divide her attention between them fairly, while making a conscious effort to favour her cousin over Cameron, just enough – or so she hoped – to convince Cameron that she was not interested in furthering their relationship. She did not wish to do anything to encourage his apparent belief that their brief friendship, while occupying adjacent apartments on the Algarve, constituted a holiday romance, or that it might become something more lasting. She had no time in this busy stage of her life – with her A'-level course just around the corner, the football season about to start, church activities and, of course, Jonah (whom she considered far more interesting company than any spotty teenager) –

for romantic entanglements. Moreover, if she had wanted a boyfriend, she would not have chosen one who lived fifty miles away from her home. This was far enough to be inconvenient, but not so far as to prevent him expecting frequent dates.

'I hear you and Lucy met on holiday?' Dominic said to Cameron. He was mindful of being, in some sense, the host, and thought that he ought to show an interest in all of his guests, however unwelcome they might be.

'Yes,' Cameron confirmed. 'Our apartment was just above theirs.'

'Actually, it was your uncle's apartment that was above ours,' Lucy said pedantically. 'Yours was the next one along. And that reminds me,' she added. 'I meant to ask: how *is* your aunt Glenys? And the kids?'

Cameron's uncle had fallen to his death from the hotel balcony, leaving a widow and three young children.

'They're OK,' Cameron said dismissively. 'Granny Wendy has moved in and taken charge. She's good at that.'

'You don't sound as if you like your gran much,' Lucy suggested, detecting the antipathy in his voice.

'She's OK, but she doesn't get on with my mum. So it's better for us now that she's got someone else to worry about. Mum doesn't like being organised by someone else, and Granny Wendy doesn't approve of Mum having a proper career. It's OK for Aunty Glenys to have a little part-time job, but Granny Wendy thinks army wives ought to dedicate themselves to their families and the regiment – or maybe it's the regiment first and *then* their families.'

Lucy was becoming interested, in spite of her resolve not to encourage Cameron. This was an unusually long speech for him and unusually revealing.

'Was that why your parents split up?' she found herself asking. 'Because she didn't like your dad being in the army, I mean?'

'That and about a million other things,' Cameron answered, rather flippantly, Lucy thought, but perhaps that was his way of covering up his own pain at the separation.

'It must have been awful for you when they got divorced,' she said sympathetically. She could imagine nothing worse than having parents who were unable to live together harmoniously.

'I dunno.' Cameron shrugged his shoulders. 'Actually, I always liked it best when he was away – out in Afghanistan and places – and it was just Mum and me. Dad always kept on at me to do more sport and things. She lets me choose for myself.'

'But still ...,' Lucy struggled to understand Cameron's easy acceptance of something that, to her, was a tragedy.

'Mum says she doesn't know why

she married him,' Cameron went on. 'She says she ought to have seen past his good looks and realised he was going to be useless at everything else.'

'She can't really have married him just for his looks,' Lucy exclaimed, outraged at the suggestion. 'I mean, *nobody* would choose a partner on that basis, would they? It would be ridiculous.'

'Only someone as pretty as you could say something like that,' Dominic said, thinking it was high time Lucy remembered that he was still there.

This statement certainly attracted Lucy's full attention, but not in the way that he desired. She glared at him, trying to think of a suitably scathing retort.

'What sort of stupid remark is that?' she said at last.

'An honest one,' her cousin replied, missing the signs and still hoping to please her with compliments. 'Don't you think she's pretty, Cameron?' he added, turning to his rival for support that he was confident would be forthcoming.

This was another misjudgement. Cameron, with more experience of Lucy's distinctive and decided views on certain subjects – and with the benefit of a mother who had spoken, and written, at some length on the subject of *objectification of women* – knew better than to agree. On the other hand, he did not have the confidence to deny the assertion, so he kept his peace, leaving the floor open for Lucy to treat her cousin to a short lecture.

'It's what you're like inside that matters,' she told him seriously. 'Not what you look like. You shouldn't judge people by appearances.'

Dominic smiled indulgently, still unable to take her seriously. Her tone reminded him of the teachers at his Primary School.

'Yeah,' he agreed. 'But I still think you're pretty.'

'And *I* think you're stupid to even think about it,' Lucy retorted. 'And anyway, we were talking about *marrying* someone because you thought they were good looking. That's just idiotic! I mean – no-one stays good looking forever. What if they got scarred in a fire or got a disfiguring disease or something?'

'Hey Lucy!' Dominic protested, giving a nervous laugh. 'Give me a break! Lighten up a bit, can't you? Why do you have to take everything so seriously?'

Peter and Julie stood together on the steps of the hotel, watching as the young people walked away. Peter would have liked some time to himself, but he did not like to leave Julie alone. She had come to Liverpool with the declared intention of writing a story about the ferry murder and would presumably be intent on ferreting out information from anyone that she could find who would talk to her. Peter wanted to make sure that whatever she wrote did not hamper the police investigation or expose his family to intrusive publicity.

'It looks as if that leaves just the two of us,' he observed. 'Do you have any suggestions for what we do to while away the time until they all come back for lunch?'

Julie considered the matter. She would have liked to visit the crime scenes in the hope of finding witnesses who would be willing to talk to her. However, she was sufficiently astute to realise that Peter was unlikely to give her any encouragement in this venture and that he would be more useful to her if she could gain his confidence by a less direct approach.

'I saw that there's an open-top bus

tour,' she said. 'I thought maybe that would be interesting; and it'll give us an idea of where else we might like to go later.'

'Sounds good to me.'

'It looks rather like a prison.' Lucy observed, as they stood in the street, gazing up at a large concrete building, which was one of the many privately-owned blocks of student rooms available for rent to those studying at any of the city's Higher Education establishments. It was very different from the Cotswold stone mediaeval Oxford colleges or even the Victorian newcomers, such as garish redbrick Keble and mock-Georgian St Hughes.

'It's handy for the city centre,'

Cameron pointed out.

'I don't like the look of those steps,' Lucy said, looking critically at the steep flight leading up to the building. 'But maybe there's a ramp further on.'

She led the way up a side road to what turned out to be the main entrance, noting with satisfaction that the pavement sloped up gently to a door marked *Reception*. She looked around for a pad to enable disabled visitors to open it. Not seeing one, she then looked at the door and sniffed disparagingly.

'A big wheelchair wouldn't fit through there.'

'Maybe there's another way in,' Cameron suggested.

'I expect there are rooms for

disabled students in other halls,' Dom said. 'Or maybe there's a door round the back somewhere.'

'I was thinking about people visiting,' Lucy argued. 'You'd have thought they could have made the door a bit wider, that's all. It's not like in Oxford where all the buildings are hundreds of years old.'

'It'd do me,' Cameron said, peering in at the reception area with its easy chairs and a board advertising a bar and a games room.

Lucy still looked dissatisfied, but did not make any further comment. They walked round the outside of the building, observing the open-air seating area and a secure cycle park. After a few minutes, there seemed to be nothing more to see.

'OK then. Let's have a look at somewhere else,' Dom suggested. 'I know another hall near the Metropolitan Cathedral.'

'That'll be nearer to the university too, won't it?' Lucy asked, remembering that Dom had pointed out the original redbrick university building when they had visited the cathedral two days earlier. 'What about the medical faculty? Is that near there too?'

'Sort of. It's next door to the Royal – where they took your mum.'

'Can we have a look? I'm not sure where that is. It's difficult to tell where things are when you go in a car.'

'OK. I'll take you to the student house I know and then we'll go along to see the medical faculty – not that it's very inspiring. It's just a big concrete box, really.'

'What about the Institute of Performing Arts?' Cameron asked. Where's that compared to these other places?'

Dom thought for a moment.

'If you want to see that, we'd better go to the medical faculty first and then to the student house and then along Hope Street.'

'That's the road we went on to get to the other cathedral, isn't it?' Lucy asked.

'That's right,' Dom confirmed. LIPA is near the Church of England cathedral.'

He led them uphill towards the area

of the city now known as the university quarter.

'Cameron seems very taken with your Lucy,' Julie said to Peter, as they sat on the top deck of the bus waiting for it to depart. 'I'm convinced he only told me he was interested in the course at Oxford Brookes because it gave him an excuse to call on her.'

Peter smiled. This at least was a relatively safe topic of conversation from the point of view of avoiding giving anything away that Julie could use in a newspaper article.

'I'm afraid he may be disappointed. He's got some tough competition.'

'Dominic, you mean?'

'Her dear second cousin, forty-three times removed, or whatever it is?' Peter laughed. 'I daresay he'd like to think he was in the running, but no, that wasn't who I had in mind.'

'Cameron said she was very taken up with helping to look after DCI Porter,' Julie suggested, 'but that's hardly the same thing, is it?'

'Maybe not, but that's where her priorities lie at the moment – that and embarking on a career in forensic pathology.'

'Don't you find it a bit odd – a sixteen year old girl wanting to spend time looking after a middle-aged man in a wheelchair?'

'Not really.' Then, seeing that Julie still looked puzzled, Peter elaborated.

'You have to remember that it's been going on since she was only nine. And when you're faced with the task of helping a nine-year-old to come to terms with the fact that someone that she sees as a sort of favourite uncle is suddenly paralysed from the neck down, you're glad of anything that can help soften the blow. It helped her, feeling that she was able to do something for him. So, as I say, your Cameron's got his work cut out if he's hoping that Lucy will take any notice of *him* while Jonah's around.'

'He seems determined to give it a go.'

'Well, if he's serious, I hope he's prepared to play a long game. She hasn't shown any sign of being interested in that sort of thing yet.'

'For which, as her father, you are no doubt grateful,' Julie said, with a smile.

'Well. Firstly, I'm only her wicked stepfather, so I have no right to have an opinion about that. And secondly, having already brought up one daughter through her teenage years and out the other end, I know better than to say anything one way or the other. When she's ready, it'll be up to her and nothing I say will have any effect, so it's better just to keep my head down and go with the flow.'

'Have you been married before then?'

'Yes.' Peter did not elaborate, so Julie prompted him gently.

'And your first wife ...?'

'Died.'

'I'm sorry.'

Neither of them spoke for a few minutes. Then Julie tried again to engage Peter in conversation, still hoping eventually to manoeuvre him round to the subject of the stabbing of the priest and the attack on his wife.

'So, you have a grownup daughter. What does she do?'

'She's a nurse.' Peter replied curtly.

'And is she married? Do you have any grandchildren?'

'I don't think you need to know any of that,' Peter said bluntly.

'Sorry. I was interested, that's all.'

'In case it's good background material for whatever it is you're

557

planning to write?'

The bus stopped and Julie looked down to see where they were.

'Let's get off here,' she suggested. 'The cathedral is supposed to be worth a visit.'

Dom was right. The medical faculty building was a drab grey concrete structure, which reminded Lucy more of a multi-storey car park than anything else. Its appearance was not improved by its being shielded behind temporary barriers and dominated by a large crane. Work had commenced on the building of a new hospital to replace the ageing Royal.

They turned away and headed off through the Victorian part of the university towards the easily recognisable tower of the Roman Catholic Cathedral.

'What are *you* planning to do when you finish at uni?' Lucy asked Dom. 'I mean, I'm going to do medicine because I want to be a pathologist. What do you want to do?'

'I'm not sure yet. Teaching maybe,' Dom answered.

'That's a bit of a cop out, isn't it?' Lucy commented. She was of the opinion that most teachers were people who had simply lacked the imagination to think of any other career. 'Isn't there anything else you could do with your degree? What is it you're studying?'

'English and Religious Studies.'

'Religious studies? Have you

thought of becoming a priest?'

'I'm not cut out for it.' Dom laughed. 'I don't have a vocation.'

'How do you know?' Lucy asked seriously.

'For a start, I'm not that keen on the idea of celibacy,' Dom answered, still with amusement in his voice.

'Vocations aren't always *easy*,' Lucy answered, still serious.

'Do you have a vocation to be a pathologist?' Cameron asked.

'Yes. At least ... I do think it's an important job; but I know I'll enjoy it too, so maybe that's what's making me want to do it.' Lucy always tried to be honest.

'What do your mum and dad think

about you having a job cutting up dead people?' Cameron asked.

'Let's see ...' Lucy held up her hands and counted each person off on her fingers. 'Mam's all in favour. My dad – well, according to Mam, he would have been dead against it, but she hopes that, now he's dead, he'll have realised that women don't need to be cosseted and protected from all the nasty things in life.' Lucy smiled at the surprised expressions on the two lads' faces on hearing this unexpected statement. 'And Peter says that he'd rather I did that than joining the police – which was what I wanted to do before – because at least pathologists don't get called in until Uniform have made the crime scene safe. He didn't like the idea that I might have to arrest an armed man or something.'

'Wouldn't you rather be a doctor that treats people, instead of cutting up dead bodies?' Dom asked.

'I'd rather cut up dead people than live ones, like Jonah's wife, Margaret. She was a surgeon. I'd be scared I might let the knife slip and cut something I didn't mean to! Being a forensic pathologist would be really interesting – a bit like being a detective. Plus, I'll get to work with the real detectives. It's a pity that, by the time I'm qualified, Jonah will have retired. What I'd *really* like would be to work with him on cases.'

'You don't like journalists very much, do you?' Julie asked, as they descended the stairs and alighted from the bus.

'I see them as a necessary evil,' Peter confessed. 'Although, I will admit the press and the media are useful sometimes. Like this morning, when DI Latham put out her appeal for people to come forward who had got off the ferry at Seacombe.'

'Do you think one of them killed the priest then?' Julie asked eagerly.

'That's not what the call was about,' Peter told her, choosing his words carefully to avoid giving anything away. 'They just want more witnesses, in case anyone saw anything that might help – someone talking to the priest, for example.'

'But you think it *might* have been

someone who got off before the police came?' Julie pressed him. 'Is that why they haven't made an arrest yet? I'd been thinking that it ought to have been easy to find the guilty person out of the passengers that they'd detained. Wouldn't they have been able to find blood on their clothes or something?'

'It's not for me to say,' Peter told her firmly.

'No, but you must have your own opinion. Do *you* think it was someone who got off at Seacombe?'

'I told you – it's not my case.'

'It isn't DCI Porter's case either,' Julie pointed out, but I'm sure he's got opinions. Isn't that why he went with your wife to the police station this morning?'

'Jonah can never resist poking his nose in anywhere there's a mystery. That's his business, not mine – or yours.'

They entered the cathedral grounds and Julie looked around.

'Is that the tunnel where your wife was attacked?' she asked suddenly.

Peter looked in the direction that she was pointing and saw that the police cordon had been removed and tourists were walking freely through the tunnel.

'Yes. That's right.'

'Do you mind if I have a look?'

Peter shrugged. While he felt that he *did* mind, he could not think of any valid reason for objecting. In any case, there would be nothing to prevent her coming back to view the crime scene later, when he might not be around to keep an eye on what she was doing.

Julie stepped forward, taking out a small camera from her bag. She photographed the tunnel entrance and then took some more snaps as she walked slowly through it and came out into the sunshine on the other side. Peter followed, cursing himself silently for his foolishness when she took a photograph of him emerging from the shadows into St James' Gardens.

'You're not planning to publish that, are you?' he asked coldly.

'Not if you tell me not to. But don't you think it would make a rather poignant shot? The victim's husband re-visiting the crime scene?'

'I'm not in the business of providing you with poignancy,' Peter grumbled. 'And,' he went on, with sudden inspiration, 'I don't think your Cameron would like his mother to be exploiting Lucy's family.'

'Ouch!' Julie looked at him with new respect. 'You don't pull your punches, do you?'

'Not where my family is concerned.'

'Does that extend to DCI Porter?'

'Lucy would certainly say so.'

'Only I was really hoping you'd be able to tell me a bit more about him. It wouldn't need to involve you or Lucy or your wife – just some background about his police work and how he copes with his disability, that sort of thing.'

'And then you'd write all about it and sell the story to the papers?'

'That's what I do. I write stories and sell them to newspapers. But they don't have to be intrusive or damaging – just helping people to know more about what's going on, and helping them to understand better too.'

'Hmmph,' Peter snorted sceptically. 'If you want to write about Jonah, you'd better talk to *him*.'

'So, what sort of performing is it you want to do?' Dom asked Cameron, as they approached the imposing front entrance to the Liverpool Institute for Performing Arts.

'I'd like to be an actor,' Cameron told him. 'But I'm also interested in the behind-the-scenes stuff. Anything creative, really. I'd quite like to be a screenwriter.'

'You mean, turning books into films?' Lucy asked.

'Maybe. But I was thinking more of writing my own original stuff.'

'What would you write about?' Lucy asked.

'They say you ought to write about what you know,' Dom said, feeling that, as a student of English Literature, he ought to be able to offer advice to a budding writer. 'What do *you* know about?'

'You could write about army families,' Lucy suggested. 'How about having a boy whose dad wants him to go into the army, but he doesn't want to?'

'I'm not sure—,' Cameron began. This was rather too autobiographical for his liking.

'Hey! That's a good idea,' Dom interrupted. 'Yes! I like that. Then you could either have him choosing to do something else and having a big bust-up with his dad. Or, better, why not have him giving in and joining up and being killed in action. And you could have his dad feeling guilty. Maybe his mum didn't want him to be a soldier either and she blames his dad.'

He waved his arms around enthusiastically. Cameron opened his mouth in another attempt at stopping the flow, but Dom continued.

'No, wait! I've got it! He doesn't get

killed, just badly injured. And his dad has to look after him. That's it! His mum can't cope and leaves home and his dad has to live with him and look after him, all the time blaming himself for what happened. And the boy tells him he wishes he was dead and asks him to–'

'NO!' Lucy shouted. Stepping in front of Dom and turning to face him with both arms raised. 'That's a horrible story! You were going to say that he wants his dad to kill him, weren't you?'

'I was just saying that assisted dying is an interesting subject for a film to explore,' Dom said, taken aback by this outburst. 'And all the more because of the father's feelings of guilt about having forced his son into a situation where he–'

'But you were saying that disabled people would be better off dead!' Lucy shouted, blinking fiercely to keep back the tears. 'There are enough people who think that way, without making a film about it. Don't you see …?'

Dom put out his arm and laid his hand on her shoulder, but she jerked back to avoid his touch. Then she turned round and strode angrily away, still fighting back the tears. Dom stood still for a moment, not knowing what to do. Then he hurried after her.

'Lucy! I'm sorry. I didn't mean …,' he began. Then the reason for her reaction dawned on him. 'Please Lucy! Wait!' he said, grabbing at her arm.

She angrily shook his hand away and quickened her pace; but Dom's long legs enabled him to keep up with her easily. She debated whether to break into a run, but decided that rapid walking was more dignified. She wanted him to know that she was angry, but not how much his remarks had upset her.

'Why do you have to take everything so seriously?' Dom asked. 'It was just a bit of fun, making up a story. I wasn't talking about people like your mum's disabled friend.'

Lucy stopped abruptly and turned to face him again.

'Jonah,' she said, very deliberately. 'His name's Jonah – not *our disabled friend*. And, yes, you were talking about someone exactly like him. And you were saying that his life wasn't worth living.'

'No, I wasn't,' Dom insisted. 'I was saying that someone in that situation might *think* that his life wasn't worth living – and that it would be interesting to explore that idea in a film. And I was talking about a young, active guy, with his whole life in front of him. Don't you see how much worse it would seem for someone like that than for ...' he searched for an appropriate description that Lucy would not take offence at, '... an older man– '

'Jonah's *not* old,' Lucy protested.

'– with a career that he can go back to,' Dom finished, ignoring the interruption.

'And Jonah *was* active before he got shot. He went swimming and cycling and he won prizes for growing things in his garden, and I remember him climbing up into my treehouse with me. It's *exactly* the same for him as what you're talking about.'

'OK then. Suppose it is. It's only an idea for a film. You can make it turn out however you like. Why not make it show people how life could be worth living after all?'

'Yes!' Cameron put in. 'You could give him a girlfriend who shows him that she still loves him even with his disabilities.'

'That's a stupid idea,' Lucy told him bluntly. 'He wouldn't need more people telling him they love him – he's already got his dad for that. What he needs is to have a *purpose* for his life – a job, a way of contributing to society.'

'OK then,' Dom sighed, wishing that he had never suggested this scenario. 'What sort of job could our hypothetical cripple do?'

'We haven't decided yet what his disabilities actually are,' Lucy pointed out, nobly refraining from criticising her cousin's use of the derogatory word *cripple*.

'My dad has friends who had legs and arms blown off in Afghanistan,' Cameron suggested. 'How about that?'

'Good idea,' Dom agreed. 'I think the girlfriend is a good idea. We could have his dad being so prostrated with guilt that he can't see how his son can ever walk again, but the girlfriend pushes him to make an effort. Maybe she has to fight to get the right bionic legs for him. Or–'

'Losing his arms would be a bigger problem,' Lucy said, getting interested in spite of herself. 'There are all sorts of things to help you get around if you can't walk, but you need your hands for dressing and feeding yourself.'

'You're right,' Cameron agreed. 'Why not have him being a bomb-disposal expert and a bomb he's trying to de-fuse blows up in his face, blowing off both arms? It could be quite good visually, showing him trying to do things like picking things up in his mouth instead of his hand, and things.'

'And,' Lucy added, 'he could have disfiguring facial injuries that make people stare at him in the street, so he doesn't want to go out.'

'Which would also be a reason he wouldn't expect the girlfriend to want him anymore,' Dom added. 'But she's like Our Lucy and doesn't care about outward appearances, so it all comes out OK in the end.'

'Is that the ferry *you* were on?' Julie asked Peter as they stood up to alight at the Pier Head.

He looked over the side of the bus and saw the dazzle ferry approaching the landing stage.

'Yes. They must have finished their examination and allowed it back into service.'

'I suppose we don't have time to go

on it?'

'No. It's nearly lunchtime. We'll have to be heading back soon.'

They walked round the building that housed the booking hall and the Beatles Story exhibition, and stood leaning on the rail overlooking the floating landing stage, where a crowd of expectant passengers was waiting to board.

'Inspector Johns!' Peter turned at the sound of his name and saw Lauren Schofield descending the steps behind him, a warm smile on her face.

'Ms Schofield,' he mumbled back discouragingly.

'Your wife's not with you? I hope she's alright?'

'Yes. She's fine,' Peter replied.

'She's *helping the police with their enquiries* as they say,' Julie added brightly, wondering who this newcomer might be, and hoping that she might be a source of information for her article.

'Won't you introduce me to your friend?' Lauren said, still addressing Peter.

'Julie – this is Ms Lauren Schofield. Lauren – Mrs Julie Price.'

They shook hands. Then Lauren produced a business card and handed it to Julie.

'I'm with the Echo. I've been reporting on the stabbings. If you have any views on them I'd love to hear about them.'

Julie smiled. Then she felt in her jacket pocket and took out a similar card, which she offered to Lauren.

'I'm a journalist too – freelance. I've had a few pieces in the nationals – the Guardian, the Indie ...'

Knowing that Peter was listening, she was careful only to list quality papers, in the hope of reassuring him that she would not sensationalise any information that she obtained from him.

Lauren took the card, still smiling pleasantly.

'And how did you manage to persuade Peter to talk to you? He was very reluctant to speak to me.'

'My son met the whole family when they were on holiday,' Julie explained. 'And he insisted on coming up to see that they were alright. We came up with DCI Jonah Porter. Peter's wife is his

PA.'

'Really? You mean *the* Jonah Porter – the police hero? He's here?' Lauren's eyes opened wide at the prospect of another angle to her story.

'He won't thank you for using that kind of language,' Peter told her. 'Call him a master detective if you like, but he doesn't consider himself a hero.'

Lauren looked at her watch. 'Can I treat you both to lunch? There's an Italian place just round the corner that I can recommend.'

'I'd love to. Maybe we could work together?' Julie answered, before Peter could say anything. 'I was thinking of writing something about the background to the case. I thought I might get it into one of the Sundays.'

'Great! Peter? Would you like to join us?'

Peter hesitated. He was loathe to leave the two journalists alone together, but he wanted to get back to his wife. Bernie – especially now that she was in the company of the irrepressible Jonah – could not be trusted not to overdo things. He decided that it was infeasible to keep Julie under constant surveillance and that if she wanted to speak to Lauren she would do so, whatever he did to try to prevent it.

'No thanks,' he said at last. 'I'd better be getting back. Don't forget that you promised not to publish anything without letting us see it first. Oh! And if you value your life, whatever paper you're thinking of writing for, you'd better not make it the Sun. And, before you draw yourself up to your full height and say that you'd never dream of such a thing, be aware that I can trawl the internet with the best of them, and you have form.'

'A girl's got to eat,' Julie smiled back at him. 'And when you're freelance you can't afford to be picky.'

'I'm not sure that our Bernie would see it that way – or any of the other good people of Liverpool either. You *do* realise that it hasn't been sold here since Hillsborough, don't you?'

'I'm sorry!' Lucy's conscience suddenly smote her, as she realised that they had walked past the Institute for Performing Arts without giving it a second glance. 'We never stopped to look at the Performing Arts Institute. Cameron – do you want to go back and see it properly?'

'No. It's OK. I've seen where it is, which is the main thing. I don't suppose there's much more to see that isn't in the prospectus.'

Lucy looked at her watch.

'We ought to be getting back to the hotel anyway. It's nearly lunch time. How far is it? She asked Dom.

'Not that far. But do you have to go back? I'd like to treat you to lunch, to make up for upsetting you back there.'

'But I need to–,' Lucy began. Then she remembered that Nathan was there and he would expect to be the one to feed Jonah. 'I suppose I could ring them and let them know,' she amended.

25 THE MEETING OF OUR LIVES

Bernie and Jonah arrived back at the hotel before Peter. Jonah, always so careless of his own welfare, insisted that Bernie should rest while they were waiting for him to join them for lunch. Bernie, who was annoyed with herself for feeling tired after what she considered to have been a morning of inactivity, grumbled but eventually agreed to take a lie down. Jonah followed her into her room to make sure that she complied.

Nathan tried to accompany them,

determined to fulfil his obligations as his father's primary carer, and loath to allow him out of his sight. However, Jonah had other ideas and sent him on an errand to buy fruit. Nathan strongly (and correctly) suspected that this was merely a ploy to get him out of Jonah's hair, but fruit was part of Jonah's carefully regulated diet, so he did not argue.

Jonah pushed the door closed behind him with his chair and then turned to face the bed. Bernie was sitting on the side, intent on checking emails on her laptop.

'Put that thing away,' Jonah ordered, 'and lie down. You look done in.'

Bernie sighed and reached over to

put the computer down on the dressing table. Then she lay down on her back, with her head propped on the pillows. A stab of pain hit her as she lowered herself into the recumbent position. Jonah brought his chair over to the bed and positioned it so that he could look down on her face. She stared back at him.

'Satisfied?' she asked.

'You could try to have a nap,' he suggested mildly.

For answer, Bernie put out her hand and undid the Velcro fastening that held his left hand in position on the key pad that controlled his chair. Then she picked up his hand and laid it on the bed.

'That'll teach you to order me

about.'

'I'm your boss. I'm allowed to order you about.'

'Not when we're both on leave.'

They sat in silence. Bernie looked down at Jonah's hand, lying motionless on the bed. He had a gold signet ring, which she had seen many times before, but never thought about. She took hold of it and slid it off his finger. It slipped easily over the bony knuckle. Lack of use had made Jonah's muscles – including those in his fingers – shrink. Bernie examined the engraved design. An intricately curling letter 'J' was intertwined with an equally intricate 'M'.

'Is this your wedding ring?'

'Not exactly. We got it when we got engaged. In our young days, there wasn't a place in the wedding ceremony for the groom to receive a ring – only the bride.'

'Mmm. That's what I always thought. Stephen and I never thought of getting a ring for me to give to him; but Peter has a proper wedding ring from Angie. Maybe that was her idea.'

'What about when you married Richard?'

'Oh, we did it all the equality way then. We got matching rings.' Bernie pulled up the string from inside her shirt and showed Jonah the two rings that still hung on it. That's his,' she said, pointing. 'Richard had one in the same design. The other one is the engagement ring that Stephen gave to me. It was his gran's – Stan's mum. He bought a wedding ring, but we were students, so he couldn't afford a diamond engagement ring. He showed me this one, and I said I liked it because it had Liverpool colours.'

She slid the signet ring back on Jonah's finger.

'There you are! I can't have Margaret thinking I'm trying to steal you, can I?'

Jonah smiled at Bernie speaking as if his late wife were still around and might become jealous of her.

'What prompted all this sudden interest in wedding rings?' he asked.

'Lucy was asking about these, when I showed her the knife mark on the locket. She seemed to think it was odd that Peter and I re-used our wedding rings when we got married.'

'I don't think it's odd,' Jonah said, maintaining a straight face with some difficulty. 'It's utterly bizarre!'

'Just practical,' Bernie insisted. 'And, after all, we were only really getting married to regularise Peter moving in with us and to make it easier for him to have parental responsibility for Lucy.'

'I don't believe that was all it was,' Jonah said, 'even if you do,' he added, seeing Bernie opening her mouth to protest.

'It was, though,' Bernie insisted. 'Only now ...' she paused. She had not been intending to tell Jonah about Peter's grand gesture. 'Only now, Peter's had my name added to his ring.

It's got Angie's name engraved – in the inside – and now he's had mine put there too. He went out and got it done yesterday, while he was waiting for me to be discharged.'

'And tell me about the locket. Where does that come in?'

'It was an old one that I found lying around the house. I put a photo of Richard in it.' Bernie paused, wondering whether to go on. Jonah, sensing that there was more to be said, waited in silence. 'I was going to put one of Peter in as well, to even it up.'

'Only now DI Latham has confiscated it,' Jonah observed. 'I thought you didn't seem that keen on handing it over to her.'

'It doesn't matter,' Bernie assured

him. 'I'll get it back eventually.'

'It could be some time,' Jonah warned her, 'if she's serious about keeping it as an exhibit for the trial. Would you like me to ask her to give it back in the meantime?'

'Don't you dare! I'd never be able to look myself in the face again if I thought I cared about what happens to a silly second-hand bit of jewellery.'

'With significant sentimental value,' Jonah pointed out.

'I don't do sentimental.'

'I'd hate to be parted from anything that was a memento of Margaret.'

'It's alright for you. You're a man. If you get sentimental, everyone says how nice it is that you aren't afraid of showing your feelings. I'd just be a silly woman who can't control her emotions and is, therefore, unreliable.'

Jonah looked unconvinced, so she continued.

'Look – it really doesn't matter. I'll get the thing back eventually.'

She stuffed the rings on their string back inside her shirt and leaned back on the pillow looking up at Jonah.

'What happened to Stephen's wedding ring?' he asked suddenly.

'I told you, he didn't have one – just like you and Margaret.'

'No, I meant the one he was going to give to you. You said he bought one. Where is it now?'

'You know, I've honestly never thought about it,' Bernie shook her head with a puzzled expression on her face. 'Stan and Sylvia were given all his personal belongings, of course. They gave me back the presents I'd given him, but they never said anything about the wedding ring and I never thought to ask. I can't believe they wouldn't have offered it to me – or at least told me they'd found it. I think it must have got lost somehow … or …'

'Or?' Jonah prompted.

'Maybe he threw it away.'

'Why on earth would he do that?' Jonah asked, wishing very much that he had never raised the question of the whereabouts of the ring. Like the elephant's child[5], he was now

---

[5] Just So Stories, Rudyard Kipling, Macmillan & Co., 1902.

regretting his 'satiable curiosity and worrying that he had let out a genie that would be difficult to persuade back into the bottle.

'Probably the same reason he threw *himself* off the top of the engineering tower.'

'Which is something we'll never know,' Jonah said firmly.

'Yes,' Bernie admitted, 'but if he threw away his wedding ring first, it *is* suggestive.'

'Yes. Suggestive that he didn't know what he was doing. I will *not* have you saying that it confirms your stupid idea that he might have topped himself because he couldn't face a lifetime with you.'

'You have to admit it's a possibility.'

'No. I don't have to admit anything of the kind. And for someone who renounces all sentimentality, you seem to be allowing your emotions a remarkable amount of influence over your reason on this particular subject. People who are depressed don't behave rationally, so it's pointless you trying to rationalise why he might have done it.'

'Even if he didn't kill himself to get away from me,' Bernie persisted, 'there's still the question of why *I* wasn't enough to stop him wanting to. I'm sure if Peter had ever been considering suicide, just knowing that Angie was there for him would have prevented it.'

Jonah sighed.

'You won't let this go, will you?'

'Sorry.'

'No. *I'm* sorry. I should never have brought up the question of the ring.'

They remained silent for several minutes.

The door opened and Peter's head appeared round it. He had met Nathan in the hotel lobby and been told that Bernie was resting; so he had come in quietly to avoid disturbing her. Seeing that Jonah was there too, he greeted them. Jonah turned his head, but, with his hand still off the controls of his wheelchair, he could not turn to face Peter.

'Nathan told me Bernie was resting,' Peter said, coming in and sitting down on the other side of the bed, 'but I didn't really believe him.

You're a better man than I am, Jonah!'

'I felt I had to stay to make sure she didn't try to make an escape on a rope of knotted sheets,' Jonah joked. 'And she's been punishing me for it. You'll have to give me my hand back now, missy, or Peter will report you for abuse!'

'Just mind you behave yourself in future,' Bernie teased.

She gently lifted his hand and replaced it on the control pad, carefully fastening the strap to keep it in place.

Over lunch, Jonah filled Peter in with the news of the finding of the knife, the fingermark in the ferry toilet and, most significantly, Bernie's recognition of the Solari brothers.

'If they didn't do it,' he said confidently, 'I'm certain they're involved somehow.'

'But they *can't* have attacked *me*, even if they killed Father Nick.' Bernie pointed out. 'Father Liam said they didn't leave until after it had already happened.'

'They could have got an accomplice to do it. It would have been easy enough for one of them to get a message out to another member of their gang. Were they alone at all, do you know? Could they have made a phone call or sent a text without Father Liam knowing? Come to that – did anyone think to ask Father Liam whether they did? Everyone has their phones out all the time these days. They could have texted under his nose without him noticing.'

'Father Liam left them in the study while he introduced me to Father Nick's mother,' Bernie told him. 'So, yes, I suppose they could have communicated with someone else during that time.'

'There you are then!' Jonah cried triumphantly. 'Now we just need to work out a motive for them killing Father Nick – and I bet it's connected with whatever it was that made him take that trip on the ferry. They were trying to prevent him getting to wherever it was he was going. I vote we go over and talk to that parish priest that you thought he might be going to see this afternoon.'

'Dad!' Nathan protested. 'How

many times do I have to tell you? This *isn't* your case!'

'I'm with Nathan there,' Peter agreed. 'DI Latham will talk to him. We've done our bit by telling her about him.'

'She was sending her sergeant to do it,' Jonah grumbled. 'She looked a bit wet-behind-the-ears to me.'

'Whatever you think, Dad, it's *her* job – not yours. Besides, you can't just turn up at that fellow's house demanding to speak to him.'

'That's where you are wrong, Nathan,' Jonah said. 'He's a man of the cloth, living in a house that belongs to the church. He'll be used to having all sorts of people calling on him unannounced at all times of the day and night. Don't forget, my dad was a pastor and I lived in the manse for twenty-five years. We always had to be ready for unexpected visitors.'

'But what would you say to him? Why would he agree to speak to you?'

'He might think I was considering converting to Roman Catholicism,' Jonah suggested. 'Or Bernie here could have had a sudden urge to make her confession.'

'Don't act daft, Dad!'

'I'd also like to reconstruct Father Nick's journey,' Jonah said, apparently irrelevantly. He had realised that Nathan and Peter were not to be convinced and had decided on a new tactic for achieving his aim. 'From leaving the presbytery at St Wilfrid's to arriving at Father Aidan's – I've checked on the web, by the way, and his full name is Father Aidan Duffy – presbytery in New Brighton.'

'That won't be easy, Bernie observed. 'For a start, we don't know how he got from Dingle to the Pier Head. His Trio pass would have let him get the bus for nothing, but equally, he could have walked. And then, when he got to the other side, was he planning to get the bus from Seacombe or to stay on to Woodside and get the train from Hamilton Square?'

'And we don't even know that he *was* aiming for the presbytery in New Brighton,' Peter added.

'Well, at least let me go on your famous Mersey Ferry,' Jonah pleaded.

'So I can see where it all happened. And once we're over there, we might as well go on to New Brighton and see Father Aidan.'

'I'm not sure you would be able to see the scene of the crime,' Bernie said apologetically. 'It all happened on the upper deck.'

'Which is reachable only by steep staircases,' Peter added.

'And we'd have to check the tide tables before we could even be sure that you could get on the boat in the first place,' Bernie continued. 'They warned us that, at low water, the ramp might be too steep for wheelchairs.'

'Besides,' Peter put in, hoping to forestall any further argument from Jonah, 'the ferries are only every hour and the bus took quite some time to get us to New Brighton on Saturday. It'd take us all afternoon – or longer.'

'That's what's so odd about Father Nick being on the ferry in the first place,' Bernie said thoughtfully. 'If all he wanted was to get to New Brighton – or anywhere else on the Wirral for that matter – why did he go on the ferry? There are trains every few minutes that would have been much quicker.'

'Could he have arranged to meet someone on the boat?' Nathan suggested, becoming interested in spite of himself.

'He didn't look like someone who was meeting someone,' Peter said. 'I mean, you'd expect him to have been looking around to see if he could spot them, not head down all the time, counting his beads.'

'I always thought he was worried about something and was trying to make up his mind what to do,' Bernie agreed.

'And that's why he went by the scenic route,' Jonah suggested. 'He wanted to give himself time to think it through – or to pray for guidance. Presumably you *can* use those bead thingies to pray for guidance?'

'Yes, Jonah,' Bernie smiled. 'You can offer the rosary for any intention you like. The words aren't important; it's just something to do to keep your mind on God. I suppose, it's a bit like what the evangelicals call *waiting on the Lord.*'

'OK,' Jonah summed up. 'So he was trying to make up his mind about something that was bothering him. And, in all probability, he was going to see Father Aidan to ask for his advice. Whatever-it-was cropped up after he told his mother that he definitely wouldn't be leaving the parish that weekend, which makes it very likely that it was something to do with the Solari boy's death. He gave him the last rites. What exactly does that mean?'

Everyone looked at Bernie.

'Well,' she said slowly. 'It would definitely include extreme unction – that's anointing with oil – but, assuming that the lad was conscious, he'd probably also have offered to take his confession and give him absolution, and then holy communion. That's what I remember from when my Dad died.'

'And would the rest of the family be there for the whole time?' Jonah asked eagerly. 'Including his confession, for example?'

'I'm not sure. It would probably depend on whether the dying person wanted them. I left the room for Dad's final confession, but I don't know if that would always happen. Why?'

'I was just wondering if the Solari boy could have said something to the priest that his brothers wouldn't want him to know about.'

'Or asked him to do something that they would prefer him not to do,' Peter suggested, momentarily forgetting that he had promised himself not to get involved.

'And he didn't know what to do about it, so he was going over to see his old, trusted parish priest,' Jonah continued. 'But the brothers followed him and saw to it that he never got there. I still think we should go and see Father Aidan. If the ferry's out, how about the train?'

'If you *must* go,' Nathan sighed, realising that his father was not going to give up his idea of visiting the priest. 'Let's take the car.'

'That's more like it,' Peter conceded, bowing to the inevitable. 'At least then we won't have Bernie spending the whole afternoon jumping on and off trains and buses and ferries and probably walking for miles as well. With the car, we can come straight home whenever we like.'

'Don't be ridiculous, Peter,' Bernie protested. 'I'm absolutely fine. I had a rest like a good girl this morning, remember?'

'And now you're going to take it easy this afternoon as well,' Peter insisted with uncharacteristic firmness. 'If you're so set on getting back to work next week, you're going to have to spend a bit of time this week allowing your body to recover.'

Bernie pulled a face, but did not argue. She could see the force of Peter's words, but was not prepared to concede out loud that he was right.

'This looks like the place,' Bernie said, as they pulled up outside a brick-built church in a back street of New Brighton. 'And I think the presbytery is round the side, there.'

She got out and stood beside the car, looking towards the church, while Peter unfastened the straps that secured Jonah, in his wheelchair, in the back, and Nathan positioned the ramp to enable him to descend from the vehicle. Two figures emerged from the building and turned to the right towards the gate leading to the presbytery. Bernie recognised the shorter of these as Mrs Allerton, Father Nick's mother. Her companion was a middle-aged man dressed in a cassock and clerical collar, whom she supposed must be Father Aidan. She stepped forward and hailed them.

'Mrs Allerton – Bernadette! How're you doing?'

Bernadette Allerton looked surprised and for a moment did not appear to recognise Bernie. Then she smiled and came towards her.

'Bernie! I was so sorry to hear about what happened. Are you alright?'

'Yes,' Bernie assured her. 'They've stitched me up and there's no serious damage. It's a case of *it only hurts when I laugh!*'

'Father Aidan,' Bernadette turned to the priest, who was waiting patiently beside her. 'This is Dr Bernadette Fazakerley. You remember, I told you she found Nicky, and now *she*'s been attacked too.'

'Pleased to meet you, Dr Fazakerley,' Father Aidan said, holding out his hand.

'And *we*'re pleased to meet *you*,' Bernie responded. 'But, please, it's *Bernie* – especially in present company, *two* Bernadettes will be far too confusing. And now, let me introduce to you my husband, Peter Johns, our friend, Nathan Porter and Nathan's father, DCI Jonah Porter, who is *very* keen to talk to you.'

Father Aidan greeted them all warmly and invited them into the presbytery for tea and scones.

'I don't know what more I can tell you,' Father Aidan said to Jonah, when they were all settled in the large living room. 'As I told your colleague earlier, Father Nick didn't tell me what it was that was bothering him.'

'But you *do* think he had something on his mind,' Jonah asked quickly, pouncing on his words. 'Had he spoken to you?'

'I was called away to a sick parishioner on Friday evening. A very sad case. His wife is developing dementia and he had been caring for her. When he became ill himself, he wouldn't go into hospital because it would have meant leaving her on her own. A neighbour called me, because the wife was convinced that he was dying, but she wouldn't hear of calling an ambulance. One of the very few things she could remember was his insistence that she should never let them take him away. Anyway, the long and the short of it is that I didn't get back until after midnight. And I had such a time of it trying to convince the wife that her husband really needed hospital care more than the ministrations of a priest, that I never even checked my mobile until the following morning. I discovered then that Father Nick had tried to ring me on the landline and then on my mobile. I remembered afterwards that there had been a call while I was driving home, but I was so whacked that I just dropped into bed without remembering to check who it was from.'

'Did he leave any message?' Jonah asked eagerly.

'No.' Father Aidan shook his head.

'At least – he only said he'd try again later. That was on the mobile. He just put the phone down on the landline.'

'So he *did* say something on the voicemail. Do you still have it? Or have you deleted it?'

'I think I still have it.' Father Aidan got out his phone and called up the voicemail. 'Yes! Here you are.'

He held the phone out towards Jonah. Bernie intercepted it and switched it to loudspeaker before setting it down in front of him. They all listened intently.

'… your advice. Never mind. I'll call again. Bye!'

Then a mechanical voice took over with instructions for re-playing the message, saving it or deleting it. Bernie pressed *1* to play it again. There was a pause, then crackling sounds and then the voice of a young man, sounding rather hesitant.

'Father Aidan. It's Nicky here. I was hoping to get your advice. Never mind. I'll call again. Bye!'

'Not much to go on,' Peter said, 'but I agree, he does sound as if he's worried about something.'

'And this was late at night, after he'd been at the Solaris' house administering the last rites to their youngest,' Jonah added. 'It could be suggestive – or it could just be that he was upset at officiating at the death of someone so close to his own age. It must have been difficult for him to know what to say to the family.'

'You're not wrong there,' Father Aidan agreed. 'I only wish I'd checked my voicemail before turning in. He maybe only needed someone to confide in.'

'He said he wanted *advice*,' Jonah said, thoughtfully. 'I may be wrong, but that sounds more as if he was uncertain what to do about something. I was wondering ... I don't know much about these things, but do dying people ever ask their priest to do things for them? Things that they might have done themselves if death hadn't intervened, or things they wish they'd thought of before it was too late – righting a wrong, perhaps?'

Seeing Father Aidan's puzzled frown, he went on.

'I remember my dad once – he was a Baptist minister – being given a message from a dying man for his sister. They'd quarrelled, years previously, and he wanted my dad to tell her he was sorry and he didn't hold it against her any more.'

'I see the sort of thing you mean,' Father Aidan said slowly. 'Yes. It wouldn't be that unusual for a dying person to ask a priest to go on that sort of errand.'

'And I was thinking,' Jonah continued, 'that a priest might agree to do something in order to ease the mind of a dying man, and then, afterwards, he might start wondering whether he really *ought* to do what he'd promised. And then he might be faced with the dilemma of either going back on his word or doing something that he now saw was wrong.'

'Such as?' Peter asked sceptically. He was used to Jonah's flights of fancy, but this one seemed more implausible than most.

'I don't know ... something that involves someone else, who might get hurt. Well, for example, if the dying man had an illegitimate child whose mother is married and whose father doesn't know he isn't the father, then it could cause all sorts of trouble if he wanted to provide for the child in his will.'

'That's not very likely in this case,' Bernie pointed out. 'The Solari lad was only twenty-two.'

'No, but you see the sort of thing I

mean.'

'Yes,' Father Aidan agreed. 'I do. I could imagine that might make a young, inexperienced priest – or even an old one like me – have pause for thought.'

'*And*,' Jonah went on, 'if anyone else knew about the priest's promise, they might want to stop him carrying it out.'

26 A BROTHER DECEASED

They were about halfway through the Wallasey tunnel when a distinctive smell pervaded the interior of the car. Peter, who was seated in the back with Jonah, looked towards his friend with an enquiring smile on his face. Their eyes met. Peter's expression changed to one of sympathy and Jonah smiled back sheepishly.

'I'm afraid there's been an unscheduled evacuation,' he said. 'I should have known better than to be tempted by the full English breakfast.'

Since his spinal cord injury, Jonah had no conscious control over his bowels. Bowel movements occurred as reflexes in response to physical prompts of which he was unaware. Usually he was able to restrict these to appropriate times by carefully controlling his diet and by regular stimulation of the bowel each morning, using suppositories, supplemented by *digital stimulation*[6], delivered by one of his carers. Any change to his routine or diet brought with it the danger of an embarrassing accident.

'We're nearly back,' Bernie assured

---

[6] See, for example, https://www.spinal.co.uk/wp-content/uploads/2015/07/Bowel-Management.pdf

him from the front passenger seat.

Nathan, for whom this was a new experience, remained silent, colouring with embarrassment. He told himself that at least it had not occurred while they were still in the company of Father Aidan and Mrs Allerton. Only His father's intimate friends need ever know about the incident. He gripped the steering wheel unnecessarily hard and silently cursed the heavy traffic.

Peter leant over and briefly placed his hand on Jonah's shoulder in a gesture of reassurance.

As soon as they were out of the tunnel, Bernie opened the window, and soon the atmosphere in the car became less intense. Not far now, but all the traffic lights seemed to be against them. At last, a green light appeared at the final junction before the hotel and Nathan put the car into gear. They lurched forward and then jerked to a halt as the engine stalled. Nathan let out more expletives under his breath, angry with himself for allowing his agitation to affect his clutch-control. By the time he had re-started the engine, the lights had changed again and they had to wait for a whole cycle before it was their turn again.

Jonah caught Peter's eye and then rolled his eyes to the ceiling. Peter grinned back in acknowledgement of a shared frustration of fathers with the behaviour of sons.

'Here we are! We'll soon have you sorted now!' Nathan declared as they turned into the hotel forecourt, becoming suddenly garrulous in an effort to cover his embarrassment. 'Don't you worry — we'll get you up to our room right away and-'

'Cut the cackle can't you?' Jonah growled, finally giving way to his frustration, firstly at the situation and secondly at his son's reaction to it. Why couldn't he stay calm, like Peter and Bernie?

They pulled up next to the wide paved area in front of the hotel's main entrance. From here wide, shallow steps led up to glass doors. To the right there was a slope for wheelchairs. Bernie and Nathan got out and came round to the back of the car, while Peter started undoing the straps that held Jonah safely in place. As soon as he was released, Jonah manoeuvred the chair towards the back door, where he had to wait for Nathan to finish securing the ramp in place to allow him to descend from the vehicle.

Once Jonah was safely out on the pavement, Peter held out his hand towards Nathan.

'Give me the keys,' he said. 'I'll park the car and then come up and give you a hand.'

Nathan nodded and handed over the car keys. While this was going on, Bernie reached inside and took out a small suitcase from a rack attached to the inner wall of the car. Then she stepped back to allow Peter to start putting the ramp away prior to taking the car to the hotel car park. They turned to start up the slope to the hotel entrance, but they were interrupted by the sudden arrival of Lucy, who came running towards them and put her arms around Jonah's shoulders.

Returning to the hotel with Cameron and Dom, she had seen the car pass them at the entrance to the forecourt and had run to catch up with them. She had seen Jonah coming down the ramp and something about the expression on his face and the demeanour of his companions had told her that all was not well. As she hugged him from behind and pressed her face against his, her nose told her what the problem was. She gave him a reassuring squeeze around the neck and then turned away and walked towards the left-hand end of the hotel steps. Her aim was to draw her two escorts away, in the hope that they need not become aware of what was going on.

Sure enough, when the two young men, who had felt it beneath their dignity to break into a run in order to keep up with Lucy, reached the steps, they came to join her, ignoring the little party who were now making their way up the slope to the right. Lucy turned to face them.

'You'd better be heading back, Dom,' she said. 'Your mum will be thinking you've left home, if you're not careful!'

Dom felt that he was being dismissed – as, indeed he was. Lucy's mind was currently fully occupied with ensuring that neither of the young men found out about the incident, which she felt sure would lower Jonah in their esteem. He briefly debated with himself whether to argue, but decided that it would be more dignified to accept the situation.

'I'll make tracks then,' he said cheerfully. 'See you tomorrow?'

'If you like,' Lucy replied absently. Her attention had already passed to considering how to get rid of Cameron.

Peter finished stowing the ramp and closed the back of the car. He was just climbing into the driver's seat when he became aware of Julie Price at his elbow.

'Shall we have dinner together

again? Meet you in the dining room in half an hour?'

Peter had no particular desire to have the Prices present at their evening meal, but he did not have the energy to argue and was in a hurry to relieve himself of the car and get up to Jonah's room to help Nathan with the messy business of cleaning and changing his father. He did not trust his wife to remember that she was supposed to be taking things easy.

'Better make it an hour,' he replied. 'We've got a couple of things to do first.'

He pulled the door closed and started the engine. Julie nodded and smiled, then stepped back to allow him to move off. Then she turned round and headed over to the other end of the steps where Lucy and Cameron were standing, making rather awkward conversation.

'Hi Lucy,' she called cheerily. 'Did you get to see everything you wanted at the university?'

'Yes thank you,' Lucy replied, speaking in the formal tone that she adopted towards adults whose advances she wished to discourage. 'I'd better be going,' she added, relieved at the thought that Cameron would now be obliged to stay with his mother rather than following at her heels. 'See you later.'

'How're you getting on?' Julie asked, turning to Cameron.

'OK,' he grunted.

'Managing to hold off the amorous cousin?' she continued brightly, ignoring his evident reluctance to discuss his love life.

Cameron sighed and turned to walk up the steps. Why did parents always ask such stupid questions?

'Dr Fazakerley!' DI Latham got up from the leather-bound sofa in the hotel lobby, where she had been awaiting their return, and greeted Bernie as she and Nathan accompanied Jonah in through the automatic doors. 'Might I have a word?'

'Of course.' Bernie turned to Nathan and handed over the case that she was carrying. 'Take this. You'll find everything you need in there.'

Then she turned back to address the inspector.

'Shall we go over there, out of the way?'

She led the way to a corner of the room, well away from the reception desk, where they could talk without being overheard.

'Would you like to join us?' Sandra Latham looked enquiringly towards Jonah.

'Sorry. Not just now,' he answered regretfully, stopping only briefly before heading purposefully towards the lift. 'Things to do, I'm afraid.'

There were two lifts, side-by-side. One had its doors open and they could see two young men dressed in dark suits standing inside with two of the small trolley cases favoured by executives for business trips. When they saw Jonah approaching in his wheelchair, one of them put out his hand to prevent the lift doors closing.

'It's OK,' Nathan called out. 'We'll wait for the other lift.'

'Once my chair is in a lift, things always start feeling dreadfully crowded,' Jonah added by way of explanation. 'Thanks, all the same.'

Nathan breathed a sigh of relief as the man nodded and the doors closed. It would not be long now before they were in the privacy of their own room. He pressed the button to summon the other lift. The display lit up to indicate that it was on the second floor and on its way down. There would not be long to wait.

'Wait for me!' Lucy called from behind them.

Nathan turned and saw her hurrying across the lobby. She reached them just as the lift doors opened. Soon they were on their way. In the confined space, the smell became very obvious and Nathan gave a silent prayer of thanksgiving that they were alone. What would those two young businessmen have thought, if they had been there? And there was no knowing what his father would have said to them by way of explanation. Nathan cringed at the idea that Jonah might have treated two complete strangers to a lecture on the physiological causes of faecal incontinence.

Lucy stood behind Jonah and put her arms around him, resting her chin on his shoulder so that their cheeks were touching. For a few moments nobody spoke. Then Lucy suddenly looked round, noticing for the first time that they were depleted in numbers.

'Where's Mam?'

'DI Latham wanted a word,' Jonah told her. 'I expect she'll be up in a minute or two.'

They reached the door of the room that Jonah and Nathan were sharing. Nathan, still feeling flustered, fumbled the key card and inserted it the wrong way round. Lucy stepped forward, calmly took it out of the slot, turned it round and re-inserted it to unlock the door. She depressed the handle and led the way in, holding the door for Jonah and Nathan to enter.

'Good,' she said, eying the case in Nathan's hand. 'You've got the emergency kit. The first thing we'll need is the plastic sheet to protect the bed.'

She crossed the room and pulled the duvet off one of the pair of twin beds. She deposited it on the floor in a corner of the room and returned to the bed to smooth out the sheets. Nathan meanwhile had put down the case on the other bed and opened it. Sure enough, lying on top of an array of other items, there was a plastic sheet. He picked it up and took it across to Lucy, who unfolded it and spread it over the bed, tucking it in at the sides to keep it firmly in place, and carefully smoothing out the creases before positioning the pillows on top.

Satisfied with her work, she straightened up and stepped back to make room for Jonah to bring his chair alongside the bed. He positioned it carefully before pressing a switch on the control panel to make it recline so that he was lying level with the bed.

'Ready?' Lucy said, looking at Nathan, who nodded in response. He did not know quite what to make of Lucy's quiet and confident efficiency, which he was conscious contrasted with his own fumbling ineptitude when dealing with his father's physical needs.

Together they gently rolled Jonah off the chair and on to the bed. Then

Nathan returned the chair to its upright position and moved it out of the way into a corner of the room.

'Can you give us a lift?'

Nathan turned round to see that Lucy had already taken off Jonah's shoes and socks, and was undoing his trousers ready for their removal. He came over and lifted his father's slight body so that Lucy could pull off trousers and pants without chafing his skin.

'Is it OK for us to turn you over now?' Lucy asked. 'We need to get you cleaned up.'

'Yeah. Go ahead.'

Nathan gently rolled Jonah on to his front and Lucy carefully adjusted the pillow to make sure that he could breathe freely. Then she went over to the other bed and looked in the case. She found a pack of latex gloves. She put on a pair and offered the pack to Nathan, who followed suit. Then she selected a roll of toilet paper and a pack of baby wipes, which she took over to Jonah's bed. Nathan watched, feeling rather inadequate.

'Could you run a basin of warm water for us?' Lucy asked, looking up from contemplating Jonah's rear end and noticing Nathan standing over her. 'Or – better – there's a washing up bowl in the emergency kit. Fill it up and bring it over. And there should be some J-cloths in there too and some liquid soap.'

Nathan obediently searched in the case and found, nestling near the bottom, a small plastic washing up bowl. He emptied its contents – a plastic carrier bag containing a spare pair of pants and trousers – on to the bed and carried it through to the bathroom. When he returned he saw that Lucy had cleaned the worst of the excrement off his father's buttocks with toilet paper, which she had deposited in a plastic bag. She pulled off her gloves and sealed them in another bag before putting on a clean pair for the next stage of the process.

Then she took the bowl from Nathan and placed it on the bedside cabinet. He watched as she methodically sponged Jonah clean with the warm soapy water.

'You've done this before, haven't you?' he said at last.

'Mmm,' Lucy replied absently, having momentarily forgotten that he was still there.

'Does it happen often?' This was a new danger associated with allowing Jonah out alone, which Nathan had not previously thought of.

'No,' Lucy replied defensively.

'Maybe once a month,' Jonah added, realising that this was something that Nathan was not going to let go without being given all the facts. 'It's not a big deal – just a matter of being prepared, as you can see.'

'But ….' Nathan found it hard to put into words the anxious thoughts that were going through his head. 'Has it ever happened while you were working?' he asked eventually.

'Only twice.'

'In six years!' Lucy added forcefully, still on the defensive.

'But how did you manage?' Nathan asked. 'I mean–'

'The same as I am doing now – my carers sorted me out.' Jonah said brusquely, in danger of losing his temper with Nathan's questioning.

'But what about your colleagues – and members of the public – how did you explain …?'

'There were no members of the public present on either occasion,' Jonah answered, with a sigh. 'As for my colleagues? They knew that it could happen. They'd been briefed.'

'You mean, you told them?'

'Before I went back to work, I prepared a fact sheet for everyone who was likely to be working with me. It explained what I could and couldn't do and what extra help I was going to need from them.'

'Including …?'

'Including the possibility that my bowel management routine might not always be one hundred percent effective at preventing motions being passed at inappropriate moments – yes,' Jonah confirmed testily.

'It won a prize,' Lucy told Nathan. 'I remember Margaret showing me the certificate.'

'A prize?' Nathan looked round in astonishment.

'Your mum showed it to the R and

D[7] department at her hospital trust,' Jonah explained, 'and they used it as the basis for a template for other people with spinal injuries to customise for when *they* went back to work. They won an innovation award for it.'

'I suppose it didn't occur to you to give *me* a copy?' Nathan grumbled, feeling that he had been rather left out of something that, it appeared, had been discussed far and wide, except with him. 'If it was such a useful document.'

'I thought you already had quite enough hands-on experience of my limitations.'

'Hmmph!' Nathan snorted. 'You managed to conceal this particular

---

[7] Research and Development

aspect of your life from me very effectively, didn't you? Why didn't you say anything about …?'

Jonah recognised the truth of Nathan's words, but could not quite bring himself to apologise for not having had the frank discussions with Nathan that he had had with some people far less close to him. He sighed.

'Look Nathan,' he said at last. 'Please try to understand. This parent-child role-reversal is just as difficult for me as it is for you.'

Nathan was spared having to formulate a response by the arrival of Peter, who slipped quietly into the room without knocking. He looked round, smiling at the sight of Lucy, who was now carefully applying cream to

Jonah's anal region, and nodded towards Nathan.

'Where's our Bernie?' he asked, noting her absence.

'DI Latham wanted a word,' Jonah told him.

'At the station?' Peter asked sharply.

'No – downstairs, in the entrance hall. You must have walked right past them.'

'Good.' Peter's features relaxed. He had not liked the idea of his wife being spirited away for another gruelling police interview and perhaps missing her evening meal. 'Any idea what it's about?'

'As you can imagine, we didn't stay to find out,' Jonah said, grinning up at him.

'Well, now I'm here, what can I do to help?'

'You could take these and sluice them out in the toilet,' Lucy said, pointing at Jonah's discarded underpants. 'And then they need to be washed properly – the trousers too.'

Bernie arrived just as Jonah was returning his chair to the upright position after having been replaced in it, clad in fresh pants and trousers. She smiled to see her family back together again and everything apparently back to normal. Jonah immediately demanded to know what DI Latham had wanted with her. She sat down on the bed, next to the emergency kit suitcase, into which Lucy and Peter were tidily stowing away the, now cleaned and neatly re-folded, plastic sheet.

'She's updated me on the investigation so far,' Bernie told them. 'DS Simpson has been over to speak to Father Aidan – as he told us – but, you'll be delighted to hear, Jonah, that you were much more effective in extracting relevant information from him.'

'I *thought* she was a bit of a greenhorn,' Peter put in. 'Too much education and not enough experience.'

'Yes, well, apparently all she managed to get out of him was that he hadn't spoken to Father Nick for over a month and had no idea what he might have been worrying about. So Sandra Latham was very interested to hear about the missed calls and the voicemail message.'

'Good thing we went over there,' Jonah remarked complacently, pleased to find his obstinacy vindicated, 'but that couldn't have been all she wanted to talk to you about.'

'No. She's also been talking to Father Liam and to the Solari family about Monday morning, and to the Solari brothers about what they were up to on Saturday. They all agree that they were in the presbytery from half past nine, or thereabouts, until eleven. Father Liam confirmed that they were alone for a few minutes while he introduced me to Mrs Allerton, and he says that, when he came out of Father

Nick's study, he found the older Solari boy – his name's John-Paul (after the pope) and people call him J-P – in the hall, just closing the front door behind him. Apparently, he said he'd just stepped out for a breath of fresh air because he was upset about his brother's death. I think that's code for needing a cigarette.'

'But it could have been to get away from the others – out of earshot of his mother, for instance,' Jonah said excitedly.

'Your theory that they may have contacted a confederate and got them to follow Bernie when she left the presbytery is starting to look more plausible,' Peter conceded.

'No need to sound so disappointed

about it,' Jonah chided, grinning at Peter, clearly back on form and enjoying himself. 'Just because I have this wonderful gift for intuitive induction ...'

'Just because you have a big head!' Peter retorted

'Boys! Boys!' Bernie scolded. 'Play nicely. Now, where was I? Oh, yes! Both the Solari brothers – that's J-P and his younger brother, Greg – admit to having been on the ferry. However, they claim they never even saw Father Nick and had no idea he was on board. Sandra has got Charlotte Simpson going through all the photos that people gave them off their phones and things, in case there's any evidence there that contradicts that.'

'What about the fingermark in the toilet?' Jonah asked eagerly. 'Have they matched that up to either of the Solari boys?'

'I was coming to that,' Bernie smiled. 'Apparently they made rather a fuss about giving their fingerprints, but their mother insisted that they co-operate with the police; so now we have a full set from both of them to compare with that partial print on the tap.'

'And?' Jonah prompted.

'And the results will be through tomorrow.'

'Although, of course,' Peter added, 'if *you* had been in charge, everything would have taken only a tenth of the time that it takes normal people. In fact the results would probably have been through even *before* the prints had been taken!'

Jonah treated Peter to a withering look.

'Go on,' he urged Bernie. 'There must have been something else to make Latham come out to see you.'

'I was coming to that,' Bernie said, with a smile. 'What she had really come for, as you so astutely point out, was to ask a favour. They're burying the youngest Solari boy tomorrow and she'd like us to attend the funeral. She's hoping that whoever it was who attacked me may be one of the guests and we might possibly recognise them – either from the ferry (if they happened to be there as well) or following me or hanging around near the cathedral afterwards. Oh! That's another thing I forgot to say. They've found a pair of latex gloves in one of the litter bins in St James' Gardens. And, before you ask,' she added, smiling at Jonah, 'they've sent them for DNA analysis, but no results yet.'

'If they left the gloves behind in the Gardens then they could hardly be loitering near the cathedral when we arrived,' Peter commented. 'They'd have been long gone, out the other way.'

'I don't know,' Jonah mused. 'They could have got rid of the gloves and then come back through the tunnel to throw us off the scent.'

'Or, I suppose they could have

come round the long way,' Bernie mused. 'Even after the police cordon went up – to check whether they'd actually killed me or not, or just to see what people were saying about it.'

'Much more likely they just scarpered,' Peter said. 'But never mind. I'm game to go to the funeral if they think it might do some good. What time is it?'

'Eleven in the morning, but Sandra would like us to get there early. Apparently, there's a little sort of vestry affair that leads off the entrance vestibule. She's arranged for us to wait with her in there, so we can watch people arriving. Then, after that, we'll sit at the back of church, as if we're just ordinary parishioners coming along to support the family.'

'It sounds as if she's got it all well-organised,' Jonah said appreciatively. 'What time do we need to be there to make sure we arrive before any of the family?'

'Ah!' Bernie said. 'I was coming to that. I'm afraid you're not invited. The idea is for us to blend into the background, so that we can mingle with the congregation without drawing attention to ourselves. She thinks you would be too likely to be noticed.'

'It's your larger-than-life personality that's the problem,' Peter joked. 'It means that you just can't help standing out in a crowd.'

Jonah frowned, but he saw the validity of the argument, so did not protest.

'The most useful thing you could do,' Peter suggested, knowing how much his friend would have liked to have been present at the kill, so to speak, 'would be to keep Julie Price out of the way. We don't want her showing up asking questions about why we're attending the funeral of a complete stranger.'

'There's Dom too,' Lucy added, 'suddenly remembering her cousin's parting words. 'He's expecting to spend the day with us again, I think.'

'Why don't you ask Dom to show you and Julie the sights?' Peter suggested to Jonah. 'He can't very well refuse to do something for the great hero, and she'll be only too pleased to get the chance to spend some time with you. She's got it in mind to write a piece on you and your work and what an inspiration you are to us all. She might even invite her new friend, Lauren-from-the-Echo, to tag along. They were talking of a joint article for the Sunday papers. That'll make two journalists fewer to be getting under the feet of the police.'

'And make sure Cameron goes with you,' Lucy added, belatedly remembering the last member of their party. 'But what are we going to tell them about where Mam and Peter and I have got to?'

'That's easy,' Peter told her. 'We simply tell everyone that the police want us to answer a few more questions.'

'To help them identify who killed

Father Nick,' Bernie added. 'After all, we *are* going to an identity parade of sorts.'

27 THE FRAGRANCE THERE WAS SWEET

'Are you sure you didn't recognise anyone?' Sandra asked Bernie in a low voice.

'Quite sure,' Bernie whispered back.

They were crammed into a small anteroom – little more than a walk-in cupboard – next to the entrance to St Wilfrid's Church. Sandra had closed the curtains that hung at the small window so that they would not be seen by anyone approaching the church from outside. This also meant that they were in relative darkness, while the vestibule through which visitors had to pass to enter the church, was bright with sunshine from the open doors. They could see out through the crack in the almost-closed door, but it was highly unlikely that anyone would see in and notice them watching.

'And neither of you did either?' Sandra asked Peter and Lucy, who shook their heads and murmured confirmation that all those who had so far entered the church were unfamiliar faces.

'OK. Now, I've just heard that the hearse has set off from the chapel of rest. That means that the coffin is going to be here soon. The close family are going to enter behind it and process down the aisle. We're going to slip into the church now and sit at the back. Bernie – I want you at the end of the pew so you can see them as they go past. You'd better wear this to hide your face.'

Sandra handed Bernie a black felt hat with a wide brim that flopped down in front of her eyes when she put it on. She grimaced, but did not argue.

They crept out from their hiding place, trying to act normally, as if they were acquaintances of the deceased coming to pay their respects. Peter led the way to the first unoccupied pew. (As usual, the church had filled up from the back.) Lucy followed him, then Sandra and finally Bernie took up her post next to the aisle.

The organ, which had been playing quietly since soon after they had secreted themselves in the broom cupboard, changed to a new tune. The congregation turned to watch as the coffin appeared, carried on the shoulders of four men in dark suits. Bernie kept her head bowed as the Solari family processed slowly down the aisle.

'That's Gregory,' Sandra whispered in her ear as the first of the brothers approached, 'walking next to his mother. The one behind is John-Paul. I don't know who the girl is.'

Bernie, looking out cautiously from under her hat, recognised the young woman who had been with the family when they arrived at the presbytery the previous Monday. She waited until they had all passed and the congregation had turned back to face the front before replying to Sandra, speaking low to avoid being overheard.

'I assumed she was their sister – although she doesn't look much like it – or else the wife or girlfriend of one of the lads. She was there with them when they came to see Father Liam.'

'Are you sure? He never mentioned anyone apart from Mrs Solari and the boys.'

'She fell against me in the scrum in the hall. I'm sure it was–,' Bernie broke off as she remembered something else. The odour that she had smelt as the hand seized her from behind in St James garden! The sweet, floral smell that she had not been able to place.

She had smelt it in the hall of St Wilfrid's presbytery – and she had smelt it again just now, as the funeral procession passed. It was not coming from the flowers that lay on top of the coffin, as she had supposed. It must be some perfume worn by the young woman who had just walked down the aisle on J-P Solari's arm.

'What is it?' Sandra asked.

'I'll tell you later – after the service.'

At the end of the funeral service, the family processed out again. As they passed, Bernie sniffed the air, confirming in her own mind that the smell that accompanied them was the same as she had encountered on those two previous occasions. They sat down and waited, to give the family time to get into the cars that would take them to the cemetery for the interment. Members of the congregation who were not accompanying them there were invited to wait in the social club adjoining the church, where refreshments were being provided. As people started to get up and move towards the door, Sandra, too, got to her feet.

They trooped out, trying to mingle inconspicuously with the other members of the congregation. Once they were outside the building, Sandra led the way to where her car was parked, in a side road a few hundred yards from the church. They all got in and then she turned to Bernie.

'Now, tell me what it was you saw

back there.'

'It wasn't anything I saw,' Bernie explained. 'It was the smell. You remember – or maybe it was DI Lucas that I told – there was a distinctive smell when whoever it was grabbed me. I smelled it again in the church – when the Solari family went past – and then I remembered that I also smelled it in the Presbytery when that young woman collided with me in the hall. I'm convinced it's the scent that she wears.'

'So, you're telling me,' Sandra said slowly, 'that it was that girl who attacked you in St James' Gardens?'

'I think it probably was.'

Sandra sat for a few moments, thinking. Then she switched on the engine.

'Right! I'm going to take you back to your hotel, and then I'm going to find out who that girl is and what her relationship is to the Solari boys. My guess is that she's J-P's girlfriend and he sent her after you when he recognised you in the presbytery and assumed you'd recognised him from the ferry.'

'So, you're saying that J-P, or Greg, or both of them together, killed Father Nick and then they tried to get me killed because they thought I'd seen something that would incriminate them?' Bernie asked as the car moved away.

'Yes,' Sandra confirmed. 'And I'd be willing to bet that the reason they killed him was to do with something he saw or heard while he was at their house the night before, giving brother Ben the last rites. So the other thing I'm going to do now is to get a search warrant to go through it to try to find out what that was.'

'You're not intending to search Mrs Solari's house today?' Peter asked incredulously. 'Not the day that she's buried her youngest son? This long after the event, another day or so can't make much difference.'

'I suppose not,' Sandra sighed. 'Yes. I'm sure you're right. And, thinking about it, it would be better to wait until we know who that girl is and where she lives. Then we can search both houses at the same time, instead of giving them a chance to get rid of anything that she may still have that would link her to the attacks.'

They pulled up outside the hotel and Peter, Bernie and Lucy got out.

'I'll drop by later,' Sandra promised, 'and let you know where we're up to.'

28 COME AWAY WITH ME

Bernie, Peter and Lucy were sitting on one of the beds in Jonah's room, watching the breakfast news programme, while Nathan was helping his father in the bathroom. A breaking news item caught their attention.

'Police have arrested three people in connection with the Mersey Ferry Murder, following dawn raids at two separate premises in the Dingle area of Liverpool this morning.'

The screen showed two men –

presumably the Solari boys – with heads bowed, being led from a Victorian terraced house into a waiting police car. They were holding up folded newspapers to shield their faces from the camera, but Bernie caught a glimpse of Mrs Solari's anxious expression as she stood on the doorstep watching them being driven away. It would not be long before their identity was known and broadcast to the world.

'The suspects – two men and a woman – are said to be local residents and members of the congregation at the church where the murdered priest used to officiate.'

The picture changed to show two police cars parked outside a block of flats. A young woman emerged, flanked by two uniformed police officers.

'That's DI Lucas,' Bernie said, pointing at the screen as a tall man in a blue suit walked across the pavement to join them. 'You haven't met him, Jonah. I wonder if he's come round yet to the idea that the two cases are connected.'

The camera zoomed in to show a close-up of the young woman's face, and Bernie recognised her as J-P Solari's companion at the funeral the day before. She looked different – the police had clearly arrived before she had applied her makeup that morning – but her mass of blond hair, slim figure and large bust were unmistakeable.

'We can now take you over to our

MYSTERY OVER THE MERSEY

Merseyside reporter, Janice Crosby, who is at the scene of one of the raids with DI Sandra Latham, the officer in charge of the operation.'

The scene changed again. Once more, they were in the street of terraced houses. Sandra Latham was standing in front of a low wall, with people coming and going behind her.

'Do you think you now have the murderers of Father Allerton under lock and key?' the reporter asked.

'We have arrested three people in connection with his killing, and they are being taken away for questioning under caution.'

'And do you believe that they are also responsible for the stabbing in St James' Gardens on Monday? Are the two attacks linked?'

'We think that is very likely, but we continue to keep an open mind.'

'We've seen your officers taking away a number of items from this house and from the flat of the other suspect – can you tell us what they are?'

'Not at this moment in time. We will be having a press conference later in the day and I may be able to tell you more then.'

'Thank you very much. And now – back to the studio.'

'What was all that?' Jonah called out from the bathroom. 'Did it say that DI Latham has made an arrest?'

Peter got up and walked over to the interconnecting door. He pushed it ajar so that they could talk.

'Yes. She's taken both Solari boys and the girl in for questioning. Officially they haven't released their names, but that's definitely who it is.'

'And they're searching a house and a flat,' Bernie added, coming up behind Peter and putting her arms round him. 'Presumably it's the Solari family home and the flat that the girl lives in.'

Peter's mobile phone rang. He fished it out of his pocket and answered it. It was Sandra Latham.

'She's on her way here,' Peter reported to the others. 'She wants to come up and speak to you, Bernie.'

'OK. Better tell her to come to our

room.'

'Ask her to wait until I'm ready,' Jonah called out. 'We won't be much longer.'

'OK.' Peter thought quickly. He knew that Jonah did not want to be excluded, but he also knew that his morning routine should not be disturbed. In addition, he was aware that Julie Price would be on the lookout for them in the restaurant, hoping to question them about the new developments in the case over breakfast. 'Tell you what: Bernie – you go across to our room and order some breakfast to be brought up for all of us; Lucy – you go with your Mam; I'll give Nathan a hand here and then we'll all have breakfast together while you and Sandra talk.'

29 LAY ASIDE THE GARMENTS

'I wanted to bring you up to date with what's been going on,' Sandra told Bernie, as they sat together in the room that Bernie and Peter shared, waiting for the men to join them. 'We've made some interesting finds and we'd like you to come down to the station to have a look at a few things.'

'Of course, I'll be happy to come – after breakfast. It should be here any minute.'

The door opened and Peter and

Nathan came in, each carrying a chair from the other room to supplement the two that were provided. Lucy declined an offer from Nathan to fetch one for her from her own room, declaring that she was perfectly happy sitting on the bed. Jonah followed them in and positioned his wheelchair between Bernie and Sandra. Peter set his chair down on the other side of Bernie, and Nathan sat next to him, giving his father a hard look (which he pretended not to see), but saying nothing about how inconvenient it was going to be for him to feed Jonah when he was not permitted to sit next to him.

'Now, Sandra,' Jonah began. 'Tell us all about it.'

Before she could begin, there was a knock at the door, signalling the arrival of breakfast. Peter got up and took charge of the trolley, handing out plates and serviettes and offering round slices of toast. Nathan poured tea for Jonah in his plastic cup and buttered a piece of toast for him. Then he got up and came round to stand behind Jonah's chair in order to feed it to him. Lucy bit into her own toast, devouring it rapidly in the hope that Nathan would allow her to give Jonah his breakfast cereal while he caught up with the rest of the family.

'The girl's name is Ashley Fisher,' Sandra told them, accepting the cup of tea that Peter held out to her and putting it down on the chest of drawers next to her chair. 'She's J-P Solari's girlfriend. She has her own flat, which I gather he sleeps in a lot of the time, although in theory he's still living with his mother. Anyway, that's who she is. Father Liam eventually remembered her coming with the family to the presbytery on Monday. He says that it slipped his mind because, by the time he got back after introducing you to Mrs Allerton, she had disappeared.'

'Which all fits in with the theory that she went out and lay in wait for Our Bernie to leave,' Jonah cut in excitedly.

'Yes,' Sandra agreed. 'We've got teams of officers searching both houses, and we've already taken away all of Ashley Fisher's clothes, so that we can examine them for traces of blood. We've also taken away a large quantity of rather interesting pink tablets from J-P's room in his mother's house.'

'Ecstasy?' Jonah queried.

'Quite possibly. We're getting them analysed, but I think it's safe to say they aren't cough sweets.'

'So, is the idea that Father Nick found out that the Solari brothers – or J-P on his own – were running some sort of drugs racket and they were afraid he'd tell the police?' Jonah asked.

'That seems like a reasonable working hypothesis. But first, we want to see if we can establish that it was Ashley who attacked Bernie – and that's where you come in,' Sandra added, turning to Bernie. 'Ashley's wardrobe is quite extensive and it's going to take us forever to check every garment for blood spatter, so I'm hoping that you may be able to identify what it was that she was wearing on Monday.'

'I'll do my best – but I have to warn you, I'm not very good with clothes. Her dress was rather tight – figure-hugging, I suppose you'd call it – and it was a sort of blue colour, I think, with something shiny on it, sequins maybe or gold braid. I don't know. The only other thing I remember was her shoes – great tall things with platform soles and high heels.'

'Don't worry. We've got the whole lot down at the station, so you only have to have a look through it and tell us which dresses are the most likely. I've asked Father Liam to come in too, so he can look at them as well.'

'Have you thought of asking the girl herself what she was wearing on Monday?' Peter asked mildly.

'We will do that, of course,' Sandra said, wishing very much that she had thought of this stratagem. 'However, we'll still need your wife's corroboration. If Ashley is guilty, she may well try to fob us off with the wrong dress.'

'Now, tell me – have you got the results back on the DNA test of the gloves you found in the park?' Jonah asked, 'and what about that fingermark in the ferry toilet, and the–'

'They couldn't find any traces of tissue on the insides of the gloves to test for DNA,' Sandra answered, putting up her hand to stop the flow of

Jonah's questions. 'The blood on the outside, however, is Bernie's. The partial fingermark on the tap in the ferry toilet could be a match for Greg Solari – or it could belong to someone else. Our fingerprint expert says he couldn't stand up in court and swear that it was Greg's; it was too incomplete. We've checked the blood on the knife that we found in St James' Gardens and it matches Bernie's; so at least we know we've found the weapon. However,' she paused for dramatic effect before continuing, 'the most interesting piece of forensic evidence is the new fingermark that has turned up on the very tip of the handle. It looks like the attacker – presumably Ashley Fisher – took off the gloves after burying the knife and then noticed the end of the handle still sticking out and pushed it down with her finger.'

'And is it a match? Jonah asked eagerly. 'If it is, you've got her, haven't you?'

'I've given orders for her fingerprints to be taken the moment she gets to the station,' Sandra answered with a smile. She liked Jonah very much and found his enthusiasm infectious, but she could not help thinking that it must be quite nerve-racking for his team to be constantly trying to keep up with his demands for instant results. 'But remember, it's only a single, partial print. It may turn out to be inconclusive, like the one on the tap.'

There was a hesitant knock at the door. Peter got up and opened it. He saw Cameron standing in the corridor, looking rather anxious and embarrassed, while his mother was engrossed in a text message conversation on her phone. She looked up when Peter's head appeared round the door.

'We missed you at breakfast,' she said. 'Have you heard the news?'

'Yes. We're about to go down to the police station. They need to ask us some more questions.'

'All of you?' Cameron asked. 'Lucy too?'

Peter smiled and turned to look at Lucy, who signalled back silently that she did not wish to be left alone with Cameron.

'Yes,' he said firmly. 'We all need to

go. I'm sorry about that. If you and Lucy had something planned, I'm sure it can be put off until this afternoon.'

'We promised Aunty Dot that we'd call on her again before we go,' Lucy said hastily. 'We've only got today left. Hadn't we better do that this afternoon?'

'Yes!' Bernie's conscience smote her. In all the excitement, she had forgotten about her aunt. 'We absolutely must go and see her before we leave.'

'Maybe after you get back from your auntie's?' Cameron pleaded.

'OK,' Lucy conceded. 'I'll send you a text when we've finished there.'

'And are you going to tell us who those people are who've been arrested?' Julie wanted to know. 'Did you recognise any of them from the TV pictures?'

'I'm afraid that is not being made public yet,' Sandra intervened, coming over to the door and showing Julie her warrant card. 'You will have to wait until the official announcement, like everyone else.'

'As you like,' Julie shrugged. 'I'm sure my friend Lauren will be able to identify the house, and the neighbours are bound to talk, but … Well, we'll be going then. See you later.'

When they got to the police station, they found DS Simpson waiting for them with Father Liam.

'I got her to show me the dress she

was wearing on Monday,' she said to Sandra, as soon as they were all settled together in an interview room. The inspector had phoned her sergeant with Peter's suggestion for speeding up the identification of the garments. 'But Father Cosgrave says he doesn't remember it.'

'Let's have a look at it then,' Sandra said.

Charlotte Simpson held up a transparent plastic bag containing a dark green dress. Bernie took one look at it and shook her head vigorously.

'No. That definitely isn't it. It was a pale-ish blue colour. I'm sure of it.'

'That's right!' Father Liam agreed. 'Blue and gold.'

'OK then,' Sandra sighed. 'It looks

like we'll have to go through this lot.' She indicated four large boxes, lined up against the wall.'

'Another brilliant idea comes to nothing!' Jonah commented cheerfully. 'We should have known she'd lie to us.'

'While we're looking through these boxes, there's something else I'd like you to have a look at,' Sandra said to Bernie. 'We found these on her dressing table.' She picked up three small bottles and handed them to Bernie. 'Are any of them the perfume you remember smelling when you were attacked?'

Sandra and Charlotte donned gloves and started sorting through the mounds of clothes looking for anything that might be described as blue and gold. Meanwhile Bernie unscrewed each lid in turn and took a cautious sniff of each scent.

'Yes. Definitely. That's the one,' she said, holding out the second bottle towards Sandra. 'Pear drops and air freshener. That's what I smelt in the Gardens and in the hall of the presbytery and then again at the funeral. Is this the one she says she was wearing on Monday?'

'No,' Charlotte replied. 'She said it was the first bottle you tried – the one with the pink top.'

I suppose that's something, anyhow,' Sandra said, with a sigh. 'But, of course, she'll only say that thousands of other people must wear that perfume – and she'll be right.'

'Doesn't the fact that she lied mean that she's probably guilty?' Lucy suggested. 'I mean, why else would she bother?'

'It could be an honest mistake,' Peter pointed out. If she really *wasn't* running round knifing people that morning, it may not have been significant enough to her for her to remember what she was wearing or which perfume she'd put on.'

'What does she say she was doing after she left the presbytery?' Jonah asked.

'She claims she went to see her mother, who lives just round the corner from the church, and then went shopping.'

Jonah opened his mouth to

comment, but Sandra continued, anticipating what he was going to ask. Their eyes met and he smiled acknowledgement that she had acted exactly as he would have done.

'I've sent a DC over there to talk to the mother, but I've not heard back from him yet. However, I'm assuming that she wouldn't have told us that if it wasn't true or else she'd already fixed it up with the mother to lie for her.'

'If it's only a few streets away from the presbytery, she could have gone there for a few minutes and then come back to wait for me to come out,' Bernie pointed out. 'Assuming that Father Liam told them why I was there, she'd know I'd be bound to spend a reasonable amount of time talking to Bernadette Allerton.'

'That's what I thought,' Sandra agreed, still sifting through the boxes of clothing. 'We can only hope that the mother isn't in on the conspiracy and tells us that her daughter left after only a short time. If she insists that she stayed all morning, it may be difficult to get her to change her story.'

'Could this be the dress?' Charlotte held up an evening gown made of blue satin with a yellow pattern of ivy leaves winding round it.

'I don't think so,' Father Liam said doubtfully.

'Definitely not,' Bernie agreed decisively. 'It's too long, apart from anything else. I remember being able to see an awful lot of leg when she careered into me in the hall.'

'This then?' Sandra pounced on what looked like a scrap of fabric lying at the top of one of the other boxes. She held it up to reveal a garment that Bernie would have considered to be a long tee-shirt, but which was probably a dress. It was made from a thin knitted material, which was presumably sufficiently elastic to enable it to stretch over Ashley's voluptuous body. It was light blue in colour, with thin stripes of gold lamé running down the front.

'Yes,' Bernie said, 'I think that's it. What do you think, Father?'

'I don't know that I'd like to swear to it,' he said slowly,' but, yes – yes, I think that's what she had on.'

'Good,' Sandra said with satisfaction. 'Get it sent off for forensic examination right away, Charlie. Now, let's see if we can find the shoes she was wearing.'

It appeared that Ashley had a collection of shoes nearly as large as her wardrobe of clothes, of which many had platform soles and almost all were high-heeled. Bernie eventually managed to narrow the search down to three pairs, which Sandra bagged up and sent off to be examined for any traces that might indicate that they had recently been in St James' gardens.

'It's even possible that some blood could have spattered on to them,' she added as she handed over the bags to Charlotte. 'Tell the labs I need a report by the end of the day. I want some definite forensic evidence before we run out of time for questioning those three.'

Her phone rang. For the next few minutes, the others were on tenterhooks trying to make sense of the ensuing one-sided conversation.

'Thanks. And you *are* sure about that print? Good. The dress and shoes will be with you any minute. Hope to hear about them later today. Bye!' Sandra concluded the call and looked round with an expression of triumph on her face.

'Go on,' Jonah urged. 'Spill the beans. I can see you've got news.'

'Forensics have actually got their finger out for once,' Sandra replied, smiling with satisfaction. 'They say that the marks in blood left by the gloved hand on the knife are the right size to have been left by Ashley.' She paused dramatically before continuing. 'And they've already got a match for that fingermark on the end of the knife.'

'Ashley's?' Jonah asked excitedly.

'No. J-P's.'

'But how?' Bernie asked. 'I mean – he couldn't have been there. Father Liam confirmed that he didn't leave the presbytery until eleven.'

'So it must either have been made later – after he left the presbytery – or else have already been on the knife before you were stabbed,' Peter said.

'And we'd secured the crime scene by quarter to eleven,' Sandra added, 'which means that it would have been impossible for him to get to the place where the knife was buried.'

'I reckon it was his knife,' Jonah said confidently. 'He handed it to Ashley and told her to lie in wait for Bernie and use it to silence her. One or other of them must have wiped it clean to prevent him being identified, but they missed that one print on the very end of the handle.'

'Yes,' Sandra agreed. 'That's my reading of the situation too. So now I think I'm ready to interview those three and ask them to explain themselves.'

30 AN AGE OF TWISTED VALUES

Sandra was not sure how he managed it, but she found herself agreeing to allow Jonah to sit in on the interviews. He was a remarkably difficult person to say *no* to, she reflected – which was probably a contributing factor to his success as a detective. She hoped that her superiors would accept that he was sufficiently far removed from the case not to have a conflict of interests and that the fortuitous presence of such an experienced officer from another force would be beneficial to the enquiry.

Bernie, Peter and Lucy left the police station with the intention of calling on Joey before going on to visit Aunty Dot after lunch. Nathan was given a seat in the staff rest room, where he settled himself with a cup of coffee and a pile of back issues of *POLICE* magazine.

'We'll be back at lunch time,' Bernie said to Jonah as they left. 'Aunty Dot will never forgive me if we don't take you along and introduce you to her.'

'I can't see why she would want to meet *me*,' Jonah grumbled, concerned that he might be dragged away before they had finished interviewing all the suspects.

'It's to restore her street cred with

the bingo club,' Peter said, straight-faced.

'You'll understand when you meet her,' Bernie assured him, seeing Jonah's look of bewilderment at this unexpected statement.

'Just imagine what Our Bernie might be like when she's ninety-seven and starting to become a bit eccentric,' Peter told him. 'That's Aunty Dot.'

'Then I shall look forward to making her acquaintance,' Jonah said solemnly. 'Now, let's cut the cackle and go and talk to these villains of yours,' he added turning to Sandra.

John-Paul Solari looked even more like a Mafioso than ever, sitting next to the duty solicitor in one of the interview rooms. He had a sullen look on his swarthy face and he scowled at Sandra, Charlotte and Jonah as they entered the room. Sandra introduced them all before sitting down opposite J-P and motioning to Charlotte to start the tape recorder. After making the formal introductory statements and repeating the standard caution, she addressed J-P.

'Why did you follow Father Allerton on to the ferry on Saturday?'

'I didn't. I didn't even know he was on it.'

'I see. In that case, why were you and your brother on the ferry? Where were you going?'

'Nowhere in particular,' J-P shrugged. 'Just a day out with my brother. Nothing wrong with that, is there?'

'The day after your other brother died? I would have thought it was more natural to stay with your mother to see she was OK.'

'She had her friends round – a load of old women from the church. We wanted to get away from all the weeping and wailing.'

'OK. You went for a day out to Wallasey. You boarded the ferry not far behind Father Allerton. That's been confirmed by the man checking tickets at the ferry terminal. Are you sure you didn't see him?'

'Yes. Like I said, we never even knew he was on board.'

'Did you see this woman?' Sandra

showed J-P the photograph of Bernie that had been taken by the police photographer on the day of the murder.

'Yes. We were behind her in the queue for the boat.'

'And did you recognise her a few days later, when you were at St Wilfrid's presbytery?'

'I may have done.'

'And did you think she'd recognised you?'

J-P shrugged. 'I never thought about it.'

'So you didn't think she'd recognised you and might tell us that you were on the ferry?'

'Why should I care?'

'Because you didn't want us to

know you were there. Why didn't you come forward when we asked for people who got off at Seacombe to get in touch?'

'I never heard about that.'

'You and your mum and brother were left alone in Father Liam's study for a while. Why did you go outside instead of staying with them?'

'Like I told you before – I wanted some fresh air. My kid brother just died, remember!'

'And your girlfriend, Ashley, went with you?'

'She remembered she'd promised her mum she'd call round; so she went off.' I went with her as far as the door.'

'So you went out to see her off, not for fresh air?'

'Both of them things. What difference does it make?'

Sandra reached into her brief case and drew out a large transparent plastic bag full of pink tablets.

'Now, Mr Solari, tell me about these.'

J-P said nothing, merely scowling belligerently across the table.

'Mr Solari?' Sandra said again. 'These were found in your bedroom. We've sent a sample to be analysed, but from their appearance, they are a brand of Ecstasy that has been cropping up a lot in nightclubs all around Merseyside recently. I'd like to know where you got them and what you were planning to do with them.'

'I don't know nothing about them,'

J-P blustered, raising his voice a little and glancing towards the solicitor. 'I never saw them before your lot picked them up. It's a police plant.'

'That's a very serious accusation to make,' Jonah said quietly, speaking for the first time. 'And not a particularly sensible one,' he went on. 'After all – why would the police try to frame you for possession of drugs when they have a rather convincing case against you for murder?'

J-P looked round wildly.

'What's the cripple doing here, anyway?' he demanded. 'What business has he got asking me daft questions?'

'DCI Porter is a very senior detective from Thames Valley Police,'

Sandra said smoothly. 'He is here to observe the operation. If he had any doubts about the conduct of the search of your house, it would be his duty to report them. So, I'll ask you again – where did these come from?'

'I told you – I don't know!' J-P growled. 'They're not mine. Someone else put them in my room.'

'Your brother, Greg, perhaps?' Sandra suggested.

J-P said nothing. He continued to glare across the table at Sandra and Charlotte.

'And what about Father Allerton?' Sandra asked quietly. 'Was it you or Greg who knifed him?'

'I told you!' J-P responded angrily. 'We never even saw him!'

'You were the only two people on board who knew him. He'd been at your house the night before. Did he find the drugs and threaten to tell the police about them?'

'No! I told you – I never saw them pills before. I don't know how they got into my room. I never touched the priest.'

'Alright. Let's try something else.' Sandra laid down another photograph on the table in front of him. 'Have you seen this knife before?'

'No. I never,' J-P replied at once, after glancing briefly down.

'Have a better look,' Sandra urged quietly. 'We found one of your fingerprints on it.'

'I told you – I never saw it before.'

'This is the knife that was used to attack Dr Fazakerley in St James' Gardens.' Sandra told him.

'Well it can't've been me. I was still at St Wilfrid's.'

'How do you know what time it happened?'

'It was in the Echo – said she was down the ozzy by eleven.'

'The ozzy?' Jonah enquired.

'The hospital,' Sandra translated. Then she addressed J-P again. 'Father Cosgrave has confirmed that you and your mother and brother didn't leave the presbytery until after the attack on Dr Fazakerley; so shall I tell you what I think happened?'

J-P shrugged.

'I think you recognised Dr Fazakerley and thought she'd recognised you. Maybe you thought she'd seen you with Father Allerton on the ferry. So you went outside with Ashley and you gave her your knife and told her to see to it that Dr Fazakerley couldn't tell anyone.'

'I never. It's not my knife.'

'It's got your fingerprint on it.'

'Must be a mistake. I never touched it.'

And so it went on. J-P Solari refused to admit to anything. Whatever evidence Sandra presented to him, he did not try to explain, he simply insisted that it was untrue, that he was not involved in any way, that the police were either mistaken or deliberately planting evidence to implicate him. Sandra, Charlotte and Jonah left the interview room feeling decidedly dissatisfied with the way things had gone.

'How do you think a jury will react if he sticks to his story like that?' Sandra asked Jonah, when they were safely outside the interview room. 'The only real evidence we have to link him to either murder is the fingerprint on the knife.'

'Hard to tell. If he managed to find a fingerprint expert willing to cast doubt on that print, then I think he might well convince them that he was the victim of a police frame-up. What about the drugs angle? If you can get evidence that he's a pusher, that might strengthen his motive for killing Father

Nicholas and also make any jury less sympathetic towards him.'

'He doesn't have any form in that respect. The best link we've got so far is that he works as a barman in one of the nightclubs where that particular brand of ecstasy has been turning up quite regularly recently. We've never been able to prove the punters weren't bringing the stuff in with them, though. We've had officers in there watching out for any deals going on, but nothing doing.'

Greg Solari appeared much more likeable than his brother – and much more nervous under police questioning. His eyes darted around the room all the time and he turned towards the duty solicitor for reassurance before answering almost every question. His nervousness did not, however, lead him to make any admission of guilt. There was one moment – when Sandra sprang on him the discovery of his fingermark on the tap in the ferry toilet – when Jonah thought he might be going to crack, but he recovered himself.

'So, I went to the lavvy before we got off at Seacombe? What's the big deal about that?'

'We know that whoever killed Father Allerton washed the blood off his hands in there afterwards,' Sandra told him. 'If that wasn't you – did you see anyone else there? Was there anyone waiting when you came out, for example?'

'Not that I noticed, sorry.'

'OK then,' Sandra said equably. 'Let's talk about something else. She reached down and brought out the bag of Ecstasy tablets, placing them on the table in front of him. 'Tell me about these.'

'What about them?' Greg asked defensively.

'We found them at your house. Are they yours?'

'No. Why should they be?'

'Your brother said he'd never seen them before, so I wondered if they were yours.'

'J-P said that?'

'Yes,' Sandra nodded.

'They were in his room,' Jonah

added helpfully, 'but he reckoned someone else had put them there.'

'You mean he said I was trying to frame him?'

Jonah lifted his eyebrows in a questioning manner as if to indicate that Greg should draw his own conclusions.

Greg looked at each of the police officers in turn. Then he sighed and nodded his head.

'OK. I'll tell you about them tablets — but that's got nothing to do with what happened to Father Nick or that Fazakerley woman.'

'Go on,' Jonah said encouragingly. 'We're listening.'

'J-P was keeping them safe for some mate of his. I don't know his name.

'Do you think Father Nicholas could have seen them while he was at your house last Friday?' Jonah asked casually.

'I don't think so. He never went in J-P's room.'

'So he didn't threaten you or your brother that he was going to report you for possession with intent to supply?' Charlotte asked sharply, undoing Jonah's patient efforts to gain Greg's confidence.

'No. Like I said, he never saw them.' Greg relapsed into a sullen silence, answering Sandra's questions in monosyllables until she gave him up as a bad job and decided to move on to their third suspect.

'I think you may be able to persuade Greg to talk,' Jonah said to Sandra in the corridor afterwards. 'My reading of the situation is that he'd quite like to come clean, but he's too much under his brother's thumb to dare to say anything. If you can convince him that telling the truth will be better for both of them, he may decide to make a clean breast of things.'

Ashley Fisher looked very forlorn and vulnerable, sitting on a hard wooden chair in front of a bare table in another interview room. Her mass of golden curls fell untidily over her face and shoulders and she kept pushing them back with a hand on which two of the nails were broken. Her eyes were red and puffy with crying. When they entered the room, she looked up at Sandra with pleading in her eyes, like a young child hoping to avoid punishment.

'How much longer is this going to take?' she asked, with a light tremor in her voice.

'That depends on how long it takes before you tell us the truth,' Sandra replied coldly. She was not convinced that Ashley's distress was genuine, and strongly suspected her of putting it on in the hope of gaining sympathy. 'Let's talk about Monday morning, shall we?'

'Monday morning?' Ashley asked, wide-eyed, as if the date meant nothing to her.

'Yes. You went with your boyfriend and his mother and brother to St Wilfrid's presbytery. Tell me about that.'

'J-P's kid brother died last week – you knew about that, I suppose?' Ashley sniffed, dabbing her eyes with a paper handkerchief.

'Yes. He told us. And so did Father Liam and this lady here,' Sandra said, showing Ashley the photograph of Bernie. 'Dr Fazakerley. She was sitting in the hall when you all arrived. She remembers seeing you with the others. Do you remember her?'

'Not really.' Ashley shook her head. Her expression was that of a small child, wanting to help, but unsure what was expected of her. 'I remember bumping up against someone in the crush, but I didn't notice her face.'

'Well, she was there, and she saw you and your boyfriend and she saw him staring at her as if he recognised her. Did he say anything to you about that?'

'No.' Ashley shook her head again.'

'Why did you leave before Father Liam got back to his study to talk to you all?'

'J-P's mum didn't want me there. I only came along because he asked me, like, but she said I wasn't real family. So I decided to go.'

'How did you feel about that?' Jonah asked sympathetically. He was as distrustful as Sandra of Ashley's show of naïve distress, but had decided that pretending that he had

728

been taken in was the best way of putting her off her guard. 'It must have been hard for you to be told that you didn't belong – when you were only there to support your boyfriend.'

'Yes,' Ashley agreed readily, 'but, to be honest, it was a bit of a relief, like, too. I'm not that keen on talking about corpses and funerals and that.'

'But you came with J-P to the funeral,' Jonah said gently. 'That was brave of you. He's lucky to have a girlfriend who sticks by him like that.'

Ashley nodded and favoured Jonah with a tearful smile.

'I'd do anything for him. We're going to get married – just as soon as his mum, like … gets over Ben's death.'

'Going back to Monday morning,'

Sandra intervened. 'You left the family in Father Liam's study and went off. Is that right?'

'Yes. Well,' Ashley paused and looked confused. Jonah guessed that she was trying to remember how much they had said when they had been asked about this before and to guess what J-P might have said in his interview a few minutes earlier. 'Actually, J-P came out as far as the front door with me. So that we could say goodbye properly, like – you know.' She giggled nervously.

'OK. You said goodbye on the doorstep,' Sandra repeated, 'and then what? Where did you go?'

'Like I said before – I went round to my mum's for a bit, and then I went to the shops.'

'How long did you stay with your mum?'

'An hour? Hour and a half?' Ashley shrugged. 'I can't remember.'

'Your mum says you only stayed about ten minutes,' Charlotte said coolly.

'I'm sure it was longer than that,' Ashley insisted, flushing red and looking a little flustered. 'Maybe not quite as long as I said, but half an hour at least.'

'And then you went shopping,' Jonah intervened again, speaking kindly and looking directly into Ashley's eyes. 'Where did you go? Which shops?'

Ashley thought for a while before

answering.

'TJ's,' she said at last.

'You'll have to tell me where that is,' Jonah said. 'I'm new to Liverpool.'

'TJ Hughes is on London Road,' Charlotte told him. 'Near the university and the hospital.'

'That would be quite a walk from St Wilfrid's, wouldn't it?' Jonah suggested.

'I got the bus.'

'I see. Thank you. That's all very clear now.'

'But I'm afraid I don't believe a word of it,' Sandra cut in. She was becoming impatient with Jonah's *softly softly* approach. 'I think you went back to St Wilfrid's and waited outside the presbytery for Dr Fazakerley to come out; and then you followed her to St James' Gardens and stabbed her from behind with this knife.'

She put the photograph of the knife on the table, looking down at it and then up into Ashley's eyes. Ashley looked startled and as if she might be about to cry again.

'I never!' she protested. 'And I never saw that knife before either.'

'Dr Fazakerley says different. She says it was you.'

'Then she's lying.' Ashley's face took on a sulky look.

'Ashley,' Jonah said gently. 'You know how you said you'd do anything for your boyfriend?'

Ashley nodded, sniffed and dabbed her eyes again.

'Well, the best way you can help him now is by telling us the truth. I don't think he killed Father Nicholas. And I don't think he hurt Dr Fazakerley either. But I do think he's got himself mixed up in some things that he shouldn't have and that he's probably regretting right now. And I think he was frightened that Dr Fazakerley might tell us about him being on the ferry and he asked you to help him to stop her. So now, how about it? Will you tell us what really happened?'

Ashley hesitated. For a moment, Jonah thought that she was going to give in and tell them all about it. Then she seemed to remember something — maybe something that J-P had told her or maybe just the fact that, whatever else she told them, if she admitted to attacking Bernie, she was going to be in serious trouble.

'I went to see my mum and then I went down the shops,' she repeated. Jonah suspected that this was the story that J-P had rehearsed with her and instructed her to tell.

'Why did you tell us that you were wearing that green dress on Monday?' Sandra asked, hoping to catch her out by changing the subject. 'Father Liam and Dr Fazakerley both agree that you had a blue dress on when you were at St Wilfrid's.'

'Maybe I did. I don't remember. What's the big deal, anyway?'

'They have identified the right dress and I've sent it for forensic examination. They'll be able to find even tiny traces of blood on it, and if they do, we'll know that you *did* try to kill Dr Fazakerley. So it will be a whole lot better for you if you tell us the truth now, instead of waiting for us to get the evidence to prove it was you.'

'It wasn't me. I went to my mum's and then I went down the shops, like I told you.'

And so it went on. After that one moment when it looked as if she might be about to unburden herself to the sympathetic policeman in the wheelchair, Ashley, like the others, stuck to her story and refused to be drawn into any admission of involvement in the events on the ferry or in the gardens.

They all ate lunch together in the police canteen. Sandra Latham knew that she was stretching the rules considerably, but she had picked up on the need for Jonah to keep to regular mealtimes and this seemed to be the easiest way. It also gave her a chance to ask his advice on the best way forward to break the current impasse.

'I don't think you've got much chance of getting J-P to budge,' he told her, dodging Nathan's attempt to put a forkful of baked potato into his mouth. 'My reading of the situation is that he's the strong character and the others are frightened of him. He's convinced himself that, if he just says nothing, we won't be able to prove that it was him.'

'And our problem is that he may well be right,' Sandra agreed.

Jonah nodded, chewing the mouthful that Nathan had succeeded in inserting while Sandra was speaking.

'So, if I were you, I'd concentrate on the others,' Jonah resumed after swallowing. 'Greg wants to talk; I'm convinced of it. And you might try working on Ashley as well – ask her about the inconsistency between her explanation of why she left and J-P's.'

'Her mum wasn't expecting her,' Charlotte contributed. 'So J-P's story that Ashley remembered she'd promised to call doesn't stack up.'

Jonah took Nathan with him to the disabled toilet after their meal, to empty the urine bag, which he kept concealed in his trouser-leg.

'I've got something I want you to do for me while we're visiting Bernie's Aunt,' Jonah said, as soon as they were alone. 'Have a look at this.' He turned his computer screen so that Nathan could see the display. 'There must be somewhere in Liverpool that you can get one of these.'

Nathan paused in what he was doing to peer down at the object on the screen.

'It doesn't have to be identical to this one,' his father continued. 'Just make sure it's plain on both sides, so there's room for the engraving.'

'Engraving?'

'I have it on good authority that,

somewhere in the city centre, there's a jeweller's shop that does engraving while you wait. I want you to get it done and bring it to me when we do my physio this evening.'

'You couldn't persuade your authority to be more specific, I suppose?' Nathan asked dubiously.

'I got the info from Bernie who got it from Peter,' Jonah explained. 'And you're not to mention any of this to either of them – it's supposed to be a surprise.'

'If you say so,' Nathan sighed. Subterfuge was not his forte. 'I'll see what I can do.'

31 I COME TO MAKE CONFESSION

'I'd like to introduce you to our great friend, Jonah Porter,' Bernie told Aunty Dot, when they visited her that afternoon. Dot looked at Jonah and smiled broadly.

'I've been reading about you in the papers. I hope you're going to be a bit less stubborn about filling me in on this murder case you're all mixed up in. Our Bernie is being very difficult about giving me the low-down.'

Jonah felt an instant affinity with

Dot. Unlike so many people meeting him for the first time, she completely ignored his disability and spoke to him as a normal adult – except that her turn of phrase was not quite what one might expect from a ninety-seven-year-old woman. He saw at once that her teasing words had an underlying seriousness and that she intended to find out more.

'Actually,' he said, after a moment's thought, 'I was wondering if you might be able to help us.'

Dot leaned forward in her chair, her eyes sparkling.

'I'm at your service,' she said seriously. 'So long as you don't expect me to go chasing after any criminals and bringing them down with a rugby tackle. My sprinting days are over, I'm afraid.'

'Mine too,' Jonah grinned back at her. 'No. What I was hoping for was some ideas about the young priest who got himself killed. You must have been at a few death-beds in your time, I'm guessing?'

'You could say that.'

'Father Nick spent Friday evening at the house of a young man who was dying,' Jonah told her. 'He gave him the last rites. What exactly does that mean? I was brought up as a Baptist, so I don't know much about how they do things in the Roman Catholic Church. Why would the family want a priest to be there when he died?'

'He'd want to be in a state of grace

when he died.'

'Now that's something that I'm not very clear about. What exactly does being in a state of grace mean?'

'He'd want to have the priest hear his confession and give him absolution.'

'Ah! And this confession – that would be done in private?'

'Yes – although,' Dot giggled, 'it wouldn't be the first time a confession got overheard. I remember, when I was doing my nurse training, getting hold of a stethoscope and putting it against the side of the confessional in our church and listening in. Nobody confessed to anything very exciting,' she added in a disappointed tone.

'So other members of the family

might have been able to hear what the dying man said?' Jonah asked eagerly.

'I wouldn't be at all surprised.'

Jonah nodded, a look of quiet satisfaction on his face.

'Now, a priest is forbidden to tell anyone about anything he hears during confession – is that right?'

'Yes. The seal of the confessional is sacred.'

'What if ...,' Jonah said slowly, '... what if a penitent confessed to something that involved other people?'

'How do you mean?'

'Well. Suppose there was a group of people involved in some sort of conspiracy ... I don't know ... a gang of burglars, perhaps. If one of them confessed, would the priest be able to do anything to stop the others carrying on stealing things?'

'I'm not sure about that one,' Dot put her head on one side as she thought about this. 'You'd have to ask a priest about that.'

'I don't want to know the official answer. What I'm interested in is what an ordinary lay Catholic might expect that the priest might do.' Dot looked puzzled, so Jonah continued. 'I'm thinking about the other gang members. If they knew that the first one had confessed to a priest, would they be worried that the priest might turn them in to the police or something?'

Dot thought for a few moments.

'You're suggesting that this young

man that your Father Nick visited the day before he was killed might have been in some sort of gang?'

'Something like that. And if he confessed, and named the other gang members, might they be worried about what Father Nick might have been going to do?'

'Well,' Dot paused as if thinking again. 'The nearest thing I can think of is when I was about Lucy's age. A group of us girls got it in for Sister Hildegarde, our French teacher, and we played all sorts of rather nasty jokes on her – like hiding her reading glasses so that she wouldn't be able to give us our vocab test. As I remember it, another girl, who had nothing to do with it, got the blame for that one. I eventually confessed to my parish priest and he wouldn't give me absolution until I'd apologised to them both and, more importantly, told the other girls that I'd tell on them if they didn't stop persecuting Sister Hildegard.'

'And did you?' Lucy asked, thinking how difficult she would have found it to threaten to grass on her schoolfellows.

'I did – in the end! That was the end of that friendship. One of the girls never spoke to me again after that.'

'But in the present case,' Jonah mused, 'Father Nick couldn't tell the dying man that he had to sort out his friends. Under the circumstances, he'd want to give absolution without any strings attached, wouldn't he?'

Dot nodded.

'And then, he'd be left with the difficult question of whether or not he was permitted by this *seal of the confessional* to do anything to prevent the other gang members from continuing to injure other people by their actions,' Jonah finished, looking round with an expression of satisfaction on his face. 'And the gang members might be very worried that he might decide that the least worst option was to break the seal and tell the police, so that they could be stopped.'

He paused briefly, manipulating the controls on the arm of his wheelchair and looking down at the computer screen. Lucy, looking over his shoulder, saw that he was sending a message to Sandra Latham: *ask them about Ben Solari's confession*.

On the way back to the hotel, Lucy's phone buzzed, indicating that she had received a text. She was sitting in the back of the car with Jonah, while Peter was driving and Bernie was in the front passenger seat. She frowned as she saw that the sender of the message was Jonah. Why was he communicating in such a round-about way? She opened it.

'Do you have any pictures of Peter or your dad on your phone?' it asked.

She looked up and saw Jonah watching her. He smiled encouragingly and inclined his head towards Peter and Bernie. Lucy understood that he wanted to have a private conversation with her, which they would not be able to hear. She saw that he was typing with one finger and then, after a few seconds, his screen turned round so that she could read, 'I want a mugshot of each of them.'

Lucy nodded and then looked down again. Jonah watched as she bent over her phone, scrolling through the collection of photographs that she had stored there. After a short while, she held it up to show a head-and-shoulders picture of a man in his fifties. Jonah recognised it as a copy of the portrait of Richard Paige that stood on the mantelpiece in their Oxford home. He nodded and smiled, indicating that this would do for his purposes – whatever they might be.

Lucy turned back to her phone and hunted again. Most of the pictures that featured her stepfather were photographs of other people, with Peter as a minor player on the sidelines. Eventually she found the one that she had taken on his most recent birthday, smiling as he opened the present that she had given him. She showed it to Jonah. Again, he nodded and smiled. Then he turned his screen towards her again and she read, 'offer to help Nathan with my physio this evening. I have a cunning plan.'

They were just coming out of the lift to go to their rooms after the evening meal when Jonah's phone rang. It was Sandra Latham with the latest news of the case. They hurried into the room that Bernie and Peter were sharing, so that the conversation would not be overheard.

'Your suggestion was spot on,' Sandra told Jonah. 'As soon as I mentioned his brother's confession, Greg came clean and told us everything. At least – he told us his version of everything. According to him, it was all J-P's idea and he just went along with it because he was scared.'

'That could be true,' Jonah said. 'J-P certainly struck me as the dominant character in that family.'

'Yes, well, according to Greg, all three brothers were involved in J-P's drugs business, to a greater or lesser extent. On the day he died, Benedict told Father Nick all about it.'

'Which explains why poor Father

Nick was so distracted on Saturday,' Bernie put in. 'He was trying to weigh up the need to do something to stop J-P's drugs racket from endangering any more young people against the imperative not to break the seal of confession.'

'Greg overheard and told J-P about it. J-P decided they had to do something to stop the priest going to the police; so they went round the following day to talk to him – at least, that's what Greg says J-P said they were going to do. They saw him leaving the house and followed him down to the Pier Head and on to the ferry. Greg insists that he still thought they were just going to talk to Father Nick and persuade him not to turn them in.'

'But it was Greg's fingermark on the tap, wasn't it?' Lucy said. 'Doesn't that mean that *he* was the one who killed Father Nick and got blood on himself?'

'You don't have to be the murderer to get blood on your hands,' Bernie pointed out drily.

'That may be a bit of a problem for us,' Sandra admitted. 'J-P is still denying everything – which may be our best hope of convincing the jury that he's got something to hide – and Greg says that J-P killed the priest and he – Greg – got blood on his hands afterwards when he tried to help him.'

'That could be true,' Peter said. 'The killer wore gloves, remember? So he probably avoided getting blood on himself.'

'We've taken away the clothes that both Solari boys were wearing on Saturday,' Sandra went on, 'but they've been washed since, so I doubt if anything will show up – especially since they were standing behind the victim and wearing short-sleeved tee-shirts so their clothes will have been shielded from any blood spatter. That reminds me! Forensics have found minute traces of blood on Ashley Fisher's dress. No DNA match yet, but it's looking very promising that we'll be able to pin the attack against Bernie on her. Greg claims to know nothing at all about that incident, but he confirmed that J-P used to own a knife just like the one that we found.'

'And J-P's fingermark on that puts him right in it,' Jonah commented.

'And once you convince a jury that he was behind the second knifing, they'll probably accept Greg's claim that he was the leading light in the first attack too,' Peter agreed. 'In my experience, juries don't like defendants who refuse to answer questions. They tend to assume they've got something to hide.'

'The trouble is, Greg may not be as innocent as he's making out,' Sandra argued. 'There's no doubt he was frightened of what the priest might tell the police. It looks to me as if he was laundering the proceeds of J-P's drug dealings through the tattoo studio that he owns. He stood to lose his business as well as his liberty if it all came to light. And, in addition, he's absolutely terrified of his brother. He begged me to keep him in custody because he's afraid of what J-P's heavies might do to him if he's allowed home. It wouldn't surprise me at all if both mur- attacks,' she corrected herself hastily, 'were done by other people under J-P's direction.'

'Maybe the DPP will go for *conspiracy to murder* against all three of them,' Bernie suggested. 'From my point of view, at least now we know for sure there's nobody else out there trying to get me!'

Peter reflected to himself that, if J-P Solari really did have a gang of *heavies,* as Sandra has put it, backing him, his wife could still be in danger. However, he said nothing. They were going home tomorrow. Surely nothing could happen between now and then?

32 NOW, AS WE PART AND GO OUR SEVERAL WAYS

Jonah insisted on going down to the police station the following morning to say farewell to Sandra Latham and her team. Nathan argued that this was unnecessary and might interfere with the investigation, but Jonah was in a determined – or, as Nathan described it, stubborn – mood and everyone fell in with his plan.

Sandra Latham greeted them cheerfully.

'I'm glad you came,' she said, smiling round at them all. 'After we spoke yesterday evening, there was a development.'

'Oh?' Jonah raised his eyebrows interrogatively.

'Mrs Solari came in, demanding to speak to her sons.'

'And?'

'It looks like she's been doing some thinking on the QT and worked out a lot of what's been going on. Anyway, she put the fear of God into J-P and he's admitted everything.'

'Really?' Jonah asked in surprise. 'I must say, I never expected *him* to crack.'

'Neither did I,' Sandra admitted. 'I don't know what his mum said to him, but whatever it was, it scared the crap out of him and he sang like a canary.'

'When you're brought up a Catholic you never quite forget the possibility of eternal damnation,' Bernie told her. 'However lapsed you may be, it's always there at the back of your mind.'

'So, who did what?' Lucy wanted to know.

'Both Solari boys now agree that J-P killed Father Nick. J-P told us that Greg held him still and covered his mouth to stop him crying out. At first, Greg stuck to his story that he didn't know what J-P was intending until it was too late, but he gave in, in the end, and admitted to helping. J-P admits to giving the knife to Ashley and telling her to follow Bernie. At the moment,

761

Ashley's still holding out, but when we confront her with the new forensic evidence and she knows that J-P has confessed, I don't think it'll be long before she changes her tune.'

'Her best bet now is to claim that she was so deeply under her boyfriend's influence that she didn't really know what she was doing,' Jonah agreed. 'If her solicitor knows what he's talking about, he'll tell her that and she'll 'fess up.'

'J-P has also given us a lot of information about his drugs business,' Sandra added. 'The drug squad are highly delighted. It's the biggest breakthrough they've had for years.'

'Would you mind telling Bernadette Allerton about that?' Bernie asked.

'She might like to know that *something* good came out of her son's death.'

Cameron was waiting for them when they got back. He told them that he and his mother would be leaving shortly, and asked Lucy to walk with him down to the Pier Head for a final look at the waterfront before they parted. As they walked off, side by side, Jonah looked up at Bernie quizzically.

'I don't think there's anything in it,' she told him. 'At least, not as far as Lucy's concerned; I can't speak for Cameron. She's allowed Dom to *friend* her on Facebook too. But I think they're both going to be disappointed if they think she's going to allow them to become more than chums – at least for the foreseeable future.'

Cameron placed his arm tentatively around Lucy's shoulders as they leaned on the rail watching the ferry tying up at the landing stage.

'There's still three weeks before school starts again,' he said, hopefully. 'Why don't you come over to Gloucester for a day? I could show you round.'

Lucy did not answer, so he tried again.

'Or I could come to see you in Oxford. I could get the train, so we wouldn't have my Mum hanging around. Perhaps you could take me on the river? I've never tried punting. Or–'

MYSTERY OVER THE MERSEY

'That's funny!' Lucy exclaimed, apparently oblivious of what he was saying. 'The ferry's facing the opposite way round from before. I wonder why.'

'I never got to see Oxford Brookes like I meant to this week,' Cameron tried again. 'Would you show me round if I come over sometime?'

'Yes, if you like,' Lucy murmured absently. 'On Saturday, it docked facing downstream every time. I noticed because it meant we got *on* at the starboard side and *off* at the port side, and the boat turned round twice between Seacombe and Woodside. Today – did you notice? It's facing upstream and the people are boarding on the port side.'

'What's the big deal?' Cameron

demanded, losing patience. 'I was talking about us meeting up again.'

'I know. I'm sorry. Yes – send me a message on Facebook when you're coming and I don't mind showing you round Oxford.' Lucy continued to watch the ferry as it cast off and started to move away. 'This is the same service *exactly* as the one we went on last week. So I don't see why it's the other way round this time.[8]'

Cameron, feeling increasingly frustrated that she appeared to find the vagaries of the Mersey Ferries more

---

[8] I owe thanks to Merseytravel (http://www.merseytravel.gov.uk), who kindly confirmed that the direction of docking of the Mersey ferries depends on the state of the tide.

interesting than himself, tried to think of something to say that might engage her attention. Before he could do so, his thoughts were interrupted by a voice calling his name.

'Time we were making tracks,' Julie Price called out, as she crossed the wide paved area to join them.

Cameron took his arm from around Lucy and turned round to face his mother. 'OK Mum. Just coming.'

'I'll come back to the hotel with you,' Lucy said, giving the ferry a final thoughtful glance before turning to greet Julie. 'We'll need to be going soon too.'

'Peter!' Bernie called from the bathroom as she packed her

toothbrush and face flannel into her sponge bag. 'Have you any idea where this came from?'

Peter put his head round the door and looked at the object that his wife was holding out to him.

'Never seen it before. What is it?'

'It looks like one of those boxes that jeweller's put things in. It was in my sponge bag. Are you sure you didn't slip it in there?'

'Quite sure. I know better than to give *you* jewellery. What's in it?'

'I haven't opened it.'

Peter stood in the doorway looking meaningfully from the box to Bernie and back again.

'Oh, alright.' Bernie lifted the lid and

took out a long gold chain, which she held up for Peter to see. Dangling at the bottom was a large, heart-shaped locket. Peter put out his hand and took hold of it. He read the inscription on the front. It was a single word: *Richard*. Then he turned it over and saw that there was another word on the back: *Peter*. He looked up at Bernie and their eyes met.

'Open it,' she said quietly.

He did so and they both stared down at the two photographs attached to the two inside faces of the locket. Peter immediately recognised the portrait of Bernie's first husband. The other picture was of Peter himself, but he was not sure when or where it had been taken.

'It must be Jonah,' Bernie said at last. 'I told him I was planning to get a picture of you to go in Richard's locket. He was all for getting Sandra Latham to give it back to me, instead of keeping it as evidence. He must have–'

'But how?'

'With a little help from his friends!' Bernie laughed. 'I bet Lucy had a hand in it. She could easily have slipped it into the spongebag yesterday evening. And Nathan probably bought the locket while we were at Aunty Dot's.'

She shook her head slowly, smiling at the thought of this conspiracy. Peter reached over and took hold of the knotted string hanging round her neck. He pulled it up and eased it over her head.

'You won't need this anymore,' he said as he untied the knot and slid the two rings off on to his palm, 'Now that you've got a proper gold chain for them.'

Bernie picked up the diamond engagement ring and slipped it on to the chain. Then she took hold of the Celtic Knot wedding ring, hesitated for a moment and then put it on her finger.

'I think perhaps it's time I started wearing a visible symbol that I'm spoken for,' she said with a smile. 'Especially with the likes of Jonah Porter around!'

THANK YOU

Thank you for taking the time to read MYSTERY OVER THE MERSEY. If you enjoyed it, please consider telling your friends or posting a short review. Word of mouth is an author's best friend and much appreciated. Thank you,

Judy.

A NOTE ON THE CHAPTER TITLES

The titles of chapters within this book are taken from hymns. The references below are included so that the interested reader may explore them. I have tried to include at least one source for the lyrics and, where possible, links to where a recording and additional background information may be found. For those that are included in *Singing the Faith*, published on behalf of the Trustees for Methodist Church Purposes by Hymns Ancient & Modern Ltd, 2011, the relevant hymn number is given. Please do not read anything into the choices of hymns, which in many cases are quite contrived. Inclusion of any hymn in this list, should not be taken as endorsement of the sentiments contained therein, either by the author or by Bernie and her friends. I hope you enjoy exploring them.

1. *Shall we gather at the river* is the first line of a hymn by Robert Lowry, an American Baptist minister. The lyrics and some background information may be found here: http://www.cyberhymnal.org/htm/s/w/swgatriv.htm. A recording may be found here: https://www.youtube.com/watch?v=F8EIjGXtCLk.

2. *Ye who have waited long* is a line from the fourth verse of the original version of *Hills of the North Rejoice*

by Charles Edward Oakley. This hymn has been revised by the editors of *English Praise* to bring it in line with twentieth and then twenty-first century thinking. This line now reads *lands of the setting sun*. It is 172 in *Singing the Faith*.

3. *An ever-present help and stay* is a line in the third verse of *Sing praise to God who reigns above* by Johan Jacob Schütz, translated by Frances Elizabeth Cox and Honor Mary Thwaites. It is 117 in *Singing the Faith*.

4. *Thy wounds they are deep* is a line from the hymn *I met the good Shepherd* by Edward Caswall, an Anglican clergyman who converted to Roman Catholicism. The words and other information about this

hymn may be found here:
http://www.hymnary.org/text/i_met_th
e_good_shepherd.

5. *As we question* is the start of the third verse of *When, O God, our faith is tested* by Fred Kaan, a minister of the United Reformed Church. It was written as a response to the anguish of parents on the sudden death of their son in a drowning accident. More on the background to this hymn may be found here:
http://www.singingthefaithplus.org.uk /?p=855. It is 643 in *Singing the Faith*.

6. *In the strife of truth with falsehood* is a line from the hymn *Once to every man and nation* by James Russell Lowell, which was written in 1845 as a protest against America's war with

Mexico. The lyrics may be found here: http://www.hymntime.com/tch/htm/o/n/c/oncetoev.htm. A recording may be found here: https://www.youtube.com/watch?v=gh8lwG4UaY8.

7. *What's the news* is the title of an anonymous hymn reportedly sung during the Ulster revival of 1859. The words and music may be found here: http://www.hymnary.org/text/wheneer_we_meet_you_always_say.

8. *O happy home* (or *Happy the home*) is the beginning of a hymn by Carl Johann Philipp Spitta, translated by Sarah Laurie Findlater. Words and music may be found here: http://www.hymnary.org/text/o_happy_home_where_thou_art_loved_the_

de.

9. *Faith of our mothers* is the title of a hymn by Arthur B Patten, an American congregational Church minister. Words and music may be found here: http://www.hymnary.org/text/faith_of_our_mothers_living_yet.

10. *I come to the garden alone* is the opening line of *In the garden* by Charles Austin Miles, a pharmacist from New Jersey. Words and music may be found here: http://www.hymnary.org/text/i_come_to_the_garden_alone.

11. *Questions without answers* is part of the opening line of a hymn by Tim Hughes. There is a recording here: https://www.youtube.com/watch?v=X

kdKJqQkYeo. The lyrics may be found here: http://www.ap0s7le.com/list/song/1160/Tim_Hughes/I've_Had_Questions. It is 632 in *Singing the Faith*.

12.   *Out of the depths* are the opening words of Psalm 130. There are several metrical versions, including one by Martin Luther (http://www.hymntime.com/tch/htm/o/d/i/odicthee.htm) and one by Orlando Gibbons (https://www.youtube.com/watch?v=yETRxtYIL-E).

13.   *And, Lord haste the day when my faith shall be sight* is the first line of the last verse of *It is well with my soul*, by Horatio G Spafford. The lyrics may be found here: http://cyberhymnal.org/htm/i/t/i/itiswel

l.htm. There is a YouTube recording here: https://www.youtube.com/watch?v=9 HLyhEdh92E and a Wikipedia entry here: https://en.wikipedia.org/wiki/It_Is_We ll_with_My_Soul.

14.   *I cannot tell* are the opening words of each verse of a hymn by William Young Fullerton, which is set to the well-known *Londonderry Air*. The lyrics may be found here: https://www.hymnal.net/en/hymn/h/9 34. There is a recording of a choral version here: https://vimeo.com/52533113. It is 350 in *Singing the Faith*. More information about the hymn and its author may be found here: http://www.singingthefaithplus.org.uk

/?p=2055.

15.　*The gift which he on one bestows* is from Charles Wesley's hymn *All praise to our redeeming Lord*. This is 620 in *Singing the Faith*. The words may be found here: http://cyberhymnal.org/htm/a/l/allprai 3.htm and you can listen to a recording here: https://www.youtube.com/watch?v=b hE-Moyghul.

16.　We are pilgrims on a journey, and companions on the road are the first two lines of the second verse of Brother, sister, let me serve you (formerly Brother let me be your servant) by Richard A M Gillard. This hymn, also known as The Servant Song may be found here: https://www.youtube.com/watch?v=E

eCDkxTqpjQ. It is 611 in Singing the Faith. The lyrics are available here: https://thepoetryplace.wordpress.com/2009/04/10/the-servant-song/.

17.   *Here, O my Lord, I see thee face to face* is the opening line of a communion hymn by the Scottish hymn-writer, Horatius Bonar. Words and music may be found here: http://www.hymnary.org/text/here_o_my_lord_i_see_thee_face_to_face.

18.   We are here to help each other is another line from The Servant Song (see 16 above).

19.   Why hast thou cast our lot in this same age and place, and why together brought to see each other's face – part of Charles Wesley's hymn All praise to our redeeming

Lord (see 15 above).

20.   *Peter, do you love me?* Is a hymn by Daniel B. Williamson. There is a recording here: https://www.youtube.com/watch?v=AVzPVontigc. The only source of the lyrics that I have located is this: http://www.namethathymn.com/hymn-lyrics-detective-forum/index.php?a=vtopic&t=7621.

21.   *Morning has broken* is the first line of a hymn by Eleanor Farjeon. It is 136 in *Singing the Faith*. There is more information about the hymn and its author here: http://www.singingthefaithplus.org.uk/?p=1660. There are several recordings available online, including this one: https://www.youtube.com/watch?v=h

5D3LEjGF8A.

22.   *Seek and ye shall find* is the second line of the second verse of the hymn, *Seek ye first the Kingdom of God* by Karen Lafferty, based on Matthew 6:33. Words and music may be found here: http://www.hymnary.org/text/seek_ye_first_the_kingdom_of_god_and. A recording may be found here: https://www.youtube.com/watch?v=S1Y8Naj3RFk.

23.   *Our researches lead us* is a phrase from the hymn, *When our confidence is shaken*, by twentieth-century Methodist hymn-writer, Fred Pratt Green. Words and music may be found here: http://www.hymnary.org/text/when_our_confidence_is_shaken. It is 622 in

Singing the Faith.

24. *O Love that wilt not let me go*, is the opening line of George Matheson's most famous hymn. Words and music may be found here: http://www.hymnary.org/text/o_love_t hat_wilt_not_let_me_go. A recording may be found here: https://www.youtube.com/watch?v=n t69WDtYNLo. It is 636 in *Singing the Faith.*

25. *Jesus stand among us at the meeting of our lives* is the opening line of a hymn by Graham Kendrick. The words and a recording may be found here: http://www.grahamkendrick.co.uk/so ngs/item/30-jesus-stand-among-us. It is 30 in *Singing the Faith.*

26.   *Rejoice for a brother deceased* is a little-known and no longer sung hymn by Charles Wesley. It may be found in the *Funerals and Memorials* section of the Methodist Hymn Book, © The Methodist Conference, 1933. Words and music may be found here: http://www.hymnary.org/text/rejoice_for_a_brother_deceased.

27.   *The fragrance there was sweet* is part of a line from the hymn *When Mary poured a rich perfume*, by Carolyn Winfrey Gillette. The lyrics may be found here: http://www.carolynshymns.com/when_mary_poured_a_rich_perfume.html.

28.   *Come away with me* are the opening words of a hymn by Mary Nelson Keithahn. The lyrics and

some information about the hymn and its writer may be found here: http://www.hymnary.org/text/come_away_with_me_to_a_quiet_place.

29.   *Lay aside the garments that are stained with sin* is a line from the hymn *Are You Washed in the Blood?* by Elisha A Hoffman. The lyrics, tune, and some additional information may be found here: http://www.hymnary.org/text/have_you_been_to_jesus_for_the_cleansing. A recording may be found here: https://www.youtube.com/watch?v=h9oW91lv8D8.

30.   *In an age of twisted values* is the first line of a hymn by Martin Leckebusch. Some information about the hymn and its author may be found here:

http://www.singingthefaithplus.org.uk/?p=1990. It is 703 in *Singing the Faith*.

31. *Forgiving God, I come to make confession* is the first line of the second verse of the hymn, *Almighty God, we come to make confession*, by Christopher J Ellis. It is 419 in *Singing the Faith* (http://www.singingthefaithplus.org.uk/?p=2823).

32. *Now, as we part and go our several ways* is the third line of the hymn, *O God our Father, who dost make us one*, by William Vaughan Jenkins. A rendition of the tune, Morecambe, may be found here: https://www.youtube.com/watch?v=JnZ2Dg1VsdM. It is 688 in the Methodist Hymn Book, © The

Methodist Conference, 1933, and 778 in Hymns and Psalms, A Methodist and Ecumenical Hymn Book, © Methodist Publishing House, 1983.

A NOTE ON THE LOCATIONS

Most of the locations and institutions that feature in this book are real. Their inhabitants and employees, however, are purely fictional. In particular:

- the excellent Royal Liverpool Hospital does not have a trauma surgeon by the name of Elvira Yorke, and she is not based on any actual surgeon employed there or anywhere else;

- there is no St Wilfrid's Catholic Church, and neither this church nor the church in Toxteth attended by the Fazakerley family is based on any existing church in Liverpool or anywhere else;

- none of the police officers mentioned in this story are based on real members of Merseyside Police or of any other police service.

Interested readers are encouraged to take a trip on the Mersey Ferry and to visit the other attractions mentioned in the book. Information and maps can be found on the Visit Liverpool website: http://www.visitliverpool.com.

MORE ABOUT BERNIE AND HER FRIENDS

Bernie features in eight other books.

- **Awayday**: a traditional detective story set among the dons of an Oxford college.

- **Changing Scenes of Life**: Jonah Porter's life story, told through the medium of his favourite hymns.

- **Despise not your Mother**: the story of Bernie's quest to learn about her dead husband's past.

- **Two Little Dickie Birds**: a murder mystery for DI Peter Johns and his Sergeant, Paul Godwin.

- **Murder of a Martian**: a double murder for Peter and Jonah to solve.

- **Death on the Algarve:** a mystery for Bernie and her friends to tackle while on holiday in Portugal.

- **My Life of Crime:** the collected memoirs of DI Peter Johns.

- **Sorrowful Mystery**: Jonah investigates a child abduction and Peter embarks on a new journey of faith.

You can find them all on Judy Ford's Amazon Author page:
https://www.amazon.co.uk/-/e/B0193I5B1M

Read more about Bernie Fazakerley and her friends and family at https://sites.google.com/site/llanwrdafamily/

Visit the Bernie Fazakerley Publications Facebook page: https://www.facebook.com/Bernie.Fazakerley.Publications.

Follow Bernie on Twitter: https://twitter.com/BernieFaz.

ABOUT THE AUTHOR

Like her main character, Bernie Fazakerley, Judy Ford is an Oxford graduate and a mathematician. Unlike Bernie, Judy grew up in a middle-class family in the South London stockbroker belt. After moving to the North West and working in Liverpool, Judy fell in love with the Scouse people and created Bernie to reflect their unique qualities.

As a Methodist Local Preacher, Judy often tells her congregation, "I see my role as asking the questions and leaving you to think out your own answers." She carries this philosophy forward into her writing and she hopes that readers will find themselves challenged to think as well as being entertained.